THE
SACRED
CLAIM

THE
SACRED CLAIM

JOE HARTWELL

Previously published by Joe Hartwell:

HUNTED DOWN

Maria Christopher is a fifteen-year-old schoolgirl. She is very popular at school, but at home her religious parents are strict and controlling.

Discovering that she is pregnant, fearing the reaction she is likely to encounter at home, Maria claims that she was visited by an Angel who advised her that she has been chosen to be the mother of God's Second Son. She also states adamantly that she is still a virgin.

Many years earlier, local Parish priest Father Giuseppe Bonelli was also visited by an Angel who told him that one day he would identify the girl who would become the mother of God's Second Son. The Holy Messenger advised him that it would be his duty to look after her along her journey, and protect her.

Police Inspector Paul Retberg is a practical police officer, and an avid atheist. When Maria Christopher and Father Bonelli receive death threats, apparently from Christians, he is called to investigate.

The threats continue and attempts are made on the girl's life. Retberg is ordered by his chief superintendent to arrange special protection for the girl and the priest, but even as the police inspector and priest are forming this unlikely alliance, a far more formidable danger develops. Devil worshippers begin to gather, fearful of the girl and her unborn baby.

As the birth of the child approaches, the Satanists plan an unholy attack. Father Bonelli and Inspector Retberg must move the girl to a secret location, but initial efforts fail leaving them with just one option. The baby will be born in a remote location on the North East Coast, in an old barn occupied by farm animals.

The priest, a few parishioners, and police officers led by Inspector Retberg, form an army to protect The New King. A fierce conflict ensues, a battle from which not all Retberg's officers will emerge in one piece.

PROLOGUE

On the 25th of March 1986 Father Giuseppe Bonelli, parish priest at the Church of St Michael, celebrated his seventieth birthday. He decided on a quiet gathering which was held at his own private house next to the church, and bang-opposite the hostel that he had managed for the previous ten years. JackDaw House was a sheltered accommodation for young ladies who had lost their way in life, many having got into trouble during their very early teens.

Some other priests from neighbouring parishes had popped in to congratulate him, and to share in the celebration with a drink or two... or maybe three. Other clergymen were there too. They also enjoyed a drink. There was even the Bishop from the West Midlands. He could knock them back.

Father Bonelli may have been seventy, but he kept himself fit with a three-mile jog every morning before breakfast. He was as physically fit as a man half his age. He had the looks to go with it, too. Slim and muscular, the sleeves of his T-shirt stretched over bulging biceps. He had a strong face with no noticeable wrinkles, and no bald patch although he kept his slightly greying hair short.

And he could take his drink. He was used to heavy drinking sessions having been in the army for twenty years before joining the priesthood.

But there was one evening, many years ago now, when a particularly heavy drinking session took place, and he lost a bet with a soldier who had the metabolism of a hippopotamus. After more than a few beers – followed by a modest number

1

of shorts – he started to feel a bit dizzy and sick, so he decided to go back to his own quarters to sleep it off...

And it was then that he was visited by an Angel.

The Holy Messenger, appearing as a man doused in shimmering blue light and hazy, white smoke, gave him instructions – and these were from *The Top*.

He was to leave the army immediately. He was to become a priest. He was then to wait for a girl who would also receive instructions. She was carrying God's Second Son, and it would be his duty to look after her and protect her. No timescale was given.

"How will I know her?" he asked the Angel. His own voice seemed to echo in his ears.

"She will know you," the Angel advised him. "Don't worry, she will come to you."

The Angel mentioned that there would be sceptical people. The girl would need to be wary of these groups. They might disbelieve her but, after all, they were mere people, albeit misled.

However, the Angel warned him, there would be a much more formidable threat...

Disciples of Satan were at large and had already been warned of the Second Coming. Once they heard that the Holy Child was on the way, they would be afraid and would have no qualms about kidnapping the girl, torturing her and ultimately killing her.

The Angel told Bonelli, in no uncertain terms, that it was these evil people he needed to be prepared for. They had the power to invoke one of Satan's most sadistic demons. Therefore, *he would need to be willing to sacrifice his own life for her if necessary.*

Then the Angel disappeared in a flash of light, leaving behind a puff of white smoke.

Bonelli was so sad to leave the army. All his comrades,

including his older brother Lucci, were also saddened and more than a little surprised. The army had taught him lots of things, and had given him a lot too, so his conscience was a little prickly when he found himself falsifying records, enabling him to take a handgun, about a hundred rounds of ammunition and, just in case, a few grenades.

And so there he was, on his seventieth birthday.

Waiting, but still believing, that one day, maybe very soon, the chosen young lady would appear.

CHAPTER ONE

Amidst a deafening roar from the home crowd, Maria Christopher took her place in front of the net. She placed the ball delicately in the palm of her right hand and held her left hand outward to assist with balance. There was a sudden hush all around the court.

The hush was then broken with somebody calling out, "Come on, Maria!"

Then sharp *shushing* sounds from other people before absolute silence was resumed once again.

There were people in the crowd who had made note of the date, the 25th April 1986, because it was on the cards that a memorable occasion, moreover an historical event, was about to take place.

It was the Senior Netball County Championship semi-final, and if Maria's school, Our Lady's Senior Girls' School, won, it would be the first time in their history that they had qualified for the final in any major tournament.

At the moment, Our Lady's were losing 33–32, but with just seconds remaining, and with the umpire looking at her watch and holding the whistle to her lips, their opponents, Blackfriars Seniors, committed an infringement defending their net.

When the umpire released a sharp, angry blast on her whistle, some of the visiting supporters cheered, thinking that she had blown for full time, but soon became silent when they realised that the whistle indicated a penalty which allowed two free shots to Our Lady's School.

The captain of the team, a burly sixth-form girl by the name of Geraldine Knox, immediately signalled to Maria, a fifth-former, and the youngest girl selected for the match. The team was mainly made up of girls from the sixth form, but at five-foot-nine Maria was still the tallest, slimmest and fastest player, and was widely acknowledged as the best shot at netball.

So she took up her position undaunted, and placed the ball in her hand ready to make the first of her two shots. Her long, dark hair was tied into a ponytail. She tossed it to one side, indicating a nonchalant kind of confidence, while inwardly making an effort to control her nerves. She knew she only had to score one point for the game to go into extra time, but to score both points would win the match for Our Lady's School, who would then progress to the final to be played in a month's time.

All the other players stood around behind her in a semi-circle, and after an initial moment of complete silence some members of the home team called out words of encouragement.

This caused a general din to build up again from all around the ground where other students and parents were gathered together to watch the match.

More shushing. Silence again.

The umpire signalled to Maria for her to play.

She launched the ball which sailed through the air, travelling upwards, then dipping at precisely the correct degree, ending up going cleanly through the rim of the net without even touching the sides.

The crowd roared, the noise rising to a deafening pitch. Maria's head was in a whirl. She was beginning to feel light-headed, perhaps from the excitement, she thought. The score was now 33–all, and she knew that even if she missed her next shot, her team was still in the match.

Another team member, Maria's best friend, Diana, passed the ball back to her, and when the crowd became quiet again,

Diana called to her, only just loud enough for Maria to hear.

"You can do it. Take two deep breaths."

Maria concentrated as hard as she could, but suddenly there was a weird spasm in the pit of her stomach.

"Oh, no," she whispered to herself. "Trust me to get the butterflies now."

The referee gestured to her, a little impatiently now, to take her second shot.

She took Diana's advice. Deep breath, composure, another deep breath.

"One, two, three," and she launched the ball again, a little blindly this time as nerves inexplicably took a sudden hold.

The whole school seemed to hold its breath as, again, the ball sailed through the air, but this time it tipped the edge of the net's rim. As if in slow motion it began a circle, spinning as it travelled round the rim. There was a gasp from the crowd as the ball, agonisingly, seemed to slow down. For one tiny fraction of a millisecond, it stopped.

Then it dropped through the net.

The home crowd exploded into a roar that was now so loud that Maria felt like she was going to faint, and indeed she would have fallen if it wasn't for her teammates rushing to grab her, then without standing on ceremony holding her aloft. Again she thought it must be the excitement of the moment as her stomach churned like a cement mixer. The other girls hugged her and kissed her in celebration, and the crowd around the court rose from their seats and surged forward.

Then Maria found herself just plonked back onto her feet again, but as her teammates were hugging and kissing, and congratulating each other, she tottered and started to feel really strange. She felt faint and dizzy.

Then to her dismay she realised she was going to vomit.

She was scared now. What was happening to her? She had experienced sickness before, but nothing like this. Surely the excitement of the occasion alone couldn't do this to her.

The feeling of dizziness intensified. She staggered again, nearly falling.

"Maria, are you all right?" she heard somebody shout above the noise.

She had no time to reply. She had to run.

The pavilion, she decided, nearly a hundred yards away, was her nearest hope, or everyone in and around the ground would be witnessing her vomiting.

Despite her increasing giddiness, and to everyone's astonishment, she suddenly broke away at a sprint, her long legs taking her right across the court, into the field beyond and towards the pavilion. She hardly heard the shouts of amazement that followed her. She heeded them not. Instead, her brain went into autopilot as she reached the pavilion and crashed through the doors, only just making it to the toilet in time before the first torrent of bile, mixed with bits of half-digested orange, came up in a frothy gush. It was during the second bout of retching that the door to the pavilion flew open and many of her teammates and friends came rushing in, all calling for her.

Then, as suddenly as it had started, it was over. No sickness or dizziness.

Maria flushed the toilet and opened the cubicle door to see all her friends gathered around with looks of concern on their faces. She then emerged and they stepped aside to let her through to the wash basins. With vomit still dripping from her chin, she leaned over one of the basins, looked round at her friends and managed a grin.

"Well, we won, anyway," she said, turning on the cold water tap. "That's the main thing."

"Thanks to you," said Diana. "But you..."

Diana made a gesture towards the toilet.

Maria shook her head and even managed a laugh.

"Oh, don't worry, it's nothing," she said as convincingly

as she could. "I hope I'm not coming down with that stomach bug that's going around."

She finished washing her face, grabbed a few paper towels and turned towards the changing rooms. All the girls laughed with relief as they followed her, but one of them stood still for a moment longer, a look of puzzlement on her freckly face.

"What stomach bug?" she whispered to herself. "Nobody's sick."

CHAPTER TWO

The incident following the netball match was not the first time that Maria Christopher had been sick so unexpectedly and suddenly, but on the two previous occasions the intensity of the vomiting hadn't been as bad, and the time of day was different. Each time it had occurred in the early hours of the morning while getting ready for school, but fortunately each time she had been washing in the bathroom and had been able to use the toilet quickly without her parents knowing anything about it.

But during that morning, the day after the netball match, it happened again, this time without warning. She was still in her bedroom and so had to dash across the landing into the bathroom. Fortunately nobody was in there. She had no brothers or sisters to worry about, her father normally left the house early each morning, and her mother was occupied downstairs in the kitchen.

But it was only now that a really disturbing thought occurred to her.

A month or so earlier she had been at a party with her friends when she met a lad, maybe two or three years older than herself. Everyone had been drinking quite a lot during the evening and were crashing out, one by one, all over the place. The parents of the girl who was throwing the party were away so all the friends had agreed to keep the mess to an absolute minimum. They promised to help tidy up afterwards, which would include airing the whole place out to get rid of tobacco smoke – or any other kind of smoke.

Maria got talking to a boy. They got on really well. She liked him, even though he was noticeably shorter than her. They even had a discreet little kiss and cuddle. She was enjoying herself now. It was a good feeling to get close to someone. And drinking red wine, with her glass being frequently topped up, she was getting quite pleasantly pissed.

The music wasn't too loud, so they were able to talk for a while without the need to shout.

Then he suddenly held onto her tightly.

"Let's go upstairs," he said to her in a breathless sort of way. "Nobody will notice. We can find a bed to lie down together and get a bit more comfortable."

"Okay," she replied, smiling.

She was not a naïve kind of girl, but she was beginning to experience a warm and cosy safe feeling developing inside her. She felt like she was now impervious to danger. Looking at him he seemed to be falling asleep anyway, so any kind of danger did not really occur to her. She felt very drowsy and all she wanted right then was to snuggle up somewhere and go to sleep.

Holding hands, they left the room, zigzagging between dancing couples along the way, and those gyrating students were too drunk themselves to notice what anyone else was doing. And with the music getting suddenly louder, most of them were falling around laughing wildly.

Still hand-in-hand, and heading carefully up the stairs, Maria looked at the boy and laughed.

"I don't even know your name," she said.

"Tobias," the boy replied, as they reached the top of the stairs.

"I'm Maria," she said.

He did not seem to hear or be particularly interested. He peered through an open bedroom door.

"Look," he said. "Nobody in here."

They went into the room and Tobias closed the door behind them. Maria instantly flopped down onto the bed. Her head rested on a lovely soft pillow.

"Ah, sleep," she mumbled to herself, already feeling herself drifting.

She had been a little drunk before, but this seemed different to anything she had experienced previously. She felt like she was floating, and all sounds were like distant echoes. She thought she could fly like a bird. Maybe, she laughed to herself, she should try it sometime. Why not? Next open window she saw, she decided, she would jump out. She was sure she could fly. Flapping her arms would be easy. She began to laugh louder.

She heard him laugh, too, but it was a sort of breathless cackle, and a strange shuffling sound made her turn her head towards him and open her eyes. What happened then, she wasn't quite sure. She struggled to recall as her memory became hazy.

*

She sat on her bed, now in her own bedroom, trying to piece together what happened that night. Tobias had taken off his trousers and underpants. She remembered being vaguely surprised at what she saw. It wasn't erect as she imagined it should be, and it was really small.

He was huffing and muttering to himself. "This has never happened to me before."

The next thing she noticed were his testicles. They were not small, but huge instead.

In fact, the size of a pair of lemons.

"Don't worry," she had said to him. "It doesn't matter. Just lie down next to me."

"Don't laugh at me," he snapped at her suddenly.

"Who's laughing?" she said. "I don't care, it doesn't

matter."

Again, she just rested her head and closed her eyes.

Apparently giving it up as a bad idea, he lay down next to her.

"I'm sorry, I'm so sorry," he started saying, and he kissed her on her cheek. "I promise I'll be better next time."

"All right," she mumbled. "It's okay."

He managed a glancing kiss on her lips, but she could not stay awake any longer. She fell into a very deep sleep.

And when she woke up in the very early hours of the morning, Tobias was gone.

*

As she continued to think deeply about that occasion, still sitting in her own room at home on her own comfortable bed, she said one word out loud. "NO."

No, she thought, shaking her head. She couldn't possibly be pregnant because she hadn't had sex. She had never had sex. She was now just a month away from her sixteenth birthday and she was still a virgin.

Or was she?

Then she breathed a sigh of relief as she remembered something else. She had not missed a period. She began having periods at the age of twelve, and they had been as regular as clockwork ever since.

But still, was it possible that Tobias had managed it while she was asleep, and had had sex with her?

Without her even noticing? Or remembering anything about it afterwards? If so, it would have been an astonishing occurrence.

It was a pity there wasn't a reliable kind of home pregnancy test available. In years to come she felt sure there would be, but of course that was of no benefit to her now.

She was in two minds as to whether to just go straight to her doctor, or perhaps the nearest pharmacist, and simply request a pregnancy test, but how humiliating and embarrassing.

"No," she said again, repeating in her mind, she was sure she could not be pregnant because she was positive she had not had sex, and she had not missed a period.

With that thought clearly established in her mind, she settled down for bed.

*

The window of Maria's bedroom was slightly open, and during the night a gentle breeze began to blow, causing a rustling of the trees outside, and billowing the curtains slightly. A bright light from somewhere began to glow, possibly from a car's headlights. Maybe a car had been parked up the road with its headlights left on.

Maria suddenly sat up in bed and was about to get out to close the window, when a shadowy shape began to shimmer from outside.

She couldn't speak. Even though she was sitting up, for some strange reason she felt like a pillow was being pressed over her face preventing her from calling out. She kept watching the window and as she did so the shimmering shape from outside began to gradually seep through the window, like a bubbly liquid, and having completed its entrance through the window it appeared to solidify.

Then, the shape of a person gradually began to emerge, and completed its transformation into a man.

Maria stared, transfixed, at the man standing there. A big, powerful-looking man, all muscly with a bare smooth chest, was standing there, now actually inside her bedroom. And he was shimmering in a bright light that almost dazzled her.

Again, Maria tried to speak, to call out, to cry out, but

still she felt like a pillow was being squashed over her face muffling her attempts at making any sound at all, and now even restricting her breathing.

Then the man spoke to her...

"Maria." His voice was quiet but deep. "Maria, you have been chosen..."

The girl began to shake with terror. She was petrified but still she could not cry out or scream, which is what she wanted to do.

"Maria," the shimmering man went on. "God has chosen you."

And then, all of a sudden, it became clear to her. Of course, this was merely a ridiculous dream, and this vision, she supposed, was an Angel. She stopped being scared. She even laughed aloud, and with that at last she found her voice.

"Chosen?" she shouted. "Chosen for what?"

"*For the Second Coming,*" the Angel's voice suddenly boomed at her.

Raising his voice still further he added, "There is to be a miraculous event, one last time before the End of all Things..."

"The End?" said Maria. "Oh, no." She found herself hoping that that wouldn't happen before the County Championship Netball final.

"... and you," the Angel continued, "will bear the child. Even as we speak, God's child is growing inside you."

Maria roared with laughter. "I don't believe you," she shouted.

She was positive now, that this was a bizarre dream. The very idea of God choosing her to be the mother of his child, to her, was hilarious.

"Believe what I tell you, Maria." The Angel was booming again, and the shimmering of light seemed to be getting even brighter.

"Rubbish! Just clear off, will you?" She shielded her eyes

from the light with her hands but now, inexplicably, she was starting to feel breathless again and, once more, she was having serious trouble with breathing.

"It'll be God's child," the Angel insisted. "It'll be a..."

Bang, bang, bang, bang, bang.

That sudden noise interrupted the Angel. He looked around him as if taken by surprise. Maria also looked around her. What was happening now?

The Angel resumed. "What you have to do now is..."

Bang, bang, bang, bang, bang.

"Maria." Not the Angel's voice now, but her father's.

The Angel disappeared just as the bedroom door flew open.

*

Maria's father rushed into the room and switched on the light. He was sure he heard his daughter's voice calling. He saw that she was in an almost impossible, twisted position in her sleep with her face pressed down into a pillow, with another pillow on top of her. She appeared to be choking, suffocating.

He rushed over to her, pulled the bedclothes right off her, then put his arms round her, pulling her round so that she faced upwards. Her breathing then immediately returned to normal. Her eyes fluttered open, but only momentarily as she murmured something in her sleep which sounded something like, "Nobody will ever believe me."

Then she turned over onto her side in a naturally comfortable position and went back to sleep.

Maria's mother appeared in the doorway.

"Is she okay?" she said.

Maria's father looked at his wife.

"Bad dream, I suppose," he told her. "Seems okay now."

"It's draughty in here."

The curtains were still flapping slightly, so Mrs Christopher crossed the room to close the window.

Then Maria's parents each gave their daughter a kiss on her forehead and left the room together.

CHAPTER THREE

When Maria woke up the next morning, she had no immediate recollection of the Angel's visit. Instead, her mind returned to the dilemma she had considered, that on one hand she could not be pregnant because she had never had sex and not missed a period, but on the other hand there were certain symptoms, together with a nagging doubt that persisted in her head.

And to make matters seem worse, on visiting the bathroom, she noticed some light yellowish discharge she had never seen before.

"Oh, no," she groaned to herself. "What could this possibly be?"

This was something she would definitely need to discuss with her doctor. Worries were beginning to build up.

Then she heaved her shoulders, trying to decide what to do. First things first, she told herself.

Putting the anxiety about the discharge to the back of her mind for now, something else occurred to her.

She remembered reading somewhere that a very close examination could detect if a girl was a virgin. There was a membrane deep inside the vagina.

"The hymen," she said to herself, clicking her fingers. By examining this, her doctor could give her absolute reassurance.

With complete confidence on the matter, she concluded a pregnancy test would not be needed. Just a test to prove she was still a virgin would be enough.

After some further thought she decided she would go and see her own doctor. Maria would tell her the reasons for her concern and ask for a close examination. She looked in her bag for her school timetable. She was sure she had a 'free', (a study period) that morning and, sure enough, there it was, from 8.30. The doctor's surgery opened at eight, but early appointments were always snapped up quickly.

She looked at her watch. 7.45. She would set off from home as though she was on her way to school, then take a detour, calling in at the doctors' surgery in order to make the earliest possible appointment.

She wished she had such a thing as a mobile phone. She had heard that in America all the kids carried around what they called cell phones, and she thought that in the future every schoolgirl in England would have one, too, but again, that was absolutely no help to her in her present predicament.

"Maria!" came her mother's voice from downstairs. "Keep your eye on the time or you'll be late for school."

"Okay, Mum," she called back. "Just going."

She quickly gathered everything up into her bag, dashed out onto the landing, then went quickly down the stairs.

"Bye, Mum!" she called out as she went through the front door, and just as she was closing the door behind her she heard her mother's voice again.

"But you haven't had any breakfast."

Having got to the end of her road, instead of walking towards the school she went in the opposite direction towards the town, and that road would lead to the doctors' surgery.

Once she got there, she was able to make an early appointment with her own doctor, a woman, Doctor Walters.

A few moments later she was sitting in the doctors' waiting room.

You have been chosen.

For some reason, those words suddenly flashed into her mind, and for just a split second she had a vision of something shimmering inside her bedroom window.

But then it went from her mind completely, and no matter how hard she tried she could not remember it, or understand it. She dismissed it from her mind and glanced at a clock on the wall as she waited.

She didn't have to wait long. Her name was called out and she went down the corridor, politely knocking on the door before entering the doctor's room. The doctor smiled up at her and typed something in on her keyboard as Maria sat opposite her, naturally a bit nervously. Dr Walters opened up a file containing Maria's medical record.

The doctor glanced at these briefly, then back at the girl sitting opposite her.

"So, Maria," she said quietly, "what can I do for you?"

God has chosen you.

Again, a deep but quiet voice in her head and, once more, that shimmering vision inside her bedroom window, only this time it had taken on a shape, like that of a person, but...

"Maria," the doctor said kindly. "I said, what can I do for you?"

Maria shook her head in confusion. After a moment or two, she coughed to clear her throat, then began to speak slowly and carefully.

"Thank you for seeing me so promptly, Doctor Walters," she said, "but I've come here this morning to ask you if I can have my vagina examined."

Doctor Walters then sat back in her seat, her eyebrows raised.

"Why, Maria?" she asked. "Are you experiencing some kind of discomfort? Itching perhaps, or soreness?"

"No, Doctor," said Maria. "You see, if it's possible, I want confirmation that I am still a virgin."

Doctor Walters raised her eyebrows still further, not able to disguise surprise.

"I don't quite understand," she said. "Are you telling me

that you cannot remember if you have had sex?"

"Yes, that is what I'm saying."

Maria went on to explain to the doctor about the encounter she'd experienced with the boy at the party about a month earlier. For now, she wouldn't mention about the sickness. She thought that if she could just confirm that she was still a virgin, then there was no real need to discuss anything irrelevant.

"Oh, I understand," Doctor Walters nodded. "So you require assurance that he didn't do anything without your consent while you were asleep."

Maria bowed her head and felt her face going crimson with embarrassment. But she nodded.

"That's about it," she confirmed.

After a moment, the doctor asked, "And do you do any cycling or horse riding?"

"No," Maria said with a nervous laugh. "But what's that got to do with it?"

"Those kinds of activities, if often enough and sufficiently vigorous, could break your hymen. But if you don't pursue those kinds of activities, then the hymen should still be intact..."

"... if I am still a virgin." Maria completed the sentence for her.

"Exactly," the doctor said, then after another moment, she stood up and walked round to the other side of the room where there was a couch,

"If you can lie down here," she said, as she pulled a screen around the couch. "Remove your lower garments and let me know when you are ready."

Maria did this, then called out, "Okay, ready."

The woman doctor appeared with what looked like a stick with a bobble on the end. Maria thought it looked like a large cotton bud.

"Just relax," Doctor Walters told her, "but part your legs as far as you comfortably can."

As well as being a brilliant netball player, Maria was a good dancer and could perform the splits, but she didn't think it was an appropriate moment to show off, so she parted her legs to what she thought was a reasonable position. She then gritted her teeth slightly as the probe went up inside her. It was wiggled around for a moment before it was, thankfully, withdrawn.

"Okay," the doctor said with a long sigh. "Put your things back on then come and sit down again."

Maria was a bit surprised at this. She somehow expected the doctor to simply tell her that everything was okay, and that she could go now. Why she evidently wanted some sort of discussion about it, Maria had no idea. She approached the doctor's desk once more and sat down. The doctor was typing something again, this time producing a printout on a pre-headed form.

"Right then." Doctor Walters swivelled her chair round. She seemed to look at the girl long and hard before continuing.

"The membrane inside your vagina, the hymen, is intact, so you will no doubt be relieved to know that you are still a virgin. However..."

Maria looked up at the ceiling and released a huge sigh of relief.

"Thank God," she gasped.

"However," the doctor continued, "may I ask you some questions about this encounter?"

"Why? What's wrong?"

"This boy you met. Do you still have contact with him? Can you speak to him?"

"No," Maria said. "I don't know him. All I know is his name is Tobias, or at least that's what he told me. I don't know where he lives, or anything."

"Someone at the party may know him," Doctor Walters persisted. "A friend of yours perhaps."

Maria was beginning to feel stressed again.

"What's wrong?" she repeated.

"You..." The doctor paused again as if deep in thought. "You do have an infection there, and there's some nasty discharge. Have you noticed...?"

Maria remembered the yellowish dribble of something she had noticed that morning.

"Just occasionally," she murmured. "Recently..."

"Perhaps in your..."

"But I thought you were satisfied that the boy didn't do anything to me."

Doctor Walters made calming gestures with both hands, and released a long, slow breath.

"I didn't actually say that. What I said was you are still a virgin."

Maria shook her head in confusion. "I don't understand." She felt like crying now.

The doctor made more soothing gestures.

"He may have started," she explained, "but failed, or fell asleep himself."

Maria decided, at that point, not to go into too much more detail. For example, the unusually small size of the lad's private member.

Not being a mind reader, the doctor added, "Maybe he was so drunk he couldn't get adequately prepared, so did not fully penetrate you, but this infection can be transmitted without a full penetration."

Doctor Walters stopped there. She could see that Maria was becoming upset and confused. She turned back to the form she was completing, typed a few more things and pressed a button on her printer. Two pieces of paper appeared from it. She pulled them out of the machine, leaned across the table and handed them to Maria.

"One of those is a prescription for you to take to the

chemist," she explained. "Just a special cream to apply at the end of each day."

Maria looked at the printouts in her hand.

"And the other one?" she asked.

The lady doctor took another long breath.

"I've booked an appointment for you at the Bridge Street Clinic," she said

The young teenage girl looked bewildered and shocked. "A VD clinic?"

"It's only a precaution," Doctor Walters said, "but I'm afraid I do have to tell you that I suspect that you have contracted chlamydia which, as I said, is a sexually transmitted infection."

Maria's head was now buzzing with confusion and anxiety.

"My God, this is serious," she muttered.

"Well, in itself, it's not terribly serious," the doctor explained, "but it can get serious if not treated. It could be cleared up with a course of antibiotics, but the consultant at the clinic will be able to explain more to you."

"But..."

"All I can say at the moment is unfortunately you do show some of the symptoms of the infection known as chlamydia, and I would like to eliminate the possibility of anything more serious."

As if in a very bad, intense dream Maria stood up and picked up her bag.

God's Child is growing inside you.

"God," Maria gasped, putting her hand to her forehead. It was that same voice again. She knew it from somewhere, and that glimpse of something, some*one*, standing inside her bedroom window...

She moved and staggered slightly towards the door. The doctor watched her with great concern.

As Maria made her way to the door, Doctor Walters made

a gesture as though just remembering something else.

"Also," she said, "just part of the procedure, they will want to carry out a pregnancy test."

"What?" Maria suddenly froze. "But..."

"Just another precautionary procedure," the woman added hastily. "Merely routine. A letter will then be sent to me as your GP, to confirm the test results."

This was getting steadily worse for Maria, having initially been told she was still a virgin. She now believed it was a bad dream and at any moment she would wake up out of it.

But before she left the doctor's room, she said, "So if Tobias has passed chlamydia onto me, what symptoms would he have? Would it be something I could have seen?"

Doctor Walters bowed her head over her table then looked up.

"The most common symptom in a man who has chlamydia," she said, "and most noticeably, is an enlarged and swollen scrotum."

As Maria went through the door, she suddenly felt so faint she thought she would fall. She closed the door behind her and momentarily leaned on the wall.

There is to be a miraculous event, one last time before the End of all Things...

She understood now. It came back to her. It was a dream she'd had.

The previous night she'd dreamt that she had been visited by an Angel. But what the Angel told her could not possibly be true because she could not be pregnant.

And still she clung to the belief that she was a virgin.

CHAPTER FOUR

The next morning, Maria Christopher found herself sitting in the waiting room of the Bridge Street clinic. She had pee'd into a pot and handed it to a nurse for the pregnancy test, and had submitted herself for a probing examination to confirm whether she had contracted chlamydia. That had all happened twenty minutes ago, and she felt sure that the results, along with explanations and advice on these, should have been given to her by now.

At last there came a call from a doorway up the corridor.

"Miss Christopher, if you could come this way please."

Maria could feel her heart pounding. What would they tell her? That everything was all right? She had a terrible feeling that it was not going to be that simple. Then she had a sudden, quite silly, thought of just running out of the building, and pretending that none of this had ever happened. She wouldn't have to listen to what they had to say. But she knew that this problem – if there was a problem – was unlikely to go away all on its own.

With one deep breath, heaving her shoulders, she calmed herself down and walked steadily towards the open doorway.

"Come in," said the nurse.

Maria went in and the door was closed quietly behind her. She looked around the room and the nurse stood to one side. Then she noticed another young woman in plain clothes sitting at a desk.

The woman gestured to a chair opposite her, inviting Maria to sit down.

"Good morning," said the young woman. "I'm Doctor McLoughlin."

"Hi, there," said Maria in a carefree manner that she was far from feeling.

"I've been looking at the tests," said Doctor McLoughlin. "The results are detected very quickly."

"What's the outcome?" said Maria. She could sense that this was going to be bad.

The doctor looked at her seriously. "Maria," she said. "You are pregnant."

The teenage girl sagged in her seat. There was something like a loud, heavy buzzing noise suddenly going off in her head. Her breath came in short gasps. She felt dizzy, sick and more than a bit scared.

"Oh, my God," she breathed.

Her head began to ache, a dull, throbbing pain. Moments passed by.

Then she became aware of the fact that Doctor McLoughlin was continuing to speak, but she hadn't heard a word since being told she was pregnant. She tried to speak herself but then found she couldn't do that either. Her mouth and throat had suddenly become tight and dry.

The doctor, realising that Maria was in a state of shock and panic, stopped speaking too and more moments of silence were allowed to pass.

"Maria," the doctor began again. "There are options open to you. Perhaps you…"

"Options?" Maria just gazed at her.

What options could there be? What to call the baby?

"Yes," the doctor said quietly. "For example, whether you want to have the baby, and if you do, if you want to keep it…"

"I don't believe this is happening," Maria muttered. "It must be a mistake."

"But in any event," Doctor McLoughlin continued, "you

should first allow yourself time to discuss this with your parents."

Maria gazed at her and shouted, "My parents? Absolutely no way. Are you kidding?"

"They'll have to know sooner or later. You won't be able to hide your condition for long."

The young girl, without realising it, had that very moment turned into a young woman. She was normally a tough cookie anyway, but from now on she would really need to stick up for herself. She glared at the doctor defiantly, ignoring her suggestion.

"Look, this is a mistake" she snapped. "My GP examined me and told me that my hymen is intact. I'm still a virgin."

"I will be sending my reports and the results of the tests over to your GP this morning," said Doctor McLoughlin. "I agree that the hymen is still mostly intact, but there's a very slight break, and even the slightest split..."

"... and," Maria continued, "I have not missed a period."

Doctor McLoughlin did look surprised at that, her forehead wrinkled.

"That is puzzling," she said. "There is no mistake about the pregnancy test, however, which is positive."

"No, please." Maria leaned forward and held her tear-stained face in her hands.

"... and as for your hymen," the doctor continued, "even the tiniest slit would allow semen to pass through. Also, I noticed Doctor Walter mentioned in her notes to me, that the boy you were with was quite drunk, and she suspects that he was unable to attain, and/or, maintain... how shall I put this...? Readiness, ability and yet..."

"You listen to me," Maria said. "Nothing could have happened. If it had, I would have remembered it."

"Not if you'd been drugged," the doctor said.

Maria looked at the plain-clothed doctor, stunned. She

opened her mouth to speak, but again, found that she could not.

"And also, I'm afraid," the doctor added with a reluctant expression, "you do have chlamydia."

Up until that moment Maria had been attempting to fight back the tears, but at that point she gave up the fight. She put her face in her hands and sobbed.

Then the doctor took a long, slow breath and said, "This boy who you were with, we will need to examine him. Can you ask him to come to this clinic, please?"

"I don't know him." Maria was now just able to talk. "I have no contact details. All I know is he told me his name was Tobias. We lay down on a bed together, I went to sleep, and when I woke up he was gone."

"Can you give me any information about him at all?" the doctor persisted.

Maria made a visible effort to pull herself together.

"While I was still awake," she said, "he exposed himself, but it was rather unusual..." she paused, wondering whether to say more.

"Go on," the doctor urged.

Maria told Doctor McLoughlin what she considered to be strange about the dimensions.

The doctor considered this for a moment, then said, "Anything else?"

"Yes," said Maria. "His scrotum did seem to be a bit swollen."

The doctor nodded.

"That is one of the symptoms of chlamydia in a man," she said. "As for you, your condition is not too serious provided it is cleared up quickly, and for that I can prescribe for you a course of antibiotics."

Maria just looked at her and released another hefty sigh.

"But I do need to examine that boy," the doctor concluded.

"Try to find out from your friends, or anyone else at the party, if they know him, and how to get in touch."

Maria just nodded.

"And as for your pregnancy, I will send my notes over to Doctor Walters, together with the results, date and time of the tests, and no doubt she will want to see you to discuss options."

"Thank you," said Maria at last, and with her head spinning and her stomach churning, she got up out of her seat and walked out of the surgery.

And as she did, a now-familiar, deep but quiet voice, seemed to embed itself firmly into her brain.

You have been chosen.

God has chosen you.

God's Child is growing inside you.

There is to be a miraculous event, one last time before the End of all Things.

*

That evening, Maria Christopher sat alone in her bedroom, having told her parents that she was tired and wanted an early night. During the afternoon she had intended to call Doctor Walters again to say she wanted to be examined again, with a magnifying glass if necessary, but then wondered what the point of that would be. So far she hadn't mentioned anything to her own GP about the full circumstance of the night of the party, her morning sickness, or the results of the tests at the clinic. Doctor McLoughlin had told her that the test results would be sent over to Doctor Walters who would then, presumably, call her in for a further consultation, and to discuss her options.

What she needed to find out now, though, was who and where, Tobias was. If nothing else he needed to be urged to seek medical advice. Whether he would agree to, that she didn't know.

She went downstairs, told her parents she needed to call one of her friends, then brought the phone up to her own room and plugged it in there.

First she called her best friend Diana.

Diana's mother answered but passed it quickly to Diana when she recognised Maria's voice.

"Hi, Di," Maria said, as cheerfully as she could when Diana answered.

"Maria," came the friendly response. "Are you okay now?"

Maria had told everyone that she had been feeling a bit unwell ever since the netball match, and had an appointment with her doctor.

"Oh, it's nothing," she said with a tight laugh. "I've probably just been working too hard."

Diana laughed. "As if," she said.

Maria laughed, too, but then said, "Listen, Di, you remember that party at Julie's a few weeks ago?"

"Oh, yeah..." Diana seemed to hesitate. "I remember. What happened to you? It was getting late, about 3 am. We were all looking around for you but you'd disappeared. I kept on meaning to ask you about that, but just forgot I suppose."

"Di, I need to ask you..."

"So what *did* happen to you, then?"

After a pause, Maria said, "Listen, Di, I need to tell you, I met a lad but he disappeared on me."

"Typical guy," Diana said. "I hate guys like that."

"It's not like that. I think he really liked me, but maybe he was just a bit shy."

But even as Maria said those words she knew it was a lie. She thought of the way he had suddenly exposed himself. Not something that she wanted to tell Diana about.

"So what was his name?" Diana asked.

Maria paused for a moment. "Tobias," she said. "At least, that is what he told me."

"Hmmm." There was another pause, then Diana said, "I'm sure that with a name like that I would have remembered him. What did he look like?"

"Slim, like me," Maria said, "but an inch or two shorter, and with dark, wavy hair."

"Sorry, Maria," Diana said, "but I just don't remember him."

"Okay, thanks anyway."

"Why don't you call Julie and ask her?"

They then wrapped up their conversation with fond goodnights.

Maria thought for a long moment before making her next call, then at last called the host of the party. But Julie didn't know Tobias either, and couldn't remember him at the party.

"Maybe a gatecrasher," she suggested with a laugh. "I'll ask around."

"Ok, Julie," said Maria. "Thanks, anyway. Goodnight."

"You, too, sweetie."

Very slowly and deeply troubled, Maria got ready for bed. As she did so she began to consider all her options.

Telling her parents…?

"NO," she said out loud. "Totally out of the question."

The absolute row that would ensue from telling her parents just didn't bear thinking about.

An abortion…?

The laws had changed now regarding terminations. If she carried the baby to full term, which she estimated would be towards the end of December, she would be just five months away from her seventeenth birthday, but even now she could arrange an abortion without her parents having to know.

Yes, that would have to be the answer. She took in a deep breath and heaved her shoulders as she did so. On reflection, in the morning, she would make another appointment with Doctor Walters, and then put the plan into motion. Slightly comforted by the idea, she settled down into bed and soon went into a very deep sleep.

CHAPTER FIVE

When the following morning arrived, though, she had the strangest feeling. She surprised herself with the following thought...

Hold on just one moment. Do I really want to have an abortion?

And that afternoon, when she got home from school, she went straight up to her bedroom. Her mother called up to her asking if she wanted anything to eat or drink, but Maria told her she had got a ton of homework and just wanted to get it out of the way.

During that day at school her teachers had noticed, for once, how inattentive she had been all day, saying very little to anyone and, when she did say something, it was wrong, causing sniggers from many of the other girls. Maria may have been the best netball player out of the fifth, *and* even the sixth form, but at geography she was crap. On one occasion, when asked for the capital city of Malta, in an absentminded voice, she told the surprised geography teacher that it was Cyprus. This brought about howls of laughter from the other girls, and earned her an angry expression from the teacher, together with a hundred lines: *The Capital City of Malta is Valletta. Not Cyprus.*

But at the moment she had more pressing issues on her mind than worrying about capital cities of different countries. She had been agonising all day over her decision to have an abortion. She had, so far, not contacted her doctor again. She could hardly believe this herself but, in fact, she was beginning to change her mind about that. For some reason, amazing to herself, she was actually starting to warm to the idea of having a baby.

If that was her decision then, after all, Doctor McLaughlin was right. She would at some point have to tell her parents. But what they would have to say about it didn't bear thinking about.

And *God*, she thought. What would they *do?*

They were an extremely strict Catholic family. Maria, though, hadn't been to church for a couple of years. For a while, her parents had attempted to force her to go, using a series of outrageous arguments, but eventually gave up as these methods caused their daughter to become even more wilful and stubborn.

Maria felt that her questions about religion had not been adequately answered, being told, "Happy are those who believe without proof."

Whereas it was good, she thought, that her parents upheld family traditions and values, her father wouldn't give an inch here. He described the Catholic faith as "a package deal". You either adhered to all of it, or none of it. It was all or nothing. You couldn't simply choose what parts you liked and reject the bits you didn't agree with. He believed that each person was undergoing some sort of test. Some people thought it was tough.

"It wasn't meant to be easy," was Mr Christopher's abrupt reply to that one.

"*Why did Jesus get crucified?*"

"To prove how much his Father in Heaven loves us."

That doesn't make sense to start with, but anyway...

"*If God loves us so much, why does he let us suffer with disease, and wreck our homes with hurricanes and floods?*"

"We'll understand more when we die and go to Heaven."

And as for people having sex outside marriage, that was

not just the limit. That was way beyond the limit.

He described unmarried people having sex as "living like animals". And to commit adultery, well those people, in his eyes, should repent quickly and sincerely.

So not much leeway there.

Maria smiled to herself, but then became serious again as her thoughts returned to her present situation. Her parents believed strongly that bringing children into the world was a wonderful and beautiful, thing, but to do so outside of wedlock went against all their beliefs, so Maria could easily predict how this news would go down.

'Like a lead balloon' would be putting it mildly.

And another thing, increasingly as the day wore on, she had been thinking about her dream she'd had about the Angel who informed her that she was to give birth to the Child of God.

She could still hear that deep, but quiet, voice in her head…

"You have been chosen."

… and the other things he had told her.

Then the notion suddenly dawned on her. *Hey, maybe it wasn't a dream.*

She considered the facts.

Fact Number One: she was pregnant but she honestly could not remember having sex. Doctor McLaughlin had told her she could have been drugged which would have accounted for not being able to remember what happened.

That, she decided, was rubbish, coupled with…

Fact Number Two: she had not missed a period.

(It is worth noting here that when Maria started having her periods, she noticed that she only had one period every *two* months. A visit to the doctor, a referral to hospital and tests etc., revealed that only one of her ovaries was active. She was just twelve at the time and was told it was not uncommon in a girl so young, and not to worry, the other ovary would soon begin to work. Now, just one month from her sixteenth birthday, and she still had not *noticed* any change there.)

Fact Number Three: Doctor Walters examined her and advised her that her hymen was intact, and therefore she was a virgin. However, Doctor McLaughlin said she detected the tiniest split in the membrane, and that could possibly explain the pregnancy.

But that, too, Maria concluded, was nonsense. So sure was she on that point that she felt there was little point in re-visiting her own GP, Doctor Walters, to be examined again. When her GP saw the test results from the other doctor, no doubt she would call the fifth-form student in for a further examination if she thought it was necessary.

And 'Fact' Number Four: although as yet not proven, was the visit from the Angel. And that notion that had dawned on her persisted. She said to herself, out loud this time, "Maybe, just maybe, it wasn't a dream."

Some of her schoolmates looked at her in surprise, but she ignored them, unaware that she had just spoken out loud in her geography class.

And on her way home, that thought persisted. Could it really be true?

Could it really be that she was going to give birth to the Son of God? The Angel may have just said *Child* of God, but Maria decided that *Son* of God would sound more convincing if she was going to tell anyone.

Tell anyone? How absurd would that be. What was she thinking?

Maria laughed to herself for the first time since the netball match.

Having carefully examined all the facts, God's child or not, she was prepared to face the conclusion that she was going to have a baby. The situation, then was perfectly clear...

She *would* have to tell her parents.

But when she got home, and went straight to her bedroom, a curious expression appeared on her face. A plan was developing in her mind. She sat on her bed as she went over it.

She would have to be so convincing, she told herself. If she told her parents this story, she would have to go the whole hog. No holding back, full conviction, no wavering. And having done it she would have to stick with it, swearing to it, and being prepared for intense questioning, and over a very long period of time.

Was she up to it?

Yes, she decided. *She was!*

Still sitting on her bed, she began a kind of rehearsal, silently going through the words in her head. She heaved up her shoulders, preparing in her mind's eye, going for broke.

And the story was this:

An Angel appeared telling her that she had been chosen to be the mother of the Son of God. She *then* began to experience symptoms, like morning sickness, but she knew she was still a virgin. She went to the doctor for an examination to confirm her virginity, just in case anyone thought she was lying. As requested, the doctor closely examined her and confirmed that she was still a virgin. And it was this point, in her mind, that absolutely settled it.

The exact sequence of these events wasn't exactly right, but she didn't think that mattered.

She grinned to herself. She had been thinking about this all day, but now at last she had made up her mind.

She was going to do it.

She looked at her watch. It was now early in the evening and her father was still not home from work. She would have to wait for him to come in. She wanted both her parents together, then she would go downstairs so that they could all have their tea together. Then she would tell them.

A chill ran down her back with the thought of it, but she

made a visible effort to get herself together.

"Don't chicken out already," she told herself. She had to stand firm. Even then she knew there was stormy weather ahead.

But at that moment she had no idea of *how* stormy it would get.

CHAPTER SIX

Eventually Mr Christopher arrived home. Shortly afterwards it was teatime and Maria went downstairs, saying hello to her father. She abruptly avoided him when he went to give her the usual hug. Somehow, she couldn't face hugs and kisses, not until her story was told. Then, if he wanted to give her a hug that would be okay. She had a horrid feeling, though, that he would want to give her something but it would not be a hug.

However, for now, he was merely surprised.

"Are you okay?" he asked her kindly with a smile. "You seem a little bit jumpy."

"Um…" It was too early to say anything. She wanted tea out of the way first.

"I'm all right," she said quietly. "But I do have something I need to tell you both."

"Well? What is it?"

"Please, let's have tea first."

Maria's parents looked at each other with concerned faces. Tea was eaten in almost complete silence, all three of them exchanging anxious looks with just occasional questions like "How was school today?" and from time to time Maria's parents murmuring something to each other, while at the same time worrying about what it could be on their daughter's mind that was making her so tense. Her mother considered for a moment that maybe her daughter was unwell, but on the other hand she seemed to be eating as hungrily as usual.

Finally, Mrs Christopher put down her knife and fork, took a sip of orange juice, then looked across the table at her daughter.

"So Maria," she said at last. "What's up?"

Maria also placed her utensils down quietly, took a deep, deep breath, then slowly exhaled, slightly puffing out her cheeks. One final decision, she briefly thought to herself, then no turning back. She went for it.

"Mother, Father," she began, graciously nodding to each of her parents. "I'm going to have a baby."

A second of stunned silence, then Mr Christopher began to choke on a piece of grilled sausage. Mrs Christopher jumped out of her seat and gave him one hefty smack on the back, which expelled the sausage piece with some force. The chewed-up piece of food went like a bullet across the table, hitting the mayonnaise bottle with a loud *splat*. Maria's mother then staggered back to her seat, while her father gradually got his breath back.

Maria looked at each of her parents in turn, backwards and forwards for a full minute before one of them spoke.

Then, as one, they both stood up. Maria stood up, too. She just thought it was the right thing to do. The meeting was going roughly in accordance with her prediction, with both her parents, especially her father, looking as though they were about to explode. Her father's face, in fact, had turned a hideous shade of purple.

Her mother then approached her daughter and grasped her shoulders in her hands. She began to shake the girl. Maria wondered what this action was supposed to achieve.

The woman continued with the shaking. "You stupid, stupid, silly, stupid, foolish, stupid girl," she yelled. "You..."

"Stop it!" Maria shouted back at her, pushing her away.

Then her father spoke. "We are a respectable family," he said with a noticeable effort at controlling his temper. "This will bring shame upon us. How dare you do this to us. The way we've brought you up is..."

"Who's the father?" Mrs Christopher interrupted her husband.

"Mum, Dad." Again she gestured to each of her parents, now using the less formal address. "I need you both to calm down for a moment, and just listen to me."

At that point her father lost control of his temper.

"What's there to listen to?" he shouted. "You've gone off with some random bloke, you've had a shag somewhere, probably in the back of a car up a country lane, and you've been caught out. Are there any other details to add to this sordid, disgusting story?"

Maria faced her father defiantly, with her hands on her hips.

"How do you know all of that?" she shouted back at him. "Making out that I'd go for a shag with just anyone who happened to come along."

"Well, haven't you?" her father roared.

"Thanks a lot, you prat."

Mr Christopher, a man well-liked at work, a respectable man in his community, opened his mouth for some further comment, but no words came out. Only some croaking noise.

Mrs Christopher let out a loud moaning sound, sat down and picked up her orange juice.

"How could you do this to us?" She began to sob.

"Won't you please listen to me now?" Maria said firmly, but amazingly calmly. "I really need to tell you something."

"Tell us something?" Maria's father started looking around him with an expression on his face like a man in a daze. "Tell us something?" Then he looked at his wife. "She wants to tell us something." Then back at Maria again. "Oh, yes, please do tell us something. You've been shagging left, right and centre, and got pregnant. But really, never mind all of that. What do you want to tell us?"

Although this meeting was going more or less as she

expected, her father's last outburst really annoyed her.

"If you will just shut up and listen to me for a minute," she said firmly, "then I will tell you something – something really wonderful."

Mr Christopher gazed at his daughter, then at his wife. When at last he spoke, it was as if his bottom jaw had become partially paralysed.

"Our daughter's gone mad," he managed finally.

"Will you please just listen to me," Maria was shouting again now. "I haven't been shagging at all. *I'm still a virgin.*"

Mr Christopher then decided to sit down. He took his place, opposite his wife, leaned forward and put his head in his hands. He then looked at his wife, opened his mouth to speak, but once more, words just failed him.

Maria looked at her two stunned parents just sitting there, the two of them completely speechless, but it was while neither of them could think of anything more to say just then, that she took the opportunity to really deliver her story.

"I *am* still a virgin," she repeated. "And to confirm this I went to Doctor Walters to be examined, and she confirmed my hymen is still intact." The girl, growing in confidence by the minute, decided to hammer home the main ingredient again. "I *am* a virgin."

Her parents gazed at her, looked at each other, attempted words to say, but they were still only able to make incoherent babbling sounds.

"Believe me when I tell you…"

"So…" her father interrupted her, shouting, finding words at last. "How do you account for being pregnant, you stupid girl?"

Maria panted for breath. After a long pause, though, she recovered and made a visible effort to compose herself. She faced her father, and the look of sheer defiance on her face at that moment utterly stunned him.

And she knew now that this was the moment. She faced her parents and with amazing confidence she spoke quietly, but firmly, virtually in a monotone.

"I have been chosen," she said. "Chosen by God to give birth to His Second Son."

Mr Christopher turned to his wife. There was a minute of painful silence, after which he was just able to speak in a husky whisper.

"A termination," he said. "That's our best bet."

Mrs Christopher considered this for a moment, then nodded. "Then a visit to a psychiatrist," she added.

"You're not listening," Maria said. She had predicted this so she was well prepared. "I'm not having an abortion, and you can't make me. I know the law. And even if you could make me, you'd both go to Hell for killing God's Child."

Her mother, still seated, gazed up at her with shock and pain in her face. She struggled to speak, and when she eventually managed the words, her voice was unsteady. Her words came out in painful gasps. "So – what makes – you think – you are going – to have – God's Child?"

"Oh, Mum," Maria said, her expression at last breaking into a serene smile. "I was visited by the most lovely Angel, and He told me."

Then her father really did look like he was on the brink of a catastrophic explosion.

"We can't tell people a complete load of bollocks like that," he shouted at her. "Nobody's going to believe that. People would just think you're bonkers, but come to think of it…"

Maria's mother looked at her husband, then at Maria, then back at her husband.

"Oh, Holy Mother," she said, letting out a huge breath. "It would be better than saying she's been sleeping around and doesn't know who the father is."

Mr Christopher gazed at his wife in wonder. "Please don't tell me that you're prepared to go along with this outrageous story? This totally insulting lie?"

It was Mrs Christopher's turn to hold her head in her hands.

"What choice do we have?" she said.

Maria laughed with relief and happiness. Just at that moment she had a premonition of the future. Everything was going to be all right.

A long moment of complete silence elapsed, after which Maria spoke again.

"Okay, well, that's my news," she grinned at her father, and in an attempt to lighten the atmosphere, she added, "and how's your day been?"

If she'd expected a laugh from him at that point, she was disappointed. The glare he gave her made her involuntarily turn away. On reflection, she thought it unwise to tarry.

"Oh, well, I'm really tired," she announced. "I'm off to bed now for an early night. School tomorrow as usual, you know. Goodnight."

She walked gracefully out of the dining room and closed the door quietly behind her. Her parents sat opposite each other at the dining room table, for a moment in stunned silence.

Then they looked at each other and both said simultaneously, "Bloody hell."

CHAPTER SEVEN

The next morning, and only a mile away, a distinguished guest arrived at the ancient Church of St Michael. The parish priest there was in for a pleasant surprise.

Father Giuseppe Bonelli enjoyed his drink, but he was a good priest and was still sober enough on a Sunday to deliver a meaningful and heartfelt sermon. Fit and strong-looking for his seventy years, he'd just returned to his house after his usual early morning, three-mile jog.

He did much of his own housework too, but he hired a housekeeper who also helped with the church, and the hostel that he managed, JackDaw House, a sheltered accommodation.

One of his ex-army comrades was his brother Lucci. Although two years older than Giuseppe, they looked almost identical, and anyone from a distance seeing him at Father Bonelli's front door just then, would have thought it was the priest.

Lucci knocked at the door and waited. He occasionally paid his brother a visit during the week, but not usually this early in the morning. There was, in fact, a particularly important reason for this visit. He carried with him a briefcase, and inside that was an extremely special parcel. He knew that when his brother saw what was in it, his eyes would almost literally light up.

He glanced at his wristwatch. Just gone 8 am. He knocked again.

He was just about to go around the back of the house and look in through the kitchen window, when he heard the sound of the catch on the door. Then the door opened.

Giuseppe stood there, still breathing quite deeply following his run.

"Oh, it's you," he said in his mother tongue.

(When there was just the two of them, they always spoke in Italian.)

Lucci laughed. "I love you, too," he said as he stepped forward.

The two brothers, as always on greeting, hugged each other.

After a moment, Giuseppe leaned back to look into his brother's face, almost like looking into a mirror.

"It's great to see you," he said. "Come on in."

They went straight through to the kitchen. Giuseppe filled the kettle and switched it on. After a few minutes of general conversation, they took their cups of tea into the living room and sat down opposite each other.

Lucci placed his briefcase on the floor between his feet.

"Still no word of the mum-to-be, then?" he inquired, referring to Giuseppe's statement he had made prior to leaving the army.

"None so far," Giuseppe conceded, bowing his head. "But I know, I just know, it's going to happen soon. I can feel it in my bones."

Lucci looked at him seriously.

"You've been saying that for over ten years now," he pointed out with a faint smile.

"I know, but it is getting closer," Giuseppe insisted. "Believe me, Lucci. Don't ask me how I know. I just do know."

Deep in thought, both brothers placed their teacups down onto the coffee table.

Lucci looked at Giuseppe long and hard. Then he reached down to his briefcase and unzipped it.

"I've brought a little present for you," he said.

From his briefcase he took out a leather pouch. It was about eight inches in length and tied with laces. He passed it to Giuseppe who stared disbelievingly into his brother's eyes as he reached out with both hands to take it. It was much heavier than it looked. He placed it across his knees then carefully began to untie the laces. He pulled the top of the pouch apart and looked inside.

He then released a sudden breath that sounded like a gasp of fear, as he saw the three horrible, nasty objects therein.

"My God," he whispered. "I can hardly believe it. You got them."

"Anything for you, dear brother," Lucci told him with a smile as he reached for his teacup again and took a sip of the steaming drink.

"And no doubt about it? The genuine articles?" But even as Giuseppe said those words he could sense that the ancient, gnarled objects he held in his hands were genuine.

"You insult me." Lucci feigned indignation. "I'll tell you the story of how I stole them."

"Fill me in later," Giuseppe said. "But how can I ever thank you?"

"Also, I'll explain what you have to do with them," Lucci continued.

"I already do understand most of the ancient scrolls."

"Yes, the ones that include what Jesus said during the last supper..."

"I know." Giuseppe was in full flow now. "Words not mentioned in *The Bible*, words that explained how his blood would banish demons, words explaining why he *had* to be crucified."

"Listen to me," Lucci told him, "Even as we speak there are men, evil men, followers of Satan, who believe just as strongly as you do..."

Giuseppe looked at him, his brow wrinkled in surprise.

"... but with completely different intentions, of course."

"Tell me."

"When the girl you speak of emerges, they will be afraid of her," Lucci warned. "They are already afraid, even before they know who – or where – she is."

"The Angel said she would come to me," Giuseppe reminded his brother.

"The evil people will eventually know her too. They will make attempts to take her, ultimately to kill her, and the child."

"I will protect her," Giuseppe said determinedly. "I will give my life for her if necessary."

"My beloved brother," Lucci said, reaching out his hand and touching the priest's arm. "I pray it doesn't come to that, but I've learned that they are planning the most atrocious evil, if they are unable to reach the girl themselves."

"But what? How?"

"By invoking the most terrifying, evil spirit this world has ever witnessed. If these followers of The Devil are not successful, then a demon will be summoned."

"But these..." Giuseppe placed his hand upon the pouch, as if for protection.

"Yes, but you will need to identify somebody who can carry out the instructions," said Lucci, "just in case anything happens to you first."

"But who? Who can it be?"

"You must find someone," Lucci continued. "Someone who will do the deed correctly, and carry out the actions in exactly the right sequence."

"But..." Giuseppe was struggling with this. At that moment he had no idea at all who such a person could be.

"And," Lucci held up one hand with his forefinger extended, "the person must understand that they will only get one chance, and by carrying out these instructions it is almost certain that they will lose their own life in the process..."

"My God."

"... but a place in Heaven will be assured."

Giuseppe opened his mouth but no further words came out.

Lucci wanted to help all he could.

"You were saying that the mother of God's Son will make herself known to you," he said. "Well maybe the person who will assist with this ultimate fight against evil, they will somehow become known to you too."

Father Bonelli's head was in a whirl. He knew something about The Devil's demons having learned about them from the Jesuits who he had studied with for more than three years. In all, there were seventy-two demons, each one with a different evil power and rank among the gutters and sewers of Hell.

"Do you know which demon they are planning to invoke?" he asked at last.

Lucci thought for a moment, then he said, "While I was working under cover in Jerusalem, spying, I heard something. I didn't catch the name but apparently he initially appears as a boy of about twelve, then he grows to over eight feet in height, then he changes his form into a..."

"Bael." The name fell from Giuseppe's lips.

Lucci looked at his brother in shock.

Bael was the most evil and terrifying of all The Devil's demons. He was the most bloodthirsty, barbaric monster, thriving on mayhem, disaster, misery, agony, mutilation and death. One of the people invoking this sadist would have to offer a sacrifice, usually an arm or a leg, sometimes both legs which would just be torn off.

There was only one being in the entire Universe more deplorable than Bael...

The Devil himself.

CHAPTER EIGHT

As Maria Christopher made her way to school that morning she could hardly believe how happy, relieved and relaxed she felt. This could only be, as she told herself, because she really was going to give birth to the Saviour of the World. She was beginning to believe it now, and that the appearance of the Angel in her bedroom really did happen and was not merely a dream as she had originally thought. Also, she decided, by believing it herself, she was going to make other people believe it, too.

As she went through the school gates, she was met by three of her friends, Diana, Julie and Becky. On seeing her they rushed to her, and there followed the usual greeting between them. Warm hugs.

"Feeling a bit better now?" Becky asked. She was a freckly girl with a high-pitched voice.

Maria tensed up slightly. "What do you mean?" she asked.

"Well, yesterday you were a bit off. Not exactly on top form."

The other two girls laughed as they all walked together towards the school entrance.

"I did lose concentration slightly," Maria conceded. "But I'll be fine today."

"Yeah, well, that's okay, then," Julie laughed. She was a big girl with broad shoulders and almost as burly as Geraldine Knox of the sixth form. But as well as playing netball, she was a fine tennis player and had qualified for the first preliminary round at that year's Wimbledon Juniors' event.

"That's right," said Maria. "So will you guys give me a break?"

"But today in geography, we've got to list towns and cities in Spain and Portugal," Julie continued, "so don't get them mixed up... Unless you actually *want* detention."

Maria stayed quiet and smiled to herself. How ridiculous would that be, she thought. The mother of the Son of God being put on detention. How dare they even think such a thing!

"You might be asked to name the capital city of Spain, for example, or Portugal," Diana suggested.

Diana was Maria's very best friend. Maria looked at her just then and thought, such a pretty, blue-eyed blonde, and so sweet and pleasant. Why wasn't *she* the 'Chosen One'?

Diana looked puzzled for a moment, wondering why Maria was gazing at her so intently, but then she said, "If it's Spain, the capital city is Madrid. And the capital of Portugal is...?"

"What?" Maria broke out of her daydream

"Capital cities, you daft twit. The capital city of Portugal is Lisbon."

"And not Cyprus," Becky said with a serious face and holding up her forefinger.

All the girls laughed as they entered the school and made their way up the corridor leading to their lockers.

"Listen, guys," Maria said suddenly as they reached their lockers. "I've got something really important I need to tell you all. At lunchtime, if we can all meet up and sit together."

"Hey, we love secrets," Julie said. "Tell us now."

At that moment, though, a rowdy group of girls from the third year bustled by, all shouting as they went, and pushing and shoving each other boisterously. Maria turned to look at them as they went past, then she turned back to her friends.

"No, not now," she said. "At lunchtime."

"It is a good thing, though, isn't it?" said Becky with a

slightly worried face.

"Guys," Maria said with a smile as she looked round at her friends. "I promise you. It's the most amazing thing you've ever heard."

*

Maria believed that telling her friends she had been chosen to be the mother of the Son of God was going to be relatively easy after the discussion she'd had with her parents the previous night. Following a fairly uneventful morning in class, she arrived in the dining area ahead of the three other girls. She got a tray, then put as many different edibles onto it as she could. A plate containing a good helping of beef casserole, and another plate with an equally large helping of apple crumble for dessert. She picked up a serving spoon and topped it with as much custard as the plate would hold. For some reason, she felt particularly hungry, then remembered with a grin that she was now eating for two. As an afterthought, before finding a table for herself and three friends to sit, she added two chunky bread rolls to mop up the gravy of her casserole, got two large knobs of butter to go on those and a jug of orange juice. Satisfied that she had fitted all she could onto the tray, she chose a table for four, and as far over into the corner that she could find. She placed her tray down, then sat down and began to look round for the arrival of her friends.

She didn't have to wait long. Julie arrived first, saw Maria, waved at her and went to the serving hatches. She arrived at the table with a salad, a plain yoghurt and a small glass of blackcurrant juice. She gave a wide-eyed stare at what Maria had selected.

Jokingly she remarked, "You're not eating for two, are you, by any chance?"

Julie fully expected her friend just to laugh, so her reaction was most unexpected. Maria looked up, startled, and just for a moment looked like a naughty child who had been found out. The very next moment, though, she recovered, and did laugh, but it was a very nervous kind of gesture.

Julie had a weird feeling about this now. Looking up, she saw Diana and Becky arriving. They were standing by the serving hatches, deep in conversation.

"Oh, just a minute," Julie said to Maria. "I've forgotten my mayonnaise."

With that she went back to the serving hatches, got two sachets of mayonnaise, then whispered over to Diana and Becky, "Hey, you guys."

Diana and Becky looked at her inquiringly.

"I think I know what Maria's big news is," she said.

"You do?" called back Becky.

Julie made frantic shushing gestures at her, then cupped a hand to one side of her mouth. "Yes," she said. "I think so." Then she mouthed the word, "Preggers."

She then made her way back to the table leaving Diana and Becky staring after her with their mouths gaping open.

"Oh, no!" gasped Becky. "Poor Maria."

Julie got back to the table and sat down, moments before Diana and Becky arrived. They sat down opposite the other two, placing their trays carefully on the table.

For a couple of minutes they began to eat their lunches in silence, Maria pondering over Julie's ill-timed joke, and regretting her involuntary reaction to it.

It was Diana who broke the silence.

"So, Maria, my dear," she said. "What's the big news, then?"

"Yes, come on, out with it," said Julie, confident that she already knew. "We're all agog."

Maria looked at each of her friends in turn, then after a pause she said, "I'm keeping this quiet for a while," she began, "but eventually everyone will know. I've already told my parents, and now I'm only telling you." After another short pause, she said very quietly, "I'm having a baby."

Julie suddenly sat up erect, and looked at Diana and Becky in turn with a big expression on her face which said, "I told you, I told you, I told you..."

"Oh, Maria," was all Becky could say, holding her hands over her freckly face.

"Well, congratulations, I suppose," said Diana. "But who's the father?"

Maria leaned forward to speak confidentially, and all the girls huddled together.

"Promise to keep this to yourselves for now?" she said.

"Okay," said Becky.

"Of course," said Diana.

"Oh, definitely," said Julie, while in her mind beginning to suspect one or two possibilities.

"I am actually still a virgin," Maria told them quietly.

Each of Maria's friends suddenly sat back in their seats. Becky became completely rigid. Her mouth opened and closed but no words came out.

Diana's facial expression was one of puzzlement. She, too, found words difficult. She did utter the one single word, "But..."

After a moment, though, Julie did manage to speak.

"You're having us on, of course," she said.

"Nothing of the kind," Maria told them cheerfully, now gaining back her confidence. "I have a test result and an attached letter from my doctor saying that I have been thoroughly and carefully examined to conclude that my hymen is intact, and this confirms that I am still a virgin."

Her three friends just stared at her.

"Of course, if you don't believe me," Maria said disdainfully. "If you think I'm lying..."

"Oh, don't be a little idiot," said Diana. "Clearly it is what you believe…"

Maria suddenly became serious and leaned back in her chair.

"I am a virgin," she said in a clear, steady voice. "But I am having a baby, and I have been visited by a messenger of God, a lovely Angel, who told me that I am going to be the mother of the Son of God."

While Maria was saying this she was getting so carried away that she didn't notice Mrs Keen the science teacher taking a seat at the next table. Neither did Maria seem to be aware that her voice had risen in pitch and had grown considerably in volume.

"Shush," Diana said, waving her hand frantically up and down in front of her mouth. "You don't want everyone to hear this wild story, do you?"

"I will be telling everyone soon," Maria said still quite loudly, "and it's not a wild story. I'm having a baby, a boy, the Son of God, and…"

"Christ Almighty." Becky found her voice at last. "You really do believe all this, don't you?"

"If you're calling me a liar…" Maria's voice was getting even louder.

"Of course not," said Becky. "If that's what you say, then I believe you."

"What about you, Di?" Maria looked at Diana.

But at the moment Diana was distracted. Both she and Julie had noticed how Mrs Keen kept turning towards them, with her head repeatedly twitching in their direction.

"All right, whatever you say," Diana said. "Just please keep your voice down, will you?"

Maria looked at Julie who was making frantic jerking gestures at Mrs Keen.

"Do you think she heard us?" Becky asked.

"Of course she did," Julie said through gritted teeth. "Unless she's completely stone deaf."

At last Maria calmed down, and slowly continued with a bit more of her dinner.

Then Julie said in a hushed voice, "Look, Maria, has this got anything to do with that boy you were asking me about? Tobias? The one who disappeared?"

Maria told her friends what happened that night, now six weeks ago. Then she reminded them of her being sick after the netball match. She had thought of the possibility it was morning sickness, but she couldn't remember having had sex. She went to the doctor who examined her and confirmed to her that she was still a virgin. After that she was visited by the Angel. He told her she was to give birth to God's child. She *then* took a pregnancy test that showed positive. (She slightly strayed from the truth here with the exact sequence of events.)

"Hold it, hold it…" Julie held her hands up and shook her head. "Go back a bit. Could you honestly not remember if you had sex with this Tobias bloke?"

"To be honest," Maria reflected, "No. But, you see, he couldn't have done."

Again the three friends gazed at each other.

Maria looked down with a look of embarrassment, took a sip of orange juice, then looked up again.

"He exposed himself, but he was having some sort of difficulty," Maria said quietly, not wanting Mrs Keen to hear that part of the story.

"What do you mean?" Julie said.

"Well, you know, he was trying to get himself started but just couldn't."

"I hate that," said Becky.

Diana and Julie gave Becky a brief look, neither of them quite knowing what aspect of Maria's statement she hated.

"The point is," Maria continued in a hushed voice, "no

matter how much he tried he couldn't get hard, and his dick seemed so small." She held up her hand, made a fist of it, then stuck out her little finger and wiggled it around. "I've never seen such a tiny one."

"How small?" said Becky, suppressing a grin.

"About one inch," said Maria. "If that."

"I know size isn't everything," said Becky. "But there is a limit, you know. You want a…"

"Oh, shut up for a minute," Diana snapped. "But I suppose if he was that small…"

"Even so," Julie began, "You could still…"

"Even so," Maria interrupted her, "there was something wrong with him."

"What Julie was going to say," said Diana, "is that some lads who have a small one when flaccid are still able to attain a fair-sized erection."

"That's true," Becky continued. "My current boyfriend, if he goes swimming in the sea…"

"Oh, for goodness sake, Becks," said Diana.

For a brief moment, Julie, Diana and Becky laughed, but the next moment they were serious again. And they noticed Mrs 'Eavesdropper' Keen was turning round and now twitching her head in their direction more than ever.

All four girls huddled together again.

"And another thing," Diana said in a confidential voice, "you said you told your parents this story?"

Maria nervously took another sip of orange juice. "Yes," she said.

"And?"

"They're fine with it."

"*Fine with it?*" the three friends gasped in unison.

"Well, not exactly fine with it," Maria conceded. "But I've shown them reports from the doctor…" (Another slight departure from the absolute truth.) "… and so I suppose they believe that part of it."

"Believe that part of it?" Julie's voice accidentally rose for a moment, but then she continued more quietly. "So, for the difference it makes, what part did they *not* believe?"

"Well," Maria looked up at the ceiling as if the answer was written up there, "they weren't entirely with me about the whole *Visit From An Angel* statement that I made."

"Curious, that," Becky remarked, unexpectedly.

Maria gazed at her, while Diana and Julie just grinned at each other.

"What do you mean, Becks?" she said.

"Well," Becky paused for a moment, obviously in thought. "I thought Catholics would believe anything they were told, especially something like that."

"Sad to relate," Maria said with a sigh, "I'm afraid not."

All the girls sat in silence for a moment, then Julie, first to finish her lunch, put her plates and cutlery together on her tray. She then looked round and saw Mrs Keen's head turning in their direction again, clearly listening.

"I think we should continue this discussion outside after school," she told her friends quietly, then more loudly for Mrs Keen's benefit she added, "Okay, I'll see you guys later. I'm off to the library now to check out some stuff for my history project."

With rather curious looks at Maria, the other two girls finished their lunches, got up from the table and left her sitting on her own.

With a satisfied smile to herself, Maria finished her casserole, and mopped up the gravy with the two buttered rolls. Then after a few gulps of orange juice, with a look of sheer glee on her face, she began work on the apple crumble and custard.

It was strange, she thought to herself, she never really liked custard before. Now, though, she had a real craving for it.

CHAPTER NINE

Mrs Daphne Roland was a very slim and elegant lady in her mid-forties. She was the school headmistress. She sat in her office after lunch going through some reports, adding her notes on the last page of each one. She had her favourite pupils of course, although she knew that she wasn't supposed to, and she was mindful of the need to keep such feelings to herself. She did her best to make the summary for each pupil as fair as possible. She remembered that she had once been a schoolgirl herself, so if one of the girls was found guilty of having a cigarette behind the cycle shed, she would deliver a lecture about health issues, but would be inclined to leave it at that. No song and dance.

She had a big surprise coming, however, about one of her favourite pupils.

There came a sharp rapid *knock-knock-knock* at her door. She tutted and sighed, not appreciating any interruption, but ready and willing to be polite and patient to whoever it happened to be.

"Come in," she called out.

The door opened. She suppressed another tut and sigh as the short, plump figure of the middle-aged science teacher, Mrs Holly Keen, appeared.

Mrs Keen swiftly entered the headmistress's office and closed the door quietly behind her, as if not wanting anyone else to know that she was making this visit.

Mrs Roland gestured towards the chair opposite her. The science teacher nodded her thanks and sat down. Moments passed while the headmistress finished the note that she was on. Mrs Keen breathed through stiffened nostrils, a little impatiently, while Mrs Roland appeared to be reading what she had just written, smiling with satisfaction to herself.

Finally, the headmistress placed the report down in front of her and looked up at the science teacher.

"Yes?" she inquired, taking a sip of water. "What is it?"

Mrs Keen took a deep breath.

"Daphne," she began. "I trust that you would know that I could not be accused of eavesdropping?"

Mrs Roland suddenly spluttered on her sip of water. She then took a handkerchief to wipe her mouth, then looked at the science teacher.

She could hardly help smiling, knowing that the plump woman did have a reputation, among other teachers and pupils, of being an unbearable eavesdropper. However, she managed to conceal her impatience, and she nodded politely.

"Certainly, I know you," she said.

"But at lunchtime," Mrs Keen continued, "I heard something, purely by chance, and I'm afraid what I heard cannot remain ignored."

"Holly, really, I..."

"And, Daphne, it is my duty to report such a thing to you."

"All right, then," said Mrs Roland, still maintaining her patience. "What is it?"

"The reason for me having to tell you, you will appreciate and understand when I tell you all I have learned, and made you aware of the facts..."

"Okay. Tell me."

"... and I'm sure you will thank me when I've enlightened you of the circumstances."

"Just tell me, please." Daphne Roland did not often raise her voice, but her patience was beginning to run out now.

"Several circumstances, in fact," the plump science teacher went on, "but one particular one, the main one I would consider…"

"Is this to do with one of the girls?" said the headmistress. "If so, without beating around the bush any further, tell me right now what's happened."

"It's about a fifth-year girl," Mrs Keen said at last. "Maria Christopher."

Involuntarily, the headmistress looked down at the report in front of her, as it seemed, by some strange coincidence, to have that very same name printed at the top of it. Then she looked squarely into the science teacher's eyes.

"What about Maria?" she said. "What do you think she's done?"

"Never mind what I *think* she's done, Daphne," Mrs Keen continued. "I'm afraid there's no doubt about it whatsoever."

"What, then?" Daphne Roland's voice was raised again. The headmistress took another sip of water to steady her nerves.

"I have to inform you," Mrs Keen began her longwinded rambling again, "that it has become my unhappy duty to tell you, as much as I regret to do so, and I assure you of the reliability of these facts, and also if I might be allowed to add…"

"*Holly!*" Daphne Roland shouted. For the first time in the history of Our Lady's School, the headmistress shouted in her office. "What on earth are you babbling on about?"

Mrs Holly Keen looked at her. "Really, Daphne," she said. "What I came here to tell you as promptly as I could, and without undue delay…"

"HOLLY!" It happened again. Twice now in less than a minute.

"She's pregnant." Mrs Keen got there at last. "A fifth-form girl. Maria Christopher."

Mrs Roland sat there in silence and glanced again at the near-perfect report she had in front of her on her desk. Again she read through the note that she had written on the back page, just moments before:

"The behaviour and work rate of this student, I would describe as exemplary. This is illustrated by her exam results together with her attendance record. She is a credit to this school, representing us in sports events at the highest level. She could try harder in geography, but I am still happy to add..." etc., etc., etc.

Then the headmistress looked squarely at the science teacher who was waiting for an appropriate response to her statement.

Because of the time lapse, the plump middle-aged woman then felt a need to repeat the statement. "As I say, she's pregnant."

The expression on Mrs Roland's face was that of sheer impatience.

"Nonsense," she said at last.

"I'm telling you what I heard," Mrs Keen said stiffly. "What I mean is, what I could hardly help hearing. Maria and three of her friends discussing it over lunch."

The science teacher was holding her arms out with the palms of her hands turned upwards, as if to say, 'What could I do about it?'

Daphne Roland leaned back in her chair and laughed softly.

"I think," she said, "that you have become the butt-end of a silly joke. I'm guessing that they could see you listening to their conversation and deliberately gave you something to chew over."

The science teacher's face went bright red.

"That's not the way it was, I assure you," she snapped.

"My friends and I used to do that sort of thing," the headmistress continued, still laughing, and looking out of the window with a glazed expression on her face as she reminisced.

"If we thought a teacher was listening, we would invent the most amazing stories."

"No," Mrs Keen protested. She felt indignant now.

"On one occasion," Mrs Roland went on regardless with her fond memories, "we'd got involved in a bank robbery, and…" The headmistress laughed aloud.

"No," Mrs Keen was getting annoyed now and spoke firmly. "That's not how it was at all. I could see they had their heads pressed together having a private natter before I sat at the next table."

"At which point you decided to go and sit somewhere else," Daphne Roland said with a derisive smile.

"There was nowhere else to sit just then," Mrs Keen said defensively, "and what I accidentally heard was said before they realised I was there."

"Hmmm." Mrs Roland looked down at Maria's report again. From her date of birth, she knew that the girl was only a few weeks away from her sixteenth birthday, but if this story was true then a report would still have to be made.

"If what you say is true," she said, "I would need to inform Social Services, so first I would need to make sure her parents are aware."

"They are already aware of it," the science teacher said promptly.

Mrs Roland shook her head.

"It seems like you heard a great deal for someone who was not eavesdropping," she commented dryly.

Mrs Keen suddenly went an even brighter shade of red.

"Really, Daphne," she said angrily. "I can assure you…"

The headmistress held up her hands.

"I apologise," she added hastily. Then after a moment of reflection, she continued, "Oh, well, I suppose I had better call for the girl and check the facts with her."

Mrs Keen had difficulty in suppressing her feelings. "Check

the facts with her?"

"Yes, I think so." Daphne Roland looked absentmindedly out of the window for a moment. "And check that she clearly understands all her options before I notify Social Services."

"Yes, of course." Mrs Keen also seemed to go deep into thought. "After all, calling Social Services can't be a decision you would take lightly."

"Indeed not."

At least the two women were in agreement on that point.

"Unfortunately, social workers have a reputation for causing conflict and breaking up families rather than helping to keep them together."

"Alas, that is true from what I've heard."

The headmistress smiled at her colleague and let out a heavy breath.

"Right, then," she said. "Was there anything else?"

There was another long pause, then the plump Holly Keen pulled another pained expression.

"Actually," she said, "there is something else. Something rather extraordinary and perplexing."

"What is it now?" said Mrs Roland with all the remaining patience she could muster.

The science teacher leaned forward slightly to speak confidentially, as if she suspected that there was somebody else hidden in the office.

"I definitely heard Maria Christopher telling her friends that she has been closely examined by her doctor," she whispered, "and..."

"*Stop, stop, stop,*" The headmistress held up her hands and was almost shouting again. "If what you are about to tell me is tantamount to a breach of confidentiality, then I must ask you to keep whatever it is to yourself."

"But I feel I have to tell you," Mrs Keen protested, "because this might signify some serious mental disorder."

"NO, please stop."

But having started, the woman was plainly determined to finish, which she did in a flurry. "She said her doctor confirmed that she is still a virgin."

The headmistress leaned over with her elbows on the desk, her eyes squeezed tightly shut and her hands clasped firmly over her ears. But she could still hear the other woman's voice rattling on. For a brief moment she considered leaning even further forward, grabbing Mrs Keen with one hand, while clamping the other hand firmly over her mouth.

"And," having got this far Mrs Keen seemed determined to complete her report. "And," she repeated, "*and* she made the statement quite clearly that she was visited by an Angel who told her she was to give birth to the Son of God."

Mrs Daphne Roland, headmistress of Our Lady's Senior Girls' School for nigh-on ten years, and elegant at forty-eight years of age, held her hands up, then banged her head three times on the desk. Then she looked up at the science teacher and spoke quietly.

"Really, Mrs Keen," she said. "I am surprised that you should utter such a stupid thing."

"But…"

"Leave this matter entirely with me," Mrs Roland said firmly. "I will discuss details with Maria before talking with her parents or Social Services, but I am convinced now that you have had your leg pulled."

"But…"

"Put bluntly, the girls have taken the piss out of you."

Mrs Holly Keen forced a polite smile and stood up. She nodded courteously towards Mrs Roland, then without another word walked out of the office leaving her headmistress with a severe headache.

CHAPTER TEN

After the science teacher had left the office, Mrs Daphne Roland sat at her desk for a few minutes completely perplexed and wondering what to do next. It was quite possible, in fact probable, that the nosy science teacher had become the butt-end of a schoolgirl gag, but this would have to be investigated.

Maria Christopher was just weeks away from her sixteenth birthday. Nevertheless, even if it was just a day before her sixteenth birthday, there was a process that the headmistress of the school was duty-bound to adhere to. And if it turned out that Maria was pregnant then plans would have to be put in place, and questions would need answers.

For example, would Maria want to remain at the school and continue with her studies? Support would be offered to her if she wanted to.

And who would care for the baby? Mrs Roland knew her parents and she doubted whether strict Catholic people would want anything to do with a baby born out of wedlock. But Maria would be entitled to have her views considered, too.

Would she want to have the baby adopted, or – Mrs Roland shuddered at the thought – would she decide on an abortion?

Maria Christopher, as mentally and physically strong as she was, would need advice and support. To this end, a representative of the Education Authority would arrange a meeting with the schoolgirl's parents and Social Services. The views of each of these people would naturally be quite polarised. Each one would be considered carefully, but in the end it would remain Maria's decision.

The headmistress drew a deep breath. No good speculating, she thought. She needed to speak to the girl. She looked at her watch and deduced that all the girls would now be on their way to their first afternoon classes. She observed the data on her computer screen and scrolled her way through the names of all the girls in each class. A grid appeared at last at the bottom of the screen that showed her where all the classes were scheduled to be. Maria Christopher, she knew, was in class 5F, and they were in their history lesson for the first period that afternoon. She picked up the telephone and dialled for the admin office. When the call was answered she requested that Maria Christopher should be asked to come and see her at once.

Mrs Roland didn't have to wait long. After five minutes there came a soft knock on the door of her office.

"Come in," she called out.

Maria came in looking somewhat apprehensive, so her headmistress spoke softly.

"Come in, my dear, close the door behind you and sit down." She gestured to the chair opposite.

Maria did as she was told.

"Is there anything the matter, Mrs Roland?" she asked quietly.

The headmistress took a deep breath.

"I do need to speak to you," she said. "It has been brought to my attention…"

"Have you been speaking with Mrs Keen?" Maria asked. "We noticed her ear-wigging at lunchtime."

Mrs Roland smiled, partly out of relief.

"So you were having her on?" she said. "Nothing but a silly prank. Oh, well, I suppose I…"

"Not at all," said Maria. "My friends and I were having a private conversation, but I'm quite happy to share my wonderful news with you."

Mrs Roland did not expect that. "Maria, I have to say…" but she didn't need to make any further comment or ask any questions. The fifth-form girl just rattled on.

And having discovered what this meeting was all about, Maria regained all her confidence. After all she had been expecting this and so had everything ready. Answers to questions were, by now, well rehearsed. She relaxed and continued cheerfully.

"Mrs Roland, I am having a baby."

From there she went on and told her headmistress every detail of what had happened so far, embellishing her story with some extra details, while the headmistress of the school sat there, beginning to doubt the evidence of her own ears. She was apprised of the whole story that culminated in the fantastic conclusion that a visiting Angel told her that she would give birth to God's Second Son towards the end of December of that year.

After hearing all of that, for the first time in her whole career, the head of the school sat there not knowing what to do or say next. A full two minutes passed containing only silence, but during that time Maria sat there facing her, unwavering, confident and unafraid.

"Maria," said Mrs Roland at last. "You will understand that I need to discuss this with your parents, and I'm afraid that Social Services will need to be informed."

"I don't see why," said Maria. "I'm quite capable…"

"I'm sure you are. But…"

"And they might want to take my baby. I won't let them."

Mrs Roland made calming gestures with both hands.

"No," she said. "If you made the decision to keep the baby…"

"Of course I'm keeping him," Maria said. "I've just said, I've been chosen to have the Son of God. Do you really think I'd want to get rid of him?"

"Nevertheless," Mrs Roland said, "you will require support and advice. Even adults need some sort of support when a baby is due, then even more so after the baby is born."

Maria just looked at her.

After another moment of deep reflection, Mrs Roland said, "Okay, Maria. Return to your class now, and I shall contact your parents, requesting to meet them before contacting Social Services."

Maria nodded, then got up from her seat and went to the door. Her hand was on the door handle when Mrs Roland spoke again.

"Before you go," she said, "Just one other thing..."

"Yes Mrs Roland."

"Have you been given an actual date yet for when the baby is due?"

"Yes," Maria said, smiling. "The twenty-fifth of December."

And with that she left the office leaving the headmistress of the school with a very puzzled expression on her face.

But Maria did not go back to her class just then. There was only another fifteen minutes to go until afternoon break, so she went to the library instead. She decided that she would go in search of her friends later.

CHAPTER ELEVEN

By the time that her friends came out into the quadrangle for their mid-afternoon break, Maria was still nowhere to be found. They were aware that she had been called out of class to see Mrs Roland, but they hadn't seen or heard anything of her since.

Julie looked around her and saw Diana and Becky walking with their heads close together in private conversation. She walked briskly towards them, calling to them as she did so. The two friends looked round, both wearing very troubled expressions on their faces.

When she reached them she spoke quietly. "So you haven't seen her, then?"

Both Diana and Becky shook their heads.

"She was called to the head's office," said Becky. "But that was well over an hour ago. She can't be still in there now, surely. She must have gone home."

"She wouldn't go home without telling us what's happened," Diana said.

"Where is she then?" Becky looked around her nervously. "And I wonder what the head wanted her for."

"My guess," Julie began in a hushed voice, "is that Mrs Keen heard every word that Maria was saying at lunchtime and went to report everything to Mrs Roland."

"The nosy bitch," said Becky. "I hate her."

"But if it's true that Maria is pregnant," Julie continued, "then her parents would have to know…"

"Maria said they already know," Diana reminded her.

"… and Social Services."

"Maria's sixteen now," said Becky, "so they can mind their own business."

"Nearly sixteen," Diana corrected her. "And Social Services will come in like a herd of bulls in a china shop and make it their business."

There was a moment of silence, the three girls huddled together, all with worried faces.

Then Julie said, "So what do you two make of Maria's story? Being visited by an Angel, and having God's child?"

"I believe her," Becky said immediately.

"You believe her?" Julie said. "You believe she was visited by an Angel, and that she is going to give birth to the Son of God?"

"Why would she make up such a story?" Diana said, not committing herself to saying if she believed it or not.

Julie looked at Diana with her head on one side. "Obviously she's afraid of being called a slut, being up the duff."

"Rubbish," Diana snapped. "If that's the case, she could have just gone for an abortion without saying anything to us, and she could have done so without her parents needing to know too."

That argument did leave Julie stumped, and the thought did then occur to her that *if* Maria truly believed that she was the Chosen One, she wouldn't readily opt for a termination.

"Well, maybe she…"

But Julie's reply was interrupted by a call from a few yards away.

"Here, you lot!"

They all looked round. There was the burly sixth-form prefect, the captain of the netball team, Geraldine Knox, striding towards them.

"I was calling you," she barked at them. "Why didn't you answer me?"

"Sorry, Gerry," said Julie. "What can we do for Your Royal Highness?"

"Cut the cheek, you," Geraldine snapped. "I'm trying to find Maria. She's your friend, isn't she? So tell me where she is."

"She had to go and see Mrs Roland," Diana told her.

"And why?" the burly prefect demanded.

"A private matter, I think."

"Nothing to do with the rumours, I hope," Geraldine said. Maria's three friends looked at her, their worried expressions intensified.

"And what rumours might they be?" Julie asked nonchalantly.

"Well," Geraldine Knox looked around her, then said, "I've heard it from a reliable source that she's knocked up."

The three friends looked at each other with looks of alarm. It was clear then, that someone other than Mrs Keen had overheard their conversation, and that would mean the news spreading around the school like wildfire.

It was Becky who, at last, unexpectedly broke the ensuing silence by saying, "Rubbish. Maria is a virgin."

Geraldine Knox visibly jumped backwards with surprise.

"And how, in God's name, would you know that?" she gasped.

"Because she told us," Becky answered truthfully, looking at the sixth-form girl like it was the most obvious thing ever.

"She told you she was a virgin?" Knox said. "When? Two years ago?"

Diana and Julie gave Becky imploring looks.

"No," said Becky. "She told us this very day."

Geraldine Knox's face registered even more surprise.

"And why would she announce to you this very day that she was a virgin?"

Becky opened her mouth to speak but Diana interrupted her.

"What Becks is trying to say, is that we all heard a rumour that Maria had a bun in the oven, but when we broached the subject she laughed it off and told us that if she was expecting then it would have to be the Immaculate Conception."

Julie smiled at Diana, admiring her quick thinking, and she had to admit now that there could actually be a thread of truth in that statement.

But Geraldine was not convinced and looked from one to the other noticing their tense body language. She was about to quiz them further when there was another shout. They all looked round and there was Maria coming towards them.

"Hi, guys," Maria called out, apparently totally carefree. Then, noticing the sixth-form girl standing there, she added, "What's up, Gerry?"

The burly prefect shook her head impatiently.

"I just wanted to check that you're okay for netball training tomorrow afternoon," she said. "Just in case you'd forgotten, we're playing in the County Championship final in three weeks' time."

"Don't worry," Maria smiled. "I hadn't forgotten."

"And I want all my players on their best form."

Maria's friends grinned at the words 'my players'.

Maria laughed. "Okay."

Geraldine continued, "Look here, we're playing the League Champions, St Angela's Seniors, and we've all got to play our best if we're to stand any chance at all of beating them."

"I'll see what I can do," Maria said. "But I must make sure that it doesn't coincide with any of my appointments."

"What appointments, you little fool?"

Maria looked at her, then at her friends. They were all making pleading faces at her that said *Please don't tell her.*

But Maria looked back at their captain and said, "I may as well tell you because eventually everyone will know. I'm pregnant."

Geraldine Knox then recalled the incident following the semi-final match where Maria suddenly became ill and had to dash off. That made perfect sense now.

She strode right up to the fifth-former and gritted her teeth.

"You little idiot," she hissed at her. "You absolute, stupid moron."

To her further annoyance, Maria just looked at her, smiled and shrugged her shoulders.

Geraldine felt like slapping her.

"Becky told me you were a virgin," she almost choked.

Maria laughed out loud.

"Well, that's true," she said. "I am."

"Oh, I see, it's just one big joke to you, is it?" The burly prefect was getting really angry now. "Here we are, going into the final of a major competition for the first time in our history..."

"Okay, but..."

"... and there's a chance for me to lift that trophy in front of a crowd of a thousand people, but then..."

"Yes, but you see..." Maria was trying to get a word in.

"... but then one of my players decides that it's more important to go off for a quick shag in the back of a car up a shady country lane."

"Take it easy," Maria laughed, having to raise her voice. "Will you please listen. I can still play. I'm only a few weeks gone."

"And," Knox continued regardless, "don't you know, there is the possibility that TV reporters will be there? This is a really big deal."

Maria and her friends looked at her. The big sixth-form captain was virtually in tears now. This netball final meant everything to her. She so badly wanted Our Lady's Senior Girls' School to win, and she knew that the best chance of that would be if Maria Christopher was in the team.

Maria was still standing in front of her. She smiled and put her arms around her.

"I said I can still play," she said. "And..." She allowed a little moment to pass as she looked round at her friends. "...and I promise you, *we will win.*"

CHAPTER TWELVE

That afternoon, once again, on returning from school, Maria went straight to her bedroom, opened her bag, and pulled out everything she needed to begin her homework, although she felt it was getting increasingly difficult to concentrate on such trivial things. Her mother popped her head round the bedroom door, first to ask her if she wanted anything to eat or drink, but then to inquire as to whether her daughter had had any further thoughts about having a baby.

Maria replied with a brief "No, thank you" to the first question, and an even briefer "No" to the second one, but then after a moment, added, "Actually, Mum, I was called to Mrs Roland's office today."

"Oh?" Maria's mum's face appeared round the door again.

"Yes, I was telling a few of my friends my wonderful news, and…"

Mrs Christopher gritted her teeth. She would hardly have described this news as wonderful.

"… and Mrs Keen, the science teacher, was listening, and reported me to the head."

"So what did Mrs Roland have to say, then?" asked her mother. "Knocked some sense into you, I hope."

"Well, she asked me when the baby was due…"

Mrs Christopher tutted loudly and glanced up at the ceiling.

"… and she told me she would be getting in touch with you shortly. Will that be all right?"

Mrs Christopher let out a sharp, irritated breath.

"Oh, yes, of course," she said with heavy sarcasm. "That's just great." And she quickly glided away and went downstairs.

But neither Maria, nor her mother, realised how quickly that contact would be made, and just an hour or so later the doorbell went with a cheery *ding-dong*.

A few minutes later, Mrs Christopher and Mrs Roland were sitting opposite each other, chatting over a cup of tea which Maria's mother had hurriedly made, during which time Maria had decided it would be judicious to stay out of the way so had remained upstairs in her bedroom.

At last, having exhausted all the initial pleasantries, Mrs Roland carefully placed her cup down on the coffee table and became serious. She looked at Mrs Christopher.

"I have to say, Mrs Christopher, I am here to discuss the serious situation I have just been made aware of," she began, "that your daughter, Maria, is pregnant."

Mrs Christopher shook her head.

"I really don't know what else I can tell you," she said. "She's being very stubborn about it I'm afraid and refuses to divulge the identity of the father."

"Quite so." Mrs Roland coughed uncomfortably. "She has also told quite a story to me," she added quietly. "First she claims – actually insists strongly – that her doctor has examined her and has subsequently confirmed that Maria has never had a sexual relationship."

"Don't tell me you believe that?" Mrs Christopher interrupted her.

"I confess," Mrs Roland said, looking downwards, "I don't know what to believe."

"I will speak to the doctor."

"I'm afraid you can't."

"I'm her mother," Mrs Christopher interrupted her. "I have the right to see her doctor, and..."

Mrs Roland held up her hand. "I'm sorry, but we have to

appreciate that any consultation between her and her doctor is confidential."

"But she's not yet sixteen!"

"Even so, she does have a right to privacy, and the right to make a decision whether she keeps the baby, has it adopted, or..." Mrs Roland's throat suddenly tightened up.

But Mrs Christopher guessed what the third choice was. "An abortion?" she said. "That would be best, I think. Both myself and my husband agree on that point."

"But at the end of the day, it's Maria's decision," Mrs Roland said. "And actually, she could have had a termination already without even consulting you, and you may never have known anything about it, but she has chosen to tell everyone."

"So you do believe her?"

Mrs Roland drew a deep breath.

"Mrs Christopher," she said. "Your daughter is saying that she was visited by an Angel who has told her that she is carrying God's Child, and so..."

"I asked you, do you believe her?"

"She is an excellent pupil at her school, and has many fine qualities, including honesty."

"Will you answer my question?" Mrs Christopher shook her head impatiently. "Do you believe her?"

Mrs Roland bowed her had and smiled.

"It makes little difference what I believe," she said. "The thing is, *she* really seems to believe it herself, and if that's what she says I'm not going to call her a liar. Also, if she does believe it herself, I wouldn't imagine that she would choose to have an abortion."

"But if she persists with this story," Maria's mother was close to tears now, "and if the story gets out..." Her words trailed away as she began to imagine awful things, like *What would the neighbours say?* And *What would her friends at the church think?*

Then she found her voice again. "How embarrassing," she said.

Mrs Roland looked at Maria's mother with very mixed feelings.

Then she said, "But, you see, Maria isn't at all embarrassed. On the contrary, she's actually quite pleased, happy to be having a child, excited even. She wants to have this baby. It is really rather extraordinary."

"She's not the one who's got to tell my friends at the church."

"She wants to tell everyone," Mrs Roland told her. "She wants to shout it from the rooftops."

"It sounds like you really do believe all this nonsense," Mrs Christopher said.

The headteacher just looked at her blankly, and said, "And the due date is the twenty-fifth of December."

Mrs Christopher held her head in her hands.

While this conversation was progressing, Maria, who had been upstairs in her bedroom, decided to descend quietly and sit on the stairs, and she smiled with satisfaction as she listened. Everything was going to plan. They were picking the idea up slowly, but she was more confident than ever now that if she just stuck to the story, it would eventually be accepted.

However, the conversation continued along a different track.

"Mrs Christopher," said Mrs Roland, "despite my own personal feelings, as you must appreciate, as headmistress of the school, I do have certain responsibilities and obligations. Maria is sixteen next month, but as she is still only fifteen I do have to advise Social Services."

"Oh, no," said Mrs Christopher, holding her hands over her face. "Not them, please. They'll only make matters worse."

"I'm sorry," Mrs Roland added, "and again, despite my own thoughts, if Maria insists on this story, and chooses to repeat it to Social Services, I feel certain that they will consider mental health issues. They may even ask, for example, has she fallen recently, and banged her head severely?"

Still sitting on the stairs, Maria nearly roared with laughter but she was able to stifle her mirth just in time by clamping both her hands over her mouth.

There was a pause before her mother replied.

"She has never had such an accident," she confirmed, "and up until now she has always been sensible, reliable and, as you say, totally truthful."

"I'm glad we agree on that point, at any rate," said Mrs Roland, looking into her teacup, deep in thought. "Coupled with the fact that, so she claims, she has never had a sexual relationship, I cannot help wondering if…"

"This is incredible," Maria's mother gasped. "You really do believe these outrageous claims?"

Outside in the hallway, sitting on the bottom step now, Maria was ecstatic. She was actually winning somebody over, and that person was the headmistress of her school.

"I really don't know what to believe," said Mrs Roland. "But I will inform Social Services. I will tell them of the conversation I had with Maria, and of this conversation."

"But…"

"I think they may wish to visit Maria at school, before they pay a visit here," added the school headteacher, standing up at that moment. "Thank you very much for a lovely cup of tea."

And before she went out into the hallway on her way to the front door of the house, Maria scooted back up the stairs just in time.

CHAPTER THIRTEEN

It was the next day, a Tuesday, that Mrs Roland contacted Social Services to fix up an appointment for them to visit the school. However, it wasn't until the Thursday that they made the visit, represented by a middle-aged Indian lady, Mrs Hosanna, accompanied by a much younger Irish lady, Miss O'Grady.

When they were shown into the headmistress's office, Mrs Roland looked from one to the other. For a reason she couldn't have given if asked, she took an instant dislike to Mrs Hosanna, and as for Miss O'Grady, she didn't look much older than Maria in the fifth year in her school.

"Tea?" Mrs Roland inquired as they came in and sat down. "Coffee?"

"No, thank you," said Mrs Hosanna. "If you don't mind, we'd like to save time by meeting... um... Maureen... straight away."

Mrs Roland gritted her teeth. She felt that her instant dislike of Mrs Hosanna was justified, if the woman couldn't even get the girl's name right.

"Maria," she said stiffly. "The girl, her name is Maria Christopher."

Mrs Hosanna looked at her impatiently, as if a name was of no consequence at all.

"Perhaps," Mrs Roland continued, "you'd like me to fill you in on some details before you meet her. Her background..."

"No need," Mrs Hosanna said abruptly. "It's actually best if we hear as little as possible from you."

"Really, I..." The headmistress thought that when Mrs Hosanna was a schoolgirl, when they were teaching basic manners, she must have been away that day.

"... or anything from anyone else," the social worker went on. "We will talk to her, we know how to approach these situations, you see. We are trained professionals and we will make our own assessments, and then provide the necessary recommendations."

"Very well." The headmistress picked up her telephone, quickly dialled the number of the front office, then requested for someone to go and fetch Maria from her classroom.

They didn't have to wait long. Five minutes later Maria was there, calmly facing the ladies from Social Services. Again, Mrs Roland noticed how confident, undaunted and unafraid she looked.

Mrs Hosanna began by asking a few very basic questions, the answers to which she already knew. Her name, age, how long she'd been at the school.

Miss O'Grady had been introduced as someone training in the department. The younger woman said very little. Maria glanced at her occasionally during the conversation and noticed how the trainee always looked away nervously. The fifth-form girl even formed the opinion that the young woman seemed a bit dim to be in a position like that. But Maria just smiled to herself. With her quick-thinking brain she began to think of ways she could turn this whole situation to her advantage.

But then Mrs Hosanna's whole manner abruptly changed. Maria expected something like this. She wasn't quite sure what it was supposed to prove, but she was ready to be thrown one way, then suddenly the other, probably in an attempt to catch her out.

The questions became rapid, but the sharp, young schoolgirl was equal to it.

"So do you and your boyfriend have intercourse regularly?"

"No," Maria said firmly. "I've never had sex as I've already told you."

"But you're having a baby?"

"Yes," said Maria. "I've explained that, too. Please pay attention."

Mrs Roland couldn't help smiling.

Mrs Hosanna breathed through flared nostrils.

"You must have an idea when it was conceived, though," she said impatiently.

"Must I?"

"Well, unless you're having sex so frequently…"

"Will you get this through your noddle before one of us dies?" Maria said. "I – have – never – had – sex."

Maria said all of that slowly, deliberately and sternly, but afterwards she couldn't help grinning broadly. She turned her face away momentarily. The next instant she was serious again and staring at the young trainee who looked afraid and turned away.

"I shall overlook that statement," Mrs Hosanna said. "You must be honest with me. I repeat, you must know when the baby was conceived."

Maria looked seriously at her again. "Yes, I suppose I must," she said.

The middle-aged Indian lady was now pumping air out of her nose with increasing irritation.

"Ah," she said. "So you admit it. You did have a sexual relationship?"

"No, never."

"That's impossible."

"That's your opinion," Maria advised her. "You're entitled to it. I disagree. I've never even had an orgasm."

Mrs Roland was just taking a sip of water at that precise moment and nearly choked on it.

Maria glanced at her and made an apologetic gesture.

The headmistress nodded back. Actually, she had been listening to all of this with great interest, and with some admiration for Maria who was standing up to this interrogation really well.

Mrs Hosanna, however, did not appreciate this communication going on. She noticed the exchange of glances and nods between the girl and the headteacher at that moment.

The Indian lady from Social Services looked at Mrs Roland.

"Perhaps it would be better if you weren't here," she said.

"NO!" Maria shouted suddenly. She was aware that her headmistress was on her side. She also knew she was entitled to have an adult present during this meeting. "I want her here. I'm not continuing with this meeting without her."

"All right, all right," Mrs Hosanna held her hands up. Then after a few deep breaths she continued with the questions.

"So, who is the father of your baby?"

"My child will be the Son of God."

"You said you knew when it was conceived."

"No. You did. And I'd prefer it if you did not refer to God's Second Son as *it.*"

This time Mrs Roland managed to hide her smile behind her hand. True or false, Maria was giving this woman a run for her money.

Mrs Hosanna was beginning to show signs of getting cross.

"Look, answer the question," she said sharply. "Tell me how long ago…"

"I don't know exactly," Maria said nonchalantly. "Six weeks ago, I guess."

"Right," said Mrs Hosanna, looking at Mrs Roland as if she'd just won a massive victory. "So was that when the Angel appeared?"

"No. The Angel appeared only a week ago, after I realised I was pregnant."

For the first time in the social worker's career, she appeared to get stuck. She was not sure what question to ask next.

Maria laughed. It was like playing chess, when you were in such a strong position that you knew you were going to win. If her opponent didn't resign, she could rub her nose in it. She went for the kill.

"I've already stated, I've never had a sexual relationship. I am a virgin as my doctor can confirm."

Beads of sweat popped out on Mrs Hosanna's forehead. She was visibly struggling to pull herself together, and by now her nerve was being torn to shreds. Then completely unprofessionally (she cursed herself for it afterwards) she challenged the girl and said, "If it really is true that you are going to be the mother of the Son of God, you must have been given some special kind of power."

"Possibly," said Maria with a devilish grin. She was actually starting to enjoy this now. She looked again at the nervous Miss O'Grady, who looked away again, perhaps fearing that the girl's story might, after all, be true.

Maria could tell that the young trainee was afraid of her, but this was no time to show mercy. Instead it was time to be totally ruthless. She was going to give the young woman the shock of her life, and the reaction might even frighten Mrs Hosanna whose nerves were already somewhat frayed.

Apart from being a popular student, and the school's most gifted netball player, Maria Christopher possessed two amazing and uncanny gifts. Whether it was some part of being the Chosen One, she didn't know, but these were skills she'd discovered, and had begun to develop, when she was still a very young child. She very rarely used them now, though. Some people, even grown men, had been shaken up when she had demonstrated these talents.

One was that she was able to move her eyes independently of each other and make them quiver so wildly that the pupils and irises became nothing but a blur. Then she would roll her eyes right up so only the whites were showing.

And two, she was a ventriloquist. She could make her voice sound like it was coming from another direction and make it sound deep and gruff... like a man's voice. Even her headmistress had never witnessed anything like what happened next.

She faced Miss O'Grady with her back to Mrs Hosanna.

"Look into my eyes," she told the nervous lady.

"I... I... I'd rather not," the young woman stuttered.

"DO IT!" A loud, deep, gruff voice came so suddenly, apparently from behind her, that it made Miss O'Grady spin round.

"Okay, let's stop this nonsense now," said Mrs Hosanna. "We..."

"SHUT UP!" came the loud voice again. Then Maria said in her own voice, "You wanted a demonstration, and by God you're going to get it."

Even Mrs Roland looked quite shocked.

"Now, look into my eyes," Maria told Miss O'Grady, "or you'll be very sorry."

The young social worker trainee did as she was told, as if hypnotised.

"That's it," Maria said softly. "Keep looking, keep looking, keep looking..."

Maria began to move gradually closer and closer to Miss O'Grady, shuffling her seat quietly as she did so, until they were barely three inches apart. Then she closed her eyes, but kept talking softly, "Keep looking, keep looking..."

And then suddenly she opened her eyelids revealing two quivering orbs, both twirling in opposite directions, and at precisely the same moment, a loud, deep, man's scream, "Aaaaahhh!" from behind her.

Poor Miss O'Grady fainted. She fell off her chair, smacked her face on the edge of Mrs Roland's table on the way, before ending up, face down, on the floor, completely unconscious.

"Good Lord," was all Mrs Roland could say.

Mrs Hosanna rushed to Miss O'Grady's side, knelt on the floor next to her, then looked up at the fifth-form schoolgirl who was now sitting there grinning back at her. There was even a rasping little giggle, too, like the girl from *The Exorcist*.

"I don't know what that was all about," said the middle-aged social worker, "or what it was meant to prove..."

"Take a hike," Maria advised her calmly, speaking in her own voice again.

"We will relinquish this part of the meeting now," Mrs Hosanna said in an attempt to calm herself, "but I will be making an appointment to meet with your parents as soon as possible to discuss with them my very serious concerns."

Maria abruptly became serious and stared back at her.

"Take a hint," she told the woman quietly. "Do not piss me off."

Miss O'Grady was now regaining consciousness, and after another moment Mrs Hosanna helped her up onto her feet. Mrs Roland winced at the sight of Miss O'Grady's face which now had a nasty red and blue swelling developing on the left cheek where it had come into violent contact with the edge of the table.

Mrs Hosanna looked at the headmistress.

"Thank you, and goodbye," was all she said before she, and her young assistant, staggered together out of the office, Mrs Hosanna's arm firmly around the younger woman's waist to support her as they went.

After they left, Mrs Roland looked at Maria.

"I didn't like them at all," she said. "Totally unprofessional. I do wish I'd never called them now."

"Oh, well, it can't be helped," Maria said as she stood up. "May I go back to my class now, Mrs Roland?"

"Of course you can, my dear," said the headmistress, and

she watched the girl as she went to the door.

But just before the door was opened she said, "Is it really true, Maria? Were you really visited by an Angel?"

Maria smiled back. "It's the God's honest truth," she said.

And with that she left the head's office leaving Mrs Roland with a very curious smile on her face.

CHAPTER FOURTEEN

Father Giuseppe Bonelli returned to his house, having taken his regular three-mile jog. He was just very slightly out of breath and having opened his front door he leaned forward for a moment, sucking in air, with his hands on his knees. He continued to rake in deep breaths as he stood up straight, put his hands on his hips, then stretched backwards.

The Italian priest, now seventy years of age, had always been keen on keeping fit. As a young man he followed in the footsteps of his older brother, Lucci, and joined the army where the fitness regime, along with the strict discipline, suited him admirably. With all the strenuous exercises and tasks, he learned to keep all his options open.

Gaining skills and knowledge of maintaining equipment and machinery in turn led to the further option of electronics studies. He enjoyed this so much he concentrated on it for three years.

But he had always been very interested in religion. His belief in God began to grow and he started going to church regularly. The true church, he believed, was the Catholic church. Or to be more accurate, the True Catholic church was the church as it originally was, not with the New Mass of today, contaminated by modernists who insisted on a watered-down version to appease people who thought that The Catholic religion was too strict. They changed the words within the Mass making it meaningless.

Giuseppe Bonelli, though, defied the bishop by continuing to say the Old Mass. Modernists scoffed at what they called the

Latin Mass, but the old priest explained repeatedly it did not matter what language it was said in, just so long as the words were of the True Faith. He had been a firm believer for a long time.

Then came his calling.

He still remembered clearly the night he was visited by an Angel who told him that his true vocation was in the priesthood, and that one day he would meet the girl, or young woman, who had been chosen to give birth to God's Second Son.

Bonelli remembered his responsibility too, that he would accompany her throughout her journey, protecting her, and even be willing to sacrifice his own life if necessary to protect her.

And he could recall how surprised Lucci had been when he suddenly left the army. That was over forty years ago. He had been a priest in his present parish for nearly thirty years now and had no idea how long it would be before he identified the Chosen Lady, but he had been assured by the Angel that she would make herself known to him.

And his belief in this never wavered.

Still a little breathless after his run, he went into the house and closed the door quietly behind him. He went to his little kitchen to make himself a cup of tea, then with cup and saucer in hand, went into the living room, sat down in his comfy reclining armchair, and switched on the television.

He found himself watching a chat show where the host of the show, a glamorous-looking woman named Patti Bonner, had invited two people to sit with her. One was an elegant lady in her fifties, and she introduced herself as Anna Gabriella, a devout Christian. She also mentioned that she was still working. She had been a midwife for over thirty years.

The other guest on the show was a slim man in his thirties. He was dressed in neat, casual clothes. He introduced himself only as Geoff. He was an atheist.

Watching them on his television set, the old priest heaved a hefty sigh. There was obviously going to be a debate on whether or not God existed.

Did life as we know it evolve over billions of years? Or, did man simply spring into existence just a few thousand years ago?

Father Bonelli took a sip of his tea and smiled. He had heard all the arguments, challenging his belief. Admittedly there were questions regularly posed by atheists where he stumbled over the answers, but to him it mattered not. He just knew what he believed.

Atheist Geoff started the ball rolling.

He looked at the audience and said, "Christians will have us believe that this planet is only a few thousand years old, whereas there is scientific proof of creatures that lived here millions of years ago."

The camera zoomed in on Anna Gabriella who laughed mockingly.

"That's utter rubbish," she said with a snort. "I know very well that there were creatures here millions of years ago, but I don't see how that contradicts my beliefs."

"And what are your beliefs?" asked the pretty Patti Bonner, tossing her blonde hair to one side.

"I believe that the Son of God, Jesus, was born over two thousand years ago to save us."

"Save us from what?" asked Geoff.

Anna ignored this question. She just shook her head with an irritated expression, as a person would do when a fly lands on their nose.

"He died on the cross," she went on. "And now we are approaching the time when God's Second Son will be born."

Father Bonelli suddenly sat up. He wanted to know if this woman actually did know something.

"Approaching the time?" asked Patti with a puzzled face. "What do you mean by that? And His Second Son born? For what purpose?"

Anna appeared to go into a trance, her eyes rolled in their sockets.

Breathless *oohs* and *ahhhs* came from the audience.

"For the chosen few," Anna's voice went into a low monotone, "for those who follow Our Lord, and don't deny His existence. They will be led to His everlasting Heavenly Kingdom."

Geoff gestured to the audience, laughed and said, "But what about the rest of us?"

Some of the audience laughed. Others remained in an uneasy silence.

Anna smiled at the atheist.

"You can't have it both ways," she told him. "This is your chance, possibly your last chance, to repent."

"Repent? Why do I want to repent?"

"You either believe or you don't," Anna continued, again ignoring the question. "No sitting on the fence here."

"Who's sitting on the fence?" Geoff's voice rose in annoyance. "If you ask me, it's all crap."

"I will pray for you, Geoff," Anna said quietly, "because you know it's not yet too late to kneel down and pray for God's forgiveness."

There was a general gasp from the audience. Again, some of them laughed, but they became silent when Patti Bonner spoke again. The glamorous show host gestured to Anna.

"You're talking as if the end is nearly upon us," she said. "Like it's the end of the world."

"This is all complete bollocks," Geoff cut in. "It's a scientific fact that the Earth will continue for another twenty billion years before it is either swallowed up by the Sun, or is hit by a giant meteorite and explodes into a trillion pieces."

Once more Anna ignored him, and the camera zoomed in on her even closer. After another moment, though, she said, "Like I said, it's not too late, yet, to repent."

Father Giuseppe Bonelli didn't wait for any more. He excitedly bounded out of his seat and turned the volume of the television right down. He deftly thumbed through the phone book, reached for his telephone, and with trembling hands he began to dial.

"I desire to speak to the producer of the BBC Live Patti Bonner chat show, please," he said when someone answered.

He waited a full minute, drumming his fingers on the coffee table.

"What can we do for you, chum?" came a crackly voice at last.

Father Bonelli gave his name and contact number, then he said, "A woman called Anna Gabriella is on your Patti Bonner show. When she comes out, can you please ask her to call me. It's really important."

"Will do." The line went dead.

The old priest looked at the telephone receiver in his hand with a very thoughtful look on his face. He had a feeling inside him now that told him that something incredible, but rather wonderful, was about to happen.

And very soon.

CHAPTER FIFTEEN

On the first day of May, early that morning, Maria Christopher jumped energetically out of bed and said, "Rabbits," a superstition she'd had for as long as she could remember, to bring her good luck for the month. At breakfast, she thought to herself with a smile, she would have to remember to take a pinch of salt and throw it over her shoulder, but for now she satisfied herself with a touch of the side of her wardrobe which, of course, was made of wood.

And it was a Sunday. Although her parents were devout Catholics, she had not been to church for a very long time. From this morning on, though, she decided all that was to change. Moreover, people were going to notice the change. The mother of the future Holy King would surely be expected to go to church.

She went to the bathroom, had a quick shower, then dried herself briskly. She was in a very happy mood. Things were going her way and she was comfortable with the decisions she had made. Also, she was feeling generally well, with less morning sickness as time went on as her body gradually adjusted to her pregnancy; and having finished the course of antibiotics for her chlamydia, all those symptoms had now disappeared too.

Another thing, it would be her sixteenth birthday soon. The 25th of that month to be exact, therefore precisely seven months before the birth of God's Second Son.

Things couldn't possibly be more exciting. The previous Friday afternoon she had visited her doctor again. She laughed with excitement as she remembered, all of a sudden, she was now booked in for a hospital appointment on the first of July for her fourteen-week scan.

She went back to her bedroom, got dressed in a modest, grey, knee-length dress and black stockings. She tied her hair into a bun, then went downstairs for breakfast. She prepared herself two slices of toast, made a pot of tea, then sat down at the table. She was scooping some marmalade onto the toast when her mother came into the dining room and sat opposite her.

"You're dressed smartly for once," said Mrs Christopher. "For a Sunday, I mean. Any plans for the day?"

"Well, this morning," Maria said with a mouthful of toast, "I'm going to church." And looking up at the clock on the wall, she added, "I'd better get a move on. I'm going to the early one."

Mrs Christopher's eyebrows raised in surprise.

"When did you last go to church?" she asked.

"Too long ago." Maria took a sip of tea.

"Why are you going now, then, all of a sudden?"

"I have to repent." Maria looked at her mother sitting opposite, then she added with a grin, "And anyway, don't you think that the mother of the Son of God should go to Mass? At least occasionally?"

"So you're persisting with this ridiculous story?" her mother said irritably.

"That *ridiculous story*, as you call it," Maria said defiantly, "happens to be true"

"Angels don't just appear to people. Not anymore."

Maria nearly choked on her next sip of tea.

"Not anymore?" she laughed. "But they used to? Is that it? Mum, you are hilarious."

"Well, what I mean is..."

"Oh, and by the way," Maria said, pointing her finger at

her mother's reddening face. "Mrs Roland believes me."

"She does not," her mother gasped, pouring a cup of tea from the pot that Maria had prepared. "She says she doesn't know what to believe."

Maria laughed again.

"Oh, well," she said. "I suppose that's better than calling me a liar." Then she gritted her teeth and added, "Like some people I could mention."

There was an uncomfortable pause, then Maria's mother said, "Look, why don't you go to the later Mass with me and your father?"

"No," Maria said firmly. "I need to go on my own."

"Why?"

"Because I want to speak to the priest after the Mass, and I..."

"Well," Maria's mother persisted, "I could speak to him with you."

"No," Maria said loudly. "I don't want you butting in."

"Maria!" Her mother banged her cup down. "How dare you speak to me like that. That was very rude."

Maria bit her bottom lip.

"Okay, I'm sorry," she said. "But I need to speak to the priest on my own."

Mrs Christopher picked up the milk jug, then put it down on the table again with a loud bang.

"And by the way," she said, "I'm not calling you a liar, but I do think you must have had some very intense kind of dream."

"And I suppose I *dreamed* that Doctor Walters confirmed that my hymen is intact and that I am still a virgin?"

"Oh, right..."

"Call my doctor if you don't believe me," Maria shouted. "Go on, phone her."

"It's Sunday."

"Tomorrow, then."

"The doctor would not discuss it with me as I think you know very well."

Maria looked at her for a moment longer, then returned to her toast and marmalade, washing mouthfuls down with sips of tea. And she glanced up at the clock again.

"So you're off to the early Mass?" her mother said with a hefty sigh.

"Yes," said Maria. "I'd better get a move on."

"Then you're going to see the priest? I think it's Father Giuseppe Bonelli who usually says that early Mass."

"Is it?" Maria shrugged her shoulders. "I wouldn't know."

Then Maria's mother sat up rigid, as if a thought had suddenly occurred to her.

"Oh, please don't tell me," she said, "you're not going to tell that poor old priest your fanciful yarn?"

Maria closed her eyes as though in silent prayer.

"I don't want an argument with you now," she said. "I just want to think nice, serene, *holy* thoughts."

Then she opened her eyes as if she'd just woken up, and got up from the table.

"Please excuse me," she said. "I must get ready now."

And with that she left the dining room, leaving her mother swaying backwards and forwards in her chair, and staring blankly into her cup of tea.

*

During Mass at the nearby Catholic church, the elderly Italian priest entered into a very long sermon. Most of the congregation were gradually falling asleep by this time, but Maria remained attentive. The words to the sermon, while it sent the people around her to sleep, were having completely the opposite effect on her.

She could hardly believe what she was hearing. The most astonishing coincidence – or perhaps not coincidence at all.

Father Giuseppe Bonelli was saying that God's Second Son would appear again as a newly born infant, and it would be a natural birth, the baby having grown in a young woman's womb.

Some of the congregation, mainly men, woke up when they heard that, and began to fidget, while woman gasped and looked shocked. But Father Bonelli, seemingly unaware of the effects that his words were having on his flock, continued.

"The young woman will naturally feel the pain of childbirth," he said suddenly loudly. "And it is my solemn belief that all this will happen quite soon. Our Saviour may already be on his way."

"Utter bollocks," Maria heard some guy behind her muttering.

"And," Father Bonelli allowed a moment of silence to pass before he imparted the next part of the sermon, looking at some of the faces in front of him individually, "I feel that he is quite close to us."

Maria felt a sudden tingle fill her whole body, but it was a lovely, exciting chill just then, especially as the priest appeared to gaze directly at her, just momentarily, as he said the words, "he is quite close to us."

After another long pause, he spoke suddenly loudly again, a method that many priests use to wake people up on a warm May morning. It had the desired effect as he almost shouted, *"The New King will be sent by Our Blessed Lord to guide us through troubled times, our final times, our final hours..."*

The people in the front row drooped forward with a moan, while others gasped a collective sigh of woe at these totally depressing words, which appeared to be, if taken literally, tantamount to telling them that the world was about to end.

"Miserable git." Maria heard that man behind her again.

"Mad as a March hare," some other guy next to him said. "It's a scientific fact that…"

Maria could contain herself no longer. She jerked herself around to face the two nerdy looking dudes.

"Shut up, you bunch of prats," she hissed, then she turned back round to face the altar again. And she actually smiled to herself as an amusing thought entered her head. If only those guys realised that they had just been addressed by the mother of God's Second Son.

And when the time came, she went to receive Holy Communion, and as Father Bonelli gently placed the Holy Eucharist on her tongue, their eyes met briefly.

There was a connection, Maria was sure of it.

"Body of Christ," he whispered.

"Amen." To Maria, her own voice seemed to reverberate around the whole church

After the Mass had ended, and most people had 'gone in peace', Father Bonelli stood in the foyer talking individually, albeit briefly, to many of the congregation as, one by one, they filed out of the church. Maria joined the end of the queue. She wanted to be last. Eventually she found herself standing right in front of the elderly Italian priest who now seemed so tall to her. He appeared to be looking at her rather intently. His eyes narrowed and, looking down, her reached out to her. She let him hold her hand.

"Do I know you, my child?" he said so quietly it was barely above a whisper.

"No, I…" But she suddenly changed her mind. "Yes, you know me," she told him. "You have spoken about me."

"Spoken about you?" The priest squeezed his eyes shut in an effort to remember. "My dear child. When have I spoken about you?"

"Just now," Maria smiled. "What I mean is, about half an hour ago."

"You do seem familiar to me, and I know your voice."

"I've been here before," she explained, but she refrained from adding that that was more than two years ago.

"And I've spoken about you?" He was still holding her hand.

She looked at his hand holding hers and she was surprised that it looked like the hand of a younger, stronger man, but then considered that the rest of him was hidden by his cassock, so she had no real way of knowing, yet, what kind of physique he had. His face, however, was of a man, she guessed, who was in his late sixties. Perhaps even seventy.

"Father," she said, looking round her to ensure there was now nobody else left in the foyer. "What I'm about to tell you is amazing, but I swear it is true. I am going to have a baby."

"My dear young girl...!"

"My doctor has examined me and confirmed I am still a virgin," Maria continued, "and yet I am to have a child, a Holy Child, a boy, the Son of God, and this, Father, has been confirmed to me by one of God's messengers. An Angel."

Father Giuseppe Bonelli, priest of the parish for nearly thirty years, looked at her for a long, hard, moment. His eyes welled up with tears.

Then he collapsed to his knees in front of her. She looked around her worriedly, praying that nobody would have a reason to return to the foyer, having forgotten a glove or their keys, or...

"I have waited so long," the priest sobbed, gazing up into her face as he knelt before her. "Over forty years since I was told..."

"Told?" Maria blinked at him, her eyes also getting moist.

"Yes, I, too, was visited. I was told that this day would come. That was over forty years ago."

"Bloody hell," Maria gasped, "I mean, goodness gracious."

"I prayed and prayed, every day." Bonelli was crying

freely now, with a mixture of happiness and relief. "And now our wonderful, loving God has rewarded me."

Maria thought that she was going to have to offer some kind of evidence, or at least be asked to swear on the Holy Bible, but that didn't seem necessary now. The priest believed her without question. She was still confused, though.

But the priest, evidently reading her mind, continued. "It's been explained to me," he said. "You would identify yourself to me, and then it would be my job, my responsibility, to look after you during your long journey."

She assumed that *the journey* he referred to was merely the general experience of living through the pregnancy until eventually giving birth.

"Will you please get up onto your feet now?" she said to him.

"I must honour you, obey you, I will worship you, and carry out your every command."

"In that case," Maria laughed, "I command you to get up onto your feet. Now!"

The priest proved how fit he was for a seventy-year-old man and sprung to his feet quickly.

"And," she added, pointing a forefinger upwards, "never kneel in front of me like that again. It is not necessary."

"I've offended you..."

"No," Maria said. "You haven't. Just please don't kneel for me again."

"Okay," said Bonelli, "but it is God's command that I look after you, at least until the Holy Infant is born."

"That's great," said Maria. "I already feel happier and safer, but I have to tell you, there are people who don't believe me."

"Always, there will be non-believers," the priest muttered, shaking his head sadly, "but no matter. I will confirm the truth, but all in good time. Do you currently live with your parents?"

"Yes." She took out a little notebook and pen from her handbag, wrote down her name and address, tore out the page and handed it to him.

He took it and examined it, smoothing the paper in his hand as if it was the most precious thing on Earth. When he looked back at her she could see his eyes were welling up with tears again, evidently with joy.

"It's important we remain in touch," he told her.

"Okay," she agreed readily enough. It would appear, now, that one way or another, they needed each other.

"There may be dangers along the journey."

There was that word again, she thought. *Journey*.

"What dangers could there be?" she asked.

He looked at her seriously.

"I've been told I should be ready and willing to sacrifice my life to protect you if necessary," he told her.

"Hopefully it won't come to that," said Maria, not knowing, at that point, what dangers were in store for her along *the journey*.

And before she left the church, she gave the priest a warm hug. She was filled with happiness now, for at that moment she knew.

She really was going to give birth to God's Second Son.

CHAPTER SIXTEEN

From that point on, Maria Christopher had a feeling that everything was really going to take off. She was right, but just then she had no idea of how quickly things would begin to happen, or how much this would affect her life that, inevitably, could never be the same again.

On the Monday evening, after Maria and her parents had finished their evening meal, she moved to the door ready to scoot up the stairs to her bedroom, partly so she could finish her mountain of homework. But it was also because she had a feeling that her parents wanted a serious word with her. She had noticed the solemn looks they had been giving her across the dinner table and she knew what the topic of conversation would be.

But she was no longer interested in that kind of talk. She had made her decision and that, as far as she could see, was the end of it.

"Not so fast, young lady," her father rapped out.

Maria stopped in her tracks and stood motionless like a statue.

"What is it, Father?" she said meekly.

There was silence for a moment, then Maria turned to face her parents, and they stood side by side as if they needed joint forces to tackle this one almighty problem.

Maria had a horrible feeling that the evening was not going to turn out well.

She was right.

"First of all," her father said, already struggling to control his temper, "you can drop the sarcasm."

Maria raised her eyebrows innocently. But she knew what he meant. In better circumstances she would have addressed her father as Dad, or even Daddy. And she could guess what was coming next.

Mr Christopher breathed a hefty sigh.

"Myself and your mother have discussed the situation at some length," he said, "and we have finally made the decision that the best course of action would be for you to have an abortion."

Maria thought that this would be one of the options on offer or, by the sounds of things, the only proffered option, so she was prompt with her rehearsed reply.

"Absolutely no way," she told them firmly. "Don't you understand, I'm having the Son of God?"

Her mother then spoke as if Maria had not uttered a single word.

"You must think of your schoolwork," she said quietly. "Your life would be ruined having a baby and not even knowing who the father is."

Maria face went bright red with anger. She opened her mouth but couldn't speak.

"Or if you do know who the father is, you're not telling us," Mr Christopher ploughed on regardless.

With a visible effort, Maria controlled herself and faced her parents.

"I'm going to tell you this one more time," she said in the same firm tone as before. "Doctor Walters examined me and confirmed that I am still a virgin, but then I discovered I was pregnant. Shortly after that an Angel appeared and told me that I was carrying God's child. Right, now, if you don't believe me..."

"Just a minute," her mother interrupted her, suddenly looking thoughtful. "Why was it that you just happened to go to the doctor at that very time, to have your hymen examined?"

For once, with all her confidence and determination, Maria was stumped. She thought for a moment. She had to invent a convincing reply to this.

"Because..." she began.

At that exact moment there was the sound of the doorbell ringing.

Maria looked up at the ceiling. Saved by the bell, she thought to herself.

"I want an answer to that question," Mrs Christopher said, pointing a finger at her, as she left the room to answer the front door.

Then it was just Maria and her father in the room, and Mr Christopher was beginning to look extremely angry. He was shaking with rage, which was unusual for him. He took a stride towards his daughter so they were barely an arm's length apart.

"Now, you look here," he said. "This is what you will do..."

"You absolute hypocrite," she suddenly blurted out. "You pray to God every day, you want everyone to see what a loving family man you are, yet you would kill an innocent baby. God's baby."

"I tell you," he began to shout, "for your own good..."

"No!" she shouted back. "And if you don't believe me..."

"No, I don't believe you!"

"You're calling me a liar," she hissed through gritted teeth. "Well go fuck yourself."

Mr Christopher would live to regret what happened next but he totally lost his temper and lashed out. He caught his daughter across the face with the back of his hand. She went spinning and fell to the floor with a yell. And to make matters a hundred times worse, at that precise moment the door of the room flew open and there stood a short, middle-aged Indian woman and a much younger lady.

There followed a minute of the most awful silence.

"I'm Mrs Hosanna" said the Indian lady, and gesturing to her young colleague she added, "This is my colleague Miss O'Grady. We are from Social Services."

"Oh, Christ," Mr Christopher said, looking down at his daughter. "I didn't mean to. God knows I didn't mean to…"

The Indian lady looked at him but didn't reply. She moved forward to where Maria had fallen. The girl was sitting up now and looking around her, dazed.

"My dear," said Mrs Hosanna. "Are you all right?"

"The bastard," Maria managed to say, with a swelling appearing on the side of her mouth.

"Can you get up?" Miss O'Grady reached down to her.

"I think so. Just keep that brute away from me."

Then, when Maria got to her feet, she turned to face her father.

And the voice of an accomplished ventriloquist went into action once more.

"You have made God very angry," she growled in a husky voice that he had never heard before, and sounded like it was coming from the opposite end of the room. *"You have struck down the woman who is carrying his child."*

"Woman?" The word dropped from Mr Christopher's lips as he gazed at his teenage daughter.

In a very bewildered state, Maria's mother brought a chair over to her daughter while Mrs Hosanna and Miss O'Grady helped the girl onto it.

Then the Indian woman from Social Services turned to Mr Christopher.

"I witnessed that most violent act," she advised him, "and now I am afraid that it is my duty…"

"For goodness sake, I didn't mean it," he said. "It's never happened before and I can assure you it will never happen again."

"Unfortunately," she continued, "it is my duty to report any violence against children."

Mrs Christopher held her hands to her face in dismay.

"What will happen now?" she asked.

Mrs Hosanna drew a deep breath.

"Once I've made my report," she said, "the decision will be out of my hands, but your daughter may be taken from here once a suitable alternative accommodation can be found."

"Oh, no, please..." Maria's mother was on the verge of weeping.

The young Miss O'Grady remained silent but looked shocked by all that she had seen, and sadly shook her head.

Mrs Hosanna continued, "We came here this evening to discuss with you the welfare of your daughter in view of the fact that she is pregnant."

"But please let me say..." Maria's mother felt like her head was spinning.

"She has expressed her desire to keep the child," Mrs Hosanna rattled on regardless, "which can be considered depending on certain conditions, but she has also talked of such things that has caused us to be concerned about her mental state. However..."

"But..." Maria's father began.

"However," the Indian lady repeated the word a bit louder, "in light of what I have witnessed this evening, those issues will have to wait. A decision will be made by someone of a higher rank than myself, once I have submitted my report."

Maria, still sitting, thought that maybe, on reflection, it was time for her to say something in defence of her father. She had never planned for things to go this far.

"Actually, if I might say," she began, but then the doorbell rang again.

"Oh, bloody hell," Mrs Christopher said. "Who can that

be now?"

Again she left the room and went to the front door.

Maria's father turned to the women from Social Services.

"Please," he said. "I assure you that I have never struck my daughter before, and..."

"I'm sorry but..."

"Can't you just forget it?"

"No, but I will add to my notes that you made that request."

Mr Christopher bit his tongue, realising he had just made matters even worse.

Everyone in the room looked toward the door as it opened again. Maria's mother stood there and standing next to her was the elderly priest whom the girl's parents recognised.

And having entered, the priest sensed straight away that there was a lot of tension in the room.

"Good evening, my good people," he nodded to each of them in turn. "I hope I'm not disturbing you. As you might know, I am Father Giuseppe Bonelli, and I am here to see Maria who I met yesterday at my church."

To the surprise of everyone else in the room, Maria suddenly jumped up from her seat, rushed to the priest and hugged him. After the brief embrace, he held her with his arms outstretched so that he could look into her face. And at once he became serious.

"I see you have been hurt," he said, looking deeply concerned, and closely examining the dark swelling on the side of her mouth.

"It's okay," she told him with a careless laugh. "I'm so clumsy, I fell down the stairs."

The priest cast a disdainful glance at the girl's father as if somehow guessing the real cause of the injury. Then, looking at Maria again, he said, "If you ever need anywhere to stay..."

Mrs Hosanna interrupted him with a cough. She

introduced herself quickly, then she said, "Am I to understand from what you've just said that you can offer accommodation to this child?"

"I certainly can," Father Bonelli confirmed promptly. "In fact, if you check with your office you will see that another young girl, Debbie Shallis who is also expecting a child, has been sent there recently, and the shelter has already been visited, and approved, by yourselves. The name of the hostel is JackDaw House."

Mrs Hosanna thought for a moment, then she said, "Oh, yes, thank you. We may be in touch then." She then turned to Miss O'Grady and said, "Make a note, and confirm that we have Father Bonelli's telephone number."

The priest quickly rattled off his number to her.

"Look, this is crazy," Mr Christopher said, being careful to keep his temper in check this time.

But then there was yet another interruption as the doorbell sounded for a third time, and at the same moment they all became aware of a commotion of some description that seemed to be building up outside. People shouting...

"What the...!" For the third time, Mrs Christopher went to the door. Everyone in the room stood still and listened. As the front door of the house opened, they could hear the people from outside calling.

"We want to see the girl!"

"The Blessed One, please speak to us!"

"Maria, we adore you !"

"Is it true? Are you really to be the mother of the New King?"

Maria's mother's efforts to reply were completely drowned out, until a man's voice was heard above all the others, shouting, "Quiet, please!"

Less noise now, but still fairly audible babble.

Then came the same authoritative voice, but quieter now,

and addressing Maria's mother.

"Is the mother of the New King at home, please?"

It was then that Mrs Christopher noticed the television cameras.

"No, I tell you, it's a hoax," she shouted. "Now please, everyone, just go away."

"But we want to see the Holy Lady," someone out there protested.

Then, under these extraordinary circumstances, for a brief instant, Maria's mother lost her composure. "Why don't you all just piss off?" she yelled.

Back in the lounge, the two Social Services ladies looked at each other with puzzled faces. Maria looked at the priest.

"Somebody at the school must have blabbed," she said.

"If that's the case," Father Bonelli smiled at Maria, "it gives you your first opportunity to speak publicly."

Mr Christopher pulled an exasperated expression and gazed up at the ceiling.

"Has everyone round here gone completely crackers?" he gasped.

The two ladies from Social Services glanced at each other and nodded, as if to say that, on that one point, they had to agree with Maria's father.

"Come on, then," Father Bonelli said to Maria. "Let's go and meet your loyal subjects. You'll have to get used to this sort of thing from now on."

"I absolutely forbid it," Mrs Hosanna said irritably.

But before she could put her hand out to grab Maria by the arm, Father Bonelli was whisking her out of the lounge towards the front of the house. There was a general gasp of excitement from outside when the young girl appeared with the priest by her side. Maria's mother was shoved unceremoniously out of the way.

Maria was momentarily dazzled when a spotlight was

trained on her. Two TV cameras swivelled on their dollies and zoomed in on her to give the news editor the choice of two different angles.

Then a microphone was pushed under her nose. Her eyes were still adjusting to the bright light, so she could not see the man standing right in front of her, but she heard a nearby voice demanding, "Is it true?

Maria squinted against the light, shielding her eyes with her hand.

"God's messenger has spoken to me," she heard herself say, "I have been told."

People were getting impatient and the noise was building up again.

"Is it true?" the reporter repeated, shouting over the din, "Is it true that you are the Chosen One?"

This was the moment she had prepared herself for. She knew what she had to do, and what to say. With great firmness and confidence, she nodded. "Yes," she said. "It is true."

"Chosen by God...?"

"Yes."

But the reporter seemed to be pushing for the answer, categorically, yes or no, to the complete question.

"... to be the mother of the Son of God?"

"For goodness sake, YES!" Maria shouted back. "It is true. How many more times?"

"And, I hear you say, that you are a virgin. You've never had a sexual relationship?"

Maria, with all her nerve, very nearly slipped up here. She nearly replied, "Not that I can remember," but that would not have sounded at all convincing, so luckily for her she gave herself a moment to think, and then answered the question with, "I have never had sexual intercourse, and I can prove it. My doctor has examined me and has confirmed that my hymen is intact."

"Why did you go to the doctor to have it proved?" somebody from the back of the crowd shouted out.

This was followed by boos and hisses, and people shouting things like, "Shut up, you tosser."

"And you definitely are pregnant?" the reporter went on regardless.

"Yes, I'm now in my seventh week," Maria said growing in confidence. "I've got a note from my doctor confirming that."

She hoped she wouldn't be called upon to produce documentary evidence, since the report she received from Dr Walters also mentioned she had contracted chlamydia.

Suddenly, a man from the crowd, jumped forward, pulled down his trousers in front of her and fully exposed himself. Amidst more boos and hisses, he found himself being dragged away, and painfully kicked several times along the way too.

"This is insane," Maria's mother shouted, but she was just ignored.

Still the reporter carried on, obviously used to distraction from members of the public.

"So when is..." he paused, but then continued. "When is *the Son of God* due to be born?"

Maria's immediate answer with a happy smile was, "The twenty-fifth of December."

This produced a massive roar of approval from most of the people in the crowd. Maria was thrilled. There was no doubt, she was winning people over, but the next moment the elderly priest stepped forward and gently, but firmly, ushered the teenage girl to a position behind him, and now out of view of the cameras.

He then faced the people, the lights and the cameras, and made a statement that he had been rehearsing for this kind of occasion.

"Ladies and gentlemen, you now have the answers you came for. I know that what this holy young lady has said is true because I, myself, have been visited by a Holy Messenger who advised me that I have been chosen as the Holy Mother's guide, to guide this young mother through the coming journey."

Again, Maria wondered at the curious use of the word *journey*.

"And I can confirm positively," Father Bonelli concluded, "that come this December, on the twenty-fifth day of that month, the new Heavenly King, Our Almighty Saviour, will be born."

CHAPTER SEVENTEEN

During the following evening, Father Giuseppe Bonelli sat at a table in his living room with his new desktop computer. It was the first he had owned with an up-to-the-minute disc operating system. He was using its word processing application to prepare his sermon to be delivered to his flock during the next Sunday's Mass. However, other pressing issues were now interfering with his concentration. His massive responsibility was weighing heavily upon his mind, and what had happened recently was making it impossible to concentrate on anything else. He felt he should be doing something – something important, not wasting his time on a sermon that nobody would listen to anyway.

A thought popped into his mind of dozy-looking cretins falling asleep. He'd actually heard those morons snoring during the delivery of his sermons. The thought of it made him grind his teeth together.

At last, with a hefty sigh, he switched off the computer and sat back in his chair. He looked at the clock on the mantelpiece. Just gone 9.30 pm.

On one hand, he felt satisfied that his task so far, albeit just started, had been well carried out. He had seen the teenage girl, the mother-to-be of God's child, safely into her new accommodation where she had met the occupant of the adjoining room. The other girl, Debbie Shallis, was pregnant too, with her baby due shortly before Maria's, and she had also been placed there by Social Services, having been removed from a violent home.

It just so happened that up until that week, there had only

been two other girls living there at the shelter, but they were both leaving now, requiring a move to alternative locations. So for now it was just Maria and Debbie who had the run of the whole place, and the early indications were that they were going to be good friends.

However, Father Bonelli knew that the task ahead was going to be difficult, and fraught with all kinds of dangers and hazards. He knew, ultimately, that he may even need to move the girls to a faraway hiding place, and he certainly would do so when the time came. His instructions had been very clear, and although it was a long time ago when he had been visited by the Angel, he could remember the precise details as if they had been delivered to him the previous day. The most vivid part being that, if necessary, he should be prepared to sacrifice his own life to protect the girl who had been chosen by God to be the mother of His Child. That, of course, didn't mean that he would just have to throw his life away needlessly. Maria would need him for continual protection for as long as he, himself, could stay alive. However, if one of The Devil's disciples was trying to kill her (and he knew this could happen) then he would be prepared to fight to the death to protect her.

He decided that he would protect both girls. Debbie could be a useful diversion. Her presence and involvement could confuse any would-be assassin. He felt a slight pang of guilt, but it did not weigh-in heavily on Bonelli's conscience that, if they were targeted by the followers of Satan, he would be placing a perfectly innocent girl in danger. His plans and his instructions thereof were for the greater good.

Bonelli glanced at the calendar that was perched on his mantelpiece. He knew, too, that the danger he had been thinking of would not end when the Holy Child was born. Far from it. There would be even more danger. Evil gangs instructed by the Dark Lord himself would be searching for any baby boys born around the same time. What had happened two thousand years ago could happen again.

The old priest gritted his teeth at the thought of it. He believed that this would lead to what could be, ultimately, the final war between Good and Evil. Priest, or not, he knew what he had to do. He was determined to do it and he did not care how he did it.

He leaned forward and opened the drawer at the bottom of his bureau and moved some old envelopes to see the object he sought, hidden beneath. His mouth set in a tight line when he saw it. An army-issue revolver that he had taken and kept hidden all those years. When in the army, he had been entrusted with maintaining the records of firearms, and he had cleverly falsified various records to conceal the fact that a revolver had been issued but not returned. He originally just wanted it as a souvenir, possibly for the occasional target practice for fun, but now he was really glad that he had it. You never knew, he thought, when such a thing would come in useful, along with a hundred rounds of ammunition of course. He had a box of grenades, too, hidden in his garden shed.

Satisfied that it was still there and ready to use if needed, he rearranged the old envelopes on top of it, closed the drawer and locked it.

Father Bonelli continued to ponder over the threat posed by these followers of The Devil. He knew that most of these, after all, were just men, with very little power, other than the strength of any average man, so if they did pose any threat at all to Maria and her baby, a bullet between the eyes would be enough. But the Angel had warned of a far greater threat. If the Satanists could invoke one of Satan's demons this would present a far worse challenge. Each of The Devil's most vicious demons had different strengths and powers, but from whispers that his brother Lucci had heard, the one the Satanists planned to invoke was Bael, the most evil one of all. But whichever one it turned out to be, the demon would laugh at bullets from a gun. Bonelli may as well fire a peashooter at him – *or her* – and this is where he believed his own life would be endangered. In the Old Scriptures he had read that if a demon was summoned, it would demand a sacrifice before it slithered back to the dark gutter it had come from; and if it was Bael, a victim would have been chosen in advance. This servant would be honoured to be a sacrifice and envied among the others. If he was lucky, he might just have one limb torn off.

The priest leaned forward again and opened the middle drawer. More old rubbish got pushed out of the way to reveal the folded leather pouch of about eight inches in length. His brother Lucci had obtained it for him. He took it out, unfolded it and untied its laces. He opened it from the flap at one end, and revealed there were three large, heavy, wedge-shaped objects. They were vicious-looking metal things, gnarled and twisted with age, each one about six inches long. They were ancient Roman nails.

And Father Giuseppe Bonelli knew that these were genuine. Absolutely no doubt about it. His hands trembled as he handled these horrible things that were over two thousand years old, and they seemed to vibrate and quiver in his hand and become warm with their own incredible power that could not wait to be unleashed.

Bonelli's breath came in short gasps as he recalled how they came to be in his possession.

His brother Lucci had visited the Greek Reliquary Chapel of The Holy Sepulchre in Jerusalem where objects from the crucifixion had been stored. There were the thirty silver denarius coins bearing the head of Augustus and claimed to be Judus's payment for betraying Jesus; the pieces of wood that made the Cross; the Crown of Thorns; the sword known as The Lance of the Roman Centurion Longinus who had used it to pierce the side of Jesus; and, of course, the nails.

Knowing that his brother would like to possess such objects

as the nails, and being an obliging brother, Lucci devised a plan to steal them. First he created the necessary diversion which involved a home-made incendiary device, then he was able to break into the glass display case and steal the nails, replacing them with some other, similar-looking, but ordinary objects. From where the tourists would be viewing them, they would not know the difference.

After that, smuggling them through customs was the hardest part of the process. (Even though the methods adopted by customs, and the equipment they used, were nothing like what they would become in later years.) Still taking a big risk, though, he managed to get the pieces through, wrapped up with his clothes, and stuffed into a tightly packed suitcase with lots of other keepsakes, ornaments and the like. Then he requested that 'Handle With Care' notices were securely taped onto both sides of the case.

But his ingenuity did not stop there.

He got a small transistor radio and placed it in the middle of some clothes. Then he put a metal coat hanger a few layers above it. When the suitcase went through to be X-rayed, the picture of the two objects together on the X-ray screen caused bleeps of alarm to go off.

It was a risky ploy but, he believed, a calculated one. And it worked.

The intention was to activate the alarm. The X-ray scanner produced a single image that could have been a time bomb.

Lucci was arrested by security guards and taken in for questioning, but promptly released when nothing more dangerous than a transistor radio and a coat hanger were found.

Quickly checking his case to ensure that the Roman nails were still safe, the relieved Lucci continued on his way to board the plane, and his suitcase was carefully loaded into the hold.

And Giuseppe greatly appreciated his brother's efforts.

But there was a very special purpose for these nails. The priest was still studying them and trying to come to grips with the very precise instructions necessary for them to serve this purpose. He knew that he still had to identify a person, willing and able, to carry out these special instructions if anything happened to him. He knew he could rely on Lucci to deliver the full explanation at the appropriate time, and the necessary preparation.

The priest put them back into the leather pouch, closed it and re-tied the laces. Then he put them back into the middle drawer of the bureau and rearranged all the rubbish on top of them. Then he closed that drawer too and locked it. He drew a deep breath and let out a huge sigh.

His thoughts then returned to the serious matter in hand. There would be other practical problems as well, of course. A long time off yet, but still something to be prepared for, and that would be the actual birth of the child. Bonelli imagined himself in a far-off secret accommodation, just him and two pregnant teenage girls. Debbie's baby was due first, whereas Maria's infant, God's Child, had been given the exact date of 25th December. It could happen sooner or later, of course, but somehow he felt certain that it would be on that exact date. Likewise he imagined this being in the very early hours of the morning, while it was still dark. In some far off, remote spot it was also likely to be extremely cold. Involuntarily he shuddered at the thought of it.

He clasped his hands tightly together and looked up at the ceiling.

"Dear God," he said out loud. "Please show me the way. What am I to do? How can I cope?"

If only he had someone else with him, he thought. Another adult to help him. Somebody he could trust.

The telephone rang. It seemed so sudden that it made him jump.

He snatched up the receiver. "Yes?" he snapped.

"Father Bonelli?" came a quiet lady's voice. "Father Giuseppe Bonelli?"

"Speaking." The old priest's voice softened. "Who is speaking, please? How can I help you?"

"Father," said the lady. "You called for me the other day. Remember? You saw me on television. My name is Anna Gabriella."

Father Bonelli stared disbelievingly at the instrument in his hand, then held it back to his ear.

"Oh, yes," he said enthusiastically. "I remember now. Thank you so much for calling."

"I'm sorry I didn't call sooner," said Anna. "The idiots at the studio forgot to tell me immediately after the TV show, but then, thank God, they did remember and called me."

"That's fine, thank you." Bonelli breathed a sigh of relief. "I was thinking about what you said about the birth of God's child. You said you had a feeling it was going to happen soon."

"Yes, I do have a very strong feeling about that, Father," said Anna. "So what can I do for you? I'm always only too happy to help the Church in any way I can."

And then the most wonderful and fantastic thought occurred to Father Bonelli.

In the Holy Bible it describes a woman, a prophetess, who foretold the birth of Jesus many years before it happened, then she spent all her life waiting to hear news of her prophesy coming true.

And her name was Anna.

(Anna the Prophetess is a woman mentioned in the Gospel Of Luke. According to that Gospel, she was an elderly woman in the Tribe of Asher who prophesised about Jesus at the Temple of Jerusalem. She appears in Luke 2: 36–38 during the presentation of Jesus at the Temple.)

Father Bonelli did not believe in coincidences. Some things

were too utterly fantastic to be coincidences, and in any case there were just too many of them now. If he did have any lingering doubts at all (which he didn't) those negative thoughts would be quashed now.

The girl, Maria Christopher, really was going to give birth to *the Son of God.*

"Are you still there?" came Anna's voice. "Father Bonelli?"

"Oh, yes, Anna, I'm so sorry," he said, "I was deep in thought for a moment."

Then Father Bonelli began by telling Anna a bit about himself and his parish. It transpired that the woman lived in a town only about twenty miles away, an easy journey for her to visit when required. The priest concluded his part of this initial conversation by explaining to Anna how, and why, he had become a priest. He told her about the visit from the Angel, telling her that he had been chosen to look after the girl who was to be the mother of God's child, and how long ago this instruction had been delivered to him.

The priest had no qualms about telling this stranger all these details, for already she did not feel like a stranger. As yet, though, he was not certain of how she would react to such information.

But he need not have worried.

"Well, like I said, Father," she said, "it's going to happen very soon. I am convinced of it."

He smiled, thinking again about the Prophetess, Anna, from the Bible, and so positive now that he could totally trust her, Bonelli said in a quiet, but steady, voice, "Anna, it *is* happening."

"Father?" the woman gasped.

"I assure you, it's true. All of it."

Giuseppe Bonelli then told Anna Gabriella all that he knew, about Maria and everything she had told him. He concluded by saying how Social Services had removed her from her family home, and how he had been at the right place at the right time, ready to offer the girl shelter. He added that there was another girl staying at the hostel, and she too was pregnant and due to deliver her child at roughly the same time.

"Oh, God. Oh, my God..." Anna's voice began to rise in pitch through sheer excitement. "So it is true, I always knew..."

"Anna," Bonelli cut in firmly, "there will come a time, perhaps closer to December, when we will need to take the girls somewhere far off, in secret, to hide them until the babies are born."

Anna laughed excitedly. "Afterwards, people will not know which is which," she said. "Only we will know."

"For the time being, that will remain so," Bonelli said. "There will be people, evil people, who will be hunting for the Holy Child, and we will protect him for as long as we can, but..."

"But," the woman said, knowing what was inevitably coming next, "when the child gets older, he will have to face the people, and accept who he is and why he's here."

"To protect us, right up to The End..."

"The End," Anna said. "Father, it really is going to happen, isn't it?"

"Within our lifetime," Bonelli said quietly. "Yes."

"Oh, my God."

The priest could hear the woman whispering to herself.

After quite a lengthy pause this time, Father Bonelli said, "Anyway, I'm going to need help with the babies' births. I have assisted in delivering a baby before, but I had plenty of people around me at the time."

"Are you forgetting something, Father?" Anna's voice was rising in excitement again. "I did mention it on the TV programme. I am a qualified midwife."

"Dear Lord, I did forget," the old priest whispered. Then he said out loud, "Anna, I had forgotten. I believe now that we were destined to find each other like this, for this very purpose."

"Yes," she said. "And together we will witness the arrival of God's Second Son."

"This is like a beautiful dream coming true." Bonelli clasped the telephone receiver in both hands and gazed up at the ceiling.

"When I took my midwifery exams," Anna gasped, "I never dreamed that one day I would be delivering the Holy King. The Son of God. All my years of praying and praying..."

"Our Father, who is in Heaven..." Bonelli began to pray.

"Hallowed be Thy Name..." Anna responded.

"Thy Kingdom come, thy will be done..."

"On Earth as it is in Heaven..."

Then Bonelli said, "Anna, I wish you were here with me now."

He was suddenly feeling so happy. In fact, happier than he had felt for a very long time. "You could come and meet the girls. I pray, dear God, that you can come here soon."

Anna laughed again, also incredibly happy.

"Have you got any spare rooms in that place of yours?" she said.

"I sure have," he told her, bursting with joy now, eagerly anticipating what she was about to say next.

"Then," she concluded, "your prayers have been answered. I'm on my way."

CHAPTER EIGHTEEN

It had been many, many years since Giuseppe Bonelli had held a woman in his arms. He had forgotten what it was like. Anna Gabriella was a fine-looking woman, middle-aged, maybe late fifties, but still good looking. No wrinkles and a fine figure. She had obviously taken care of herself. No doubt the running around of her midwifery duties for thirty years had helped keep her fit both physically and mentally.

She had wavy brown hair, with very little grey, and nicest of all she was a good height so that the tall, old priest was able to hold her comfortably in his arms without having to bend too painfully.

As they embraced, for a long moment, he rested his chin on her shoulder, then leaned back and looked into her hazel eyes. She could see from the look in his slightly ageing grey eyes that he yearned for her, but she didn't pull back, priest though he was. They both believed in that same moment that God would look kindly upon this embrace. They were there to protect His Child which they had promised to do – that they were destined to do – so God would allow them this physical pleasure which they deserved. After all, it probably would not be for very long.

Anna had arrived at the hostel, JackDaw House, within an hour of their telephone conversation. She didn't have to knock on the door. Father Bonelli had been looking out for her. She had one suitcase with her, but she told him there was another larger, heavier one in the boot of her car. Bonelli happily collected it for her.

Then, while carrying all her luggage, Bonelli showed her to her room that he had quickly prepared with a quick whizzround with the hoover, fresh blankets on the bed and towels on the radiator. And there they stood, still with their arms around each other, and looking into each other's eyes like a pair of teenagers.

"You are one lovely lady," he told her. "I mean, to come over so quickly, and to be here, ready to help us."

Her face turned downwards for a moment, but her eyes still peeped upwards.

"Are you sure that's all you meant?" she said quietly.

"Well, I mean..."

"You being a priest, and all..."

"Don't remind me of that," he grunted, holding her more tightly.

At that moment he could feel a stirring from his groin area, from a part of him that had remained dormant for years – except for peeing. And for years he had disciplined himself so that if ever he did feel an erection coming on he would immediately think of something unlikely to stir sexual desires. For example, he recalled once there was some horse's muck left on the road right outside his house. He remembered saying something unpriestly when he trod in it. Thinking of that had often come in useful.

He shut his eyes tightly, trying to concentrate on the mound of horse poo, but it was too late now. He could feel Anna's warm body pressing on him and his erection was becoming established. It was beginning to throb.

"God..."

Suddenly, as if understanding the priest's turmoil, his dilemma, his anguish, Anna pushed away from him.

"I would like to meet the girls as soon as possible," she said.

"Yes." Slightly red-faced, Bonelli turned around to

straighten his trousers. "Yes, of course."

He fought desperately to control his quivering member. Pushing it down was painful so he stuck it upward with its tip just showing behind his trouser belt.

He faced her again and looked at his watch. Half past ten. He knew the girls would still be up, together in one of the rooms, probably having a late-night snack and watching a film.

"Okay, I'll just pop into the corridor and knock on the door. They should still be up."

"Oh, fantastic," she said. "I can't wait to meet them. Especially Maria."

Father Bonelli looked at her, smiled, then went to the door with his erection dwindling like a balloon with a puncture.

*

Two teenage girls sat next to each other on the couch in Maria's room. They had just finished watching a rather long film about a man who was on death row for a crime he did not commit. He was a very religious man and spent much of his time praying to God, but the execution still went ahead.

Maria and her new friend Debbie Shallis discussed the film for a while, then prepared a snack and a pot of tea to have together while waiting for the *Ten O'Clock News* to come on.

Maria and Debbie were completely different in some ways, but then very similar in others, and they were gradually becoming really good friends because of it.

On one hand, for the time being at least, Maria still had school to go to, together with all her friends, but Debbie had no school, therefore, she had no close friends. Also, whereas Maria had been taken away from her family home, Debbie had run away from hers and had left it a hundred miles behind.

Lookswise they were completely different, too. Maria was tall for her age, slim, and had long, straight, dark hair. Debbie in complete contrast was somewhat shorter and slightly plump. She was still quite pretty, though, with ginger eyelashes and freckles, and red, bushy hair.

But despite all their differences, they were very similar in one most extraordinary way, and as time went on, visibly this would gradually become more obvious. They were both pregnant with their babies due at about the same time towards the end of the year.

Debbie was intrigued with Maria's story, although as yet she found herself struggling to believe it. She tactfully decided to keep her true opinion to herself, and both girls just remained supportive of each other.

They sat together having their tea, and Maria smiled proudly when *The News At Ten* came on with the usual sound of the chimes of Big Ben.

In between the chimes, the news headlines were announced.

Bong...

"The Prime Minister announces radical changes to unemployment benefits."

Bong...

"Women demand equal pay, and an increase to maternity leave."

Bong...

"Film star legend dies at the age of a hundred and three."

Bong...

"Chelsea through to another FA Cup final following five-goal, semi-final thriller."

Bong...

"Fifteen-year-old girl claims that she will give birth to the Son of God on 25th December."

Both girls laughed aloud, but then remained quiet as they listened to the other items of news, sipping their tea as they did so. Eventually the item of particular interest came on.

"The teenage girl," the newsreader was saying, "Maria Christopher, is insisting on her story that she is going to give birth to the Son of God. She has strenuously repeated that her doctor has examined her and confirmed that she is a virgin. She also says that she was visited by an Angel. Here's our reporter, Susan Stewart, with the latest update on the story."

The lady reporter was shown holding a microphone that looked like a huge lollypop and standing outside Maria's parents' house.

"Yes, thank you, Trisha," she said. "Well, as for the doctor saying that the girl is still a virgin, we haven't had that proven, but then we wouldn't, would we, what with patient confidentiality? And as for the visit from an Angel, everyone can draw their own conclusion to that…"

"Okay, but Susan," interrupted the newsreader in the studio, "where is the girl now? Rumours have it that she's gone into hiding. Can you confirm that?"

"I can, indeed, confirm it, Trisha," said Susan Stewart. "I am standing outside the family home now, and up until Monday evening, this is where Maria Christopher was living. She is not here now, though. Only a few minutes ago we learned that she has been moved to a private dwelling, although it is believed to be nearby. A local clergyman is thought to have put her into a private shelter, and only two days ago local television reporters heard him say that he also had a visit from a Holy Messenger who told him that he had the responsibility to look after the girl."

"Did the priest offer any proof?"

"He said he would accompany the Mother of the New King on her Journey. He was asked what he meant by that, and he just replied that we are all on a journey."

"Sounds like he speaks in riddles."

"Yes," Susan laughed. "Next he was asked if he really did believe in the Child of God, and he replied that we are all children of God."

"So what do you make of it, Susan?"

"Me?" said Susan with a smile. "Personally? Well, I think it's extremely far-fetched, but I have to say that this girl is gathering support. There are people who do believe her story, that the Holy King will be born this coming December the twenty-fifth."

The TV picture returned to the newsreader in the studio.

"Thank you, Susan," she said. "And now sport. Chelsea are through to the FA Cup final to be played at Wembley at the end of the month. We now go to our sports correspondent…"

Maria laughed excitedly at the television and clapped her hands.

"So," she said proudly to Debbie. "What do you think of that?"

"Hmmm," Debbie smiled, then she said, "So, you're having a boy?"

"Yes," said Maria. "It's funny, but I just know it's going to be a boy."

"Well, actually," Debbie said, "I'm hoping for a little girl."

Both girls laughed. Then Maria took out another video tape and put it into the machine. It was a film based on a Stephen King novel, *Carrie*, about a girl with telekinetic powers.

*

About a hundred miles away there were two men watching *The News At Ten,* and they were not laughing. Both men looked very serious, and worried, and both, seemingly, had dental problems. One had a missing front tooth that gave him a permanently menacing leer, the other had black bits between his front teeth and nicotine stains.

"Probably a load of crap," said Claud Tyler, the one with the missing tooth.

"Most probably," said the other, a rather weedy-looking man by the name of Rod Spencer.

"Just a load of lies."

"Yeah."

"Can't be sure, though."

"No."

"What shall we do then?"

Rod reached for an ornament from a shelf and held the object in both hands.

"Should we go to see *Tuan?*" he said.

The ornament in his hands was an ugly figure, about twenty centimetres high, and of a man's body but with a grotesque animal's head, possibly a dog, a bull mastiff, its face in an aggressive snarl.

"Yes, we have to. We must set off immediately."

"What? Tonight?" Still clutching the ornament, Rod looked at his watch.

"Yes. We must ask him what we need to do."

"And whatever he tells us to do...?"

And finally both men said together, "... in accordance with our vows, we must obey."

CHAPTER NINETEEN

The film had only been running for a few minutes when there was a knock at the door. Both Maria and Debbie looked at the clock on the wall. Twenty to eleven...

"Who could be knocking at this time?" Maria said impatiently.

"It'll probably be Father Bonelli," said Debbie. "He sometimes goes around the place late at night before he goes back to his own house, just to make sure it's all secure. Then if he sees any lights still on, he calls out to check everything's okay."

"Yes, but why would he knock?"

"Let's see." It was Debbie who got off the couch to go and answer the door.

As Maria was stopping the video with the pause button, she heard voices from the hallway. She thought she heard another lady's voice.

"Oh, no, not Social Services," she murmured to herself. "Not at this hour."

Within half a minute Debbie was back in the lounge again, with Father Bonelli close behind, and a woman the girls had never seen before.

"Girls," said Father Bonelli. "This is Anna Gabriella. She is um..." he thought for a moment. "... she's a friend of mine. She's also a qualified midwife."

"Okay..." Maria looked from one to the other feeling rather uncertain.

"Nice to meet you," Debbie said, extending her hand.

Rather surprised, Anna shook hands with Debbie.

"You, too, my dear."

"This is Debbie Shallis," the priest said to Anna. "She's been here for a few weeks now, and her baby is due the second week in December."

Debbie gave Anna a courteous nod.

Maria just looked at the woman.

"Sorry, I don't understand this," she said. "Why are we being introduced to a midwife at nearly eleven o'clock at night, and seven and a half months before the babies are due?"

Without answering Maria's question, Bonelli turned to Anna and said, "This is Maria."

It was all he needed to say. Another sentence, like, 'The girl who has been chosen to give birth to God's Child,' would have been totally superfluous.

Anna moved towards her.

"Blessed are you, my child," she said, bowing, and doing the sign of the cross.

Maria couldn't help grinning, and put her hands together, in front of her mouth, attempting to disguise this as a reverent gesture.

Debbie stifled a giggle.

Bonelli didn't seem to notice and looked benevolently at the girls.

"Anna has a rare gift," he told them. "She predicted all of this, long before it happened, as did I, of course. It's a purely incidental thing that she happens to be a qualified midwife."

"What, you actually believe all of this?" Debbie said, smiling broadly.

Maria stared at her and made frantic, but silent, gestures at her.

"Oh, no, I mean..." Debbie tried to look serious. "Oh, yes, really good, after all, who wouldn't believe it, what with all that evidence, and all?"

But all of this time, Anna had just been gazing at Maria, not being able to take her eyes off her.

"I want to do all I can to help," she said. "Nearer the time, you see, we may need to go away, into hiding somewhere, just for a few weeks."

"Why?" said Debbie. "I'm not going anywhere."

Anna then looked round at the priest, clearly taken aback at the other girl's reaction.

"I thought you said you'd explained everything," she said, her voice barely above a whisper.

"To Maria, yes," said Bonelli. "But Debbie and I still need to have a talk about our plans."

"Plans?" said Debbie. "What plans? Count me out."

Bonelli then explained everything that he knew. From his own experience with a visit from a Holy Messenger, coupled with his premonitions, and what he'd read in the Bible. Therefore, he felt sure that there would be evil people who would want to find Maria and her baby and do them harm. Newspapers and news bulletins on TV were good in one way, even essential to God's plans, but in another way, they could be dangerous, drawing the attention of undesirable characters. Therefore, he felt sure they had two choices. Either run and hide from the danger, or face it head-on and fight it, and use what weapons they had.

He concluded with, "Until the babies are born, the best thing to do is run and hide. After that, I believe that God, himself, will guide us. Afterwards, when we're seen to be travelling with two babies..."

"Hold it right there," Debbie suddenly snapped, with her hands held up. "You're planning on using me and my baby as a diversion, to cause confusion, so if evil people do come after us, they might get me by mistake. You complete bastards."

Anna looked at Bonelli in panic. She felt then that this was his fault. He had said too much.

"No, I assure you," Bonelli said. "That is not the case. The opposite in fact."

Debbie faced him, determined, adamant.

"How?" she demanded, hands on hips.

Bonelli may have been old, but he was much younger in body and soul, and had a sharp brain having never used drugs (except the occasional magic mushroom) so he was able to think quickly.

"Any evil people," he began, "would quickly learn where Maria had been hiding, and come looking for her here, so it is more likely that it would be here they would find you instead of her."

"Then I'll go somewhere else," Debbie said.

"They would find you wherever you went," Bonelli continued, anticipating her argument, "so you'd actually be safer with us."

Debbie looked from priest, to midwife, back to priest again, and even glanced at Maria with an expression of mistrust.

"I need to think this out," she said at last. "I'm going back to my own room. I think tomorrow morning I might call Social Services and ask them to place me somewhere else."

She marched to the door, but before stepping out into the hallway, she called back, "And by the way, I think you're all bonkers."

And with that she left Maria's room and slammed the door behind her.

Father Bonelli looked at Maria, drew a deep breath, then looked at Anna.

"Leave her to me," he said. "I'll speak to her. She'll be okay."

He then went to Debbie's room and knocked on the door.

"Go away," was the immediate response from within.

"Debbie, listen to me," said Bonelli.

No answer.

"Please listen," he said.

Still no answer.

"Okay, so you're angry with me, and I don't blame you. I should have told you about my plans sooner, but I didn't. I'm really sorry."

Still no answer, but the priest heard a shuffling sound from inside Debbie's room, as though she was moving closer to the door to hear what he was saying.

"The reason I didn't tell you," Bonelli continued, "was that until Anna came, I didn't actually know what I was going to do. But I'll tell you one honest thing, and may God strike me down here and now if I'm lying: I will lay down my life to protect you *and* Maria, *and* your babies. I have already sworn to sacrifice my own life if necessary, and that is what I will do, and furthermore…"

The door clicked, then opened.

Bonelli stood there looking at Debbie, her eyes red and full of tears. She held her hand up, and in her hand was a large book. Bonelli knew straight away that it was *the Holy Bible*, and he guessed what she wanted him to do with it.

"Swear," she said quietly. "Swear on the Holy Bible that no harm will come to me or my baby."

Father Giuseppe Bonelli reached forward with his left hand and took the Bible from her. He then placed his right hand on top of it.

He looked Debbie directly in the eyes, and steadily and firmly said, "I swear on the Holy Bible that no harm will come to you or your baby as long as I shall live. And I swear that I will fight to the death if necessary to protect you both."

He passed the Bible back. She took it and held it to her chest.

"Well, okay, then," she said.

"Okay? he said. "So does that mean…?"

"You said something about weapons," she said, putting

the Bible down carefully on a little table just inside the door.

He looked at her and gave a slight nod. He now needed to speak to her in the privacy of his own house, but he had noted, from the sounds of things, that it had just started to rain.

"Get your jacket on," he told her, "and come with me."

He took her across the road, into his own house, and into the living room. He then went across the room to his bureau, took the key from his pocket and opened the bottom drawer. As he did so he explained about his army days and his brother Lucci. He showed her the gun and explained how he came to acquire it.

"My God," Debbie said, actually holding the gun. "I've never held a real gun before."

"I've got plenty of ammunition," he told her. "And I've got a few grenades, too."

Debbie just looked at him, bewildered.

"Now," said Bonelli. "I've got something else to tell you."

"What?" said Debbie, still wondering if she could really trust the old priest. "Like a secret, you mean?"

"Yes, like a secret," he told her. "You are really important to accomplish our mission, and one day soon when the time is right I will tell you this secret. Before I do, however, you must promise something to me, and that is that you won't tell anyone else about it. Not even Maria."

He then turned back to the old bureau, and crouched beside it, reaching for something else.

CHAPTER TWENTY

Rainwater from another puddle across the country lane hit the underside of the old Land Rover with a resounding thud, and as the torrential rain continued to fall, the single-speed windscreen wipers struggled to keep the narrow windshield clear. To interfere further with visibility, only one of the old vehicle's headlights was working, and the driver, Claud Tyler, was squinting through the rain-splattered glass and into the dark while keeping his speed down.

He decreased his speed still further at every bend, keeping a watchful eye out for the required turn-off.

He was a pot-bellied man with more hair on his swarthy face than on his head, and his grimace as the vehicle hit a pothole emphasised the aggressive look of his missing front tooth.

"Take it easy, Claud," said his passenger, Rod Spencer, not helping matters by lighting a cigarette. "Let's get there in one piece."

"Bloody road," said Claud. "What do we pay our road tax for?"

Rod laughed, his bony face creasing grotesquely, revealing the black bits between his front teeth, and nicotine stains from years of smoking. "I didn't know that you paid any road tax."

Claud Tyler did not have sufficient funds to pay for such trifles as road tax. Both he and Rod Spencer had been down on their financial luck for a long time, none of their ventures having paid off. In desperation, they had placed money on a horse, having been advised by a very helpful man in their local pub. They noticed that the man had ugly tattoos on both forearms, those of scaly reptilian bodies entwined. He told Claud and Rod that the horse was "a dead cert".

The horse lost. It didn't even finish the race, and from there they got drawn into a spiral of misery, always trying to recover their losses, but only succeeding in getting into more debt.

Then one night the man with the tattoos advised Claud and Rod there was a much easier road to success. He invited them to an initiation where they would promise to serve some geezer calling himself the *Dark Lord*, although they never actually met him.

Anyway, after proving themselves by performing a few 'simple tasks', they would be rewarded and would become rich beyond their wildest dreams. Their instructions would be passed to them by another man, an ugly, obese man, calling himself *Tuan*.

(Apparently, Tuan, was some Greek or Latin word, or something like that.)

Anyway, he was the one they were to report to that rainy evening.

The rickety old Land Rover bounced over a dip in the road, then splashed through another puddle.

"Jesus H. Christ," hissed Claud as the old vehicle's suspension bounced with an unhealthy bump. "What I reckon is…"

"There it is," Rod interrupted, pointing excitedly at the turning in the lane, partly in shadow, and partly illuminated by the Land Rover's single headlamp.

They took the turning and the lane narrowed. They didn't talk at all now. Claud needed all his concentration so as not to end up in the bushes or down a ditch. He also hoped that no other vehicle would come down the lane in the opposite direction. There would hardly be enough room for two vehicles to pass side-by-side.

Then after two or three minutes they could determine the illumination of a large house. It was like a stately home. When they arrived at the front of the vast property, they found themselves on a big, stony driveway that was long enough and sufficiently wide to accommodate at least a dozen vehicles. There were lamps around it, like street lamps, but it looked like the whole plot was privately owned.

They got out of the Land Rover and, hoping he wouldn't be picked up on a security camera, Rod dropped his half-smoked cigarette onto the stony ground and trod on it. The two men walked together up to the large, oak front door. The rain was still falling so heavily that even after a short distance their jackets were quite soaked. As Claud knocked on the door with the heavy, brass knocker, completely drenched, Rod mused over how this was like a scene from an old horror movie.

And then there was a brilliant flash of lightening followed seconds later by a deafening crash of thunder.

A tall, thin butler, wearing a suit and top hat, obviously some kind of uniform, opened the door.

Claud eyed him cautiously. "Good evening," he said. "We're here to see…"

"Tuan is expecting you," said the butler.

"Right. But I have to explain…"

"Follow me."

They looked at one another and nervously stepped inside, thankful for the shelter at least, and the great door was closed after them with a loud thud that seemed to echo around the whole building. Then, leaving a dripping trail of rainwater in their wake along the tiled floor, they followed the butler along a very long corridor. At the end of this, they were led through a door, then along another corridor.

Rod mulled over the brief thought that if, for whatever reason, they had to make a quick getaway, they probably wouldn't be able to find their way out again.

As they walked along the corridor they noticed grotesque pictures that were in dark, wooden frames fixed to the walls. The pictures were of snarling faces that looked half animal and half human. Some looked more like reptile creatures with their scaled bodies entwined.

Claud and Rod looked nervously at each other, thinking the same thing at the same time. Those horrible pictures were just like the tattoos on that man's forearms. The one who invited them to the initiation. As the butler continued to lead the two men along the corridor of this eerie place, they were both beginning to regret getting mixed up with this nonsense, whatever it was.

And all of these hideous pictures on the walls, seeing one after the other as they continued along the corridor, added to the spookiness of the place.

Then Claud and Rod stopped in their tracks, frozen rigid at what they saw.

A group of eight hooded figures moving towards them in a military-style, two-by-two, squad formation.

Their wide hoods completely hid their faces, and the long cloaks they wore covered their feet, if they had any, for the people were like ghosts and appeared to be floating.

The figures floated soundlessly by without turning to them.

Rod reached out and grasped Claud by the arm.

The butler stopped and turned round towards them.

"This way, please," he said, with a tone of impatience.

Eventually they arrived outside yet another door that turned out to be the entrance to what looked like a huge hall. When they stepped inside, after the door had been closed behind them, they looked round to discover that the butler seemed to have vanished, preferring to remain in the corridor.

Claud and Rod looked at each other again, still trembling from the sight of the floating, hooded figures they'd met in the corridor.

Then they heard a voice, a lady's voice, which made them look towards the opposite end of the hall.

It was then that they saw Tuan, a big man weighing over three hundred pounds, with thin, creamy-coloured hair that could not be described as natural-looking. He wore tinted glasses and a jacket that was bursting at the seams.

They recognised him, even though they had only ever met him once previously, and that was at that initiation.

He was sitting some distance away, on what appeared to be a stage. They were still a bit confused about where the lady's voice had come from, but then they understood. The big man was watching something on a large television screen.

The two men pulled puzzled expressions at one another, then began to slowly approach the stage. Despite the sounds of their footsteps on the bare wooden floorboards, Tuan did not even glance at them. He was aware of their presence, though, as he continued to watch the television intently.

The men stopped a short distance from Tuan, who was still staring unblinkingly at the television, evidently a news report programme, and it was only then that they realised what was holding the big man's attention so completely.

It was the girl, Maria Christopher.

The teenage schoolgirl. She was the one who claimed that she had been visited by an Angel, and that this visitor from Heaven had told her that she was going to give birth to the Holy Saviour. She insisted that she was still a virgin, *and* that she could prove it.

If true, the girl and her unborn baby were enemies of the *Dark Lord.*

The programme was a repeat of an earlier news bulletin where they showed, once again, the scene recorded by the local TV station. The girl was outside her former family home and accompanied by the old Italian priest. And it was this priest who seemed to strike fear into Tuan's heart, for the clergyman, too, adamantly claimed that he had been visited by "A Holy Messenger".

Claud and Rod stood close to each other, both wondering for the moment what to do or say, reluctant to speak, afraid to interrupt.

More moments elapsed where the lady newscaster explained that now nobody seemed to know where the girl was living. It had been reported that she had gone into hiding, although she was still attending school. She was currently being escorted and watched over by security guards.

"It's obvious that it's all just a pack of lies," Claud ventured at last.

"Of course it is," Rod agreed. "That girl and her friends have cooked this whole story up."

"And all having a good laugh."

Both men laughed uneasily, still waiting for Tuan to say something.

"Cheeky little bitches," Rod continued. "What I would do with them is…"

He stopped abruptly as Tuan reached for a glass dish on a little table in front of him, gathered up a fistful of peanuts, and popped a few in his mouth. Then he just sat there munching, while apparently still staring in front of him, even though the repeated news report had now finished.

Then he spoke. "What I want you to do is…" His voice was quiet, but deep.

As if lost in thought, he placed another few peanuts into his mouth, and resumed munching.

Claud and Rod looked at him. They were feeling confused and afraid, perhaps wishing even more now that they had never got mixed up with this.

"Find her," Tuan said. "Find out where she lives, and then…"

More peanuts. More munching.

"And then?" Claud said nervously.

At last, Tuan turned his head and looked at the two trembling men who were standing there like two naughty schoolboys waiting for the headmaster to pass sentence.

Two words seemed to just drop from Tuan's lips.

"Kill her."

CHAPTER TWENTY-ONE

The journey from JackDaw House to Our Lady's Senior Girls' School was actually slightly shorter than the walk that Maria used to have from her family home, so having set off for school at roughly the same time as usual, she arrived at the school a bit early.

But only to be greeted outside the school gates by a noisy mob of people. Because of all the television coverage and newspaper stories and photographs, all the people instantly recognised her as she arrived. It was difficult for her to determine at first whether they were angry – not believing a word of it – or happy – supportive and just wanting to see her, believing that she really was to be the mother of the Son of God.

The first rotten tomato came whizzing overhead, but missed by a yard, and splattered on the ground in front of her. She walked on, hurriedly, tempted to run but not wanting to look undignified.

Several police officers were there. They had been tipped off and called in. Several of the officers were standing in a line across the gates, and as Maria continued on her way through, she paused for a moment to try to hear what they were actually saying.

And through the overall din she distinctly heard an angry, old man's voice calling.

"You lying whore, I hope you go to Hell for your lies!"

Whereas another voice conveyed an entirely different view, with, "Please come to us and tell us what we need to do to be saved."

However, just as she was turning towards the school entrance, another rotten tomato came swishing overhead, a lot closer this time and missing her by only a few inches. This prompted her into a run, dignity forgotten, until she was safely through the doors.

Inside the school she walked briskly along the corridor towards her locker to sort out her books for the morning's lessons. She was soon joined by her three best friends. They seemed quite breathless. Evidently they had also been running.

"You've really caused a stir, haven't you?" said Diana. "I'm wondering if you've thought this whole thing through, you know."

Julie was busy with a handkerchief wiping some wet, red staining off her skirt.

"I've been hit by a rotten tomato," she said indignantly, scowling at Maria. "By rights, it should have been you who got this."

"I nearly did get hit," Maria assured her.

"Oh, that makes me feel lots better."

"As long as what you're saying is true, though," said Becky. "I mean, you are sure?"

Maria thought for a moment, then said, "Listen, guys, I am telling you the truth, but possibly it would be better all round if I make a public statement to say it's all been a mistake, or a misunderstanding, or..."

"Or a joke?" Diana suggested. "And in really poor taste, too."

"No, not a joke," Maria said hastily. "I could say that the Angel's visit was just a dream."

"And what about being a virgin?" Diana said, raising her eyebrows suspiciously.

Maria looked down at her feet. She hadn't thought about an answer to that one.

"Hang on, though," said Julie. "If you did claim now that

it was all a mistake or whatever, then what about the baby?"

"Well, I've changed my mind about that now," Maria confessed. "I think I might have an abortion."

"WHAT?" all Maria's friends shouted together.

"You simply can't do that," Becky cried. "Not now."

"You would go down forever in history," Julie said seriously, "as the girl who had God's Child terminated."

Maria stood there facing her friends with her hands on her hips.

"Not if I made a public announcement," she said, "that the visit from the Angel was just a dream."

"Yes, even so," Julie said, starting to get cross at the idea. "Even more so, in fact."

"Why?"

Julie felt her blood begin to boil, good friends though they were.

"Look, you started all of this," she snapped. "Now you'll have to stick with it."

Maria looked at the three girls in turn. They were all good friends, but out of all of them, Diana was her very best friend.

In desperation, Maria looked at her again, wanting, needing, some reassuring words of wisdom from her, but Diana just shook her head sadly, and at last, after a long moment of reflection, she said, "No, my sweetie. I'm afraid it can't be done."

With that, Diana, Julie and Becky dashed off to their first class of the morning leaving Maria on her own, lost in her thoughts. She leaned up against her locker and gently tapped her head on the locker door several times. But then she leaned back and smiled to herself.

She remembered one particular story from the Bible, when Jesus suffered a moment of weakness. At that point He knew that He was going to die a ghastly death, and He prayed to His Holy Father in Heaven and asked if it was at all possible to have this burden lifted from His shoulders.

But Jesus recovered from the darkness, and eventually completed his mission.

Maria put her hands together and closed her eyes in silent prayer.

Dear God, I'm so sorry, please give me more strength. I swear I will never let you down again...

Then she said out loud, "Please give me strength so I don't fail, and please also..."

"WHAT do you think you're doing?" came a sudden, loud and familiar voice.

Maria opened her eyes and looked round to see the burly figure of Geraldine Knox standing there. The sixth-form prefect and netball captain gazed at her with a puzzled face.

"Um..." Maria had to think quickly. "Oh, I was just saying a quick prayer for our final with St Angela's Seniors."

Geraldine's tone immediately softened.

"Oh, I see, very good," she said with a nod of satisfaction. "But I think we'll need more than just prayers to beat that mob."

"Yes, Gerry."

"Final practice, this afternoon, last one before the match. Right?"

"Yes, Gerry."

"And now you'd better get off," said the bossy prefect, "or you'll be late for class, and I don't want any of my players stuck in detention when they're supposed to be on the netball court."

Maria gladly went on her way, and as she went she felt relieved and happy about everything, and confident that she was going to see things through, and satisfactorily to the end.

CHAPTER TWENTY-TWO

The alarm clock bell sounded just as Police Inspector Paul Retberg had his hand on the collar of an escaped convict that the police had been tracking for more than three years.

With a groan, and wondering vaguely where his wife Donna was, he rolled over in bed and slapped his hand hard down on the top of the alarm clock.

Through squinting eyes he looked at the time. 5.45.

He would have time to have a shower, go downstairs and have breakfast, while still being able to get to the police station on time and begin his 8 am shift. Briefing his section, though – a customary start to each day known as Parade On – would commence at 7.45.

A few minutes later...

Having had his shower and shave, he got dressed, and now with a much clearer head he began to wonder again where Donna was. He went downstairs.

Before going to the kitchen, he quickly went into the lounge and switched on the TV to catch up on the news. He was just in time to hear some crap about that schoolgirl who was pregnant and was claiming that she was going to give birth to the Son of God.

The police inspector *knew* it was a lie. And it was a lie because he *knew* there was no such thing as God. Paul Retberg was an atheist through and through. He firmly believed that we evolved from apes. Plenty of evidence of that, but no actual proof. It just seemed to make more sense to Retberg than Adam and Eve simply springing into existence.

But now all this nonsense was happening very locally, and the school that the girl attended was less than a mile from the police station.

As the news item proceeded, he snorted angrily. He had no time for such bullshit. He looked impatiently at the TV screen when a reporter appeared outside Our Lady's Senior Girls' School.

"And today is the day that everyone has been looking forward to," she was saying. "The Netball County Championship final against the current league champions, St Angela's Seniors. But the big talking point is that Maria Christopher who has made these claims, will be playing. It's estimated that there will be over a thousand spectators here, and we have been told that..."

Retberg had no interest whatsoever in knowing what they had been told, and with another hefty snort he reached for the TV knob and switched stations.

"Oh, you're joking," he said under his breath.

There was no escape from it. There was the priest being interviewed. The caption at the bottom of the screen said, *Father Giuseppe Bonelli*.

"Now, is it true that you were also visited by an Angel?" said the interviewer.

"Yes," the priest replied promptly. "It's all true, and I can confirm that the new Holy King will be born on the twenty-fifth of December."

Retberg groaned, and holding his hands over his face, he stood up. Not being able to see where he was going, he strode briskly into the kitchen. He would just have time for a cup of tea, he thought, and maybe a piece of toast.

In the kitchen he removed his hands from his face.

And there it was, on the counter, a single sheet of paper with Donna's handwriting.

The note ran...

I've had it with you, you utter pig, never caring about me. We haven't got a relationship. We never have. Your relationship is with the police. Well, I hope you'll both be very happy. I wish I'd listened to my mother...

"So do I," Retberg muttered to himself as he continued to read.

... She said never marry a policeman. She's invited me to stay with her at her new house in Adelaide, so I'm going. I've seen a solicitor. He will be in touch. I want a divorce. You absolute loser. Love and best wishes, Donna. PS I'm going to do you for every penny I can get, you bastard.

Paul Retberg made a cup of tea and sipped it thoughtfully. Moving to Australia was a big step to take so she must have been planning this for a long time.

Before leaving the house, he went back into the lounge to turn off the TV, but just before he did so the priest said, "Let God into your life and into your relationship. Don't shut him out."

"Oh, shut up," Retberg said with one final snort before switching off the TV with a decisive click.

He then dashed out of the house and into his car.

*

Paul Retberg was a stout guy. He had just turned forty, and at over six feet tall he weighed a bit. When approaching a suspect, the person in question would quake in his boots. The recently appointed inspector had been questioned on allegations of police brutality, but he had never used more force than necessary to make an arrest. His face was not pretty, though. His eyebrows were permanently wrinkled into a frown and his mouth was set like he was sucking something bitter.

On entering the police station that morning, that look of bitterness was even more intense. The thought of that local girl making up stories about visits from angels was annoying enough, but the fact that some people actually believed these fairy stories was intolerable. *Outrageous!*

There was something else that had momentarily irritated him that morning, but he had forgotten what that was now. He looked at his watch as he strode briskly towards the report room.

Then he remembered. The watch had been a ten-year wedding anniversary present.

A moment of genuine sadness, but then...

"Hey, Paul!"

He spun round.

Trotting up behind him was Sergeant Ian Green.

Paul Retberg and Ian Green had worked together, and had been close friends, for nearly ten years. They had first met at the Police Training College at Shotley Gate, Ipswich, which was originally a navy barracks. From there they had joined the same section at a town in the East Midlands. Two years later they both passed their sergeant's exams and were both promoted within weeks of each other. Almost immediately they began their inspector's studies, then entered for the exam and passed that, too.

Following that, Retberg was promoted again.

Then Ian Green was offered an inspector's position in a different town, but to everyone's surprise he turned it down. He stated that he wanted to stay at his current station. There was speculation among some of the younger PCs that Retberg and Green were gay. Of course they were not. Ian Green, now in his mid-thirties, had a stunningly beautiful wife, Bella, and Paul Retberg's wife, Donna, wasn't bad either, even though she had now left him, presumably for a better life.

Retberg and Green were good mates, though.

And Sergeant Ian Green was every bit as tough as Retberg. A sturdy, although slightly shorter officer, he had been a boxer before joining the police. His nose was slightly crooked where it had been broken in one of his least successful bouts. He could take a punch or two, but he would always return them with plenty of interest, hitting hard as many captured villains could confirm. Like his inspector, he'd had to answer allegations of using unnecessary force on a few occasions, but Retberg had got him off, making statements that Green, and other officers on his section, only used standard and approved self-defence techniques. One such technique was the cross-block, and this involved applying the palm of the hand *firmly* on the assailant's chin. In the real world, though, when actually being attacked by thugs, Ian Green would repeat this process several times with considerable force, but only when absolutely necessary with a clenched fist.

Retberg looked at his watch again as they continued swiftly along the corridor.

"What's happening, Ian?" he said. "Any news? Any gossip? Any scandal?"

"We're going to be extra busy today," the sergeant replied breathlessly, trying to keep in step with Retberg. "We've got two officers off sick. Nugent is still on leave with stress, Vickie's gone off on her maternity leave and Wendy's got a hospital appointment this morning."

"Bloody hell, Ian," Retberg said. "We've got the chief super screaming at me because our arrests are well-below target. I want everyone out on the beat and pulling people in."

"The town centre beat officers can do that," Green said, as they arrived at the report room, and entered to see half a dozen officers already there, sitting on the edges of desks.

The night shift officers had finished their reports, updated their pocket notebooks and were ready for home.

Paul Retberg looked around him, then turned back to the sergeant.

"So how many have we got left on the section?" he asked.

"Eleven." Ian Green replied.

"Bollocks." Retberg observed his depleted squad and considered asking one ore two of the night shift officers to stay for a couple of hours overtime, but pairs of bleary eyes looked back at him. "Bugger it," he added.

"Including you and me," Green said.

Retberg took a deep breath.

"Right then," he said. "We cannot afford any officers sloping off to do anything non-essential today, and I must insist..."

"Sir," said one of the young constables, holding up his hand like a child in a classroom. "Todd and I have got to get some blokes together for an identity parade. We're looking for tall, thin men with long curly fringes, and wearing glasses, and..."

"Oh, for fox sake, Dutton," Retberg snapped. "We only need one of you to do that."

"But..."

"Now listen, guys. I want some arrests today. Yesterday, Toddy went to the Harpur Shopping Centre to apprehend a twelve-year-old girl for shoplifting."

"I gave her a good telling off," PC Todd protested. "Poor kid was scared shitless, sobbing her heart out. She promised never to do it again, so I gave her some advice and sent her on her way."

Ian Green hid his grin in his hand, disguising the gesture as a rub of his crooked nose.

"That's no good for our stats," Retberg said. "We need arrests."

Another young cop, a muscular lad who looked like Rambo, shifted his weight as he sat on the corner of a desk.

"What's the fockin' point?" he said. "What can you do with a twelve-year-old kid?"

"I'm not arguing with you," Retberg said loudly, holding

up his hands. "And we cannot afford any officers at all to do anything other than…"

At that moment there was a knock on the report room door, and in walked Chief Superintendent Sutton.

"Sorry to interrupt, chaps," he said, even though two of the constables sitting there were ladies, "but I wonder if you could spare me a couple of officers this afternoon?"

There was a soft chuckle around the room. Paul Retberg struggled to conceal his irritation.

"Sorry, sir," he said, "but I'm afraid we are at full stretch today. Maybe you could try the Town Centre boys and girls?"

"No," the chief super said firmly, indicating that this was more of an order, rather than a casual request. "I need experienced officers from this section."

"Any particular reason?"

The other officers in the room seemed to hold their breath. It was not the usual thing for an officer, inspector though he was, to question a request from a chief superintendent.

Sutton, though, maintained his composure and took a deep breath.

"I need them to attend a girls' netball match," he said quietly.

There was another ripple of spontaneous laughter that filled the report room.

Except that Paul Retberg did not laugh. His bitter expression intensified as he stared up at the ceiling.

Sutton continued. "Everyone by now has heard the name Maria Christopher."

There was a collective sigh all around the room.

But one officer became suddenly alert. His name was Gifford. Most of the other officers called him Giff. It had been noted he was a bit of a loner, but he took everything in, and he seemed to sit up suddenly at the mention of the netball match and in particular the name of the girl who had made the most astonishing claims.

The chief superintendent went on to explain all about death threats, and about his very real concerns that an attempt on the girl's life might be made at the school in front of a crowd of people.

"And so," he concluded while looking directly at Retberg, "I require two officers from this section to accompany me to the girls' school at two this afternoon. I will be in my office when they are ready."

"I'll volunteer if you like, sir," Gifford said unexpectedly.

"No, thanks, Giff," Retberg said. "You need to catch up on your paperwork. You're way behind…"

The chief super looked at Retberg with a puzzled frown, then shrugged his shoulders. He then turned back to the door, but as an afterthought he stopped and added, "We will be doing lots of stop-search, asking loads of questions, but we will be in plain clothes. Okay?"

Retberg made no reply. Just gave a look of defeat.

Sutton then left the report room, closing the door quietly behind him.

Sergeant Green could not help smiling.

"What are we going to do now?" he said in a panicky, high-pitched voice.

Retberg just held his head in his hands, then in a muffled voice said, "Class dismissed."

All the officers in the section filed out of the report room, all grinning while getting ready to go out on their various tasks. Gifford was the last one to leave the room, apparently lingering for as long as possible.

Then with just Retberg and Green left in the report room, Ian Green approached his best buddy, and put his hand on his shoulder.

"I suppose you and I could go," he said. "It'll only be for an hour or two."

"Ian, my old mate," Retberg said with a huge sigh and just managing a weary smile, "you are a bloody mind reader."

The sergeant nodded. He always kept a set of civvies in his locker, and he knew that Retberg did, too.

"And after all," he continued with a grin back on his face, "an hour or two of stop-search will actually be quite relaxing compared to some of the shit that we get."

"You're right," Retberg said with a firm nod. "And at the end of the day what could possibly happen at a girls' netball match?"

CHAPTER TWENTY-THREE

There was a buzz of excitement around the school grounds in anticipation of the greatest day in the school's long history. Some people, pupils and parents alike, had to keep pinching themselves to ensure they were not dreaming.

No! It was not a dream. Our Lady's Senior Girls' School really were going to be playing in the County Netball Championship final, but all eyes seemed to be on one particular player, a girl who had been hitting the headlines recently for other reasons.

A toss of a coin at a teachers' meeting during the previous week had decided the venue for the final, and Our Lady's had won that decision. The players of the St Angela's Seniors' team had jokingly declared that it didn't matter where the match was played. The current league champions fully expected to absolutely pulverise their opponents.

The Our Lady's sixth-form prefect and netball captain, Geraldine Knox, had been running 'her' players through their paces in training, and she believed that everyone, especially goal-shooter Maria Christopher, were on top form. The attention of the newspaper and television reporters didn't deter her, and it didn't occur to her straight away that apart from reporting on what could turn out to be an historic event, Maria had drawn most of this attention to herself in extraordinary ways.

The reporters and journalists were jostling around talking to people, interviewing them to get lots of different views, and as a padding for their reports, but at the same time keeping an eye out for the star of the show. She was the one they all really wanted to talk to.

Maria herself was aware of this, and so she was trying to keep out of sight, mingling with others, and hiding among them, but this was not easy as there were not many girls, even in the sixth form, who were taller than her.

Now some of the players were going off in groups to the pavilion to change into their school sports kits of white tops and navy-blue skirts, while the visitors would be wearing their usual all-red kit. The girls from St Angela's Seniors were a bit baffled at the presence of so many people from television. For them, the County Netball final was a big deal, but they had no idea that it was *that* big.

"What a palaver," said one of the players of the visiting team, as a few of them stood huddled together, looking around in bewilderment.

There was also a noticeable police presence, unprecedented at a girls' school netball match. The whole atmosphere was more like that of a great football match, like the European Cup final. The police were aware of the girl's story, though, and they had been put on alert that the fifth-former had actually received death threats. The officers were there to seek out anyone who could pose a threat, or even anybody who just looked a bit funny. The high-ranking officer, Chief Superintendent Sutton, had even ordered a random stop-search.

In accordance with the Police and Criminal Evidence Act 1984 (PACE) to submit to such a search, purely on suspicion, was not compulsory. However, Sutton had ordered that anyone refusing to be searched would be escorted out of the school grounds for whatever reason that the officer could trump up.

Inspector Paul Retberg and Sergeant Ian Green had agreed to help with this, and after some persuasion, the inspector in charge of the Town Centre beat bobbies had agreed to spare two of his officers. Two young ladies who were both probationers currently on Module Three.

Claud Tyler and Rod Spencer arrived at the school and were amazed at the atmosphere. At first they thought they'd arrived on Carnival Day. They may not have been the most gifted men mentally, but they were bright enough to realise that something was going on. They saw crowds of people of all ages milling around all over the place. News reporters were going up to people in the crowd, pushing microphones under their noses while being flanked by television crews.

"What the hell's going on?" said Claud. He grabbed the arm of one young man hurrying past. "Hey you!" he said. "What's happening here?"

"Don't you know?" said the man, trying to twist his arm free. "It's the biggest day in Our Lady's School's history."

"Why?"

"Are you thick, or what?" said the young man. "It's the final of the County Netball Championship, and the mother of the future Son of God is playing in the team."

With that he managed to twist his arm free, then he carried on in his hurried pursuit of an autograph or two.

Claud looked round at Rod.

"Well, at least we know we're in the right place," he said.

"Yeah, but at the wrong sodding time," said Rod.

Claud looked around him and nodded. His Land Rover was parked about a mile away, and in the back of the vehicle was Rod's rifle with its telescopic sight. On seeing the police officers marching around, they began to have second thoughts as to whether this was the most suitable time and place for an assassination.

"I've got a feeling we're being tested," Claud said, and looking round he noticed a man standing right behind him, wearing tinted glasses and a peaked cap. "And we're being watched, too," he added.

Rod turned round and suddenly became rigid.

"I'm not doing it," he said.

"What?" Claud was not sure what he meant.

"I'm not shooting her," Rod said. "The girl is just a cheeky kid who likes playing games, but that ain't reason enough for killing her." Then he repeated, "I tell you, I'm not doing it."

Claud looked at him and nodded, but his attention was now on the man standing behind him. The man appeared to be watching them and listening. He had produced a walkie-talkie radio receiver that he began talking into rapidly.

Realising that Claud had noticed him he started backing away, keeping his eye on Claud and Rod as he went, and still talking on the radio.

Even from some distance Rod could make out the tattoos on the man's forearms, those of entwined reptilian creatures.

"We're not alone," Claud said. "I don't like the look of him."

Rod looked round. "Me neither," he said.

"Who is he? What does he want?"

"Sent by Tuan, most likely to check on us, I bet."

"Right," said Claud, "And he heard you say you're not doing it."

The man, realising that his cover was blown, started walking away quickly, but still talking on the radio. Claud and Rod followed. They expected him to either leave the ground of his own accord or stand and face them. But he did neither. Instead, he began to lead them round in circles.

*

Meanwhile the television reporters eventually caught up with Maria. She felt the spongy top of a microphone being pushed into her face. At the same time, a camera rolled up to her.

"Hello, there." She heard a loud woman's voice right next to her. "Here we have Maria Christopher. How are you, Maria? Are you and your team feeling confident today?"

"Yes, thank you," Maria said, looking right into the camera. (She was beginning to get used to TV cameras by now.) "I am quite confident that we are going to win today."

"But don't you think that you have an unfair advantage?"

"What do you mean?" Maria smiled. Of course, she guessed what the woman meant.

"Well, I mean, having God on your side."

Maria laughed.

"No, God's not like that," she said. "He's chosen me to be the mother of His Second Son, but he's quite fair to everyone, and doesn't get involved much with games."

"What? Ever?"

"Well," Maria said, wrinkling her nose in thought, "Perhaps he did once. It was a very long time ago. I don't remember, of course. I wasn't even born then. It was the 1966 Football World Cup final, and, apparently, he did exercise some influence over a Russian linesman."

The young woman reporter laughed.

"I'm too young to remember that," she said, "but in football, you do see some footballers doing the sign of the cross, before coming onto the pitch. Do you think that would help their team win, then?"

Maria thought about that for a moment, then she said, "Well, I remember seeing a match between Brazil and Italy. Halfway through the second half, both teams decided to make a substitution at exactly the same time. Both substitutes ran onto the pitch side-by-side, and they both looked up at the sky and made the sign of the cross simultaneously."

The news reporter laughed. "Who won?" she asked.

Maria looked into the camera with a serious frown.

"The game ended in a draw," she said.

At that precise moment the captain of Our Lady's team, Geraldine Knox, came running over.

"Hey, Maria!" she shouted. "You're wanted. We're getting

ready to start."

※

Whereas Maria was goal shooter, her Captain Geraldine Knox was goal attack, and she could take shots, too, but if she could she was more likely to pass the ball to Maria who had an uncanny gift for accuracy. During the first of the four fifteen-minute periods, the fifth-form girl had had five shots on goal, with four of them going cleanly through the net. Geraldine had scored one, so that was five in all, and with two points per goal scored from open play in the goal area, that was a fine tally of ten points.

Their mid-field players (centre and wing attack) together with the defenders and goalkeeper, had also played well, but even so the St Angela's team had managed thirteen points which included a single penalty point, so were winning after the first period by 13 to 10.

During the first three-minute break, Geraldine got the other eight members of her team, including two substitutes, to stand in a semi-circle together, and while they sipped lemon squash, she gave them her thoughts on the first fifteen minutes.

"Come on, guys," she was saying. "They're not that great. We can win this."

As this pep-talk was going on Maria glanced around her, amazed at the noise from the huge number of people around the ground. She estimated at least a thousand people, not including police officers, security guards, news reporters and TV crews.

※

Two men also looking around them at that same moment were Claud Tyler and Rod Spencer, with particular interest in the man with the tinted glasses, who was still inexplicably talking on his walkie-talkie radio. And he was still obviously aware that they were following him, which Claud and Rod also found to be inexplicable. He just continued to wander, seemingly aimlessly, around the ground.

News reporters and TV crews circled the netball court. The reporters gave a running commentary about the latest situation on the match, with massive and continuous emphasis on the fact that one of Our Lady's players was none other than Maria Christopher, the girl who had made astonishing claims about her forthcoming child.

A woman was chosen randomly from the crowd. She offered her opinion of a pregnant girl being involved in such a vigorous game. Another 'expert' appeared next to her, however, saying that whether the child was God's or not, the girl was as yet only a few weeks pregnant, so playing in this game would cause no harm to her or the baby at all.

Claud leaned over to Rod and was just about to say something when a firm hand on his shoulder made him jump and spin round.

"I'm using the power of stop-search," Sergeant Ian Green advised him. "I refer to the stop-search section of PACE. This states that you do not have to submit to the search, but failure to comply means that I may request you to..."

"Okay, okay," said Claud. "There you go."

He turned his trouser pockets inside out and opened his jacket. He smiled, revealing the large gap in his teeth.

Ian Green grimaced back at him, but seemed to be satisfied enough with the search.

He then turned to Rod who also smiled, showing off all the black bits and nicotine stains. Rod was glad now that he hadn't brought with him the case that contained his rifle, complete with its telescopic sight. He was happy to turn out his pockets.

"Okay, so who are you both?" asked the police sergeant.

"Um..." Claud had to think about that. "Er..."

"We're uncles," Rod said. "Uncles of one of the netball players."

"Oh, yeah?" Green asked suspiciously. "Which one?"

"Maria," Claud said, still smiling. "Maria Christopher."

Sergeant Ian Green looked from one to the other, obviously far from convinced. He was just about to say something else, when there came a crackly voice on his radio.

"Chief super to Green."

The police sergeant held his radio and pressed the transmit button.

"Ian Green here," he said. "I copy, over."

"Get yourself down to the main entrance right now," said the crackly voice. "There's a bunch of prats down there letting off fireworks. There are people scared shitless. They reckon it sounds like a gun's going off."

"On my way. Over."

Ian Green gave Claud and Rod one more suspicious look, shook his head and set off on his way.

Claud looked at Rod, then looked around him, doing a complete 360-degree turn.

"Bugger it," he said out loud.

The man with the tinted glasses and walkie-talkie radio had disappeared.

CHAPTER TWENTY-FOUR

Things got worse for Our Lady's during the second period, and the deficit grew. They scored another ten points giving them a total of twenty, but St Angela's scored a further twelve points so they now had twenty-five.

And in the third period it got worse still. Most of Our Lady's team were starting to show signs of fatigue now, and as they went into the final fifteen minutes they were trailing 35–28.

As tired as they were, the Our Lady's girls put everything they had into it for one final supreme effort, and with their captain snapping at their heels every inch of the way, they began to catch up. At first it seemed that every time they scored, St Angela's would break away down the other end and score too, so it went 37–30, then 39–32, then 41–34, and so on.

By the halfway line there was a huge clock, and the players could see the seconds ticking away. Geraldine looked at it. Five minutes to go. St Angela's were winning 43–36.

"Come on, come on," Geraldine shouted at her players, and clapping her hands. Tears were beginning to run down her face. She desperately wanted to win. "Please, come on."

The crowd started to get noisier, Our Lady's supporters really getting behind their team.

Maria collected the ball from Diana who had come on as a centre substitute in the third period, Diana's task being to link up with the wing attack. Maria bounced the ball twice, then passed it to Geraldine who caught it in eager hands. Maria then ran towards the St Angela's goal and held her arms up cleverly anticipating the return pass from Geraldine. She caught the ball and swung her arms through the air in one swift movement, then threw it just as a St Angela's defender jumped up with her arms aloft. The ball went like a bullet, hit the wooden panel above the net with a loud *clack,* then went straight through the netted ring.

That sublime team movement, a direct result of hard graft on the training ground orchestrated by Geraldine Knox, had the desired result. It raised the spirit of the team and gave them new energy.

The crowd cheered. The scoreboard now read, Our Lady's–38, St Angela's–43.

Then the visitors went on the attack again. They wanted to restore their seven-point advantage. The St Angela's centre caught the ball and was just about to pass it to her goal attacker, when Maria, with her face set in a fierce snarl, jumped in front of her. She performed her ventriloquist gift of throwing her voice.

A sudden shout of a man's voice, *"Hey you!"* seemed to come from behind the startled girl who screeched in surprise and dropped the ball.

Maria quickly gathered it up and made a long pass straight to Geraldine who was just as surprised to find herself with a shooting chance and under no pressure at all. She turned and had the easiest shot of the afternoon to give her team another two points.

More cheering from the crowd, and even louder now.

Our Lady's–40, St Angela's–43. Three minutes to go.

Then the St Angela's captain went around passing an instruction to each of her players. They were going into lockdown – everyone into defence.

Two minutes left, still St Angela's led 43–40, and every attack that Our Lady's started was just blocked. Geraldine's players were getting exhausted, for them it was like trying to run through a brick wall.

One minute left, seconds ticking away, Geraldine was running her heart out, and sobbing at the same time, desperately trying to get an attack going. She quickly glanced at the large, glittering trophy sitting on its stand on a table by the side of the court, ready to be presented to the winning captain. She shook her head irritably when the cliché of *so near, yet so far away,* sang in her mind, and with thirty seconds left, with a desperate cry, she realised now that even if Our Lady's did get another goal, they would still lose the match by one point.

Nothing short of a miracle could save them now.

Ten seconds left, then everything seemed to happen in slow motion.

Maria caught the ball, way outside the goal area. She bounced it twice, then seemed to hold it, seemingly for ages. All her teammates were yelling at her to play the ball.

Then she hooked the ball behind her in her right hand, swung her arm back and fairly catapulted it. Everyone watched the ball as it looped over their heads.

Smack! went the ball as it hit the panel above the net, and the split second after it dropped through the net, the whistle went for full time.

Then pandemonium broke out.

The noise from the crowd of people was deafening. The St Angela's players and their supporters were celebrating, believing that they had won the game by a single point. But then the scoreboard was adjusted.

Our Lady's–43, St Angela's–43, and the umpire pointed to the centre circle, and then at her watch, indicating that the game would now re-start with extra time.

Then a furious row broke out between one of the St Angela's teachers and the umpire. In some confusion, all the players from both sides gathered round the umpire who was having to shout to make herself heard over the din. She was explaining that there are three slightly different versions of rules to netball, and on entering the competition the full rules are clearly explained. The version incorporated in this tournament was known as The Midland Senior rules that, in some ways, were similar to basketball. There was one particular rule referring to shots on goal from outside the goal area.

The umpire then actually produced her rulebook, found the relevant page and began to read out the rule, still having to shout even louder now to make herself heard.

"Goals may be scored from outside the goal area, *and these shall be worth three points.*"

All the Our Lady's girls cheered as though they had won the game. The fact that they were still in it was enough to be getting on with. They all gathered around Maria.

Geraldine Knox flung her arms around the grinning fifth-former.

"You really are a miracle worker," she said with a mixture of laughing and crying.

As they hugged with everyone else around them, Maria said, just so Geraldine could hear it, "We will win now."

News reporters and TV crews were swarming around.

"Did you get all of that?" the programme director said to the sound technician.

"Every word, George," was the response. "Loud and clear."

"Good man."

The lady newscaster could hardly contain her excitement.

"What we witnessed just now," she said, "was nothing short of a miracle. The Our Lady's girls were dead and buried with just seconds to go, but now they've forced extra time. Whether this girl, Maria, really is the Chosen One or not, she does appear to possess some special powers."

And the crowd was growing rapidly. News was travelling around that the girl claiming to be carrying the Son of God was performing miracles, and everyone wanted to see. People were forcing their way into the school ground, despite numerous security guards and police officers trying to control the situation. While some were being stopped at the gate, others were climbing over the fence at the opposite end of the school grounds.

*

Meanwhile, Father Giuseppe Bonelli was starting to get suspicious of two slovenly looking men who just seemed to be wandering around the ground, as though searching.

The old priest had arrived with Anna Gabriella and Debbie Shallis about an hour earlier. Debbie was just totally enthralled in the game. She wished that she could play.

But although it was wonderful to see Maria doing so well in the game, both Bonelli and the midwife knew that they had the responsibility and the duty to ensure her safety, especially following some nasty death threats.

(One of these threats, a crudely written letter, said that Maria would be nailed to a tree. The letter was intercepted by the priest, and so the girl never saw it. There was another one even worse than that, therefore too horrible to be printed here.)

Anyway, what drew Father Bonelli's attention to the two scruffs was that they had been searched by a tough-looking police sergeant, and the officer did not seem to be totally satisfied with their presence. There had been a disturbance with fireworks going off somewhere, and the policeman had been called away to deal with the problem.

As their attention was drawn back towards the netball match, and Maria scoring with a spectacular long-range shot, Bonelli lost track of the men's exact whereabouts, but while the players were taking a break prior to the commencement of extra time he began to scan the area slowly, and eventually located them again. They were still looking this way and that. Evidently still searching.

"I don't like the look of those guys," he said to Anna, over the noise of the crowd. "I'm going to talk to them."

Anna looked at the men, then momentarily held Bonelli's hand.

"Please be careful," she said.

"Don't worry, I will," he said, while with his other hand he felt the handle of the army revolver through his jacket pocket. "You just stay with Debbie."

They both looked at the girl who was jumping up and down, and clapping her hands. She looked at the priest and the midwife.

"Oh, I wish I was in Maria's team," she said.

After one last glance at Anna, Bonelli set off at a brisk walk, hoping that he wouldn't get stopped and searched. He was wearing ordinary clothes, except for his dog collar, but he was hoping that that would be sufficient to ward off any suspicion. He walked until he was right in front of Claud and Rod, and gave them an intense stare. They looked at him with puzzled frowns.

Then the priest spoke. "Right, guys. What's going on? Who are you?"

"Eh?"

"Do not piss me about," Bonelli hissed at them, clutching the handle of his weapon and momentarily showing the gun to them.

The brief moment was enough. They saw that the gun had a silencer fitted to it.

"I'll have no qualms about putting a bullet through you," Bonelli said. "Now who are you?"

"We're the uncles of..." Rod began.

The old priest made an angry hissing sound through gritted

teeth.

"One more wrong answer," he snapped, "and you'll get a bullet between the eyes. Now, for the last time..."

"You're Father Bonelli, aren't you?" Claud said, to Bonelli's surprise.

"Correct," said the priest. "Now, talk."

And to his further surprise, the two men looked at each other, then between them told him everything. They talked in lowered voices, but just loud enough to be heard above the general noise, while continuing to look round them, making sure that nobody else could hear. They openly admitted that they had been sent there on a mission to kill the schoolgirl, but added with the utmost sincerity that, after all, they had no intention of carrying out these heinous instructions. They concluded their story by explaining that they were being watched, and that their conversation may have been overheard by some Johnny with a walkie-talkie radio.

"It's him that we've been searching for," Rod said.

"We lost sight of him when we were being searched," Claud added.

Bonelli looked from one man to the other. He did not like their appearance at all, but he'd had many years of experience with people from all different walks of life. He could always sense when someone was lying, but he was positive now that these men were telling the truth. What power *Tuan* had over them he didn't know. Maybe that would be something to investigate another time, with the view to freeing these men from him, but right now he had his duty to consider, and that was the protection of the Holy Mother.

He visibly relaxed much to the relief of Claud and Rod.

"Okay, we'll carry on looking for him together," he told them. "But when we find him, *I'll* deal with him. Okay?"

"Okay," Claud and Rod said together quite readily. They seemed to be quite happy with this arrangement, their body language even demonstrated evidence of genuine relief. This gave Father Bonelli further confidence that they were telling the truth.

Searching through the crowd of people that were gathered around the netball court was getting more difficult as more people were arriving, but all of a sudden Claud caught Bonelli by the arm.

"There he is," he said, pointing.

Bonelli looked, and there at the opposite end of the ground, and beyond the main cluster of people, was the man with tinted glasses and peak cap as described, and still continually talking on his walkie-talkie radio.

Again the priest clutched the handle of his gun through his jacket pocket. He wasn't taking any chances. He'd never killed a man before, but if this particular individual posed a threat to the mother of God's Child, Bonelli would shoot him without the slightest hesitation.

"Right," he said, breathing hard. "I've got him."

And with that, Bonelli started working his way around the crowd, while carefully keeping his eyes on the man he was after.

Claud and Rod looked at each other, wondering whether they were supposed to follow the old priest or not. Then they nodded to each other in agreement and decided to follow.

Beyond the main crowd of people, Bonelli approached the man with the walkie-talkie, then strode briskly up to him.

"Hey, you!" he called out. "I want a word with you."

Then everything happened so fast, he would have difficulty in piecing it all together later.

To Bonelli's astonishment, the man suddenly yelled out, *"Bonelli,"* then he withdrew a snub-nosed revolver and aimed it straight at the old priest's chest.

Father Bonelli had no time to react, or to draw out his own gun. As the man's finger tightened on the trigger, Claud and Rod, now just a few yards behind the priest, looked on in horror.

Then without thinking, Rod dashed forward and ran in front of Bonelli.

The gun went off with a resounding *Bang!*

CHAPTER TWENTY–FIVE

As Rod fell to the ground with a yell of pain, the man with the gun in one hand, and the walkie-talkie still in the other, dashed off.

People to the rear of the crowd turned round in fright.

A woman screamed, "Oh, my God!" but most people further forward didn't seem to notice. They probably thought that the *bang* was just another firework going off.

Rod was lying flat on his front with his face buried in the grass.

Claud Tyler and Father Bonelli dashed to him, knelt down on either side and rolled him over.

"Oh, Rod!" Claud was crying.

Rod was still alive, his eyes were fluttering, but his face was twisted grotesquely in pain, the black bits between his teeth and nicotine stains more vivid than ever. And Bonelli saw straight away that the wound he had would mean the end of him. The bullet had gone completely through him, ripping through his side. The priest knew that with that amount of bleeding, the internal injury would prove to be fatal.

Rod lay there crying in pain, and as he looked up at the priest, he knew he was going to die. With his remaining strength he reached for Father Bonelli's hand.

"I'm sorry for everything," he said. "I don't want to go to Hell."

Bonelli reached into the inside breast pocket of his jacket and took out a little bottle of holy water. He pulled the top off the bottle and sprinkled some of its contents over the dying man. At first, Rod reacted like he'd been burned, and an angry rash appeared on his forehead, but the priest then recited some words in Latin and repeated the process. This time he sprinkled the holy water in the motion of the sign of the cross.

And now Rod remained still, and even managed a faint smile at the priest.

"Thank you, Father," he managed to say, albeit feebly as he could feel his life rapidly fading away.

Father Giuseppe Bonelli crouched over him.

"Are you truly sorry for all your sins?" he said.

Rod was at death's door now. His mouth quivered but he could no longer speak.

A woman standing nearby said, "What's happening?"

"Someone's been shot," came a reply from somewhere. "The priest is giving him the last rites."

"Oh, my good Lord."

Bonelli held Rod's hand.

"Squeeze my hand to answer yes," he said, then he repeated, "Are you truly sorry for all your sins?"

Rod's hand gave a feeble squeeze.

Bonelli leaned over further.

"Think of these words," he said, then he quickly whispered the words to *the Act of Contrition*, closely into Rod's ear.

Then he said, "Did you say those words with me? And did you understand them?"

Another squeeze, so weak now that Bonelli barely detected it.

He hurriedly continued with, "And do you denounce Satan and all his works?"

Rod grimaced. This time it was as if a little bit of life came back to him. The squeeze was stronger. It was an emphatic reply.

Kneeling by his side, Claud sobbed out loud. The words, "Please God," involuntarily fell from his lips.

And as Rod Spencer approached death, and as his physical life gradually drained away, his mind still allowed him some last thoughts and some memories. He was a ten-year-old boy trying out his first cigarette behind the school cycle shed, then he was a teenager, about fourteen, losing his virginity to an older woman. She must have been at least eighteen.

Rod was dying, but he laughed softly to himself at these memories. He was no longer afraid. Moreover, he started to feel an exciting anticipation. He couldn't see anymore, so he closed his eyes.

But he could still hear.

Father Bonelli continued to sprinkle holy water in the motion of the sign of the cross over his body, and as he did so he made a final statement.

"Through this Holy Anointing may The Lord in his love and mercy help you with the grace of The Holy Spirit. May The Lord who frees you from sin save you and raise you up."

Rod squeezed Father Bonelli's hand one last time, turned his head towards the sound of the priest's voice, and with his final breath he managed a croaky whisper, "Thank you, Father."

As two police officers approached and called out, a small group of people had gathered and formed a circle around the dying man. Many of them made the sign of the cross.

Finally, the priest leaned over a little further and whispered into Rod's ear for the last time, "Your faith has saved you."

The very next second, Rod was dead.

*

And during all of that time, neither the netball players or the crowds around the netball court were aware that a man had been shot and had just died.

And the game wasn't over yet. All the players, already

tired, were getting ready for the start of the ten-minute extra time period. Team captain, Geraldine Knox, quickly called her troops together before the re-start.

"Right," she said, with one single clap of her hands. "During the last few minutes they went into lockdown, everyone into defence. Well, we can play at that game too. And that's what we're going to do, until the very last minute, and then we're going to hit them with all guns blazing. Okay?"

"Okay!" all the other girls shouted together.

Amidst a deafening roar from the growing crowd of people, the match got underway again. The St Angela's players came at them fiercely, time after time, rapidly alternating attacks down one wing, and then the other, but all their efforts were blocked off. And when, on one occasion, their goal shooter did get through with a chance to shoot, the Our Lady's goalkeeper jumped up to her full height and just managed to tip the ball away safely.

The St Angela's captain guessed what was happening, that the Our Lady's team were absorbing the pressure, with the intention of a sudden counterattack right at the end. She briefly gathered her players together. "Watch out for that Geraldine," she said. "She's one sly, fat cow."

The match went on, and with just one minute left, there had been no further score at either end. All the players knew that if the scores were still level after extra time there would be a sudden death tiebreaker, and none of the players, or supporters, wanted to see that.

One of the Our Lady's goal defenders got the ball and bounced it twice before passing it to her centre teammate.

Then suddenly, Geraldine yelled at her players. "Go!"

Maria and Geraldine just sprinted to the opposite end of the court, and the centre player and wing attack ran behind the front two, bouncing the ball and passing it backwards and forwards between themselves until arriving just outside the St

Angela's goal area.

The St Angela's defenders gathered around Maria, holding their arms up, preventing the anticipated pass, but there was some breakdown in communication because one of them should have marked Geraldine. Instead, the Our Lady's captain found herself completely free.

Diana quickly spotted this and promptly passed the ball to her captain who caught it in eager hands. Geraldine felt the rush of blood as she turned towards the goal, her heart already pounding with the excitement and anticipation of scoring the winning goal. But at that very moment a St Angela's goal defender rushed towards her, lost her balance and 'accidentally' grabbed Geraldine's arm as she was about to shoot. The ball went a whole metre wide of its target.

"*Obstruction*," Geraldine screamed as she ran up to the umpire. "That was obstruction. Two free shots to us."

But the umpire appeared to be waving her away.

"Obstruction," Geraldine repeated. She was in tears again now. She felt she had been robbed of a dramatic, last-minute shot on goal. The rest of the Our Lady's team backed up their captain and formed a circle around the umpire, protesting.

Meanwhile, the clock had been stopped with just ten seconds left. The umpire seemed to have already made her decision, and the signal she was making indicated a drop-ball, which wouldn't have been much use with just ten seconds left, and at all costs the Our Lady's team wanted to avoid the match being resolved with a sudden-death tiebreaker.

Maria decided it was time to take action. She pushed her way forward so that she was right in front of the umpire, and struck an intimidating attitude, her face uncharacteristically aggressive. Maria gripped her firmly by the arm.

"Confer with the second umpire," she shouted over the noise.

The umpire just stared at her, pulling at her arm.

But Maria's grip tightened.

"That was obstruction," she said. "Two penalty shots to us."

"Get off, damn you." The umpire was pulling at her trapped arm, while pushing at the tall fifth-form girl with her other hand.

Then the girl's grip tightened so much the umpire cried out. She put her face close to the umpire's frightened features before, once again, rolling back her eyes, revealing just the whites.

And at the same time she growled in a deep voice, "I said, check with the second umpire."

The woman looked shocked for a moment and cried out, "Oh, my good Lord," then suddenly finding herself free, she staggered and nearly fell.

The St Angela's player who had allegedly obstructed Geraldine was protesting her innocence.

"I never touched her!" she was shouting.

The umpire, still in a state of shock and confusion went off the court, then after a brief talk with her assistant, returned and immediately pointed to the penalty area, then made two throwing gestures over her head.

There was a massive roar from the crowd. Two penalty shots had been awarded to Our Lady's School.

The St Angela's captain went up to Geraldine.

"You cheating fat slag," she hissed.

But the sturdy Our Lady's captain didn't hear her, or even notice her. The umpire had handed her the ball, and she in turn was looking round for Maria to take it from her.

Maria arrived next to her and offered her sweetest smile.

"Looking for little me?" she inquired.

Geraldine gave her the ball.

"Take your time," she told her. "No pressure. Okay?"

Maria laughed. Then she said, "But once the whistle goes

I've only got ten seconds."

Geraldine shook her head.

"No," she said. "You will be allowed time to take both shots."

The umpire signalled for Maria to get into place. Her teammates stood behind her in a semi-circle. All the St Angela's players, except the goalkeeper, stood behind their goal, all looking angry.

The crowd for once became silent, seemingly holding their breath.

Then, Maria Christopher, who had hardly put a foot wrong, or a hand, all afternoon, the girl who had stirred up the nation with fantastic claims, perhaps at last showed the first signs of stress under such intense scrutiny.

She took her shot, possibly rushing it – and missed.

The ball went at least a foot wide of the target.

A moan of disappointment came from the crowd, although a small section of St Angela's followers cheered.

One of the St Angela's players went up to Maria.

"Mother of the Son of God," she sneered. "Don't make me laugh, you cheating, lying bitch."

Maria went up to her and stared intently at her. Her eyes rolled right back again as she growled in a demonic voice, "You'll be sorry you said that. I'm placing a curse on you. Tomorrow morning you will wake up covered with yellow warts, and you will only be cured if a handsome prince kisses you."

The St Angela's girl's expression changed from a sneer, to a look of fear and utmost dread. She went back to stand with her teammates but she did not look very well.

Geraldine Knox went up to Maria as the fifth-former was getting herself together and preparing for her second shot. The team captain hadn't heard a word of that exchange with the St Angela's girl. She wasn't concerned with the opposition whinging and whining. She was only interested in winning this match, and if it turned out that the sweet-mannered Maria had a ruthless streak in her, then she could only applaud it.

"It's really true, isn't it?" she said, as if only just making a discovery. "You really are going to give birth to the Son of God?"

"Yes." Maria smiled at her. "It really is true."

Then Geraldine threw her arms around her and kissed her on the cheek.

"In that case, I don't care if you score the second shot or not," she said. "We've done so well, anyway, thanks to you."

Geraldine returned to stand in the semi-circle among the rest of the team.

Maria steadied herself, and with one foot behind the other she stood straight like a statue. She delicately balanced the ball in her right hand ready to shoot, with her left hand held out for balance.

Then she launched the ball. Two thousand pairs of eyes watched it as it sailed through the air.

It swished through the net and the whole school ground reverberated with the roar that followed, and the court itself erupted with a deafening noise as Our Lady's supporters jumped out of their seats and swarmed towards the players. Maria's teammates had gathered around her, and Geraldine was swaying from side to side with her arms tightly around 'her' player who had just scored the deciding point. The scoreboard was adjusted to read: Our Lady's–44, St Angela's–43.

The sixth-form prefect, and captain of the winning team, had tears spilling down her face again now, but this time they were tears of joy.

"You certainly are a miracle worker," she said with a mixture of crying and laughing.

"Well," Maria laughed. "About average."

Reporters and TV cameras were also jostling for position.

"Did you catch what that fat girl said?" the programme director shouted at the sound crew.

"Don't worry, George," came the reply. "We got it."

Hardly noticed by anyone, all the St Angela's girls traipsed off without shaking hands with any of the victorious team. They glumly collected their runners-up medals and trudged off to the pavilion.

All the Our Lady's players hugged and kissed each other. They eventually formed themselves into a respectable line, with Geraldine Knox bringing up the rear, and Maria just in front of her. And one by one they stepped forward to receive their winners' medals affixed to ribbons that were placed round their necks.

TV camera crews, together with newspaper photographers, crowded around them jostling for the best position.

Maria received her medal, bowing slightly to have the ribbon placed round her neck. When she stood straight again, she turned right round, scanning the crowd as she did so, with a vague thought in the back of her mind that her parents were not there to witness this proudest of moments.

And finally, Geraldine, after receiving her medal, was handed the large, heavy, golden trophy. She couldn't wait to get her hands on it. All the players gathered round.

Then the president of the British Netball Association held a microphone and spoke through the public address system.

"Ladies and gentlemen, following one of the most exciting finals that I can remember during my involvement with the BNA, can you please put your hands together in celebrating, and congratulating, our new County Champions. Our Lady's Senior Girls' School."

And in time to the massive roar from the crowd, Geraldine Knox and Maria Christopher together held the trophy aloft.

CHAPTER TWENTY-SIX

Inspector Paul Retberg and Sergeant Ian Green arrived back at the police station later than they had estimated, but it wasn't because the girls' netball match had gone into extra time.

It was because somebody in the crowd had been shot dead.

Witnesses had given a description of the gunman, but then somehow, amidst the confusion, the priest and another man who had been close by, had managed to slither away. The police would need to interview both of them.

Retberg and Green went straight to the report room. Nobody was there. Retberg slammed the door shut.

"At least we know who the priest is," said Ian Green. "Witnesses say it was Father Bonelli, so we know where to find him for a statement."

Retberg was in his most furious mood ever. He shook his head, sat down on the edge of a table, and looked at the sergeant.

"It's not that, Ian," he said. "I don't care about that. It's old Sutton."

"He doesn't blame you for what happened."

"No," said Retberg. "But now he wants us to focus our entire attention on this incident."

"He seems to think that this whole thing is linked to some recent terrorist activity," Ian Green mused.

"That, and I suspect because he is a devout Catholic, he actually believes this girl's claims."

Ian Green smiled and released a low whistle.

"What, that she really is going to give birth to the Son of

God?"

"Well, he hasn't actually said that in so many words, but he's implied it, and that he feels that we should offer her protection."

"Against the threat of terrorists?"

"Well, you see..."

Retberg's suspicions of the chief superintendent's beliefs would shortly be proven, as just then the door to the report room opened. Sutton entered the room and closed the door quietly behind him.

"Ah, I thought I'd find you both here," he said. "Listen, guys, I want you to follow this up. This whole business has scared the crap out of me."

"A shooting," Retberg said in a flat tone. "Regrettable, but we will just carry out a few routine inquiries."

"No," said Sutton. "There's got to be more to it than that. I can feel it."

"But, sir..."

"The girl, Maria Christopher, claims that she is carrying God's child."

"Oh, for the love of Mike," Retberg suddenly snapped. "Sorry, sir, but surely you don't believe that pile of absolute bollocks."

"Now, you listen to me, Paul," Sutton said, also raising his voice, almost shouting, and pointing a shaking finger, "It makes no difference what I believe. Our job is to protect lives, and this girl's life is obviously in danger."

"I don't get you, sir," Ian Green said with a puzzled frown. "A man gets shot in the middle of a field, at least two hundred yards away from the netball court, and you fear that this means that the girl's life is in danger."

"Think about it, Greeny," Sutton said, waving his arms impatiently. "Piece together what the witnesses have told us. Father Bonelli has said that he has been chosen to protect the girl. He meets up with two men who have both got criminal records involving explosives and firearms, then inexplicably they all go off together after another armed man."

"But…" Retberg was shaking his head, as though trying to blot out some sort of madness.

"Another armed man," Sutton went on regardless, "who witnesses say aimed the gun at the priest, until the man Rod Spencer, seemingly with a complete change of heart, *deliberately* got in the way, and…"

"Change of heart," Retberg scoffed. "Do me a favour."

"Yes, Paul, a change of heart," Sutton said. "To such an extent that the priest administered the last rites. Now, why do you suppose he did that?"

Ian Green looked at Sutton, then at Retberg, and pulled a puzzled expression. He had to admit, that was a damned good argument.

But Retberg was stubbornly still not convinced.

"No, look," he said. "What I think really happened was…"

Sutton raised both his hands in a silencing gesture, and shook his head, clearly tired of the argument. After a moment he continued.

"I want you guys to go and visit the priest," he said. "Get a full statement and gather as much information as you can, but ultimately I want you to offer him, and the girl, protection."

Paul Retberg stumbled into a chair, sagged forward across the table and held his head in his hands.

Sutton did not want to pull rank on the inspector, but he had to drive his point home somehow.

"And by the way, Paul," he went on, "I notice that you've put in an application for a further promotion, and that you've applied for the vacancy upstairs for chief inspector."

Retberg dropped his hands onto the table, looked up at the chief super, but didn't say anything further.

"People will need to cooperate with you," Sutton

concluded. "So it would be pretty damned good if you would cooperate with others for a change. Okay? Take a hint."

With that he marched out of the report room, closing the door – this time firmly – behind him.

Retberg and Green looked at each other, both releasing hefty sighs.

"Oh, well," said Ian Green with a shrug of his broad shoulders. "I suppose things could be worse."

Retberg attempted a laugh but it came out feebly.

"I can't see how," he muttered.

"Well," the sergeant looked at the ceiling as though trying to think of some ghastly scenario. "For instance, you could get home this evening to find that your wife has left you."

Retberg looked at Ian Green, and the expression on his face told the sergeant that he had unwittingly touched a sensitive nerve.

Then despite everything that had happened, Retberg's head jerked back as he roared with laughter.

"Oh, Ian," he said. "What would I do without such a great mate?"

"I'm so sorry, Paul," Green said.

"She went in the early hours. Gone to her mother's place in Adelaide."

Ian Green puffed out his cheeks.

Retberg reached for a writing pad off the desk. He got a pen and scribbled something down, then he tore the page off the pad and handed it to the sergeant.

"What's this?" Ian Green asked.

"It's Donna's contact number."

"Sorry, Paul," Green said with a look of slight confusion. "But why would I want her contact number?"

Retberg looked intently at the sergeant.

"If anything happens to me," he explained. "I would want you to let her know."

"But..."

"I know what you're going to say, but there would be finances to resolve."

"Oh, Paul," Ian Green laughed. "I wasn't going to say that. What I was thinking was that you're built like a tank, you're as strong as an ox, and you've got me and all your other loyal subjects around you, so what could possibly happen to you?"

*

Inspector Paul Retberg was an atheist who had been ordered by the chief superintendent at his station to interview the priest, and to offer protection to him and the girl who claimed that she was going to be the mother of God's Second Son.

He was tired, having already exceeded his preferred number of hours for the day, so was now on involuntary overtime. And he had enjoyed an exceptionally bad day.

Even so, as Sergeant Ian Green knocked on Father Bonelli's front door, he was prepared to be polite, especially to a priest. He even managed a courteous smile when the door opened.

"Oh, no, it's the police," came a woman's voice from within, followed by the sound of a door from inside the house slamming.

"Oh, good evening," said Father Bonelli, feigning surprise at seeing the two police officers. "What can I do for you?"

Retberg and Green instantly recognised the priest, even though he had melted into the crowd immediately after the shooting. They had seen him on television and in the papers.

"Good evening, Father," began Sergeant Green. "I wonder if we may speak with you?"

"But officers," Bonelli continued with his tone of innocence and ignorance. "What could this possibly be about?"

"Well, you see..."

Paul Retberg's patience was already travelling on thin ice.

"I think, Father," he said in a stiff tone, interrupting his colleague, "it would be better if you allowed us in. We are here, as I believe you know, to investigate a…"

He was about to say, 'to investigate a murder,' but just then a startled young girl's voice came suddenly from behind him.

Retberg and Green spun round and there were two teenage girls approaching. The police officers recognised one of them as Maria Christopher, but it was the other one who had called out.

"It's the police!" she shrieked. "What do they want?"

"Good evening, miss," Ian Green began, courteously tipping his cap to the girls. "We're sorry to worry you, but…"

Giuseppe Bonelli hastily interrupted.

"These good officers are investigating car thefts in the area," he said. "But as they can see, my car is perfectly safe."

He pointed at his Mazda Estate car that was parked on the driveway, while making pleading, silencing gestures to the police officers.

Ian Green glanced at Retberg and could see the exasperated expression on the inspector's face, and almost hear the breath hissing through his teeth.

"Have you seen Maria's medal?" Maria's friend said, cheerfully changing the subject.

It was only then that their attention was drawn to the large, golden medal that was hanging around Maria's neck by means of a colourful ribbon. They guessed it was her netball winners' medal.

Ian Green approached and reached out his hand. Maria showed it to him. He held it briefly and marvelled at how heavy it was.

"It's nice," he said. "Is it real gold?"

"Rolled gold," she said, smiling proudly.

"I wish I had one," said her friend.

Ian Green looked at the girl and thought for a moment that he had seen this kid somewhere before.

"Do I know you?" he said.

"Possibly," she said. "My name's Debbie Shallis. My uncle is a copper. You might know him. Robert Shallis."

Retberg approached the girls.

"Oh, yeah," he said. "Robert Shallis. He got transferred down to South London, didn't he? Wimbledon, I think."

"Morden, actually," Debbie laughed. "The joke is, people call him Bobby."

"Why's that funny?" Retberg said absentmindedly, looking round at the priest who was still standing in his doorway.

"Because he *is* a bobby," she said, laughing. Then she turned to Maria and grabbed hold of her medal.

"I wish I had one," she repeated.

"Well, I'll tell you what," Maria said, "if you like it that much I'll leave it to you in my Will, then if anything happens to me, you can have it."

"Oh, thanks. That'd be great."

Both girls ran off together, laughing merrily.

Retberg and Green turned to each other, then back to the priest.

Father Giuseppe Bonelli drew a deep breath.

"You want to know about the shooting?" he said.

The police officers moved closer to him and nodded.

"I didn't want the girls to get upset," he continued.

"That's okay," Paul Retberg said, as Ian Green got out his pocket notebook. "Now, I want the full story, from the point you met up with Claud Tyler and Rod Spencer, to the point where you gave the last rites."

"And," Ian Green added, "we want the whereabouts of Claud Tyler."

CHAPTER TWENTY-SEVEN

That evening, Father Giuseppe Bonelli decided on an early night. The girls went back to Maria's room to watch TV and to enjoy a bottle of wine that Debbie had smuggled in.

Anna, though, went back to her room on her own. Bonelli had noticed that she seemed a bit quiet, but when he asked her if everything was all right, she assured him that it was. So the old priest went back to his house and decided to read for an hour before settling down for the night.

After just twenty minutes, though, there came a knock at the door.

It was Anna.

She came into his lounge and removed her jacket. Bonelli's eyes almost popped out. She stood there in front of him, wearing nothing but a thin shortie-nightie. The priest considered her figure, and noted that she was not at all bad for a woman in her fifties. In fact, he mused, a woman of half her age would be pleased with such a figure. Looking down he saw, too, that her legs were fine and shapely.

And then...

Everything happened in a frantic rush. They wanted each other so urgently they didn't make it to Bonelli's bedroom. They collapsed onto a chair-bed that was quite elderly.

As already mentioned, the seventy-year-old man had kept himself fit, but what ensued left him a little more breathless than his three-mile run would have done.

*

Having made love to a woman for the first time in nigh-on forty years, he looked at Anna Gabriella as he held her in his arms. Her eyes were closed, but then she opened them and smiled at him, loving the look on his face. They were now in a half-sitting, half-lying position on the reclining chair-bed that had malfunctioned during the height of their passion. At first it seemed to have been standing up well to this vigorous test, remaining completely flat. But then, as if contributing its own punctuation to the event, at the precise moment of *his* climax, it had sprung up into its present position.

It mattered little to her, however. Like a much younger woman she was multi-climaxing, but with an unmusical *boing* the chair-bed had attempted to fold itself up while the couple were testing its springs. This made them both roar with laughter.

"Oh, well," he said quietly. "Sex is supposed to be fun."

"It certainly is." She found herself giggling like a schoolgirl.

Bonelli's first sexual encounter after all those years had gone at a frantic pace, urgent expressions on both of their faces, his climax coinciding with one of hers, amidst yells from him, and high-pitched screeching from her. These happy sounds woke the echoes of the creaky 1930's building. The priest squeezed his eyes shut and gritted his teeth, feeling like his insides were being gouged out, and his brain was about to explode.

Afterwards they both prayed for God's forgiveness. Bonelli wept with remorse, promising to accept any punishment. When none came he promised that such a breach of his vows would never, ever happen again. He decided that his penance should be ten Hail Marys.

After a relaxation period of approximately thirty minutes, Anna snatched his rosary beads, threw them into the corner of the room and grabbed his penis.

"Give it to me again," she demanded.

The second time they had sex it was far slower, more relaxed, less urgent, but actually more loving. It was after that, that the reclining couch went with a loud *boing!* and sprung them into their current position, where they remained just cuddling one another.

And they were both insanely light-headed and happy.

On reflection, Bonelli remembered the thoughts he'd had on having sex with Anna, and the subsequent conversation they'd had. Both of them genuinely believed that God would approve of this union. They should both, therefore, graciously accept it as a gift. A reward for what they were doing, protecting the mother of God's Second Son.

And during all of this time the television was mumbling softly to itself in the background, but when the local mid-evening news came on, they both sat up, suddenly alert. Bonelli reached for the TV handset from the coffee table and turned up the volume.

On the earlier news, there had been a report that threats against Maria's life had been sent by Christians. Giuseppe Bonelli didn't believe a word of that, of course. A man making a brief statement on behalf of his own Christian group said:

"The claims made by this girl are preposterous and blasphemous, but good Christians would never make such evil threats."

The priest let out a relieved sigh.

After a few more relatively nondescript items, the newsreader said, "And Our Lady's Senior Girls' School have won the County Netball Championship in a closely contested final against arch-rivals, hot favourites and League Champions, St Angela's Seniors. The game was decided by a last-minute penalty shot scored by none other than Maria Christopher, the girl claiming to be carrying the Son of God. We now go over to our sports reporter, Chris Hughes."

The scene then changed to the familiar surroundings of the

school grounds, and the reporter, a thin little man with jutting-out ears, rabbit-like teeth, talking into a pink microphone with a fluffy top.

"Well, Trisha," he said, "The girl, Maria Christopher, whether she's the Chosen One or not, certainly does have some tricks up her sleeve. With her team losing by seven points, and with just five minutes of normal time remaining, she inspired the most incredible fight-back, including an unbelievable shot from nearly fifteen metres. Then with the scores level, the match went into extra time."

"And I understand there was some controversy at the end of extra time?" came Trisha's voice from the studio. "Is that correct?"

"Yes, Trisha, that is correct," Chris Hughes confirmed. "With the scores still level, with just seconds left on the clock, Our Lady's captain, Geraldine Knox, claimed she was impeded in the St Angela's goal area. She rushed to the umpire, remonstrating wildly, and demanding two penalty shots. The umpire, however, appeared to be waving her away, deciding on a drop ball."

"And I understand that Maria Christopher got involved in the argument that has added to the controversy?"

"Yes, Trisha, that's true. Maria Christopher approached the umpire, nearly knocking her over, and shouting madly. Witnesses from the St Angela's subs bench said that her manner was aggressive and intimidating, and they claim that this definitely had an influence on the umpire who then changed her decision after consulting with her assistant."

"And so Our Lady's were awarded the two free shots?" said Trisha.

"That's right," Hughes assented. "Maria herself took the shots, she actually missed the first one, but after a few words of advice from her captain, she scored the second one. Then the whole place just went crazy."

"And I heard that the St Angela's girls left the court without shaking hands with any of the Our Lady's players?"

"That's true, too," said Hughes. "I noticed them leaving the court in a somewhat sour mood, but to be honest, not many other people did. Apparently though, one of St Angela's teachers, Mrs Maisie Gooch, lodged an official complaint to the tournament's organisers concerning the behaviour of Knox and Maria Christopher, but the reply that we heard back was: 'In the heat of the moment, all the players from both teams were shouting, but in the end the correct decision was made.'"

"Okay, thank you Chris."

The screen then returned to the newsreader in the studio. Looking at the camera, her face suddenly becoming very serious.

"Still on the subject of the events at the netball match," she said, "while all of this was going on, there appeared to have been a serious disturbance in a section of the crowd furthest away from the netball court. We have heard reports that a man was actually shot dead. A priest was right there on the scene and, witnesses have said, he administered the last rites to the man before he died. More details of this can be seen on your national news station. Other local news now..."

Bonelli looked at Anna. "This is getting serious," he said.

Anna nodded in agreement. "I suppose that's what the police wanted to talk to you about," she said.

"Yes," Bonelli said, "and they also wanted to know about the other man, Claud Tyler."

"How could you possibly know anything about him?"

"After the death of his friend," Bonelli started to explain, "amidst all the confusion, we mingled with the crowd, then managed to move away from the scene practically unnoticed."

"So now what?"

"The police want to interview Mr Tyler," the priest said. "They said that he might need protection."

Anna shook her head. "I don't understand," she said.

"Tyler and Spencer were ordered to kill Maria, but they refused to do it." After a pause Bonelli concluded with, "Anna, these people are Satanists. We're all in danger from them."

"But surely you can't do anything about that man Tyler."

"I've promised to help the police," he said. "Tomorrow night I've agreed to go with them to Tyler's apartment."

Anna went into silence and the priest could see from her face that she was not happy with him worrying about Claud Tyler when his responsibility was with Maria and her baby.

He released a deep breath, deciding on a change of subject.

"It won't be long now before we make the decision to pack our bags and go," he told her.

"You predicted this would happen, didn't you?" said Anna. "Just like I predicted the birth of the Holy Child ages ago."

"One man is already dead. No doubt there will be others, so now what we need to do is..."

There came three sudden, loud knocks on the door. Bonelli and Anna looked at each other.

"I'll go." Bonelli heaved himself off the couch, and hurriedly put on his shirt and trousers. He then made his way out into the hallway.

He opened the door. Maria and Debbie entered together in a rush.

Father Bonelli closed the door quietly behind them and followed them into the lounge. Anna stood up to greet them as they entered. She had put on her blouse but was still busily adjusting her skirt. Maria appeared not to notice her somewhat dishevelled appearance, but the young girl's face was red with excitement. She spun round to face the priest as he followed the girls into the lounge.

"I didn't know anything about that," she said, pointing at the television, but trying to remain calm. "A man getting shot dead?"

Bonelli held his hands up in surrender.

"I didn't want to alarm you," he said.

Maria took a moment to compose herself, then she stamped her foot.

"Look," she said, "Just answer me these two questions. Who was he? And who was the person who shot him?"

Bonelli made another surrendering gesture and shook his head. Debbie looked from one to the other.

Then Anna suddenly spoke. "Look," she said, adjusting the TV volume. "And listen."

She then adjusted the tuning, going to the national news station.

Whereas the local news talked primarily about the girls' netball match, while only mentioning the shooting in passing, the national news programme's report was from an entirely different angle. And as Anna switched the TV stations, they were just in time to catch the start of the report.

Sharon White, a newsreader who mostly reported on the national news, was in the television studio and had just completed an introduction.

"... and so now we have Chief Superintendent Sutton to tell us more."

The next TV shot was of the senior police officer who had been in charge of policing at the netball match.

"This has become a very serious and complicated matter," he said. "The reason we were there was because of death threats received by Maria Christopher, the girl claiming to be the future mother of the Son of God. Earlier on, before the shooting, one of my team, a police sergeant, had searched and questioned Rod Spencer, the man who was shot dead."

"Yes, but if we can just be clear..." said Sharon White.

Sutton continued, apparently not hearing her, and talking over her.

"This man had told my officer that he was Maria's uncle, which is obviously untrue. Spencer, and his associate – who has since disappeared off our radar – were known members of a Satanic group who have, we suspect, been responsible for the death threats to the girl, most probably, we believe, because of her claims."

"And have you any idea who the gunman was?" came Sharon's voice from the studio.

"We don't know for sure, he ran away from the scene before my officers arrived, but we believe he may have also been from the same Satanic group."

"But why would he shoot one of his own disciples?"

"Well," said the superintendent. "We have two witnesses who believe that the priest was the intended victim, but they say that Spencer appeared to deliberately get in the way, and consequently was shot. Then the priest gave him the last rites. The plot thickens further, though, on discovering that the priest is the same man who owns, and manages, the shelter where the girl is believed to be living."

"This is all very bizarre."

"We have a theory," said the chief super. "That is, in the end, Rod Spencer changed his mind and wanted out, and he actually saved the life of the priest who is caring for the girl who claims she is carrying the Holy Child. After he was shot, witnesses say they heard him begging for forgiveness and saying he did not want to go to Hell."

"So would he be saved from Hell, then?" asked Ms White from the studio, "and eternal damnation?"

"Catholics believe," said the senior officer, "that the last rites would guarantee him a place in Heaven."

"Thank you very much."

The newsreader in the studio appeared on the screen once more.

"And the netball match," she concluded, "ended in a

somewhat controversial win to Our Lady's Senior Girls' School, who are now West Midlands' County Champions. The winning point was scored by Maria Christopher, the very girl we've just been talking about, the same one who has been making all these fantastic claims."

Anna Gabriella then turned down the sound of the television.

"Now," Bonelli said to Maria. "You know as much as I do."

"Okay," said Debbie, talking for the first time. "So what do we do now?"

Father Bonelli looked at the girls, then to Anna. "What we have to do now is move as far away as possible, as soon as we can, and remain out of circulation."

"For how long?" Debbie asked.

Maria looked at her with a puzzled expression. Debbie seemed to be more agreeable to the idea than before.

It was Anna who provided the answer.

"It would be best for all of us to remain hidden until after both the babies are born," she said.

Maria appeared to go deep in thought.

"When do we go, then?" asked Debbie.

"I would suggest straight away," said Anna.

Maria suddenly broke out of her private thoughts.

"No," she said. "Not just yet. I've got a few things I need to do first."

Father Bonelli and Anna Gabriella looked at each other with looks of concern. After what happened during the netball match it was clear that Maria was now in very serious danger, and the longer they delayed moving, the worse the threat to her life would get.

CHAPTER TWENTY-EIGHT

Tuan was not very happy.

That was an understatement. He was furious. Livid.

He pointed at the young man who stood trembling in front of him, quivering in fear.

Tuan also quivered, in uncontrollable anger, at first not even able to speak.

At last, though, he did find his voice.

"You!" he managed that single word while still pointing with a shaking hand. "You," he repeated, "what part of 'kill the priest' did you not understand?"

His voice echoed around the huge hall.

The young man, Vince Hucknell, spoke quietly, trying not to be disrespectful.

"It was Claud and Rod," he said, momentarily removing his tinted glasses, wiping them on his T-shirt, then replacing them. "Blame them, it was their fault."

"No point in me blaming Rod now, is there?" Tuan growled. "Seeing that you shot him dead."

"He got in the way."

"You complete moron."

"Look, it's okay."

"OKAY?" Tuan roared the word. "I ordered Claud and Rod to kill the girl."

"Yes but I heard them…"

"And she's still alive. Then I told you to kill the priest."

"Yes, but let me explain…" Vince could guess where this was going.

"And *he's* still alive," Tuan shouted. "Then you decide to shoot Rod. You utter twat."

"But like I said, he got in the way."

"And what happened to the diversion? The fireworks?"

"Fireworks were let off, but the idiots let them off at the wrong place and at the wrong time."

"And so," Tuan made an effort at controlling himself. "What part of that account would you describe as *okay?*"

"Look," Vince said, fidgeting uncomfortably, "all we need to do now, is..."

Tuan waved his hand impatiently, dismissing the useless words uttered by the young man.

"But do you know what makes me *really* angry?" he said, hissing like a puff adder.

Vince just looked at him with no idea at all what he meant.

"Shall I tell you?"

Still Vince didn't say anything, feeling sure that Tuan would eventually tell him anyway.

"What makes me really angry is that when you shot Rod, the priest who you were *supposed* to kill then heard Rod's final confession, then gave him the last rites."

Vince shrugged his shoulders. "Oh, so what...?"

"You ignorant little turd," Tuan Shouted. "Don't you know what that means?"

Vince shook his head.

"It means that he's gone to Heaven," Tuan clasped his head in his hands at the thought of it. "It means that he got away at the last second, and it's *me* who's got to answer to..."

He broke off and looked like he wanted to bite his tongue off.

Vince looked baffled.

"Answer to?" he murmured. Then said more loudly, "You've got to answer to someone? Who have you got to answer to? I thought *you* were Tuan, The Master, *Lord...*"

The man who was known as Tuan shook his head.

"I have been awarded that title," he said, "but there are two levels of command higher than myself."

"Who?"

"Well, the man at the top," Tuan said. "You don't need me to tell you who that is."

Vince bowed his head and did a reverse sign of the cross.

"Then below Him are His seventy-two most powerful demons, each one a specialist in his own field. Death, destruction, torture... you name it."

Tuan paused there for a moment and looked up at the ceiling as if deep in thought. Then he continued. "If I fail in carrying out my duties, then one of those demons will appear. I don't know which one it would be."

"What will he do?" Vince asked. "Or she?"

Tuan gave Vince a searching look.

"I don't want to find out," he said, then raising his voice again he continued, "so I want you to get your men together and do the job properly."

"But..."

"I want both the girl and the priest, dead."

"I'll get my best men together."

"If they're anything like you, then they'll be a crowd of cretins."

Vince didn't want to argue with him, so to appear more positive he said, "Don't forget Gifford. A really good man. Or should I say, Police Constable Gifford."

"A pig?"

"Our best undercover man," Hucknell explained. "A damned useful man to have in the right position."

"Now the filth are sticking their snouts in."

"Exactly, and Giff can get us info hot off the press, so to speak. Places, dates, times "

"Okay, okay." Tuan put his hands up and began rubbing

his face.

After a moment's reflection, Vince Hucknell gave Tuan a curious look.

"So why are you so scared of this girl?" he said

Tuan laughed. It was a nasty, sardonic laugh. "I'm not scared of her," he said.

"She performs miracles, I suppose."

Another horrid, derisive laugh.

"She threw a ball through a ring from a distance of fifteen metres," Tuan said with a sneer. "Very clever, indeed, but hardly a miracle."

"Why, then?"

A long, long moment passed before Tuan spoke again, but then he said, "Just carry out my instructions." Then he pointed at the door. "Now go."

"Yes, Tuan, Master, my Lord."

Vince now seemed unsure of how to address the obese leader.

After an awkward pause he bowed his head then made his way to the door, but just as the door opened Tuan called out to him one more time.

"And Mr Hucknell. No more fuck-ups. If my arse goes on the chopping block, then I'll make sure yours does too."

CHAPTER TWENTY-NINE

It was the following evening. Claud Tyler had sat alone in the sparse living room of his first-floor apartment for the last twenty-four hours. His friend was dead and he was thinking that Rod Spencer was the lucky one. He'd received the last rites and Father Bonelli assured him that that would guarantee his place in Heaven. Claud wished that he could be with him.

Instead he was sitting alone, trembling with fear, and not knowing what to do. He knew that some of Tuan's torturers would be after him soon. He just didn't know exactly when.

He knew that, if he chose to, he could run. But he couldn't hide.

He also knew that the punishment for failure would be the usual standard method.

He would be nailed to a tree, then his throat would be slit.

For not even attempting Tuan's instructions he could only imagine that his fate would be even worse than that. So bad would it be that having his throat slit would come as a blessed relief.

After the priest had administered the last rites to Rod Spencer, he saw two men running towards them. They were in plain clothes but he recognised one of them as the policeman who had searched him and Rod earlier.

He had then swiftly followed the example of the priest and mingled with the crowd.

The rifle that his friend Rod Spencer had left in his Land Rover was now perched across a chair in his living room, but it offered him very little comfort. A handgun sat on his lap and that did make him feel a bit better, but even that would only offer a chance to escape. A temporary solution only.

He was so tired now, having not slept for so long, and his eyelids felt heavy.

He was scared to go to sleep. Even so, drowsiness gradually began to seep over him, and while still clutching the handgun, he leaned back in his chair and allowed himself to close his eyes.

He then found himself in a vast garden. It was a beautiful and peaceful place, not a cloud in the clear, blue sky. There were trees and flowers of various colours, and a stream running through the centre of the garden. A duck was swimming with ten ducklings following in a neat line. People were walking around the garden, talking peacefully to each other. Soft laughter occasionally floated to his ears, and couples who walked hand-in-hand openly showed affection to one another.

Claud Tyler felt more relaxed than he had ever done. He wished he could stay there forever, but there was a nagging worry at the back of his mind that he would need to go back to his apartment and face the danger, The Devil's henchmen.

And then Rod Spencer approached him.

His old friend looked happy and relaxed, and as he smiled Claud noticed with fascination that his teeth were perfectly white, free of any black bits or nicotine stains. Claud approached him, reaching out his hand.

"Rod," he said as they shook hands. "I thought I'd never see you again. I thought you were dead. I thought..."

Rod spoke quietly.

"I asked for permission for you to be allowed this pre-visit," he said. "I was told you would be given just a couple of minutes, just long enough for me to explain."

"Explain?" Claud said. "Listen Rod, They're after me. They're going to torture me and kill me."

"No," Rod said, taking Claud's hands in both of his.

"They won't lay a finger on you. I will be there with you."

"I don't understand," said Claud. "God knows I've done some evil things in my time."

"But you know better now," Rod assured him. "You would never have hurt Maria Christopher. You were helping to protect her."

"Yes, we both were. After we met the priest."

"That's right, and so you can be forgiven, just like I have been. And we can both atone for our wrongdoings."

"Oh, God, I'd do anything to make things right."

"In that case," Rod said, "we've got one more piece of business to finish together, then we can both be free."

"Yes, please, please, please."

"But you must be truly sorry for all your sins, just as I was."

"Yes, of course I am," said Claud. "I am truly sorry for all my sins. I hate The Devil and all his followers."

As he said these words, he remembered those spoken by Father Bonelli during Rod's last rites. He raised his voice and repeated the words that he could recall.

"I denounce The Devil and all His works. I am sorry for my sins. I am truly sorry..."

There was a sudden, almighty crash from somewhere. It made him jump but he knew he had to concentrate and keep going.

"I am sorry," he repeated. "I'm so sorry."

Another crash. He sat up straight in his chair.

He still continued to repeat the words, "I am sorry," until another, even louder, crash made him jump to his feet. He ran out to the hallway in time to see the door to his apartment crashing open.

Everything then happened quite quickly.

Two of Satan's huge thugs came in. One of them held a gnarled-looking length of chain, while the other brandished a knife with a long, vicious, curved blade.

Claud pointed his handgun at them but it was snapped painfully from his hand and thrown to the floor before he had time to pull the trigger. He watched the men, terrified.

"We're going to rip your guts out," one of the thugs advised him gruffly. "Then we're going to put this chain around your neck and drop you out of the window. After that we'll nail you to a tree, tip petrol over you and set light to you."

All these horrible intentions may well have been carried out if the thugs had lived long enough to see them through.

But it is sometimes the unexpected that happens.

Suddenly and violently the two thugs rose into the air, both struggling wildly in an invisible grip. They were then bound together with their own chain tightly around their necks until they were struggling to breathe, then set back onto the floor with a clatter.

Choking and struggling madly, and tied back-to-back, they were dragged across the floor, out the door, along the landing and towards the staircase.

Then they were thrown forcefully down the steps.

*

Paul Retberg, Ian Green and Father Bonelli arrived at the apartment block and went in via the communal entrance, just in time to see two burly figures, inexplicably chained together, crashing down the stairs.

Then the bodies lay absolutely still, and when the priest and two police officers rushed to the bottom of the steps, they could hardly believe the bizarre and horrific details.

Two gruesome-looking louts chained to each other, their ugly faces drawn into grimaces of pain still etched on their grotesque features after such a violent death. And those features looked even more ghastly because of the most horrific injury imaginable.

Their heads were twisted right round so that the horrid faces were staring backwards.

And to complete the scene of total horror, their eyes were still open.

"Necks broken," Ian Green gasped, feeling bile rising from his stomach.

Retberg looked at him. "You don't say," he said, trying to disguise his own urge to puke up.

And Father Giuseppe Bonelli noticed something else. The distinctive tattoos on the men's forearms, ugly images of intertwined reptiles.

He looked at the two police officers, gazing into each of their faces.

"Satan's thugs," he said. "This is what we're up against, and this is why we need to…"

"How did they end up like that, though?" said Ian Green.

"I think I know," said Bonelli. "My guess is…"

Then the priest suddenly stood up straight as though just remembering something.

"Tyler," he shouted, and with that he dashed to the staircase. He proceeded to run up the stairs towards the landing above, taking two steps at a time, without waiting for the police officers.

After a brief glance at each other, Retberg and Green raced after him.

By the time they arrived at Claud Tyler's apartment, Bonelli had already gone in. The door looked like it had been smashed in with a battering ram.

They went in through the hall and into the lounge.

The dead body of Claud Tyler was sitting in a natural position, leaning back slightly in a reclining armchair with his hands crossed on his lap. He actually looked quite peaceful and relaxed. The priest was kneeling in front of him, his own hands joined together as he recited a prayer in Latin.

Retberg saw that there was a rifle propped up on a chair, and a handgun was on the floor. He quickly examined them. He was careful not to touch the handles or triggers, but as far as he could tell, neither weapon had been fired.

Ian Green looked at him with a totally deflated expression on his face.

"How are we going to write this one up?" he said.

Retberg took a deep breath and shook his head.

"God knows," he replied, although even with all the evidence stacked up around him, he still didn't believe in God.

The Latin words that Father Bonelli recited in front of the late Claud Tyler were the same as those spoken during the last rites, but adjusted in sequence as the person in this case had died before the Italian priest had arrived.

But Father Giuseppe Bonelli observed the relaxed and serene expression on Mr Tyler's face indicating that he, like his friend Rod Spencer, had truly repented in the end.

CHAPTER THIRTY

The months rolled by without much more incident, and the warm months of spring became the much hotter climate of summer. Also, Maria's pregnancy was now beginning to show a little, and she was becoming quite proud of her 'bump'. She was very excited, if a little bit nervous, to be invited onto a live TV chat show entitled *Cross Examination*.

So on a warm evening of the first of July, the Allerstry Television Studio was abuzz with excitement. Ushers at the door were directing people as they poured in, inspecting their tickets as they did so. Some people tried to get through without tickets. These people were stopped but treated very courteously and generously, and were offered an alternative area where they could view the show on a big screen set up there. Speakers were also set up outside for people who couldn't get into the building at all, and the crowd in the street outside the studio was growing. Luckily for them it wasn't raining, but *un*luckily for the police, officers from neighbouring towns had to be brought in to help with crowd control and traffic jams. Thousands of people awaited the appearance of Maria Christopher, the girl who had made such fantastic claims.

Maria sat in the back of a huge limousine as she travelled towards the studio, dressed in a neat light grey jacket and skirt. She'd had her long, dark hair done specially, allowing her hairdresser to recommend something appropriate for the occasion, which turned out to be a loose bouncy half-up do. She looked calm, but as she got closer to the studio, inwardly her stomach was beginning to turn over.

Next to her sat Father Bonelli who had already pledged publicly that he would dedicate the remainder of his life to looking after and protecting this girl who he fully believed in – the mother of the Future King.

He had a toolbox that he kept on the seat next to him, and Maria kept giving it a puzzled look. She'd already asked him what it was for. He'd just told her not to worry about it. She was too curious to keep quiet any longer though.

"Tell me what that's for," she said. "What are you up to?"

"Never mind that for now," he said quietly.

"But…"

"I promise you'll find out soon enough." Then changing the subject he said, "When you come out later we'll be getting away in my own car."

Maria looked worried. The way he said 'getting away', it sounded like he expected to be leaving in a hurry.

"Where's your car now?" she asked.

"I told you," he said. "A friend of mine has parked it at the back of the studio, but don't worry, I'll lead you to it later, away from the crowds."

She felt in her jacket pockets. On either side there was a small capsule.

He looked at her. "You've got them?"

She nodded.

"You know what to do with them," he reminded her, "and when to do it?"

She nodded again.

"And the switch?"

She put her hand inside another pocket on the inside of her jacket and flicked a little switch. A blue shimmering light around the whole jacket was illuminated.

She laughed and switched it off.

"When should I switch it on?" she said.

"You'll know when." Then he pointed to something else.

"And last but not least?"

Again she put her hand inside her jacket, but this time to feel something fastened to her top, the tiniest little microphone with a wire dangling down inside her blouse.

"Say something," he said, holding an earpiece close to his ear.

"Mary had a little lamb," she said, "one day it was quite sick…"

"Okay, okay, I got you," he said. "Loud and clear."

They eventually arrived in the limo which had been laid on by the studio. People hardly noticed as Father Bonelli got out and mingled with them. The crowd was already noisy and being driven back by police, but when the teenage girl stepped out of the car, there was sheer pandemonium. Never in history, since Beatlemania, had the country witnessed such mass hysteria.

The noise was getting worse, and people were trying to force their way through the line of police officers who were all in riot gear. One young man, about mid-twenties, was determined to get through. He was within ten feet of the girl when he was brought down to the ground with a painful crash as a police officer performed a superbly timed rugby tackle. Four other policemen then grabbed the struggling man by his arms and legs, and there was no standing on ceremony when they literally threw him into the back of a police van.

Other efforts to reach the girl from then on were curtailed, but this did not prevent the shouts from the crowds reaching Maria's ears. As she had done before, she stopped to listen, and as before some of the screams were in support of her, but other were against her.

As she was promptly ushered through the front entrance of the studio building, a smoke bomb was thrown. Television coverage from outside was momentarily blocked by black and blue palls of smoke. Once more she had a pang of regret at the back of her mind that she had told the world her story. She briefly considered shouting back at the crowd telling them it was all a mistake.

Or a stupid misunderstanding?

A silly joke that got out of hand?

But then she remembered what Diane, Julie and Becky had told her – such a bid could only make matters a hundred times worse.

No, she was stuck with it. It had already gone too far to back out now. She would have to see it through.

Inside the building, she was shown through to the studio where the recording of the programme was taking place. The presenter of the show was the same lady who had introduced Anna Gabriella several weeks earlier when Father Bonelli had been watching.

Patti Bonner, was a glamorous woman in her early thirties. She had long, wavy, blonde hair. She was having final touches done to her make-up.

Some backstage guy suddenly appeared in front of Maria with a clapperboard in his hand, pushing it right into her face.

"On in ten minutes," he yapped at her, as he had a practice with the clapperboard, snapping it shut and nearly chopping her nose off.

CHAPTER THIRTY-ONE

Patti Bonner and Maria Christopher sat opposite each other with a low table in the middle with glasses and a jug of water on it. The director began making signals to the operators of the three stage cameras, counting down from five with his fingers, then somebody was heard to say, "On air."

There was then some introduction music that gradually faded out, then Patti Bonner turned her head dramatically to face camera one.

"Good evening," she said brightly. "I am Patti Bonner, and this is *Cross Examination* where politicians, clergymen and celebrities agree to appear in front of a live audience, give us some information about who they are and what they're doing, and then stand up to some brutal cross examination."

The audience laughed and applauded.

"Brutal, because it's you asking the questions."

The applause and laughter grew louder.

Patti Bonner waited for the applause to fade out before continuing.

"Of course, there are some politicians and clergymen – won't name any names – who have repeatedly refused to appear on our cute little show."

More laughter and applause.

"But," Patti Bonner said, continuing to look directly into camera one and suddenly becoming serious, "this evening we have an extremely interesting and important guest. Important because – she claims – she is going to give birth to the Son of God..."

Gasps from the audience.

"… and," the glamorous presenter held a forefinger up to camera two giving her a dramatic change of angle for TV viewers, "the due date for the birth of the New King is the twenty-fifth of December."

Patti Bonner waited for the gasps of anticipation from the audience to subside again, then back to camera one, "Ladies and gentlemen, please give a warm welcome to our main guest this evening, *Miss* Maria Christopher."

There came a mixed reaction from the audience, all very noisy but not all supportive. Maria sensed that the sceptical ones were strongly represented, and this gave the studio a somewhat apprehensive atmosphere. The three stage cameras swivelled on their stands and immediately zoomed in on the girl so those different angles could be shown to TV viewers during various parts of the show. But Maria was prepared for this and, neatly dressed in her jacket and skirt, and with her hair done up so elegantly, she sat there with confidence, one leg delicately crossed over the other. The strap of her handbag was placed over her shoulder, and her hands rested calmly on the arms of her chair.

"So, Maria," said Patti. "Please, in your own time and own words, tell us your story."

Maria took a deep breath and began to retell her whole story that she had already told several times before, to her parents, friends, teachers, Social Services and Father Bonelli.

Except that now she was mindful of the fact that this show's average TV audience was said to be over twelve million people, and this particular show was expected to draw more than that.

Even so, quite calmly, she told how she discovered she was pregnant, even though she could not remember ever having had a sexual relationship. She then explained how she went to the doctor who confirmed that her hymen was intact, proving that she was still a virgin, and finally how she was visited by an Angel who informed her that she had been chosen by God to give birth to His Second Son.

When she finished, she sat back in her seat and released a hefty, well-rehearsed sigh that indicated how relieved she was to have the whole story out in the open. There was a moment of absolute silence in the studio, but after a while muttering began to break out among the audience.

"Little liar," somebody said.

"Cheap hussy," called out a fat lady who had an ugly, large wart on her nose.

"Daughter of The Devil," from somebody else.

But an elderly lady suddenly stood up and raised her arms full-stretch into the air, and one of the audience cameras zoomed in on her as she shouted, "I love Jesus. Please lead us and deliver us from all Evil."

"Oh, shut your cake hole," said a scruffy dude from behind her.

"Okay, okay," said Patti Bonner. "Let's have some questions." And she pointed to a middle-aged man right in the centre of the auditorium. "You, sir. What would you like to ask our guest?"

The man stood up and coughed as a microphone attached to an extension from some rigging above, appeared in front of him.

"You say you were visited by an Angel," he said in a mocking kind of voice. "So what did the Angel look like?"

"Was it male or female?" somebody from the back of the audience shouted.

Maria was prepared for this line of questioning.

"Definitely male," she said, managing a smile and a nod. "And he…"

"How did you know it was male?"

People in the audience began to shout out at once.

"Was he naked, then?"

"Could you see his dick?"

"Okay, okay..." Patti Bonner held up her hands. "Please, ladies and gentlemen..."

Some members of the audience were laughing, but others made irritable shushing noises back at them.

"One question at a time, please," Patti continued. "Maria, the gentleman asked what did the Angel look like? You said he was male..."

"And someone else," Maria began defensively, "asked rather stupidly if he was naked. Let me say I could tell the Angel was male without him having to be naked."

She paused to take a deep breath, and to compose herself again before continuing.

"His chest, though, and his arms, were bare, and quite muscular-looking, but there was a bright light glowing around him so I couldn't work out any specific details. His voice was soft, but very deep and quite clear, so I could not be mistaken over what he told me."

"And can you tell us again, please, what did he tell you, exactly?"

Maria released another huge sigh. "He told me that I had been chosen to be the mother of the Second Son of God."

"And have you any idea why he said that to you?" Patti asked. "I mean why you had been chosen?"

"I have absolutely no idea," Maria replied with complete confidence.

Patti Bonner looked at camera three and pulled a comical expression of exaggerated puzzlement, then she faced the audience again to ask for another question. The fat lady with the wart on the tip of her nose thrust up her hand. Patti gestured to her, inviting her to speak.

"You said you went to your doctor," the fat lady observed, "to confirm that you were still a virgin. Why would you do that? Wouldn't you know yourself if you were a virgin?"

"The Angel told me..."

"NO!" the fat lady interrupted, pointing an accusing finger. "You said you went to the doctor *before* you were visited by the Angel."

This was the same question that her mother had asked her the night she told her parents the story. During that evening, though, at that point they were interrupted by the doorbell. The question had never come up again so, temporarily at least, she had literally been saved by the bell. Since then, however, she had prepared an answer if that question was ever asked again.

That moment was now.

Maria took yet another one of her deep sucks of air before answering.

"I was experiencing symptoms like the ones you would get if you were pregnant," she said, "like morning sickness, but I had never had a sexual relationship. I knew that if I..."

"What you said was," the obnoxious woman interrupted again, "you could not remember having sex. So, you might have done but couldn't remember, for example, if you were drunk."

"For your information," Maria said through gritted teeth, "having been examined by my doctor, she has confirmed that I am still a virgin."

Patti was eager to prevent the conversation from boiling over, although most of her shows tended to do that, but usually right at the end of the transmission.

"You were saying," she said quietly to Maria. "You knew that if...?"

"Thank you," Maria said, after an aggressive stare at the woman in the audience. "Like I was saying before I was rudely interrupted, I knew that if I mentioned these strange symptoms to someone, like my mother, she would conclude that I was pregnant, and therefore would want to know who the father was. I thought that at the same time if I went to my doctor, then I would be able to reassure my parents. And don't forget that, at that point, I didn't believe that I actually was pregnant."

Having finally finished that rehearsed response, Maria looked steadily at the fat lady hoping that her explanation was satisfactory. At least it could not be disproved.

But instead, the wart-nosed woman just leaned over to the person sitting next to her and muttered to him, "Sounds like a right Cock And Bull story if ever there was one."

Those words were clearly picked up by the television studio microphones.

Maria's keen ears picked it up, too. The cameras zoomed in on her still further as her eyes narrowed aggressively at the fat woman, and her whispered words, "You're mine, you fat witch," were also clearly registered.

A sounds technician made a thumbs-up signal to the director.

Patti Bonner did not want her show to be reduced to a slanging match, although that was good for the ratings, so she hurriedly moved on.

"More questions, please," she said pointing to a neatly dressed young man sitting in the front row. "You, sir."

The slim, young man, who wasn't very tall, stood up and the microphone suddenly appeared and sailed over him. He momentarily looked up at it, then faced Maria.

"Is it true," he began, "that you are being paid twenty-five thousand pounds to appear on this show?"

There was another general gasp of astonishment around the studio, and greater than before, but Maria was prepared for this too. Fortunately for her, because the figure was incorrect, she had been presented with a loophole which she could exploit, and therefore had every right to deny it. The sum offered was actually *thirty*-five thousand pounds.

She leaned forward slightly so that she was a little closer to the microphone.

"I can absolutely, categorically deny it," she said. "Next question, please."

The young man sat down looking confused and totally deflated.

For a moment Patti seemed to be slightly taken aback that Maria, herself, had invited the next question, but she recovered her composure quickly, shook her head and laughed. She then pointed to a tarty-looking young woman who was wearing make-up so thick it could have been scraped off with a knife. She had been waving her arms around for several minutes.

"You, madam," said Patti Bonner.

Once the microphone was positioned correctly above her head, the woman with the thick make-up said, "Surely if you are the Chosen One, you would have been given some privileges. Some sort of power, perhaps?"

"No," Maria answered. "Next question please."

"Hang on a minute," said the tart. "I haven't finished yet."

But as she continued to protest, and wave her arms excitedly, an elderly man called out uninvited, and as he began to raise his voice, the microphone on its extension rod whizzed straight over to him.

"What about the Clergy Project?" he shouted. "Some people, even clergymen, have now acknowledged that their lives have been dedicated to a false belief, namely the Virgin Birth, so why should people believe in you now, more than two thousand years later?"

Patti Bonner turned sideways and looked into camera three.

"The Clergy Project," she said, "is an organisation that counsels people who are trying to come to terms with the fact that they have held beliefs dear to their hearts all their lives, only to have all those beliefs proven to be false."

Meanwhile, cameras one and two zoomed in again on Maria. She was really in the spotlight now and under the cosh, so to speak, so she realised that if she was going to make an impression on these people then this was her moment to do it.

She looked bravely and firmly ahead, then said, "I cannot speak for a girl who lived over two thousand years ago, but as I sit here before you now I am stating the facts. I have offered proof that should satisfy you, for example what my doctor has said. However, before I leave this studio this evening I will leave you all with absolutely no doubt that I am to be the mother of God's Second Son."

Then she added, "But I tell you this, *Blessed will be those among you who believed me without proof.*"

The gasp around the studio now was like a giant pulse.

Maria's conclusion to this statement was, *"The rest of you will be damned to Hell."*

Then, unexpectedly, she stood up and pointed at the woman who had spoken previously, the tart with the thick make-up.

"Stand up," she shouted.

The woman felt compelled to stand up.

"Okay, then," Maria said to her. "What would you have me do?"

"Perform some sort of trick," said the common tart. "Some kind of magic."

"That would be a vulgar display of my power." Maria did not try to disguise the contempt she felt towards this woman.

"So you can't do it. You're a fucking liar."

Maria appeared, at first, to ignore her. Instead she pointed at the other obnoxious woman, the one with an unsightly wart on her nose.

"Now, you stand up," Maria snapped at her.

The woman did stand up with a grotesque sneer on her face, but by this time Maria was warming to her work. The rest of the audience was now in a stunned silence, wondering what was happening.

And for the first time in her career, Patti Bonner was not sure what to do.

"Okay," she said, putting her hands together, "Now let's just…"

"SHUT UP!" Maria yelled at her, then continuing to address the wart-nosed woman, she said, "And what do you want from me?"

"I agree with that woman over there," said the fat biffer. "You need to perform something completely unexplained." Then she laughed, "But we all know you can't do it."

"Oh, I can do it, all right," Maria told her calmly. "And I will. But before I do, can you prove to everyone here that I'm lying?"

"I cannot disprove you," said the woman, "any more than I can disprove the Easter Bunny."

Then all hell broke loose. Patti Bonner had been itching to intervene again, but what happened next caused so much confusion and noise she didn't know what to do or where to turn.

Maria thrust both her arms forward, one forefinger pointing directly at the tart, the other at the wart-nosed woman. The audience began to scream and shout.

Then all the lights in the studio began to flash.

First the flashing was to a steady rhythm, but then they clicked on and off intermittently.

While people were being dazzled and confused with flashing lights, Maria reached into her left-side jacket pocket, took out the first capsule given to her by Father Bonelli, and threw it down hard onto the floor in front of her.

The effect was devastating.

There was a deafening *Bang!* that shook the foundations of the studio, and a blinding flash,

A cloud of thick, white smoke began to sail over the shocked audience.

And Maria's voice could be heard shouting loudly, as though amplified through a five-hundred-watt speaker, and above the noise of the screaming audience. And with her skills of ventriloquism she had practised recently, not only was her voice amplified, but it had become very deep. The voice that the audience heard now was no longer that of a teenage girl.

It was of a man.

"DAMN YOU!" came the deep, booming, echoing voice, as she continued to shout at the two women who had dared challenge her. Both women now looked terrified, and their aggressive sneers were gone.

"You have made God very angry," continued the deep amplified voice. "For calling His Son's mother a liar. For this you will be burned in Hell."

The woman with the painted face looked petrified now. She tried to get out of her seat but was confused with the flashing lights. She lost her way, then lost her balance, and tripped over the outstretched legs of some lanky individual.

She fell flat on her face, and when she re-emerged, she had blood seeping from her forehead. There was an ugly gash she'd sustained from a collision with the back of a seat.

The sight of this in the intermittently flashing lights made it more bizarre and horrific, and caused people sitting closest to her to scream in terror.

The wart-nosed woman suffered a similar accident. She fell up against a young lad who was wearing a motorcycle jacket that had vicious studs on it. As she fell, her face scraped down the arrangement of pointed studs, until her wart was completely torn off her nose, and as she tried to stand, in pain and shock, blood could be seen spurting from the wound.

Then Maria put her hand into her right-side jacket pocket, took out the second capsule, and threw that one onto the floor just as before.

Bang!

Again, the foundations of the building reverberated like there was an earthquake.

And another blinding flash of light and cloud of smoke.

Then darkness – the lights went out completely.

And silence – apart from the odd murmur, or whimper, from the injured women.

And no further action from the cameras, and no sending of the microphones. Everything had just stopped dead.

And from the darkness, amidst the drifting smoke, the mother of the future Son of God emerged, shrouded by a florescent, shimmering, blue light.

As she walked forward slowly, she produced a torch from her handbag, similar to the ones used by cinema ushers. The audience sitting on the front row dropped forward from their seats onto their knees, bowing their heads, fearing what would happen to them if they did not openly – and willingly – worship the girl.

CHAPTER THIRTY-TWO

Maria Christopher was smiling now, and just managed to prevent herself from laughing as she stepped down from the stage. She walked along the central aisle towards the double doors at the back of the studio and out into the corridor. There she was met by Father Giuseppe Bonelli who took hold of her arm and led her through a small exit at the rear of the building, away from the crowds. The priest's own car was waiting there in a small, private car park. She got in by a rear door of the vehicle.

Father Bonelli placed his toolbag on the back seat next to her, then got into the driver's seat and began to drive, gently at first, to negotiate the heavy traffic.

He looked back momentarily.

"Just keep down for now," he told her.

She was practically lying down on the back seat as the car began to gather speed, and as she did so she glanced inside the priest's toolbag. She grinned broadly when she saw the contents therein. There were screwdrivers, a pair of pliers, bits of broken wires and various circuit boards with soldered contacts on them.

She laughed quietly to herself. Evidently, Giuseppe Bonelli was an accomplished electrician as well as being a reasonably good priest, and somehow he must have found out where all the studio light fuses and circuit boards were.

(Unbeknown to her, he had in fact shown a security man a fake ID and said he was there to test the lighting to ensure there were no failures during the show.)

And another thought came to Maria's mind. The man was also some sort of explosives expert.

"Bloody hell, Bonelli," she laughed. "What was in those capsules? My ears are still ringing."

"Oh, just some goofy little recipe my brother Lucci concocted," the old priest replied as the car continued to accelerate. "He learned a trick or two when he was in the army. Well, we both did."

And people at home who had been watching the evening programme on television were left with no picture and no sound.

So literally in the dark.

Just a message on their screens which read...

We apologise for the temporary loss of transmission.

*

Later that evening, people tuning in to see *The Late Evening News* on television, sat mesmerised at what they saw and heard. It was announced at the beginning of the broadcast as the main story.

"Maria Christopher, the pregnant teenage girl who claims that she will give birth to the Son of God, appeared earlier this evening on Patti Bonner's show, *Cross Examination*, where members of the audience were invited to ask her questions. Things were proceeding fairly well, but it was when two women in the audience became abusive that fireworks literally began to fly. Our reporter Maggie Jones has the story."

The scene then switched to the TV studio, which just two hours earlier had hosted Patti Bonner's show. Standing there facing the camera and holding a microphone was Maggie Jones, a pretty redhead in her mid-twenties, with a cheery face. She was nodding and on a signal she began to speak into the microphone.

"This evening's programme was going really well, I thought, and the audience had lots of questions to ask the young girl, Maria Christopher, fuelling discussions and arguments, referring to her claim that she is going to give birth to the Second Son of God. In fairness to her, though, she was answering the questions firmly and confidently, but the atmosphere in the studio suddenly changed when two women in the audience became abusive towards her. They called her a liar."

The newsreader cut in. "On all accounts, Maggie, she shouted back at them in a very loud voice. A *man's* voice."

Maggie Jones momentarily pressed her hands on to her ears and gritted her teeth as though she could still hear that voice.

"Yes," she said, nodding. "A man's voice and amplified to a deafening level. She made an announcement that the women had made God angry, and that they would be damned to Hell. Then everything became even more bizarre. The studio lights began to flash, then there were two horrendous explosions right here in the studio. Both women were injured in the confusion that followed. Then the lights went out completely."

"And what did the girl do?"

Maggie paused for a moment, then nodded as she picked up the question.

"She just floated," she said.

"Floated? What do you mean, floated?"

Maggie's face looked completely serious.

"I tell you, she floated, immersed in a shimmering, blue light."

"And then?"

"She disappeared," said Maggie. "I swear to you. The girl just simply disappeared."

"When you say disappeared, do you literally mean...?

"Vanished."

At that point, a recorded part of the programme was briefly shown where the girl appeared to be floating within a warm glow of blue light.

Maggie Jones appeared again, and continued, "I have with me here two people who were in the audience. First on my right I have Krupa Mistry who was sitting on the front row. Krupa, can you tell us what happened?"

The camera zoomed in on the elderly Muslim lady.

"I believe what I saw was the power of God," she called out looking around her. "*We must listen to God when he talks,*" she went on as though reciting verses from the Quran. "*We are told, believe your eyes, believe your ears, do not deny what you plainly see and hear. Your own eyes and ears will not lie to you…*"

"Yes, but…" Maggie wanted to get in another question.

"How else can we explain what happened? The girl floated, she shimmered in light, she spoke in a man's voice. It was God's voice."

The woman looked up as if deep in prayer, and her voice rose hysterically. "…and I believe we are actually going to witness the birth of God's Second Son."

"Thank you very much," Maggie Jones managed to say, but unable to match the woman's sheer emotion. "But on my left, I have Mr Barry Boldman who doesn't seem to be quite as convinced. Please explain, Mr Boldman."

The camera zoomed in again, but this time on a youngish man who was going prematurely grey, prematurely bald, and had a potbelly indicating his partiality to regular beers.

"It's all rubbish," he said. "There were weird special effects being used, and the girl was clever at throwing her voice with the use of an amplifier."

"The studio technicians say that she could not have possibly got control over sound equipment," said Maggie Jones. "I asked them myself and they said it's impossible."

"I don't care," said Boldman. "There must have been somebody else behind the scenes controlling everything."

"And the flashing lights?"

"Same thing exactly," Boldman said with a firm nod. "I guess an expert electrician, some quite clever person behind the scenes, someone who knew the electrical system of the building."

Maggie Jones pulled a puzzled expression at the camera, then back towards Boldman, she asked, "And the explosions?"

"I believe that each of those was the result of some specially prepared incendiary device which the girl had carefully concealed about her person," Boldman said, folding his arms. "They would have been prepared by an experienced explosives person, perhaps an ex-army officer."

"So," Maggie said, "you believe that Maria Christopher came here accompanied by an electrician who knew his way around, and an expert sound systems man, and an explosives expert who was an ex-army man, whereas the head of security told me there was absolutely nobody else around?"

Then she broke off as if remembering something, and added hastily, "oh, apart from a doddery old priest who said he was lost, looking for the men's room."

Maggie looked at the camera and laughed. "So it couldn't have been him."

"NO!" Krupa Mistry shouted suddenly. "It was no special effects, and how do you account for the shimmering blue light around her?"

"A small battery with a cleverly concealed switch," said Boldman. "Together with an array of coloured bulbs on a length of wire, all available for about two quid from your nearest joke shop."

"NO!" the Muslim woman shouted again, and persisted, "I saw her disappear."

"That's complete shit," Boldman shouted back at her.

"Apologies to viewers at home for the language," said Maggie Jones.

"NO!" Krupa Mistry shouted for the third time, and lunged forward with remarkable agility for a woman of her age, pointing an accusing finger at Boldman.

"Beware of the doubters," she began as though reciting more verses from the Quran. *"For they are your enemies, as they are the enemies of God. Shun them, ostracise them, for they have no knowledge, and they will envy those who have seen the light and will seek to destroy the wonderful gift that you have."*

Barry Boldman drew a deep breath, looked directly at the camera, opened his mouth and said...

... what he said was not heard by TV viewers, because just before he did make his remarks, the television producer urgently yelled out, "CUT!" and all sound was disconnected.

*

Before the broadcast of the Patti Bonner Show (it was reported afterwards) a survey had revealed that seventeen per cent of people believed in Maria's claims that she was visited by an Angel who informed her that she would give birth to the Son of God on the twenty-fifth of December.

Furthermore, some of these people had made their own claims, that they had actually witnessed miracles performed by the girl. Some of those, however, also claimed that they had witnessed other miracles performed by different people at various times. It was rumoured that Angels had appeared to them also. Most staggering of all, though, was a magician in Greece. He really could walk on water and had been witnessed doing so by hundreds of people.

A further thirty-two per cent said they did not know what to believe but were prepared to keep an open mind.

The remaining fifty-one per cent said that it was all a pack of lies, but whether people believed the schoolgirl or not, she was gradually becoming more famous, and everyone just wanted to see her.

After the live TV broadcast, and subsequently the repeats later in the evening, millions more people around the country learned about Maria Christopher and her claim to be a virgin mother-to-be. Many of these, though, still the majority, didn't believe a word of it.

Notwithstanding the number of people who did not know what to believe, the ones who still represented the minority actually believed more firmly than ever now that this girl was telling the truth, that she really had been chosen by God.

And this belief gave them reassurance and comfort, and over the coming weeks and months, the number of believers in Maria's Sacred Claim was destined to grow.

CHAPTER THIRTY-THREE

It was 2nd July, the day of Maria's fourteen-week scan. She went into St Mark's Hospital on her own. Waiting in the car park opposite the hospital's main entrance sat Father Giuseppe Bonelli, again dressed in ordinary clothes so as not to draw attention to himself. He had grown a stubbly beard to further disguise himself, with the hope that he would not be recognised from his recent TV appearances. He felt that media attention was now becoming too intrusive, and he was thinking again about taking Maria far away, along with Debbie and Anna. It would need to be a long way away from this vicinity, and in the utmost secret, at least until the New Heavenly King was born.

While the priest waited, he could see a crowd of people gradually congregating.

He thought about Maria and marvelled at how well such a young girl was coping with all this attention which brought with it some serious danger. However, during a recent interview, she may have let it slip that she was going to hospital for the scan, and many people would have guessed at what hospital this appointment would be attended.

As the priest sat in his car waiting, he was starting to get worried. The crowd was rapidly getting bigger and bigger, and somewhat noisier. He decided he would have to do something drastic to get her away safely.

He leaned across to the glove box in front of the passenger seat and opened it. There was a chunky leather case in there. He took it out, placed it on his lap and unzipped it. And there was his army-issue revolver. He took the gun in his hand, then reached across for another item. An oblong box. He opened it and looked inside to check the ammunition.

Giuseppe Bonelli was a decent shot with a firearm. Since leaving the army, he had frequently gone to shooting ranges with Lucci, and had always got an excellent score on the targets. He smiled to himself as he thought of it, but hoping at the same time that, for today at least, shooting was not going to be necessary.

While looking across the car park again at the growing crowd of people, he began to load the gun.

*

Maria Christopher walked along the corridors of the hospital and got to the pre-natal ward in plenty of time for her appointment. She didn't have to wait long before a nurse called her into the scanning room.

When invited to do so, she lay on the couch, unbuttoned her blouse and pulled it open, revealing her bare tummy that was now showing a healthy-sized bump. The nurse who was going to operate the scanning equipment squirted some lubricating jelly onto her tummy, then began to move the scanner around thereon. Maria gasped with joy as a clear image appeared on the monitor in front of her.

"Look at that," she said, excitedly pointing. "He's moving around, he's waving his arms."

The nurse smiled.

"I notice you're referring to the baby as *He*," she observed, "but I'm afraid it's too soon to confirm the sex. We will, however, be able to determine the sex of the baby when you come back in six weeks' time."

"Six weeks?" Maria said.

"Yes," the nurse confirmed. "For your twenty-week assessment."

Maria became serious as she looked at the nurse.

"With respect," she said, "I already do know the sex of my baby. It *is* a boy."

The nurse had a puzzled expression on her face as she continued to move the scanner, viewing certain aspects of the image on the screen.

"A beautiful spine," she commented. "Strong legs..."

Exactly on cue the baby kicked.

Maria laughed. "I think he heard you," she said.

The nurse laughed, too, but just shrugged her shoulders. She moved the scanner around again.

Maria saw what looked like a little flashing light.

"Is that his heart beating?" she asked excitedly. "Is everything all right?"

"Yes, that is the heart," the nurse confirmed, "and everything looks fine, and..."

She broke off suddenly and looked at Maria.

"Hey, you're the girl they've been talking about on television, aren't you?" she said. "The one who says she's going to give birth to the Son of God?"

Maria sat up suddenly and looked directly at the nurse who had become mesmerised with the young girl's stare. Maria used her uncanny gift of drawing the nurse's attention with her eyes. The nurse just looked blankly back at her, as though hypnotised.

Then the teenage mum-to-be, as practised before, rolled her eyes right back into their sockets revealing just the whites.

And her voice became deep, and she spoke in a slow monotone.

"And blessed art thou who is the first to witness the Saviour of the World. Believe in us and you will have a place with us in Heaven."

The nurse, a young Catholic woman, dropped to her knees and burst into tears of joy. Together they recited four *Hail*

Mary's, one *Our Father* and the *Act of Contrition*.

Fifteen minutes or so after, she was conveying her thanks and farewells to the nurse and preparing to leave the hospital, little dreaming of how the next hour would unfold.

*

Outside in the car park, Father Giuseppe Bonelli was certain now that there would be some sort of public order issue, exactly to what extent, he didn't know, but he was getting ready for it all the same. With no intention of injuring anyone at that moment, he placed the loaded revolver into its holster that was strapped to him but concealed beneath his jacket. He then got out of the car and walked briskly towards the crowd of people. The crowd was still steadily growing in number, and in noise. The priest estimated that there were now around five-thousand people who were beginning to spread across the car park. This was a worry in itself because his plan, once Maria was safely in the car, was to make a speedy getaway, and that would be difficult with the whole area so crowded.

As he approached the growing crowd, he could not help noticing with some trepidation that many people in the crowd were holding up banners with varying and contrasting religious messages. Some were from the Bible, and referenced chapters and verses from Mathew, Mark, Luke or John, while others were simple quotes like: *God Is All Good And All Loving* and *God's Son Will Deliver Us From All Evil*.

But there were many other different messages that made Giuseppe worry that some people were angry. They felt that Maria was a blasphemer and a threat to their own specific belief, therefore she could find herself in very real danger.

And somebody must have tipped off the police, because five patrol cars had turned up, and at least a dozen officers on foot appeared in front of the hospital's main entrance. They started pushing people away from the doors. One of them was using a megaphone, repeatedly instructing people to keep back.

"At least things can't get any worse than this," he muttered to himself.

Then he saw news reporters and television cameras appearing on the scene.

He released a hefty sigh. "I was wrong," he said aloud.

But it was about to get a lot worse than that.

Father Bonelli put his hand on the handle of his revolver under his jacket, as if for reassurance. He reached the crowd and mingled with them, confident that nobody would recognise him in his plain clothes and with a stubbly beard.

As he looked around he could sense the tension in the crowd building up. He'd already guessed that there would be some kind of unholy incident, but nothing like what actually did happen next. And it all occurred quite suddenly.

The people at the front could see Maria emerging through the doors from the hospital's main entrance. They all began to surge forward, all shouting. The noise then rose in pitch and volume until it was deafening. More police officers moved in trying to hold people back.

Bonelli moved in too, planning simply on grabbing Maria and attempting to move her away to safety, but he could see now that that was impossible.

Then suddenly a group of four men, all wearing balaclavas, moved stealthily forward together from the back of the crowd where previously they had been unobserved. They roughly pushed people out of the way. One of them had a handgun, and another had a knife that had a nasty-looking curved blade.

It was the one with the knife who attacked Maria, holding her with one arm locked around her neck, and threatening to slit her throat with the knife in his other hand.

The police officers moved forward but the man with the gun levelled his weapon at them and shouted, "Stand back, or

I will shoot."

The police officers stopped in their tracks but did not retreat.

The man who was holding the knife to Maria's throat shouted, "I'll kill her, I swear, I will kill her."

One of the police officers, an inspector, held his hands up in a calming gesture.

"Okay, okay," he shouted back. "Nobody needs to get hurt. Just let the young lady go, then back off."

The inspector began to wish that they had brought in the armed squad, but of course they had no idea the morning was going to turn out like this.

The TV cameramen jostled for position so people at home could enjoy all this action with their tea at 6 pm.

The man with the gun laughed. A horrible sneering laugh.

"We're taking the girl," he shouted, "and I will shoot anyone who gets in our way"

"And if anyone attempts to follow us," the man with the knife at Maria's throat interrupted, "I will not hesitate to slit her throat."

"Are you getting all of this?" the TV director called to the sound crew.

"Loud and clear, George," was the reply.

Bonelli's hand was on the handle of his revolver again. With grim determination he knew what he had to do, but it had to be done quickly. Once his gun was out, he would have to shoot instantly. He was confident from his shooting range days that he could score two rapid hits, but Maria was directly in front of her captor with the knife.

The priest needed eye contact with the girl, but at that moment she was so scared her eyes were all over the place.

He needed to get her attention so he could signal to her.

"You cowardly bastards," he shouted suddenly. "Let her go."

"You want a bullet between the eyes, old man?" shouted the man with the gun, not realising that the 'old man's' hand was on a gun with a fire power far more formidable than his own.

But Bonelli ignored him. He now had eye contact with Maria. He moved his hand under his jacket, while gesturing with his eyes to the man holding her.

She gave a faint nod indicating her understanding of the signal.

Then before the man knew what was happening, with a deafening scream, she thrust her elbow back with every ounce of her strength, getting him in the ribs. She then wrenched herself free, and with the other hand, with two fingers extended, she thrust these into his face. One finger found its soft target.

Half blinded and screaming in terrible pain, he made a renewed grab at the girl and stabbed the knife towards her pregnant tummy.

Bonelli whipped out his gun, aimed in that split second and fired.

The man with the knife was dead before he hit the ground. The high velocity round from such close range had exploded the top of his skill. His brains splattered everywhere.

The crowd of people were screaming and shouting in shock and confusion, but Bonelli immediately turned and fired again. This time it was the man with the gun who died. He had just aimed at the 'old man' but hadn't lived long enough to pull the trigger.

The other two men forced their way backwards through the crowd to make their getaway, but some police officers ran after them and easily apprehended them. The police inspector was talking desperately on his radio, and the TV crews were moving around excitedly.

At the same time, Bonelli knew that he couldn't just stop to talk to the police, or to give himself up for questioning. His job was to look after and protect the mother of the Unborn Prince, and he was prepared to fight to the death if necessary to do so.

He moved forward towards Maria, put one arm around her to guide her back towards the car park, and with his other hand waved the revolver around, firing two shots into the air to encourage the crowd to let them through. The noise from the crowd was still deafening, but they separated to either side allowing the old man and young girl to come through, while Maria took out her handkerchief from her jacket pocket to wipe the dead man's oozing brains off her face.

They got to the car and Bonelli began to drive, while still holding the gun. He did not intend shooting anyone else, but still felt reassured to have the weapon with him. He hated himself for doing it, but when some of the police officers stepped in his path, he aimed the gun at them. This had the desired effect of making them move out of the way, but of course he would never have actually fired at them. He had good liking and respect for the police. Even so, he was glad he had a disguise. He would need a thorough wash, shave and change of clothes instantly he got home.

He looked in his rear-view mirror and saw that one police officer had stepped out into the path behind him and was writing something – probably just the vehicle's registration number. They would soon discover the car was reported stolen. It was his own car but he, himself, had reported the Mazda 6 Estate car as stolen, anticipating this sort of situation, thereby cleverly misleading subsequent investigations.

Out onto the open road he knew he was going to have to drive fast. There would probably be police helicopters searching for them soon.

"What now?" Maria had to raise her voice over the noise of the revving engine.

"First, we'll have to ditch this car," he told her. "There's a petrol station coming up. Then we'll nick one at the garage. It'll have to be an old one, though. Modern cars can't be hot-wired."

Maria laughed.

"Thou shall not steal?" she said in a questioning tone. "Isn't that one of the Ten Commandments?"

"Yes," the old priest nodded as he negotiated a tight bend at high speed. "And thou shall not kill, is another one. As you saw, though, I killed two men just now, but that was for the greater good."

CHAPTER THIRTY-FOUR

Ten minutes later, Father Bonelli and Maria Christopher were heading west in an elderly hot-wired Vauxhall Cavalier, which seemed to run okay, albeit with a slightly noisy exhaust. Bonelli had hurriedly transferred his personal belongings into the stolen car, and Maria noticed an oblong-shaped box that he carefully tucked behind the front passenger seat. With a vague thought at the back of her mind wondering what it was, she quickly got into the seat and strapped herself in. Bonelli then got in on the driver's side, hot-wired the ignition, and floored the accelerator.

As they resumed their journey in the stolen car, they saw a police helicopter swooping down in the direction of the filling station, probably spotting Bonelli's Mazda, which by now they would have noted had been reported stolen, before being used by the car thief and then ditched.

The crew in the helicopter continued to circle overhead for a few more minutes, and having radioed into control they waited until their colleagues from below arrived to thoroughly examine the abandoned vehicle. They then started to scan the area, hoping to identify an elderly man and a young girl running away, but finally had to accept the probability that they had made off in another car and would be miles away by now and heading in any direction.

They heard a garbled exchange over the radio, a request for a search via the abandoned car's registration number on the Police National Computer.

What the helicopter crew, or any of the police officers,

didn't notice was another, much smaller, privately-owned helicopter speeding away in a westerly direction, the pilot of which was also using a radio, listening to the police, but speaking on a different channel.

The old Vauxhall Cavalier that Bonelli and Maria had stolen had a transparent sunroof, and hearing the sound from above, even over the sound of an old car with a defective exhaust, the priest looked up.

"We're being followed," he shouted to Maria over the combined noise, and gesturing skyward as he held his accelerator foot to the floor. The old banger was now doing nearly 100mph.

Maria looked up, gasping with fright at the sight of the helicopter buzzing along above them, and flying much lower than any aircraft should be operating. She then leaned over to look at the car's speedometer.

"We'll get pulled in if we carry on like this," she shouted.

"That'll be the least of our problems," he shouted back at her.

Maria noticed that while Bonelli held the steering wheel with his right hand, he continued to grasp the revolver in his left, and as the helicopter weaved through the sky above, he was repeatedly looking in his rear-view mirror. The old priest seemed to be more concerned about another threat, possibly from behind.

He guessed correctly. The new threat appeared.

As Bonelli glanced again into the rear-view mirror, he saw a car from a distance, but gaining ground fast. With the Cavalier doing nearly a hundred, he estimated that the car coming up from behind was doing at least 130.

"We're under attack," he shouted.

"What?" Maria turned in her seat to look out the rear window. "Boy, is that guy speeding?"

Bonelli then rapped out clear instructions to her.

"That box that I put behind your seat. Pull it out."

Maria did as she was told. She reached behind her. The noise was deafening now as the old car edged over a hundred, its temperature gauge creeping up. They were whizzing past other vehicles, the drivers flashing their lights and hooting angrily. The helicopter swooped even lower while the car from behind continued to gain on them.

Maria had the box that the priest wanted and held it between her hands on her lap.

Bonelli looked at it and shouted again.

"Pull the lid off, then place the box across my lap."

Maria grasped the stiff lid and pulled, then gasped in fright at what she saw. She had seen the occasional war film so she recognised a grenade when she saw one. Six of them, packed side-by-side. With the lid removed, she passed the open box to Bonelli.

But then there was a deafening *Crack!*

"What the fuck was that?" Maria screamed.

The other car had drawn level, two men glaring at them angrily, aggressively, the side window open. The man in the passenger seat was firing a handgun.

"He's going for our tyres," Bonelli yelled in panic.

The bullet, though, had narrowly missed the front tyre and had ploughed into the wing of the old car. The man was just taking aim for a second shot, when Bonelli levelled his gun at him. The split second before the priest pulled the trigger, the man looked directly at him, and a look of surprise, and then alarm, registered on his face.

Bang! The man in the passenger seat of the pursuing vehicle fell back in his seat, lifeless, a bullet hole through the side of his head.

The car he was in swerved, and momentarily lost ground on the old Vauxhall, with the driver evidently in shock. Still other cars were flashing lights and hooting angrily at the two cars that appeared to be involved in some sort of chase.

But then the driver chasing the Vauxhall regained his wits, gathered up his partner's gun, and gradually drew his vehicle alongside the priest and the girl again.

The noise now seemed even louder than before. Bonelli still had his foot hard down on the accelerator, the old vehicle now doing close to a hundred and ten, its engine valves beginning to bounce.

And as the other vehicle drew level, the priest shouted at Maria again.

"Hold the steering wheel. Just keep it straight."

In shock, Maria instantly did as she was told.

Father Bonelli took a grenade from the box. He pulled the pin, and as the other vehicle drew exactly level, for a brief second he looked into the face, *and the tinted glasses* of the driver.

And he recognised the man who had shot Rod Spencer.

Bonelli threw the grenade through the car's open window.

It bounced off the passenger seat and landed on the floor in front of the driver.

Bonelli saw the look of absolute shock and terror on the driver's face and heard the hysterical scream of a man who knew he was going to die.

The priest leaned back in his seat and jammed on the car's brakes.

As the old Vauxhall swerved and snaked across the road with smoke pumping from its screeching tyres, there was one almighty *Boom!* accompanied by a blinding flash of light. The car, now half a mile ahead, continued to move at over 100mph, but no longer a car – just a spectacular ball of flame.

Bonelli instinctively threw himself across the girl as debris seemed to fly back towards them. Mayhem ensued from behind as the drivers of other cars fought desperately with their controls to avoid the total arsehole who had just jammed his breaks on, with no time to consider the poor bastard who'd just been instantly incinerated.

The elderly Vauxhall gradually came to rest off the side of the road, skidding down a grass verge. The engine stalled with a splutter and a cough. The helicopter swooped overhead, circled twice, then to Bonelli's relief, sped away.

Maria leaned forward in her seat and puffed out her cheeks.

"Thank God it's over," she said.

"I wish it was," Bonelli said. "But I think our problems have only just begun."

He handed back the box containing the remaining grenades.

"Put the lid back on," he told her, "and chuck them behind you."

After replacing the lid, she put the box down carefully behind her seat.

The priest then reached down below the car's steering column for the wires to re-start the engine. Miraculously it did start, albeit with an engine that now sounded like it was all but knackered.

"Hey, you," came an angry voice just then.

"You complete tosser, we want a word with you," were words that were heard from a bad-tempered, portly woman.

Both the priest and the girl looked to see some angry motorists, on foot, slipping and sliding towards them down the grassy slope.

Bonelli put the car into gear and gradually let out the clutch, allowing the tyres enough grip to get up the slippery incline. With the wheels still spinning he drove off, leaving a few angry people behind, all shaking their fists. But he now drove at a far more leisurely pace, and as they went on their way, they saw two police cars speeding in the opposite direction towards the site of the explosion.

*

"Well, that was a pleasant drive in the country," Maria said as they approached their turn-off.

"Yes, it was." Father Bonelli smiled at her, glad to see that she had at least maintained her sense of humour. "We must do it again some time."

"I wonder what Anna and Debbie have been doing this afternoon."

Bonelli looked around him, almost absentmindedly.

"Not having as much fun as us, probably," he said. "I believe they spoke of going shopping."

Maria was pleased to see that the priest had put the gun away at last, into its holster inside his jacket.

Father Bonelli stopped the car about a mile down the main road that led to their own street. Off towards one side of the road was a large woody area. He looked round to make sure there were no pedestrians, then bumped the car up the kerb, and towards the trees.

Then he stopped the car and looked round at his passenger who was starting to look weary.

"Out you get," he told her unexpectedly.

"But..." Maria looked confused.

"I need to park it," he explained, "but I don't want you in the car."

"I don't understand."

"You will," he said. "Just get out now, please."

She did as she was told, then to her amazement the priest drove the old car directly into a tree at about twenty miles per hour.

"What the...!" Maria was flabbergasted.

A ghastly hissing and spitting noise came from under the car's bonnet, accompanied by some wisps of steam and smoke.

Bonelli then leaned his head out of the window and looked

back at her.

"Bloody teenage joy riders," he said with a rueful grin.

Only then did the priest get out, and as he did so Maria thought he looked a bit wobbly on his legs. He leaned in through each door, wiping the inside door handles with his handkerchief, then did the same with the steering wheel, gear stick and handbrake. He then collected the box containing the remaining grenades from behind the passenger seat.

He held the box under his arm, and after slamming the passenger door one last time, he looked at the car and patted it on the roof.

"Thanks, Buddy," he said softly.

Then he approached Maria. "Right," he said. "We've got a little walk home now."

They began walking together, and lost in their own thoughts, some moments passed before either of them spoke again. Eventually the priest glanced round at Maria.

"We really have got to move now," he told her. "Today we were lucky."

"Well, they certainly couldn't have guessed that you'd start chucking grenades at them," she laughed.

"Exactly." Bonelli was serious. "So I have no idea what they'll try next."

"But you've killed most of them now."

"No, I haven't." Bonelli suddenly stopped walking and to her surprise he caught hold of her arm. "The ones I killed were just human fodder to their leaders. Mere pawns with very little brains."

"But..."

"They're a large organisation," Bonelli went on to explain. "They'll use people, like the ones I've killed today, to find out initially what they're up against."

"Yes, but you see..." Maria seemed determined to say something.

"And now," Bonelli concluded, "*we* will be up against a far more formidable enemy."

"But look here, Father," Maria said, caught in a moment of agonising indecision. "There's something I need to tell you…"

Father Bonelli then let go of her arm and they carried on walking.

"Whatever it is that you've got to tell me," he told her, "it won't make any difference now. God knows who they'll send next, but whoever it is they will not be in the mood to mess about."

"Yes, but I do need to say…"

"We're moving," Bonelli said firmly. "I've sworn to God that I will look after you and see you safely through your journey. We'll meet up with Anna and Debbie tonight and make our plans. We lie low for now, remaining totally in hiding, but we'll be off just as soon as I can make the necessary arrangements."

CHAPTER THIRTY-FIVE

Maria's popularity quickly continued to grow and according to surveys, the percentage of people believing in her was rising.

And the people who still insisted that the girl's claims were a load of lies, even they could not help their curiosity. They listened intently whenever her latest exploits were aired on the news.

Someone suggested to her that she should employ a publicity officer. If she had taken up that advice, such a person could hardly have dreamed up a better stunt than her appearance on the Patti Bonner programme, *Cross Examination*, which actually invited people in the audience to challenge her.

Watched by over twenty million viewers in the UK alone (the largest TV audience ever for a TV chat show in the UK) the girl who had now just turned sixteen, systematically shot each one down in flames with the confidence and maturity of someone much older.

This, followed by a number of visual effects, brilliantly and invisibly, orchestrated by her guardian, Father Giuseppe Bonelli, left some people in no doubt whatsoever that she was, or would become, the mother of God's Second Son.

And now she had even more television coverage following the violent incident outside the West Midlands St Mark's Hospital. It was reported that a billion people around the world had seen the action which included the old man foiling the kidnap attempt and shooting the kidnappers. It was probably a lot more than a billion people who had seen it, though, because those scenes had been repeated on the television many times, and on numerous different channels.

And now leaders from other countries were beginning to get curious, and invitations were coming in for her to appear on chat shows all around the world, including America and Australia.

Father Bonelli, however, made a public announcement saying that Maria would not be appearing on any more TV programmes until after the birth of the Blessed Child.

He sat in the front room of his house watching yet another repeat of an earlier news bulletin.

A reporter, Maggie Jones, who was now becoming familiar with Maria's developing story, was standing outside the hospital and talking rapidly as if trying to say everything at once.

"The girl claiming to be carrying the Brother of Jesus, is believed to have visited the hospital for her fourteen-week scan, but chaos ensued as she was seen coming out of the main entrance. Masked men then appeared, one of them grabbed the girl and held a knife to her throat, while another one was seen brandishing a handgun, threatening police with it as they moved forward."

"What happened next?" came the voice of the newsreader in the studio, Sharon White, who was also getting used to hearing, and repeating, the name Maria Christopher.

"What happened was nothing short of incredible," said Maggie Jones. "And it was all captured by our cameras."

As she continued to describe the events, the recorded scene was shown on millions of TV screens around the county, an elderly man coming forward, then he, too, wielded a gun. Following a sudden struggle between Maria Christopher and the man with the knife, the old man, obviously a crack-shot and clearly experienced in handling firearms, fired twice in quick succession, first killing the man with the knife, and then the yob with the gun.

As the televised scene continued, the reporter carried on with her commentary.

"Then the old man and the girl backed away through the crowd together, while further shots were fired into the air. They got into a car which had been reported as stolen, and drove off."

"Thank you, Maggie," said Sharon White from the studio. "Now we've heard further information from the police. We have a senior officer here, Chief Superintendent Sutton."

The chief super was also becoming familiar with the events that seemed to be happening more regularly now. He appeared, looking tired and agitated.

"This is not the first time that threats have been made against the life of this young lady," he said. "There would appear to be a Satanic group whose followers have demonstrated a genuine fear of her."

"Fear?" said Sharon. "Does that mean that they believe that she really is going to give birth to a Holy Child that, I suppose, would be an enemy of their Antichrist?"

"Yes," the chief super said with a firm nod. "And all the time the girl seems to be fearless, and apparently impervious to their threats and efforts to kill her. This leads me to consider one of two possibilities."

"What are they?" Miss White's question was superfluous as the chief super was already in full flow.

"Either she is completely stupid," said the senior officer of the West Midlands Police Force, "although I find that hard to believe…"

"Or?"

"Or…" Chief Superintendent Sutton paused, "… or she really does have divine protection."

"My goodness," Sharon gasped. "And that, in turn, gives religious people all around the world more confidence to believe in her."

"I'm beginning to believe in her myself," the chief super muttered under his breath.

"Pardon?" Sharon said, holding her earpiece tightly into her ear. "I didn't quite catch that last remark. Could you repeat that please?"

"I said I'm keeping my own belief to myself."

"Oh." Sharon White in the studio sounded a bit muddled, but then she continued, "And there's also mystery around the old man who, so routinely, gunned down the masked men?"

"That's true."

"Rumour has it that he, and the priest who is the girl's guardian, are one and the same?"

"I cannot confirm that as I've never actually seen the priest myself."

"Another rumour is that he's an ex-army officer?"

"Well, there are two other updates," the chief superintendent announced, "but neither tie the priest in with this violent incident. One is that, at our request, the TV camera crew have sent us a freeze-frame of the old man holding the gun. The image was blown up and the gun has been identified by our firearms expert as an SZ1514 semi-automatic army-issue handgun, which carries a high-velocity nine-shot magazine in its handle. It's a fast and formidable weapon, but actually obsolete now. The army haven't used it for over twenty years."

"The rumour could still be correct, then," said Sharon. "And what's the other thing?"

"We've spoken to witnesses, six other motorists heading west on the A6, and now we believe that after Maria Christopher and the old man swapped cars at the filling station, they were chased by another vehicle. At high speed the other car exploded. Our forensic team combed through the wreckage, then for confirmation called in our explosive experts, and between them they found evidence that the explosion was caused by a grenade."

"Oh, good Lord…"

"Two of my officers are on their way as we speak," Sutton concluded, "in order to see the priest and to return to him his stolen car. I am sure they will take that opportunity to get as much information as they can."

"Okay, thank you," said Miss White, and after communication with the senior police officer had been disconnected, she concluded with, "And just to confirm again, Maria Christopher's baby's due date is the twenty-fifth of December."

*

Lord Tuan was beyond angry.

The man who had flown the reconnaissance helicopter chasing the old Vauxhall Cavalier, stood before him, expecting to be flayed alive. Not that the failure was his fault.

Tuan began to murmur incoherently.

"Pardon, my Lord?" the helicopter pilot said apprehensively.

"Four men dead." He spoke just a bit louder. "Outwitted by a teenage girl and some doddery old man."

"Hardly doddery," said the pilot. "The way he drove that car at such speed while firing a gun with unerring accuracy at the same time…"

"I tell you, a feeble old fool…"

"Then he started lobbing grenades."

Tuan looked at the helicopter pilot, making an impatient gesture with his hand.

"Our research has discovered he was in the army," he said. "He must have stolen guns, ammunition and explosives."

"Must have done, I suppose."

"Then we must do the same." Only then did Tuan begin to raise his voice. "Two can play at that game. There's one of your men who has a rocket launcher."

"Seems a bit drastic."

"I know people who can prepare and detonate a nuclear device.," Then Tuan shouted in a hoarse voice, *"And I will instruct them to do so if I have to."*

"Oh, shit," the pilot said in a shaky voice. "Okay, okay, whatever you say."

Then Tuan made an effort to control himself.

"That child must not be born. At all costs, the girl must die. And the priest."

"Yes, my Lord."

"So can you get more men together quickly?"

"Yes, my Lord."

"Including that buddy of yours with the rocket launcher."

"That's Giff," said the pilot. "Useful chap to have on our side – being a policeman."

"Oh, yes. I believe Hucknell mentioned him. Police Constable Gifford."

"Yes, my Lord. He can get us inside information. He has already told us that the chief superintendent has ordered police protection for the girl *and* the priest."

"We're way ahead of them," said Tuan, beginning to calm down a bit. "Well, that's something anyway. And his rocket launcher?"

"I don't know where he got the shells from," the helicopter pilot said with a hefty sigh, "but he's an explosives expert, too, and can launch one from the rear of a moving vehicle, like in a James Bond movie."

"Okay, then," said Tuan. "Get Giff and whoever else you need."

The pilot laughed. "Don't worry," he said. "The rocket launcher will sort them out. Bonelli's revolver will seem like a pea-shooter to my boys, and he won't get close enough to lob any more grenades."

Tuan abruptly pointed at the door. "Okay, now go."

The pilot went to the door, but before he left the huge hall, Tuan called out. "Let me know when you are ready."

And then the great hall was empty, except for Lord Tuan sitting there, deep in thought. And the place had suddenly become eerie and silent, save for the sound of his own breathing, and the slow ticking of a clock on the wall...

*

... and he must have gone to sleep for a short while, but he woke with a start, and with the spookiest of feelings that he was being watched. There was no other sound, but he felt someone, or something's, presence.

He suddenly spun round in his seat.

He nearly fainted at what he saw.

A thin-looking boy who appeared to be no more than eleven or twelve years old, just standing there, staring at him, a faint smile on his thin face, his short, bristly hair sticking up.

And his ears seemed to have an abnormally pointed shape.

"Who are you?" Lord Tuan shouted. "How did you get in here? I didn't hear you."

The boy laughed, but it was not a laugh anyone would expect from a boy. It was a deep hiss, that came from the back of his throat, more like the warning sound from an animal – like a cat.

"I'll tell you what I'll do," Tuan said, pointing at him. "I'll have you thrown out, but first I'll teach you a lesson."

The boy continued his guttural laughter, then he pointed back.

Tuan strode towards the boy, but after his third step he stopped.

He had become paralysed, but not just his legs. His whole body had become rigid, while the boy laughed even louder and continued to point his finger.

Tuan spoke, but even that was difficult, his throat and mouth had become as tight as a drum.

"Free me, you little bastard," he said through gritted teeth. "I command you. I am Tuan, The Lord, The Master."

Then the boy spoke in a hissing voice.

"You are not my Master, and you are not The Lord."

It was only then that the man, up until then known by the Latin name, Tuan, noticed that, not only did the boy have abnormal ears, but there was also something really strange about his eyes. Then he realised what it was.

He had narrow, vertical pupils.

Again, the likeness to a cat came to mind, and when the boy laughed again, the man saw the long, sharp, feline teeth, exposed fully when the lips were drawn back into a vicious snarl.

"My Master is Bael," the boy said.

"Oh, no, I'm sorry," said Tuan. "I did not mean to call you a little bastard."

"My Master has instructed me to leave you with a warning, not to disappoint Him again."

"No, please..." Tuan's voice was tightening up even more, and his tongue was like a lump of leather.

"If you do annoy Him again," the boy hissed, "then He will be invoked, and it will be He who visits you next time. You do not want to make Him angry again."

Tuan tried to speak, but now the paralysis had spread to his mouth and throat. He collapsed onto the floor and lay on his side. He could not even make a croaking noise.

And he was unable to scream when the boy rapidly completed his transformation into a large, snarling, black cat that leapt onto him and sank his teeth deeply into his face.

The cat tore a huge chunk of flesh away from one side of Tuan's face, also wrecking the eye socket on that side.

Now in agony, Tuan remained fully conscious, and looked up with his one good eye at the cat as it chewed on the piece of meat it had torn away.

And then the cat grew and grew and grew, until it stood on its hind legs, at least eight feet tall.

Then it began to change into something else.

CHAPTER THIRTY-SIX

Other people not too far away were enjoying a fine summer's evening. Meanwhile, there were people like Father Giuseppe Bonelli who, although were safe for the time being, knew that they had work to do and duties to perform.

He decided to call a meeting to discuss everything that had happened so far, and to begin plans for the future, one plan being to get away to safety, and spending the next few months in hiding.

Sitting together in Anna's room at JackDaw House, between them Maria and the priest had told Debbie and Anna the events of the day. The middle-aged midwife held her hands to her face in horror at the part of the story when the parish priest had thrown a grenade through the car window. In great detail, Maria described the spectacular explosion that followed.

"Bloody hell," Debbie laughed. "Oh, well, at least that's the end to that problem."

"I'm afraid not," Father Bonelli told her. "Believe it or not, we're dealing with highly organised people. All we've done so far is to wipe the floor with a few of their brainless idiots."

"So what do you think they'll try next?" asked Anna.

"This is the point I wanted to tell you about," Bonelli said while looking from one to the other. "I've been discussing this with my brother Lucci, and I'm afraid it seems that..."

At that precise moment the doorbell at the front of the house echoed through the hallway.

"Sod it." Father Bonelli left the room, went along the hallway and opened the door.

And there were the two very sturdy-looking police officers standing there, Inspector Paul Retberg and Sergeant Ian Green.

He was beginning to get used to the sight of them now, although he found himself wrestling inwardly trying to decide whether he liked them or not. It was something to do with the way they always seemed to stand so close together. At that moment he thought they looked more like a couple of rugby players, about to go down into a scrum.

Retberg and Green smiled politely and bowed their heads courteously.

The priest was wearing his dog collar and was neatly shaved, therefore looking nothing like the man who had gunned down two Satanists, had shot another man in a car, and had subsequently blown the other one to kingdom come with a grenade.

He courteously joined his hands and bowed slightly.

"What can I do for you?" he said quietly. "My fine, young officers?"

"Good evening, Father," said Retberg, bowing his head again.

Ian Green also nodded and smiled.

"Won't you come in?" Bonelli momentarily stepped to one side.

"No, it's okay," Retberg said. "It's just a quick visit."

"We have a nice surprise for you," said Ian Green.

"Oh?"

Retberg looked at Green as though slightly irritated, "What my comrade and I have come here to tell you is..."

"Look at that," Green said, stepping to one side, and pointing down the path towards the road.

Then Retberg also stepped sideways.

"Yes," he said. "We have found and returned your car."

Father Bonelli looked in that direction. There was his Mazda, and behind sat a police car.

"Good Lord," he said.

"You reported this car stolen early this morning," Retberg said. "We recovered it after it had been abandoned by the individual who stole it."

"Good Lord," Bonelli repeated. "That was exceedingly good and quick work on your part."

"The keys had been left in it," the inspector said, passing the keys to the priest.

"That's excellent. Thank you both so much."

"Not at all, Father." Retberg's broad face registered satisfaction.

"Just doing our job," said Sergeant Green.

"I thank you and congratulate you," the priest said, as he gave another courteous bow, "but have you any idea who stole it?"

"Not yet," said Green. "But I assure you that we will get him, and when we do we'll make sure he goes down for a long time."

"Goes down?" said Bonelli, feigning complete surprise. "What, for stealing a car? It's returned now, so provided it's not damaged, I'd rather just forget the whole thing."

Retberg also looked surprised, except that his emotion was genuine.

"That's very forgiving of you, Father," he said. "But the guy who stole your car used it to kidnap a young girl. And you know this particular young lady."

"No," said Bonelli, looking amazed. "The poor girl. Who was she?"

"Maria Christopher. The girl we saw with her friend about six weeks ago. I trust she still lives here and is currently in your care. She was taken from outside St Mark's Hospital."

"Unbelievable."

"And this man also shot two men."

"You're kidding me."

"Then he made off with the young girl, abandoned your car, then stole another one, we believe to confuse us."

"You don't say."

"And from there," Ian Green joined in, "he drove off at high speed, fired his gun at another car, and caused an explosion along the way."

"How could he do that?" Bonelli asked, acting superbly at being shocked and confused.

"We have witnesses who say he threw something at a passing vehicle," Retberg said solemnly. "And we now believe that that object was a grenade."

"My God, I don't believe it." Bonelli put his hand on his chest and leaned on the wall.

"As for poor Maria who was kidnapped," said Green, "we're still trying to discover her whereabouts, but it's our guess that this mad kidnapper will contact her family, or he might even call you to demand a ransom."

"Talking about me?"

From behind Father Bonelli came Maria's voice. The priest looked round, and the two policemen stared at her in disbelief.

"Miss Christopher?" Inspector Retberg said in amazement.

"Yes," she said, "but you see…"

"And I take it that you still live here?"

Retberg then pulled a puzzled expression at the priest.

"Why didn't you say that she had now returned?" he said. "You could have saved us a lot of time and trouble."

"I'm sorry, officers," said Father Bonelli. "I feel so confused. Everything's been happening so quickly, but you see her whereabouts is supposed to be a secret for security reasons. As you realise now, people are trying to kidnap her, and there have been threats to kill her."

Maria and the priest stood looking at each other.

Then she said, "Sorry, Father. I haven't told you all the details about what happened. I didn't want to worry you."

"Okay, but what on Earth...?"

"As you know I went for my scan today," she said, "I came out of the hospital and was attacked by four masked men. One had a gun, another had a knife and threatened to cut my throat."

"Oh, my dear child!" Bonelli went to the girl and hugged her.

The two police officers stared at one another in astonishment.

"But then," Maria continued with her story, "this other man arrived, shot two of the masked men, then took me away to safety. Along the way he explained that he believed in me and wanted to protect me."

"Did you say anything at all to him?" asked Ian Green.

"Yes," she said. "I told him that he had secured a place for himself in Heaven."

Sergeant Green looked upwards. Retberg removed his flat cap, gave his head a good rub, then replaced the cap.

"What then?" he asked, almost as if he didn't want to know any more.

"Well, he seemed really pleased," Maria said. "We stopped at a petrol station, and he let me go. I hitched a lift and he disappeared. I didn't see him again."

After the two bewildered police officers had gone, Father Bonelli and Maria went back to Anna's room, where both Anna and Debbie were still sitting, having heard everything that was said in the hallway.

Debbie was grinning.

"Who's the best actor?" she giggled. "Father goody-goody Bonelli or Maria?"

Maria laughed too and sat down next to Debbie.

But Bonelli was deadly serious.

"We have got to leave soon," he told them. "We are now all in extreme danger."

"Let's start planning then," suggested Anna.

Then even Debbie became serious.

"Listen," she said. "I have to admit that, at first, I thought this was all a complete load of bollocks, but I'm really starting to believe in it now."

She put her arm round Maria and kissed her on the cheek.

Then a very thoughtful look came over Father Bonelli's face, and to everyone's surprise he addressed Debbie in a very official sort of tone.

"Miss Shallis," he said. "I need to speak with you alone."

Anna and the two young girls all looked at each other in surprise.

"If you need to speak with me, Father," Debbie said, "I don't mind if my friends hear what it is you have to say."

Maria returned the hug and kiss to Debbie, and Anna gave the priest a happy smile.

But Bonelli remained serious.

"That's okay by me," he said, "but I need to talk to you about contact with your family, then if you want to tell Maria and Anna about it afterwards, that'll be up to you."

After a pause Debbie looked up at the ceiling.

"Oh, all right," she laughed.

Father Bonelli went to the door.

After a warm hug with Maria and Anna, Debbie followed him out.

Out in the hallway, the priest turned to the young girl.

"Let's go across the road," he said.

Wondering what this was all about, she followed him across the road and into his house. They went through the hallway and into the living room where he gestured to her to sit down. He sat down opposite her next to his old bureau.

"What do you want to tell me about my family?" Debbie asked. "I haven't spoken to them for nearly four months."

Bonelli looked at her seriously.

"What I have to tell you is nothing to do with your family," he said, "but I do need to talk to you privately."

She looked at him, confused.

"If you remember our discussion a few weeks ago," he continued, "I told you that you were very important to our plans... our mission... and there's a secret that you must keep."

"But you swore on the Holy Bible that no harm would come to me or my baby."

"Our Blessed Lord himself will ensure your safe return," the priest said joining his hands as if in prayer. "And I have been trying to identify somebody for a very special purpose."

"What's that got to do with me?" For a moment, Debbie felt that the priest's eyes seemed to penetrate her.

"Sometimes you can look too hard," Bonelli told her, "and you don't see what's right in front of you."

Debbie just looked at the old priest, sensing that he was about to tell her, or show her, something phenomenal.

"I am about to show you something," he said, "but first you must promise me that you will keep this secret."

"Okay," Debbie said quietly.

"You must not tell anyone."

"All right. What is it?"

"Not even Maria."

She just looked at him wondering what this could possibly be about, and feeling a bit scared now too.

The priest then reached for the drawer of the old bureau. She remembered he kept the army revolver in the bottom drawer.

"You've shown me the gun already," she reminded him.

Bonelli looked at her as, this time, he opened the middle drawer.

"What I am going to show you," he said, "is infinitely more powerful than a gun."

And he drew out the leather pouch that his brother Lucci

had given him. He handed it to Debbie. She took it in both hands and lay it across her knees.

"Untie the lace," he told her. "Open it."

She did as she was told, untying the lace bows so gently, as though expecting it to explode in her face if she wasn't careful. Then she pulled the pouch open and looked inside.

She saw that there were three wedge-shaped, metal objects, gnarled and twisted with age. She took one of them out, held it in her hand and looked at it. It was a horrible, heavy thing, and about six inches in length.

"They're horrid," she said. "What are they?"

The old priest then took something else from the top drawer of the bureau, an envelope that he placed on the coffee table in front of the bewildered girl.

"That's a letter from my brother Lucci," he told her. "Keep it close to you. It has his contact details in it. Now, if anything happens to me…"

"I don't understand what you're trying to say," said Debbie, still holding the nasty-looking metal object in her hand. "And what are these horrible things?"

"If anything happens to me," Bonelli continued, "Lucci will tell you what to do with them."

"Okay, *but what are they?*" The young girl's voice was raised in alarm now.

The priest looked at her, hesitating just one last time, before finally making the decision that she was the right person for the task.

"Nails," he said quietly.

"Nails?" Debbie said in bewilderment. "Just nails."

"What you have there are over two thousand years old," Bonelli continued, now in a low, confidential monotone. "They possess the power to defeat the most destructive evil that can be set upon us, *if* they are used correctly, and in a series of actions to be carried out in a precise sequence."

"But…"

"Those were the nails, the very same ones, that were used in the crucifixion."

Debbie looked at him in shock, a gasp of terror escaping from her lips as she nearly dropped the nail from her hand.

Giuseppe made sure the information had properly sunk in by reiterating categorically, "The three actual nails used to nail Jesus to the cross. One through each of his hands, the other one through his two feet, with one placed over the other."

*

For now, Bonelli decided to put the nails back into the middle drawer, while Debbie continued to sit there in wonder, disbelief and finally, horror.

Then he sat opposite her and told her all he knew about the nails, and ultimately about their power.

His brother learned that the nails, because they had been coated in the Blood of Jesus, were believed to possess the power to pass goodness, wisdom and holiness to those who touched them.

By the same token, though, that very same power would have the opposite effect on unholy people, and so the power could be directed to defeat evil.

Since discovering Maria, Bonelli began to remember more things that the Angel told him. The Italian priest had always known that there was an element of doubt over the authenticity of the nails because there were so many such articles around the world that had been claimed to be the genuine ones. But he had very good reason to believe that the nails he had were the real deal. The Angel actually confirmed this to him. The Messenger from God had referred to these as *the* Holy Nails and said that once the demon, who would initially appear as a young boy, had been identified, Bonelli would need to look for an opportunity where he would ambush him. With all his strength, and with the use of a mallet, he would attempt to drive one of the nails right through the evil one's head. The second one would go through his heart, and the third one directly above his genitals, thus defeating utter Evil with absolute Goodness.

Lucci warned him, however, that if the demon had the chance to turn into his most hideous, gigantic form, Giuseppe would not be able to get close enough to drive a nail though his head with a mallet.

"But not to worry," he had said. "I know of a way it can be done."

Giuseppe was intrigued to know, but so far had no idea what Lucciano was planning.

CHAPTER THIRTY-SEVEN

As Inspector Paul Retberg and Sergeant Ian Green drove back to the police station, they were both lost in their own private thoughts. The puzzlement on their faces steadily increased and they glanced at each other, increasingly more often, until eventually Retberg, who was driving, broke the silence.

"Do you know," he said, "I can't help thinking there's something funny about that little lot."

"Just thinking the same thing," Green agreed.

"And I get the definite impression that both the priest and the girl were hiding something from us," Retberg observed. "They both knew more than they were letting on."

"They were lying."

Retberg looked at his partner and compressed his lips, but then nodded in agreement that Green's rather blunt way of putting it was correct.

"When we get back to the nick," Retberg said, "I want to do a bit of digging."

"Where do we start, though?"

Retberg thought for a moment as he stopped at traffic lights.

"I want to do a search on Giuseppe Bonelli," he said. "See if he's got some kind of mysterious past."

"He's a priest," Green laughed. "What do you expect? Find out he's an ex-con?"

"Well, no," Retberg admitted as the traffic began to move again. "But there's got to be something."

They continued on their way to the police station. When

they arrived there, they entered the building, went straight to the lift, then up to the second floor, to *Police Records*.

On entering the department Chief Inspector Morris was sitting at a desk, scrolling through a record on a computer screen. He looked up at them momentarily.

"Hi, guys," he said.

"Good evening, sir," said Retberg. "We've just been to return the stolen car to the priest."

"Bonelli?"

"That's right," said Retberg. "The funny thing is, he didn't want to take any action."

The C.I. nodded and shrugged his shoulders, concentrating on the information displayed on the computer screen.

"Another thing," said Sergeant Green. "Usually when we return a stolen vehicle, the owner will immediately want to go out and look at it to make sure it's all right."

"That's true," said Retberg, smiling approvingly at the sergeant. "But he didn't, did he? In fact, he seemed hardly interested."

"So what are you saying?" asked C.I. Morris, looking from one to the other, waiting for an answer which he already knew.

"I'm beginning to wonder whether the car actually was stolen," said Retberg.

"Can we find out anything about the old priest, then?" Ian Green asked.

The chief inspector abruptly stood up and looked at them.

"Ex-army," he said. "Firearms and explosives expert."

Retberg gazed in amazement.

"How the bloody hell did you know that off the top of your head?" he said.

C.I. Morris laughed.

"You guys are not the only ones who have been trying to dig up the past on the old duffer," he said. "Most recently, the chief super."

"Sutton?"

"Precisely."

"But the description of the old man outside the hospital doesn't match," Green said.

The C.I. looked at the sergeant with a faint smile, reached up to a shelf just behind him and took from there a videotape. He pushed it into the VCR and switched on the TV screen.

"Take a closer look," he said.

The three officers stood there, looking at the screen displaying a recording from the TV news. They saw Maria Christopher coming out of the hospital. Four masked men appeared, and two of them pushed forward and grabbed her. One waved a gun around, while the other had a knife that he held to the girl's throat.

Then the old man moved forward and very quickly drew out a gun.

There was a struggle between the girl and the man with the knife.

Then the old man aimed his gun and fired.

He spun round, aimed again, and fired again.

"Two men killed instantly," said C.I. Morris.

"Each shot right between the eyes," Sergeant Green said with a grimace. "Ouch!"

Retberg nodded in agreement.

"Two accurate shots in quick succession," he said. "The guy has to be an expert. A crack shot."

"Exactly," said the chief inspector. "And now watch..."

He rewound the tape to the point just before the first shot was fired. And there he pressed the *pause* key. Then he pressed *zoom in* on the freeze frame.

Retberg and Green stared at the screen.

"My God," said Green. "It is him, isn't it?"

"Bonelli," said Retberg. "Yes, it's him, all right."

"And the gun has been identified," said the C.I. "An army issue."

"Well, that settles it," said Green. "We'll go back there right now, arrest him and bring him in for questioning."

To Retberg and Green's surprise, though, Chief Inspector Morris stood in front of them, blocking their path to the door.

"No," he said firmly.

"But..."

"Listen, guys," said the senior officer, holding up his hands. "I've got a meeting with the chief super tomorrow morning to decide on our way forward."

"I don't get it," said Retberg. "Why can't we just go and get the priest?"

C.I. Morris drew a deep breath.

"Because," he said, "we are not interested in Bonelli." Then he hesitated before continuing, "Well, we are, but not in arresting him."

Both Retberg and Green looked at him in amazement.

"Think about it, guys," he said. "The priest has announced publicly that he is there to protect the girl who claims that she is going to give birth to the Son of God."

"Yes, but..."

"And along the way, he shoots a couple of Satanists, basically two terrorists."

"But what about the other shooting?" said Retberg, "and the explosion?"

The C.I. held up his hands again.

"The chief super has made it perfectly clear," he said. "*Do not arrest Father Bonelli.*"

"What do we do then?" asked Sergeant Green.

"You may go back to see the priest," Morris told them, "but only to ask him if he would be so good as to help us with our inquiries."

Retberg heaved his chest impatiently.

"What for if we can't arrest him?" he said.

"What the chief super wants is to get the terrorists," said Morris, "and he believes that the priest can lead us to them…"

"How?"

"… and he's specifically selected you two guys as the suitable go-betweens."

Ian Green took that as a compliment and grinned back cheerfully. He thought of all the crap jobs he would get out of doing, to be replaced by a relatively cushy one.

But Retberg did not look so sure, and after glancing at Green he looked back at the chief inspector, his eyes narrowed with suspicion.

"Let's have this clear," he said. "You want us to chase after a bunch of Satanists?"

"Actually, to be more accurate," Morris concluded, "he wants the head of their organisation."

Inspector Paul Retberg drew a deep breath.

"That's going to be very dangerous," he said. "And I bet he's a right sadistic bastard too."

At that point, neither Inspector Retberg or Sergeant Green knew exactly how much of a sadistic bastard he would turn out to be.

CHAPTER THIRTY-EIGHT

The next morning immediately after parade-on, the two police officers sat down in their report room to complete the necessary paperwork prior to revisiting Father Bonelli.

Inspector Paul Retberg and Segeant Ian Green were both firearm-trained, so considering the distinct probability that they would be facing armed terrorists some time soon, it was agreed that, until further notice, they were to be issued with firearms each day. Before returning to the priest's house they needed to complete the RIF forms (Request for Issue of Firearm) which, once completed, would need to be signed by their chief inspector.

C.I. Morris was expecting them to drop by his office and so promptly signed the forms. Then Retberg and Green booked out a car and set off to headquarters where the Firearms Unit was based.

Another chief inspector was in charge of the firearms stores. He spent some considerable time inspecting the forms, and as a formality was required to contact C.I. Morris by telephone.

"Hi, Bob," he said when Morris answered. "Firearms here. I've got two of your crew here."

"Yes, that's right, Jim," Morris answered. "Retberg and Green. Two excellent chaps, and the chief super is aware of this oppo. In fact, it was the great man himself who selected these boys."

"That's good enough for me," said the firearms C.I. "And did you see any of the cricket yesterday? That's right... a great start... 192 for 3 at the close of the first day's play. Okay?

Tootle pip, old scout."

Replacing the telephone receiver, he looked at Retberg and Green across the bench, then disappeared through a doorway.

When he returned a few minutes later his arms seemed to be full of things.

First, the two 6-shot pistols were placed down carefully on the bench, then a box containing ammunition. Also there were two shoulder straps. Attached to these were holsters, and a strap with small pockets for placing spare ammunition, for twelve rounds in all.

The two officers were given records to date and sign.

Then the C.I. counted out twenty-four rounds of ammunition and gave Retberg and Green twelve each.

"Okay, kids," he said finally. "Have fun."

*

But as it turned out, Retberg and Green's visit to Father Bonelli was delayed. As they were travelling in that direction, and just negotiating themselves through the busy town, an urgent shout came over the radio.

"All available units, all available units," came the anxious voice. "Go immediately to Harkleys High Street Bank. The raid alarm in going off."

"Shit." Retberg who was driving looked at Green. "Just our rotten luck."

Ian Green reached for the radio receiver from the car's dash.

"Unit Five-Three-Two," he said. "We're one minute away. Over."

"Thank you, Five-Three-Two, although we may need armed officers. Over."

"Just so happens we are armed today," Green said, smiling and nodding at Retberg. "Over."

"Thanks, then. Anyone else? Over."

Retberg switched on the car's siren and put his foot down.

There was a lot of further crackling on the radio, then more urgent shouts.

"A member of the public has called in to confirm it is an armed robbery. I repeat, an armed attack on the bank is in progress."

On reflection, Retberg switched off the siren.

Neither Retberg nor Green had foreseen such an early opportunity to use their firearms. As the car pulled up in front of the bank, Green loaded his pistol and before getting out of the car, Retberg did the same.

"Right, then," said Retberg, remembering his training from ten years earlier, and therefore confident he knew what to do in this kind of situation. "Follow me. Stay behind me, though."

Retberg got out of the car, waving his gun in the air.

"Okay, but..." It was too late for Green to make any suggestions concerning strategy.

There was a crowd of people outside the bank looking in. They were all screaming but quietened down abruptly when they saw two police officers turning up brandishing guns.

Retberg got to the entrance of the bank and looked in. He could see just one masked man aiming a sawn-off shotgun at a terrified cashier. She was so scared that she just screamed and screamed, and the man with the shotgun was having to shout his demands at her. With that and the loud alarm bell going off he could hardly hear himself think.

Then Inspector Paul Retberg made his mistake.

He dashed in through the door, then stopped and aimed his gun at the back of the bank raider.

"I am an armed police officer," he shouted. "Drop the gun, then turn round slowly. If you do not drop the gun, then I warn you I will shoot. And then..."

A sharp, painful crack across the back of Retberg's head cut him off.

When he had dashed through the door he had failed to observe another man, also with a sawn-off shotgun, standing to one side of the entrance, and therefore hidden from outside.

The crack on the head was from the butt-end of the shotgun being brought down viciously upon him.

Retberg fell on his back, unconscious, but only for a few seconds.

When he opened his eyes he found himself looking up into the twin-barrels of the weapon.

And the masked man behind it snarled aggressively, "Let's see what this pig looks like with his head blown off." His finger tightened on the trigger.

Retberg tried to get up, squeezing his eyes shut.

Bang!

Retberg opened his eyes just in time to see the masked man with a neat hole in the middle of his forehead. The next moment the bank raider was falling backwards, dead before hitting the floor.

Looking round, Retberg saw Ian Green still pointing his smoking gun, as if expecting the masked man to come back to life, but there was little chance of that. The bullet, from such close range, had gone right through his brain, exploding out of the back of his skull.

"You should give a warning before shooting," Retberg told him.

Then the other masked man spun round and aimed his sawn-off at Ian Green.

Bang!

The second bank robber also fell, dying painlessly before he had time to scream, and he, too, had a neat hole in the centre of his forehead. A fountain of blood from the back of head splattered all over the hysterical cashier.

Retberg then stooped down to retrieve his firearm that he had dropped and replaced it in its shoulder holster, out of sight, under his jacket.

Then they picked up the fallen shotguns, and on searching the dead men's jacket pockets they found a box of cartridges. Retberg told Ian Green to put them in the boot of the car. They would have to remember to hand them in at the nick later.

More police officers arrived, and the bank raiders' corpses were routinely removed. Retberg could not help noticing the grotesque tattoos on the bank robbers' forearms. Ugly entwined reptile creatures, the same as the thugs at Claud Tyler's apartment block had.

A young beat constable turned up and approached the blood-splattered cashier, asking her if she was ready now to make a statement. In response, she just produced a series of incoherent babbling sounds.

Ian Green went out to the car and carefully placed the shotguns into the boot together with the box of cartridges. Retberg arrived behind him.

"Just remember in future," he said, "before firing your gun you must issue a warning, something along the lines of *I am an armed police officer and if you do not drop your gun, I will shoot.* Okay?"

"Yes, okay," Ian Green said, rolling his eyes skyward.

They got back into the car and continued on their journey to visit Father Giuseppe Bonelli.

CHAPTER THIRTY-NINE

Tiredness, for once, was beginning to take its toll on Father Giuseppe Bonelli, and despite his supreme fitness for a seventy-year-old man, he was looking forward to a good sleep.

The girls had gone back to their rooms, and now Anna, seeing the weary expression on the priest's face, had made an excuse to go to the bathroom. This gave him the opportunity to tell her that he'd had enough for one day and would return to his own house for some well-deserved relaxation.

At last, back in his own lounge, he released a massive sigh and pushed himself back into his reclining armchair. Almost immediately he began to doze, despite worries he had at the back of his mind about the forthcoming journey that he felt sure would be fraught with perils. Ultimately they would be facing the Satanists who had made it quite clear that they would stop at nothing to kill Maria and her unborn baby, invoking the most dangerous of demons if need be to do so.

He prayed for God's help and for his guidance. After all, it was God's Child that this was all for. He remembered very clearly the Angel's instructions. He would need to be prepared to sacrifice his own life if necessary.

He began to drift off, and then…

A vivid dream of driving his car at high speed. The girls sitting on the back seat, terrified. Anna next to him on the passenger seat, leaning over, judging his speed on the speedometer. Another car chasing them.

He threw a grenade.

Bang!

Then another grenade.

Bang!

And then...

Bang! Bang!

He woke with a start.

Bang! Bang! Bang!

He was fully awake now, but still confused.

Bang! Bang! Bang! Bang! Bang!

Somebody was knocking at his front door, and the knocks were getting progressively louder. Whoever it was knocking, evidently didn't believe in the possibility that he was out, or asleep.

He jumped out of the recliner, dashed out into the hallway and opened the door.

And there were two familiar faces, that of Inspector Paul Retberg and Sergeant Ian Green.

"More news?" he asked.

Retberg looked at him. "May we come in?" he said.

Father Bonelli sensed that this was going to be a lengthy interview and that he'd have to leave his nap until later.

He heaved a big breath. "Sure," he said, standing to one side. "Do come in."

The police officers went in. Bonelli closed the door gently, then led them into his lounge, gesturing for them to take seats.

All seated, Bonelli said, "So, have you found out more about who stole my car?"

Retberg and Green looked at each other and Bonelli noticed the smiles that were exchanged between them.

Retberg then looked at the priest, still with a faint smile on his face.

"Father Bonelli," he said. "We know that your car was not stolen."

"Not stolen?" Bonelli said with a look of innocence. "But..."

"If you were not a priest," Retberg continued, "I'd be arresting you now for wasting police time."

"I see."

"And," Sergeant Green put in, "we would at least want to question you about the shooting of two men at the hospital, then later shooting another man in a car, causing an explosion on a public highway..."

"Not to mention the theft of one Vauxhall Cavalier," said Retberg, "and disposing of the same in the woods only one mile away from here."

Father Bonelli leaned back in his chair and released a low chuckle.

"Seems you boys have been doing some investigations," he said. "Very good. I'm impressed."

Retberg and Green sat opposite the priest, allowing a moment for him to comment further of his own accord.

But all Bonelli said was, "So? What now?"

Retberg's smile slowly faded.

"Father Bonelli," he said. "Please stop wasting our time. Suppose you tell us everything."

"Then what?" said Bonelli, slightly confused now, not yet understanding what the police officers wanted.

"If you level with us," said Ian Green, "then we'll level with you."

Inspector Retberg looked at his colleague and nodded for him to continue.

"As soon as we realised that it was you at the hospital," Sergeant Green went on, "firing an obsolete army-issue revolver..." He paused.

Father Bonelli smiled. "I *am* impressed," he repeated.

"... as soon as we knew," Green continued, "we wanted to come over here and arrest you."

Bonelli looked worried.

"But," Retberg rejoined, "our chief inspector said he

didn't want us to arrest you."

For a moment Bonelli looked even more worried. He thought there must be a catch somewhere.

Ian Green raised a hand with his forefinger extended. "Not because he's a sentimental old fool . . ."

Bonelli smiled at the sergeant. "I guessed," he said, "but thank you anyway, officers."

"Provided you cooperate with us," said Retberg, "stop wasting our time, and tell us everything you know about these terrorists."

"Terrorists?" Bonelli looked unsure for a moment, but then he understood. "Oh, yes," he continued. "Terrorists."

And so then Father Giuseppe Bonelli told Retberg and Green every detail he could remember, from the point that Maria Christopher had been identified as the Chosen One, to the incident at the netball match where Rod Spencer was murdered.

This now made more sense to Retberg and Green who already knew about Rod Spencer and his partner in crime Claud Tyler who was now also dead.

The priest talked about the death threats that Maria had received, and the incident at the hospital that the two police officers also already knew about.

"These people," he concluded, "will stop at nothing to hunt the girl down and kill her."

"Kill her?" said Ian Green. "I don't get it. Why are they so afraid of a young girl? She's just a kid."

The old priest pondered for a moment, wondering whether to tell the officers about the entire religious significance of the situation. Whereas most Christian people would rejoice at the birth of God's Second Son who would lead the way through the final days before rising up into Heaven, there are other people who worship The Devil. These people lived in fear of the girl, so much so that they would want to kill her before the child was born.

On reflection, just for now, he decided on a slightly watered-down version.

"There are people who feel that she is a blasphemer," he said, "lying about being visited by an Angel in an attempt to cover up for an illicit sexual relationship, for which she deserves to be punished."

But now the sergeant looked even more baffled and shook his head. "Seems a bit drastic, though," he said, "threatening to kill her and her baby."

Father Bonelli just looked at him and shrugged his shoulders.

After a brief pause, Retberg said, "Father Bonelli, do you honestly believe that this girl is actually going to give birth to the Son of God?"

The priest looked into the faces of the two down-to-earth police officers, and again wondered how much he should tell them.

"Inspector," he said. "To you it shouldn't matter what I personally believe. Your concerns are purely with the facts, and those are that this girl has been placed in my care and there are people who are trying to kill her."

"Yes, but look here…"

At the moment there was an interruption. Another knock on the door.

"Excuse me for one moment." Father Bonelli got to his feet and walked out of the room. He marched up the hallway and opened the door.

What he saw standing there initially gave him a fright and he stood back in alarm, but the figure raised his hand in a calming gesture, and a muffled voice was heard.

"Please do not be alarmed. I mean you no harm."

The reason for the initial trepidation was that the large figure standing in front of him had a hood made of black cloth over his head. There was a slit cut in it, through which the priest could see just a single blood-shot eye.

Why? Father Bonelli did not yet know.

"I'm looking for Father Giuseppe Bonelli," came the muffled voice.

"I'm Father Bonelli, but who are you? Why are you concealing your identity?"

"That is what I am here to explain," said the perplexing figure, seemingly of a man. "And to impart important information to you if you allow me to come in."

Father Bonelli hesitated for a moment, but then he remembered there were two sturdy police officers in his house who would quickly resolve matters if need be.

He stood to one side and gestured for the man to enter.

"Thank you." The man entered.

The priest closed the door then led him into the lounge where Retberg and Green were still sitting.

When the door to the room opened, the inspector and sergeant looked round, then stood up in shock when they saw the large figure in a long greatcoat and, bizarrely, with a black cloth hood pressed down over his head.

"These are police officers," Bonelli said to the hooded man. "Anything you want to say to me may be said in front of them."

"I'm glad they're here," said the unidentified person. "It saves me from having to call them."

Retberg and Green looked at each other with puzzled faces. Then Retberg took a step forward.

"Who are you?" he said. "Take that hood off."

The figure moved back by one step, held up a hand and spoke loudly, although his voice was still somewhat muffled.

"I'm also glad you're here because I have a confession to make," he said.

"First do as the inspector tells you," said Ian Green. "Take that hood off."

"Yes I will. But please let me explain first."

"Okay, get on with it then," said Retberg, believing at that moment that they were dealing with some kind of lunatic.

"I was the one known as Tuan," the man told them, his voice quiet now.

Bonelli stared at him intently.

"That means The Master," he said. "Or Our Lord."

The man in his hood nodded. "It's Latin."

"I know my Latin, thank you," the priest said. "But actually, it's Malay."

"I am known by other names."

Ian Green leaned over to Retberg. "Probably escaped from somewhere," he whispered.

But the man went on regardless.

"I confess," he said, turning to the priest again, and bowing, "I was the one who orchestrated the attacks on you and the girl."

"You?" Father Bonelli looked confused. "So why come to me now?"

"Because of this…"

The huge figure raised up his arms, then took the bag between his hands and began to lift it off. He did this very slowly, gradually revealing the horror that lay beneath.

Father Bonelli, Paul Retberg and Ian Green watched in wide-eyed fascination, which turned to bewilderment, and then to revulsion. They reeled from the shock of what they saw,

More than half of the man's face was gone where it had been torn off. The flesh of his cheek on one side was completely absent, leaving bare bone, with his jaw and teeth on that side exposed, and the eye gone leaving an empty and shattered socket.

"Jesus H Christ," Ian Green gasped. "What the fuck happened to you?"

The man managed to speak with breaths of air escaping grotesquely out of his bare cheek.

"This is my punishment for failure," he said.

"But who actually did it?" said Retberg. "It looks like it was done by some wild animal."

"It was a messenger," said the man who called himself Tuan. "Sent from one of Satan's demons. First it appeared as a boy, then turned into a large, black, sabre-toothed cat, like a panther."

Father Bonelli's eyes narrowed as he went deep into thought.

Paul Retberg tutted and puffed impatiently, and looked at Ian Green. They were both anxious to return to the facts, and not waste time with some lunatic who talked about messengers from Hell.

But the man was not done yet.

"And I'm here today to warn you about the followers of The Devil," he continued. "They are now planning to intensify their search. They will find the girl and they will torture her and kill her."

Father Bonelli raised his hand. "But…"

"Unless," the man added, "you really do possess some kind of divine protection."

Retberg could now feel his teeth grinding together with impatience.

"The girl is carrying God's Son," Bonelli snapped suddenly. "Of course He will protect Him."

Tuan just stood there. Ian Green looked away, unable to look at that grotesquely stripped face any longer. Retberg did not want to arrest this 'Tuan' character, only because he didn't want to bring a creature like that into a respectable police station. They had all sorts of human life down there in custody, but never before a low-down, repulsive slug like this.

Father Bonelli moved forward for a closer inspection of

the savaged face.

"This boy," the priest said quietly, "and the large cat. Describe to me exactly what happened."

The man known as Tuan described in graphic detail how he was paralysed and rendered helpless as he lay on the floor in his huge hall, suffering the agony of having half his face torn off.

"It wasn't a messenger," Bonelli barely whispered, as though absentmindedly muttering to himself. "It was Bael himself. Oh, my good God. He's with us already."

The man's one bloodshot eye stared at the priest. "What? What?"

Retberg looked at Ian Green again.

"Is everyone in this town completely insane?" he said.

But the sergeant didn't reply. Instead he looked uncertain. Having heard everything that had been said so far, he did not know what to believe anymore.

CHAPTER FORTY

On their way back to the police station, the inspector and sergeant said very little to each other. They were each wrapped up in their own private thoughts and opinions, perhaps realising that those opinions were now very different.

Inspector Paul Retberg was an excellent policeman. He was very practical and down to earth, and he liked to follow procedure, where at all possible, to the letter of the law. Therefore he did not want to hear about devils and demons, or ghouls and goblins, and messengers from Hell.

Sergeant Ian Green was also excellent at his work but realised that sometimes a copper had to be flexible. He would fill in his reports and write notes in his pocket notebook using what most policemen would call their best friend – common sense.

He could sense now that even if there were no such things as The Devil, and demons from Hell, there was a very real danger brewing up. Men and women who did believe in The Devil, and were worshippers of the Dark Lord, at the very least had to be considered dangerously insane.

Before they had left Father Bonelli's house, there was one last issue, and a dilemma. What to do with Mr Tuan, or whatever his real name was. The man himself had said he would commit suicide, saying that he would be hunted down and killed anyway when it was discovered he had been to confess to the priest, and he asked Bonelli if he would consider giving him the last rites, like he performed with Rod Spencer.

But Bonelli told him that suicide was a grave sin and could

not be used as an escape route. Therefore, the last rites would not be allowed.

But beneath a tough exterior, the old priest had a soft heart and he took pity. Even though this man had ordered the killing of Maria and himself, he had confessed to his sins and did appear to be full of remorse. Seeing his destroyed face, Bonelli himself could not help feeling some compassion.

He went across the room to a cabinet and took two things out of a drawer.

A crucifix and a bottle that he explained contained holy water.

With these he went to stand in front of the man. Then speaking in Latin he appeared to perform some sort of sacrament, very similar to the last rites, and he pressed the crucifix and the holy water into the man's hands.

"Keep these with you at all times," he said.

The man nodded.

The priest suddenly spoke loudly. "Do you denounce the works of The Devil?"

"Yes," was the firm and prompt, reply.

Father Giuseppe Bonelli made the sign of the cross.

"There, now," he explained. "I've put the matter into God's hands."

"I don't understand." The man turned to Retberg and Green as though expecting them to help explain, but all they did was to turn away with looks on their faces like they were about to vomit.

"If you really are genuinely sorry for your sins, then God will protect you," the priest told him. "But if you're lying..." Bonelli held up his hand in a warning gesture, "if you're lying then The Devil can do with you what he will."

*

When Retberg and Green stopped off at HQ to return their firearms, Ian Green had to complete an additional form because he had actually fired the gun. There were about twenty questions on it.

One of the questions was: *Did you issue fair warning that you were armed and would shoot?*

Ian Green nervously pointed this question out to Paul Retberg. The inspector reminded him that he, himself, had already issued a warning, so the sharp-shooting sergeant could answer truthfully that the warning had been given.

The questionnaire then asked if any other officer, more senior if possible, could confirm this.

Ian Green wrote Retberg's name and rank, and Inspector Paul Retberg signed it.

So that sorted that out, but when they eventually arrived back at the nick, Retberg who had been driving all day glanced round at Green, and the sergeant could see the tiredness in the inspector's eyes. Before knocking off, though, they had one last piece of routine to complete.

Retberg pulled the car up in the car park behind the station.

"We'll just sign the car back in," he said, "then I'll be off. I'm knackered."

"Leave that to me, Paul," said Ian. "I'll sign it in. You go. I'll see you tomorrow."

Retberg looked at him. "Okay, cheers mate. And…"

He paused for a moment, then said, "… and I forgot to say, thanks for saving my life. I very nearly had my head blown off today."

"I had an ulterior motive for that," Green said seriously. "Things around here wouldn't be nearly as funny without you."

Retberg just managed to smile. "Thanks a lot," he said. "See you tomorrow."

With that he got out of the car and walked off. Ian Green

watched him walk across the car park, get into his own car, and drive off, giving a brief hoot on the horn as he did so. Then the sergeant took a note of the mileage, wrote it down on the vehicle's record, then got out of the car and made his way through the back entrance of the station.

It was as he walked along the corridor towards the report room that he realised how tired he felt. It had been a long, eventful day and he was looking forward to getting home.

He handed the car keys and the mileage record to Inspector Hammond who was responsible for the vehicles. He was sitting in the report room. He carelessly glanced at the document, but then suddenly sat up.

"Bloody hell, Ian," he said. "Where have you been? Off to the seaside for the day?"

Ian Green laughed, then explained to Hammond all that they had done that day. He concluded with, "And now Paul's gone home. Really knackered."

"Oh, yes, and I hear you shot two armed bank robbers," said Hammond. "Two shots in quick succession, right between the eyes. Bloody good shooting."

"Thank you, sir."

"So good, in fact, that the firearms squad have taken notice. They're always looking for a good man who's a bit tasty with a shooter."

"Thank you, sir," Green said again, "but I don't know. I joined the police force to help people, not to kill them."

"Pity." Hammond pulled a disappointed expression, then after a hefty breath, he said, "Oh, well, so you're off now?"

"Yes," said Green with his usual cheery smile. "But back tomorrow for some more fun and laughs."

Sergeant Ian Green left the police station through the back entrance, then in the car park stopped suddenly. He looked up at the sky and smacked himself on the forehead. He just realised he had forgotten something.

In the boot of the police car were the sawn-off shotguns and box of cartridges. He would need to go back into the nick, get the keys back that he had just handed in, then collect the weapons. After that he would be tied up for ages with the time-consuming rigmarole of submitting the wretched things.

Or, alternatively...

He looked around him, then with the coast clear he dashed over to the police car and tried the boot catch.

With great relief he looked up at the sky again. "Thank you, God," he said.

He had not locked the car. With a click the boot lid sprung open and there inside were the shotguns and cartridges.

Looking around him again he gathered them up, then dashed across the car park and transferred them into the boot of his own car.

He decided that he would hand them in the next day.

After returning to the police car just to shut the boot, he then set off home in his own car.

When, at long, long last he got home, he was greeted by his pretty wife, Bella. She gave him a warm hug, a moist kiss, and asked the usual questions.

"Nice day at work?"

"It was okay," he said with a faint smile, knowing that there would be more questions.

"Anything exciting happen?"

"Not really," he told her. "Just the usual routine stuff."

She leaned back and studied his face seriously.

"You always say that," she said. "Surely something completely out of the blue must have happened?"

He returned her serious look.

"Okay, if you must know," he said, "we stopped a bank raid and I shot two bank robbers right between the eyes. Then we went to visit a priest who staged the theft of his own car. He warned us of the activities of terrorists, although he believes they are Satanists, but our interview with him was interrupted by a man whose face was torn off by an evil demon who appeared as a vicious monster from Hell."

Bella looked at her husband with a slightly hurt expression.

"Oh, and I forget to mention," he added, "Paul and I have been given the task of protecting the mother of God's Second Son."

"Ha, ha, very funny," she said. "I won't bother asking any questions in future."

CHAPTER FORTY-ONE

Now it was mid-July, just two weeks before the break-up for the schools' summer holidays. Maria's bump was showing quite obviously now, and she was needing to wear loose-fitting garments so as not to attract too much attention, either at school or on her journey thereto.

But she loved her school, and most people there, so it was with reluctance, and great sadness, that she felt forced into the decision to leave. When she would be able to return, if ever, she did not know.

There were some of her personal belongings that she needed to collect from her locker but she deliberately arrived on the premises during class time, rather than on any break period to avoid seeing her friends. Such goodbyes, she decided, would be altogether too painful. She got herself a good-sized carrier bag for herself to collect her personal property.

Also she decided to arrive in disguise. She'd had enough just recently of being followed by religious fanatics, and the novelty of being interviewed by news reporters had long since started to wear off. As for Antichrist yobs trying to kill her, the thrill of that had also begun to wane.

So she tied her long, dark hair up into a bun, donned a short, curly, blonde wig, and applied plenty of make-up including bright, red lipstick. She also wore a pair of plain glasses, an old denim jacket she found in a cupboard at JackDaw House, and to complete the part of someone with really poor dress-sense, a bright pink midi-length skirt with floral patterns. All of this gave her a totally different appearance. Nobody could possibly recognise her. When she looked in the mirror, she didn't even recognise herself.

When she arrived outside the school there was a woman waiting, evidently a reporter, who was stopping people to ask questions. She wanted to find out if rumours of the girl's disappearance were true.

In her disguise, Maria scooted past her, hoping to avoid any questioning but...

"Excuse me for a moment, please," the woman called out.

Maria stopped and looked round at her.

"Could you tell me," the woman went on, ignoring the girl's impatient expression, "do you know the whereabouts of the girl, Maria, reported to be the future mother of God's Son?"

Maria's ventriloquism skills had been coming into regular use recently, and now, in a high-pitched, posh voice, and with a peculiar accent, she said, "The perthon you wequire ith no longah at thith thchool."

"Do you know her?" the woman wanted to know next.

"Not perthonally, no." Maria began to walk away toward the school entrance.

"But do you know where she's gone?"

"No," Maria said sharply. "Now pleath pith off."

Maria hurried on her way, but when she was almost out of hearing the woman reporter, having to shout now, gave it one more try. "And what do you think of these stories that she is, in fact, the Chosen One?"

Before going through the doors of the school entrance, Maria turned back towards the reporter, and shouted back, "Ith a load of complete bollockth."

Once at the school entrance she decided that, first, she would need to call in on Mrs Roland, the headmistress. She arrived outside the office and knocked on the door.

On being called in, she entered and quietly closed the door

behind her.

"Who? What?" At first Mrs Roland did not recognise Maria in her wild disguise.

"Mrs Roland," Maria said as she undid her denim jacket. "It's me. Maria Christopher."

The headmistress's face instantly relaxed.

"Ah, my dear child," she gasped. "We feared we'd never see you again."

Maria smiled and bowed her head respectfully.

"Sorry about the disguise," she said.

"Oh, no, I completely understand," said Mrs Roland. "But how are you?"

"I'm okay, thank you, but…" She paused there. She'd had to make a lot of decisions already, but this, by far, was the most difficult one, leaving the school she loved, and all her friends.

"Yes, my dear?" The headmistress sensed that the girl, so young, was struggling with the kind of decision that most adults would have trouble with.

And the genuine and sincere look of concern on the woman's face finally brought a cry of anguish from Maria's mouth. The loud sob seemed to come from deep inside her. She tried to speak but found that she couldn't.

Mrs Roland got up from her seat, went to the girl who she personally liked very much, and put her arms around her.

"It's all right," she said, patting her on the back. "It's okay to let it all out."

And for the first time in a long time, Maria cried loud and long. Everything that had happened over the past four months finally came flooding back in one big rush. It all seemed to hit her in one go.

From the point of first telling her story to her parents, and then to her friends, to this present moment with her headmistress.

There was the bust-up with her parents, meeting Father

Bonelli, and Debbie and Anna.

Then there were the numerous news reports. Some people seemed to love her, but others hated her and wanted to kill her.

But despite all of this she continued to go to school. And it was this that seemed to earn her more support. Regardless of whether they believed her or not, people were marvelling at how a girl so young, and with such a responsibility, could just continue with her life as normal. They were asking, "How could such a young girl who had received death threats, be so brave?"

There must be some kind of divine protection.

Not only that, she seemed to be able to rise above all that danger to a higher level. Over two thousand people packed into the school grounds, and millions on TV, had watched in disbelief as she played in that incredible netball match, helping her school win the County Championship.

But perhaps the most astonishing thing of all, to herself at any rate, was that she had unexpectedly made the extra friend of the bossy prefect Geraldine Knox.

After a good, long cry, Maria made an effort to pull herself together. She shook herself. Mrs Roland went to her table, got a few tissues and handed them to her.

In between her remaining little sobs, drying her eyes and blowing her nose, Maria was able to speak again.

"I'm leaving," she said. "I'm afraid I've got to go."

"Are you sure, my dear?" said Mrs Roland. "If only there was another way."

"I'm afraid not, Miss." Maria heaved a huge sigh. "Father Bonelli is taking us away to a secret location until after the baby is born."

"And then?"

Maria thought for a while and shook her head.

"I don't know," she said. "I really don't know. Possibly I'll be able to return, perhaps next year," she laughed. "I'll be a sixth-former, maybe a prefect."

"You will always be welcome back, Maria," Mrs Roland told her with a tear in her own eye. "And you will make a wonderful prefect."

"Thank you, and..."

"What about your parents?" Mrs Roland asked suddenly. "You must see them before you go."

"Yes, I know," said Maria. "I plan to visit them later this afternoon."

Another long moment passed. Mrs Roland was holding Maria's hands in both of hers.

"Oh, well, I'm off now," Maria said at last, holding up her carrier bag. "I'll just clear out my locker."

Then Mrs Roland looked at Maria with an expression of surprise.

"But my dear," she said, "I cannot believe you would leave without saying goodbye to your friends."

"But Miss, I..."

"I know who your very best friends are." Mrs Roland picked up the phone and quickly issued instructions for Diana, Julie and Becky to go to the headmistress's office immediately.

*

Fifteen minutes later, in a somewhat fraught mood, the girl with a heavy heart made her way along the corridor towards the fifth-form lockers. She was kind of grateful for Mrs Roland's motives, and her sincerity, but Maria had arrived at the school deliberately during class time so that she would not have to endure that totally painful experience. On reflection, though, by the time she got away from the school, she would have regretted it if she had not said goodbye to her friends, especially her three best pals.

They had all ended up sobbing and hugging her, and

begging her not to go.

She, in turn, was crying again, and trying to explain, between sobs, why she did have to go. They then all agreed to keep in touch. Diana, Julie and Becky made her promise that she would be back.

Even as she made that promise, however, she was not sure if she would be able to keep it.

She arrived at her locker, got out her key, and opened the locker door. Then she hooked the strap of her bag to the inside of the locker door, ready to put her things into.

And then...

"Hey, you!"

She nearly jumped out of her skin and spun round.

And standing there was the burly figure of Geraldine Knox.

"Gerry," Maria gasped. "Hi..."

"Nice wig," the sixth-form prefect remarked dryly. "It suits you."

Maria put her hands on her head. "Oh, thanks," she said.

"So you're leaving, then," Geraldine said in a rather flat tone.

"News travels fast," Maria said, blushing with embarrassment, knowing what the netball captain was thinking.

"I just saw your three friends," Geraldine continued. "Diana and Co. all sobbing their hearts out. I was going to ask them what they were doing out of class, but..."

"Oh, God." Maria looked up at the ceiling. She was finding this unbearable.

"Leaving," Geraldine repeated, clearly upset. "Without saying goodbye to me, or anything?"

"I was going to come looking for you," Maria lied. "Honest, Gerry, I was going to."

"Lying little bitch."

"I was!" Maria looked at Geraldine Knox and was amazed

to see that she, too, was crying, although the tough sixth-form prefect was trying to fight back the tears.

And Maria made a sudden rush to her. "Come here, you."

The two girls hugged one another for a long moment, swaying slightly as they did so. Then Geraldine's voice came between muffled sobs.

"I'll never forget you," she said.

"I won't forget you either." Maria found herself bawling her eyes out for the third time that afternoon. "You are one brilliant team captain."

Geraldine shrugged.

"We wouldn't have won the County Championship without you," she said.

Maria laughed. "'Course you would have," she said. "I just got in a couple of lucky shots."

Still in Maria's embrace, Geraldine leaned backwards and looked at her.

"It was a whole lot more than that," she said, "and you know it."

Maria shrugged nonchalantly, then she said, "Hopefully we can keep it going now, and there are some good kids in the fourth year. One or two of them could be worth a look-in next year."

Geraldine nodded, gave Maria one more firm hug, then stepped backwards, while wiping her eyes.

"Well, anyway," she said. "I'll be leaving, too, probably next year."

Maria looked at her, surprised. "Where are you off too, then?" she said. "I thought you were a fixture here."

Geraldine Knox laughed.

"Well, I am, really," she said. "I'll be starting my teacher's training, then I will be coming back here as a teaching assistant"

"Excellent!" Maria nodded and smiled admiringly.

"And then," Geraldine concluded with a proud smile,

"when I've completed my practical, and passed my exams, I'm going to apply for the position here as a full-time games teacher."

Maria looked at the prefect with a big smile.

"Gerry," she said, "I couldn't think of a better person to carry that responsibility for this school."

"Thanks." The sturdy sixth-former looked away for a moment, then with a note of finality, she added, "Now, you look after yourself, do you hear me, you cheeky little cow?"

"You, too," Maria laughed. "You bossy bitch."

Geraldine became serious.

"Take a hundred lines," she said, *"I must not call the house captain a bossy bitch."*

They both laughed, then for the last time the two girls hugged, both breathing hefty sighs.

"Okay, keep in touch, now." Then Geraldine turned, and began to walk away.

Maria watched her go, but when she was a little way up the corridor, the prefect stopped and turned round.

"And, hey, Maria," she called out, "When the baby's born, bring him in to show us. Okay?"

Maria waved. "Sure thing," she said. "And that's a promise," but even as she spoke those words she realised that that was another promise that she wasn't sure she could keep.

She continued to watch the sixth-form girl go up the corridor and through the next door. Then Geraldine Knox was gone.

Maria Christopher turned back to her locker, leaned forward, and momentarily rested her forehead against the edge of the shelf, and closed her eyes.

Ten minutes later she was leaving the school building for the last time. She was halfway across the quadrangle when she paused for a moment and looked back.

At that moment she could hardly accept that this really

was goodbye, and that it was unlikely that she would see this school, or any of her school friends, ever again.

*

Quite late that afternoon, Maria decided there was still one thing that she felt duty-bound to do before going away, something she dreaded doing even more than saying goodbye to her school friends, and that was, what would probably turn out to be, a final farewell to her parents.

She had already mentioned this intention to Father Bonelli, and Anna and Debbie. The priest had offered to accompany her. She thanked him but told him that this was something she had to do on her own.

As far as she could remember, there were not many of her own personal things left at the house, but she decided to bring her carrier bag just in case.

She still had her own front door key in her purse, but when she arrived at the house she knocked on the door. And she waited.

After a minute or so she knocked again. Still no answer.

She took out her key and let herself in. She stepped into the hallway, closed the door quietly behind her, then began to look around. As she did so she could hardly believe that she had been away from the house for almost four months.

Anyway, it was obvious that nobody was in and, in one way, she felt relieved at that.

Looking around the living room, dining room and kitchen, she smiled to herself, but her initial feeling of relief was mingled with sadness and regret.

She went out into the hallway again and, very quietly and slowly, made her way up the stairs.

Then she went striding across the landing and into her bedroom, pushing the door wide open as she did so, but what she saw there made her cry out in shock.

Sprawled across the bed (her bed) with the blankets pulled up to just his midriff, was a young man of about twenty. And as she stood there gazing at him he suddenly woke and sat up. And after rubbing his eyes clear of sleep he spoke in an irritated voice, and an indignant tone. But it was the words he spoke that gave Maria a further shock.

"Hey, you. Who are you? And what are you doing in *my* room?"

She simply couldn't speak. The mixture of shock and anger was overwhelming.

But she quickly pulled herself together. Any words she might have said would have been utterly superfluous. She turned back to the landing and made her way to the stairs.

It was when she was halfway down the stairs that the young man bounded out of bed, out onto the landing, and leaned over the banisters.

"Oh, I know you, don't I?" he called out. "I've seen your photo. So what do you know about that? The prodigal daughter returns."

She paused for a moment, contemplating briefly explaining to this half-wit what the word *prodigal* actually meant, but again saw very little point in speaking. She continued on her way down the stairs.

"Hey, don't get at me," he continued. "I'm just a temporary lodger."

Before she opened the front door of the house, she took out her key once more.

The young man called out one last time. "Do you want me to pass a message to your mother?"

Maria looked up at him and found her voice at last.

"Yes," she said, holding up the door key. "Tell her to take this and shove it up her arse."

She then placed the key on the little table inside the front door, and left the house for the last time, closing the door behind her with a decisive slam.

CHAPTER FORTY-TWO

At last it was the beginning of December, and time for Father Giuseppe Bonelli to keep his promise and take Maria away to a safe hiding place, leading up to the birth of her baby.

Anna Gabriella, Bonelli's close ally and invaluable assistant with her midwifery skills, would be travelling with them.

Father Bonelli had given Debbie Shallis instructions on her role, should circumstances demand it, and she had been invited by Giuseppe's brother Lucci to visit him where he would give her more details and, most intriguingly, *training*.

So with Debbie temporarily out of the picture, the plan was that the three of them would travel to Great Yarmouth and book a room in a guest house there for two weeks. It was pre-booked before setting off so Debbie would know where to find them. After joining up with them they would all travel north along the east coast together until they came to the remote seaside village of Bathlum. No pre-booking had been made for that because they didn't know exactly when they'd arrive there. Also in the middle of winter they did not foresee any difficulties with vacancies.

They remained mindful of the fact that Debbie's baby was due at the middle of the month, whereas Maria's child, God's Second Son, was due later. The exact date given was the twenty-fifth, although Debbie kept reminding them all that either baby could be born anytime between two weeks early, to two weeks late.

Father Bonelli and Anna, however, were convinced that Maria's son would be born on that exact date. They also believed that it would be during the very early hours of the morning. They planned to bring plenty of extra blankets, fleeces and towels with them, just in case there weren't enough of them at the guest house.

For their added protection and peace of mind, their new-found friends and allies, Police Inspector Paul Retberg and Sergeant Ian Green, would be meeting up with them. Those police officers were still under strict orders from their chief superintendent to provide protection for Maria and her entourage, while attempting to track down, and capture if possible, the leader of the terrorist gang who had been attempting to kill the young mother-to-be and her unborn baby.

Bonelli had decided that, when the time was right, he would advise Retberg and Green of the full threat that they all faced.

These people were not just terrorists. They were Satanists. Individually they were not much of a worry to the priest who had a trick or two up his own sleeve, but together they posed a deathly threat. The ability to raise a demon from the depths of Hell was terrifying enough, and beyond any imagination, but he was now sure that the demon was none other than Bael, the most evil of them all, and second in evil strength and power only to The Devil himself. The priest knew that, given the chance, the demon would not hesitate to kill Maria and the unborn infant, and would do it in the most hideous and cruel manner possible.

Lucci had been risking his life, spying on the Satanists, trying to discover their plans for their next attack. If discovered by the evil ones, though, he also would be subject to the most terrible and sadistic torture before being killed slowly.

Lucciano Bonelli was every bit as religious as his brother, and although not a priest, he prayed harder than he had ever done before. One of God's most impressive powers was the ability to be in more than one place at the same time, and Lucci prayed dearly for that power.

Because right then he needed it.

*

Using travel instructions, the public transport guide and a map, Debbie Shallis eventually found her way to the home of Lucciano Bonelli, but when the man she sought opened the front door of his house she stood back in amazement.

He was so like his brother that at first she thought it was the priest.

"Lucciano?" she said.

He smiled at her, understanding why she looked confused.

"Please call me Lucci," he said. "And you are Debbie? I've been expecting you."

"You and Father Bonelli are so alike," she said.

"We have been mistaken for twins," he told her. "But I am the big brother. Two years older."

He reached out and briefly held her hand while she stood there looking at him.

And he looked at her, being reminded as he did so that she was heavily pregnant. He felt guilty now that her journey had been necessary.

"Everything okay, I trust?" he said, pointing at her bump.

She laughed. "Strong as an ox," she said.

Then he let her into his house and led her through to the kitchen.

It was midday by that time and he realised that she'd had a long journey so he offered her various choices of food and drink.

"I'm sorry I took so long to answer the door," he said. "I was out the back. I've got something that's very important for me to show you."

"Okay," she said, biting into a Scotch egg.

"So when you're feeling refreshed and ready…"

He then suggested other facilities that she might need, pointing out directions.

Then he said, "… I'll be in the shed out the back."

With that, he slipped out of the door from the kitchen.

It was after her thirst had been quenched with some ice-cool shandy that she began to feel curious, and she ventured out into the large garden. She could see a shed and, from that direction, came a strange buzzing sound, and through the windows of the shed there were intermittent flashes of light.

More curious than ever, she went to the shed but as soon as she opened the door the noise and the flashing light stopped. Lucci had seen her entering and had instantly stopped what he was doing. She saw he was wearing dark goggles.

He passed her another pair of the same kind of goggles.

"Put those on," he told her.

"What are you doing?" she asked, having never seen this kind of equipment before.

"Just a spot of welding."

"Okay, but…"

"Just give me a moment."

Debbie put on the goggles and watched in fascination.

In a vice there was what looked like a thick arrow. In one hand, Lucci held something that looked like a fire poker with a cable coming out of one end, and brilliant white-hot, glowing metal at the other, hence the need of the protective goggles. In the other hand he held a long pair of grips.

But it was what was held in the grips that fascinated Debbie the most.

A six-inch long, wedge-shaped nail, very similar to the three gnarled and twisted, ancient objects that Father Bonelli had shown her.

The very same nails that were used to crucify Jesus Christ more than two thousand years ago.

"My God," she said. "Another one."

With the tip of the welding iron glowing with intense heat, Lucci placed something else against the arrow and it, too, began to glow. Debbie thought it looked like the metal was melting, but then Lucci took up the grips again, placed the arrow and nail together and touched the point where they joined with the welding iron.

Then he stopped work and switched off the equipment. He took off his goggles and signalled to her that it was safe now for her to remove hers too.

"You see, it's an experiment," he told her. "We know what we've got to do, but we're not sure yet on how to deliver it."

"But I don't understand," said Debbie. "Father Bonelli showed me the three nails."

"Yes, that's right," said Lucci, holding up his hand and extending his forefinger "They are the genuine ones, but the ones I have here are fakes that I found. Still useful for this purpose, though."

"What purpose?"

"To experiment before the battle begins."

"Battle?" said Debbie. "What battle?"

"The final battle," Lucci explained. "The battle against pure, unadulterated evil."

Debbie just looked at him, confused and unable to think of a suitable reply.

"You see," Lucci continued, "it's only now, more than two thousand years later, that we fully understand why Jesus had to be crucified. It could only be his blood, shed in that way, that eventually would defeat evil."

"But his blood?" said Debbie. "Preserved? How could it be? For over two thousand years?"

"It has been preserved," Lucci said emphatically. "And in addition to that, what Catholics believe, and what others have scoffed at, is actually true."

"What?"

"About the bread and the wine being turned into the Body and the Blood. This means His Body and Blood can still be resurrected."

Debbie shook her head in confusion "I don't get you," she said.

"Forget the modern, wishy-washy, watered-down crap that's dished out these days," Lucci said with a note of impatience. Passion brewed up in his voice as he continued, "Words of the modern Church don't mean a damned thing. We bow to so-called modern thinking, merging with manufactured religions, afraid of hurting people's feelings."

"Not your brother," Debbie interrupted. "Father Bonelli is a good priest."

"Yes he is," Lucci smiled. "He keeps to the original wordings of each part of the True Mass, not like the modern Catholics who have allowed it to change beyond recognition. But I'm afraid he's one of a dying breed."

"Oh, yes," said Debbie. "I remember my father used to refer to the *true* Catholic faith."

"Exactly." Lucci clicked his fingers in the air. "Again I refer to the bread and the wine..."

"Symbolising the Body and the Blood..."

"NO," Lucci said firmly. "During the true Latin Catholic Mass, if the sacrament is delivered correctly, it actually *is* the Body and the Blood."

Debbie just looked at him, wanting to believe it, but not quite able to.

"The three main beliefs which sets the Catholic faith apart from all others," Lucci said as he began to count them off on his fingers, "are the Body and the Blood, the Resurrection, but first and foremost, the Virgin Birth. You believe in that, don't you?"

"Sure I do," Debbie said enthusiastically. "Maria's my best friend. She really is going to give birth to the Son of God."

Lucci looked at her for a moment, hesitating, as if struggling to decide on what to say next, or how to say it.

"God's Second Child *is* going to be born," he said at last. "No doubt about that, but..."

Debbie squinted at him, her forehead wrinkled.

"Is there something else I should be aware of?" she said.

Lucci continued to study her face thoughtfully, but then shook his head and continued to talk as if she had not spoken.

"And all of this," he said, "has been deliberately arranged and planned for over two thousand years. God's Second Child being born will strike fear into the hearts of all evil people, and even The Devil himself. That is why they are trying to kill Maria and her baby."

"Because the baby is God's child," Debbie mumbled to herself.

"They believe that it is," was Lucci's somewhat vague answer.

The priest's elder brother and the girl looked at each other in silence for a moment, then Debbie's thoughts returned to the nails.

"So Jesus' blood had been preserved, then?" she said. "The blood he shed at the crucifixion. And the bloodstains on those ancient nails..."

Lucci nodded slowly. "Preserved right up until the final hours."

"Final hours?" Debbie murmured the words to herself.

"Unless..."

Debbie looked at Lucci, anticipating his next words.

Lucci just nodded again, seeing her beginning to understand. "You..."

"Why me, though?"

Lucci picked up an arrow from his worktop, similar to the

one that was still in the vice. He handed it to her.

"An arrow?" she said.

"A kind of arrow," he said. "To be fired from a specially modified weapon."

"Can't you just shoot it from a bow?"

Lucci laughed, then picked up another contraption, this time from beneath the worktop.

"Actually, from one of these," he told her.

Debbie took it from him. It was heavy and actually looked more like a snub-nosed shotgun, but had a bow fixed across its barrel.

"A crossbow," said Lucci.

Then Debbie looked at the bolt in the vice. "They are quite light," she said. "But the nails are relatively heavy."

Lucci smiled and nodded in appreciation. He was beginning to like this girl, and to trust her. She was bright, together with all the other issues that Giuseppe had mentioned.

"That is a carefully modified crossbow," he told her. "Alterations done quite cleverly, even though I say it myself."

Debbie laughed. "Just tell me how to use the bloody thing."

Lucci suddenly became serious again.

"It will fire at an increased velocity despite the added weight," he explained. "It's also one hundred per cent accurate up to a hundred metres."

"I still don't know what I'll actually be shooting at," Debbie said.

Lucci looked at her for one long moment, then he said, "Come with me."

He walked out of the shed. She followed him, still holding the crossbow, and as he led her along a footpath to the centre of a spacious piece of land, she could see what looked like a large bucket, and they were walking towards it.

They stopped at the bucket and she could see now that it was full of the pointed objects. Arrows, or bolts, welded to other wedge-shaped pointed objects.

"Here's a few I did earlier," he smiled.

She raised her eyebrows and nodded admiringly.

"Curiouser and curiouser," she grinned back.

He picked up one of the specially prepared arrows, then took the crossbow from her and showed her how to load it.

"Now, look over there," he told her, pointing.

She looked in that direction and could see at some distance a large target mounted on a stand that looked like a big, wooden easel.

"That's a long way off," she said.

"I've measured it," he told her. "From here to the target is precisely one hundred metres."

"Wow," she said.

Lucci took aim with the crossbow and fired.

Crack! And a second later a *Thud* was heard as the arrow hit the outer rim of the target.

"Wow," Debbie said again, clapping her hands. "Good shot."

Lucci looked at her and gave her a wry smile.

"Not good enough, though," he said. "*You* will have to do a lot better."

"Me?" said Debbie. "I couldn't hit that target at all from this distance."

"Well, you've got to," Lucci told her. "You've got to hit the bull's eye."

"But..."

Lucci re-loaded the crossbow, then passed it to her.

"Your turn," he said.

She looked at him with a puzzled half-frown, half-smile, but the smile faded completely when she saw that he was being serious.

She took the crossbow and held it up. It was quite a heavy contraption for a young girl to hold up with her outstretched right arm, even though she could steady it with her left hand.

"Line up the sights," Lucci told her, pointing at where to look. "Then line them up together against a point a few centimetres above the bull's eye."

"Above?"

"Yes, to allow for some dip at this range."

"Oh, yes, I understand."

She did exactly as she was told, then fired.

Crack! Thud!

Lucci looked at her shot, shielding his eyes from the bright sky with his hand.

"Bloody hell, Debbie," he said.

"Beginners' luck?" She turned towards him and gave a nervous laugh.

Her shot was a fraction below the bull's eye.

He then gave her another arrow and let her load it herself. She did that easily, then she took aim and fired again.

Crack! Thud!

This time she had over-compensated for the trajectory over such a distance, and her shot ended up several centimetres above the bull's eye.

Still Lucci nodded approvingly and watched her as she took another arrow, loaded it and fired.

There was a delay after every six shots or so, as Lucci walked to the target, removed the arrows, and walked back again.

It was on Debbie's thirteenth shot that she hit the bull's eye, bang in the centre.

Lucci Bonelli stood back and applauded.

Debbie turned to him and smiled. "Satisfied?" she asked.

"No." He became serious again. "I want you to hit the bull's eye three times."

"Oh, come on…"

"Three times," he insisted. "On the trot."

It was on her twenty-second shot that she achieved this.

She then turned to Lucci, holding the crossbow to her chest with her arms hugging it as if it now belonged to her.

"So," she said, "you didn't invite me all this way to teach me how to fire arrows at a wooden target, did you?"

Lucci drew a deep breath.

"No, I didn't," he said. "And it's about time I told you what your real target is going to be."

"My real target?"

"Yes." Lucci nodded gravely. "And you've got to hit this target three times."

"But what...?"

"It's imperative that you hit it accurately," he continued, "but to be exact, once, but in three different places. Let me explain."

Debbie looked at him, again with her curious half-smile.

Lucci spent the next two minutes explaining to Debbie Shallis exactly the nature of her mission, during which time the expression on her face gradually changed into a look of utter horror.

When he had finished, she looked at him, her face having turned pale.

"You make it sound like my life depends on it," she said.

She felt even more frightened when she saw the look that came over his face just then. An almost desperate look.

"Your life," he said. "And about five billion others."

Debbie looked up at the sky. "No pressure, then," she said.

CHAPTER FORTY-THREE

It was now the middle of December. They knew by then that the Satanists were on their track, and Bonelli also knew that evil groups could be lurking anywhere. There were people connected to Satanism in virtually every environment and every organisation. Hospitals, schools, the armed forces... anywhere. A person could be having a conversation with a Satanist at a railway station, a bus stop, or supermarket.

Therefore, any ideas that Maria might have had of giving birth to the Son of God in hospital instead of enlisting the experience of Anna Gabriella, was forgotten.

After all, Anna was an experienced midwife and, probably with Bonelli's help, she would be quite capable of delivering both babies, even if they arrived at the same time.

And so it came to be that on the 15th December, reunited with Debbie, the four of them set off, heading north along the east coast. Debbie's baby was due any moment now. Both Father Bonelli and Anna glanced repeatedly and anxiously at her developing condition and regretted not making this last leg of their journey a few days sooner. Sitting next to her on the back seat of the car, Maria put her arm around her, attempting to comfort her, realising that in just a few days she would also be puffing and blowing, with the birth of her own child by then being imminent. The two girls had become close friends and had decided to be each other's babies' godmother.

They had pondered together over who should be the godfather. Of course, the obvious choice was Father Bonelli, but the priest himself had turned down this offer. He said he'd prefer the choice to be a layperson. A man in a position of trust by all means – perhaps a policeman. The reason he gave was the fear of being accused of biased views. But another professional person who held a position of trust, and had a completely open mind, would be ideal.

*

"What absolute and complete, utter bollocks!" Police Inspector Paul Retberg said, looking at Sergeant Ian Green, exasperated.

Once again driving towards their HQ to extend their firearms issues, they had already changed into plain clothes in readiness for their drive to the north-east coast. Along the way, with their visit to see Father Bonelli still fresh in their minds, they were discussing the possibility that Maria Christopher really was going to give birth to God's Second Son.

"Okay, okay," said Ian Green, holding up his hands in submission, "but whether it's bollocks or not, the fact remains that kidnapping and murder are serious crimes."

"I know." Retberg shook his head. "And so are attempted kidnap and attempted murder. I was there at training school, too, you know."

"Right then," said Green. "So let us forget whether Maria Christopher is really the Chosen One, or not, and concentrate on our jobs."

"Ok, I suppose you're right," Retberg said. "We'll just look after them, and protect them, and along the way bring those morons to justice, as per the wishes of our chief super."

"If that's the way you want to look at it," Green said with a hefty sigh, "then I guess I can live with it."

At HQ, having been issued again with their firearms, they were surprised to be summonsed to a meeting room. On entering they saw there were several men and women sitting around a long table. The police officers quietly closed the door behind them.

At the head of the table, in full tunic, was seated the majestic form of Arthur D'Arcy, the deputy chief constable. The other people sitting around the table were in various forms of dress. Two of them looked like pilots, whereas some others looked like paramedics.

D'Arcy gestured for the inspector and sergeant to take seats. There was then some shuffling of feet under the table, of seats' positions being adjusted, and chair-legs scraping on the floor.

"Ladies and gentlemen," D'Arcy began. "An extremely serious matter has been brought to my attention, and that's acts of terrorism. An undercover operation has revealed a plan of attack."

"Yes, sir," Retberg interjected. "If I might say, though…"

"And as I was about to say," D'Arcy talked over Retberg, "in connection with the girl who has repeatedly claimed to the media that she is going to give birth to God's Child, there have been death threats sent by Satanists to her family home."

"I am sorry to interrupt, sir," said Retberg, "but death threats have also been sent by Christians, although they have denied it. One of these threatened to nail the girl to a tree."

"If I may be allowed to continue?"

"And as for Satanists, this is not the Dark Ages where people are scared of ghosts, ghouls and goblins."

"Inspector Retberg." D'Arcy raised his voice but avoided actually shouting. "Do not misunderstand me. Of course there's no such thing as demons and The Devil, but these people who call themselves Satanists are still extremely dangerous and must not be underestimated. Therefore, they must be apprehended. Our undercover man has reliably informed us that they plan an attack…"

"Yes, but…"

"… and they plan to invoke a demon whose main agenda

is destruction and mayhem."

"But I thought you said..."

"Of course there aren't any demons." Again D'Arcy managed to avoid shouting, but he was clearly irritated with Retberg's repeated interruptions. "But..."

"Myself and Sergeant Green have been issued with firearms," Retberg said, "and we will not hesitate to use them if necessary."

Ian Green nervously stifled a cough into his fist. He had not yet told Retberg that the shotguns obtained from the attempted bank robbery four months earlier were now in the boot of their car. Up until the previous day they had been in the bottom of a wardrobe in his house. He had simply forgotten to hand them in as instructed, but strangely nobody has asked about them so clearly they had been overlooked.

The deputy chief constable smiled for the first time, albeit faintly. He then gestured to the other men and women sitting around the table.

"Once we have more details of this planned attack, then these officers will be at your disposal," he told Retberg. "Their helicopters will be armed with machine guns."

"Machine guns?" Ian Green spoke for the first time. "It sounds like we're declaring war."

"It is every bit like that," D'Arcy nodded. "Whether true or false, when this girl Maria Christopher started claiming that she had been visited by an Angel, I doubt if she realised what effect this would have."

"What do you mean by that?" Green asked.

The deputy chief regarded the sergeant with a patient smile.

"Some people love her and want to worship her," he explained, "whereas others seem to hate her and want to kill her."

"We've met her, ourselves," Ian Green ventured. "To me

she seems quite sound mentally."

Deputy Chief Constable D'Arcy pulled a face as he considered this for a moment. Then he gestured to the officers around the table once again, and continued, "As I say, when we know the date of this planned attack, these officers of our Helicopter Division will be stationed within a mile of the site." He then looked at Retberg and Green, and added, "They will then await your instructions."

"And who will be advising us of this date?" asked Ian Green.

"I think I mentioned our undercover man," said D'Arcy, rubbing his chin.

Paul Retberg's eyes narrowed. "And who might that be?" he asked.

The deputy chief leaned forward slightly in his chair, and spoke discreetly, as if fearing that someone might be listening just outside the door.

"This is of the utmost secrecy," he said, looking at each officer seated around the table in turn. "You mustn't breathe a word of this to anyone outside this room, lest his cover gets blown."

Everyone nodded solemnly.

At last, the deputy chief said, "Our undercover man is... Lucciano Bonelli."

Retberg and Green looked at each other in astonishment.

Deputy Chief D'Arcy read their thoughts.

"That's right," he said. "The priest's brother."

CHAPTER FORTY-FOUR

It was late on a cold winter's afternoon when Father Bonelli, Anna and the two girls arrived in the remote village of Bathlum, which was situated about two miles inland off the north-east coast, but they could still feel the freezing wind blowing in from the sea. It was a good piece of aforethought and organisation on Father Bonelli's part that he had filled the boot of the car with items such as extra blankets and fleeces.

Anna Gabriella was well prepared too, bringing with her a cylinder containing the painkilling gas, Entonox, an equal-measure mixture of oxygen and nitrous oxide. She had also managed to acquire all the necessary pipes and face masks to go with it... (a piece of equipment she had stolen without prickling her conscience too much. It was, after all, for the good of God's Son, so she was sure that the theft would be overlooked on her day of reckoning.)

... and boxes of the strongest painkillers she could find (also stolen) in tablet and liquid form, dozens of syringes, and several packs of the smallest size nappies.

So all the practicalities had been taken care of, but then they hit a snag that they had not foreseen.

Where to stay. Unexpectedly for the winter season, there did not appear to be any rooms available in any of the guest houses.

They knocked on the door of every guest house in the whole village, and on each occasion the proprietor seemed to observe the group with suspicion.

And the housekeepers beheld an elderly man, a middle-aged woman and two young girls who were clearly in their mid-teens and, equally obviously, both heavily pregnant. Doors could be heard slamming shut, up and down each street.

"No," a slim, dark-haired man said abruptly. "We've got no rooms vacant."

Slam! went the door.

Then at another place: "We're fully booked up until the new year," said a common-looking woman with a painted face and ridiculously pencilled eyebrows.

It was the same story wherever they went.

Then Father Bonelli saw a sign hanging on a wall outside a brightly coloured building.

"This could be okay," he said in an attempt to sound encouraging.

The sign read, in large, bold print, *Rooms now available. Apply within.*

Bonelli knocked, and when the tall man answered the door, the priest gestured to the sign. "We'd like to stay for a few days if we may, my good man."

But just like the others, the man took one searching look at them.

"There's no rooms vacant," he said.

"But the sign..." Bonelli began to protest.

"It should have been taken down. We're sorry." The door was banged shut.

By now, the girls were starting to get tired, as well as shivering with the bitter cold. The priest supported Maria by putting his arm round her, and Gabriella did the same for Debbie.

Once again, the thought occurred to both Bonelli and Anna about taking the girls into hospital, but they were mindful of the need to keep Maria's whereabouts a secret until after the baby was born. As for Debbie, sceptical though she had been at the beginning, she was now with them wholeheartedly and was determined to stick with them – and the plan – right up until the end.

Then they began to pray out loud for God's help.

They were just about to give up hope, now considering going home, when the proprietor of one guest house seemed to take pity on them.

Having already refused them, he went trotting up the road after them.

"We haven't got any spare rooms," he said at first, "but there is an outhouse, out the back and across the field."

"That is very kind of you," Bonelli said, "but we will require warmth and the means to boil water."

"I'll get one of my men to set up an old oil heater for you," he said. "And we've got a camping gas unit we can lend you, too."

"What about light?" asked Anna.

The man looked at the middle-aged woman, clearly intrigued by her, but then he relaxed, guessing correctly that she must be a midwife, or at least a nurse.

"I think there are a couple of oil lanterns in there," he said. "I'll get my man to check those for you as well and get them lit."

"What about a toilet?" asked the practical-minded Debbie, still puffing and blowing, so close to her delivery.

The guest house proprietor looked at her.

"We'll get something rigged up for you," he said.

Father Bonelli looked round at the ladies.

"It's the best offer we've had," he said quietly. "It's that, or we go home and have news reporters chasing us, and getting more threats."

"Let's get on with it, then," said Maria.

The proprietor was leaning over and straining his ears to hear this muttering conversation. There was something familiar about the girl who'd just spoken, but he was not yet sure what it was.

"As long as you don't mind," he said, interrupting more hushed conversation, "you'll be sharing the barn with a few animals, but I assure you quite harmless ones. There's a few sheep, two goats called Kane and Abel, and an elderly donkey."

"Elderly donkey?" said Maria, rather intrigued. "How elderly?"

"Nobody knows," said the proprietor. "He was pretty old when we got him, and we've had him for... well, for donkeys' years."

"As long as there isn't anything else," said Debbie.

"Of course not," said the proprietor. "Except, maybe, a few field mice."

"Terrific," said Debbie. "I just love the little darlings."

*

Anna Gabriella and the two girls arrived at the outhouse in the back of an old Bedford van and, despite the rough terrain, Father Bonelli followed in his own car, the Mazda Estate car.

The outhouse looked like a derelict old barn. It was situated under the cover of a dense cluster of trees. When the priest saw it he grimaced at the idea of God's Second Son being born there, but on reflection it was probably no worse than the barn where His first son was born, more than two thousand years earlier.

The driver of the van got out, went round to the rear of the vehicle and pulled out the oil heater which looked like it had seen better days, then carried it to the front of the barn. He produced some keys, opened the barn door, dropped the heater just inside, then went back to the vehicle to fetch the camping gas unit. While he was doing that, the priest and midwife took a look around the place. The two girls looked inside the barn that was currently being illuminated by the headlamps from the van.

The driver brought in the camping gas unit, then while he was checking the lanterns and getting them working, they gazed in wonder at the animals that they would be sharing the accommodation with.

But then Debbie suddenly screamed as she saw something scuttling across the ground. A small animal of some kind, a black shape, startled by the shadowy light from the lanterns.

Debbie turned and threw her arms around Maria as she saw it too.

"Oh, my God," Maria cried out. "A rat."

CHAPTER FORTY-FIVE

On the day that Inspector Paul Retberg and Sergeant Ian Green set off to the north-east coast, they were quite a bit later than they had planned so they had to break the speed limit. They were in plain clothes, and in an unmarked car, so they were risking being stopped by the traffic cops, but they had their warrant cards so hoped that would be enough to see them through if they were pulled in. They had got issued with firearms again, and this time Ian Green was under strict instructions to give a verbal warning before shooting at anyone – or even any*thing*!

Another reason they were in a hurry was that while mindful of needing to keep Maria's location a secret, they had just discovered that her whereabouts had been leaked to the press. The chief editor of *The Daily Venus* had offered a reward of ten thousand pounds for any information leading to the location of the girl, and further amounts for photographs of her and the baby. The editor was then contacted by a proprietor of one of the guest houses in Bathlum. The man claimed he had seen her and another girl, and a middle-aged woman, and an old man. Two reporters were being sent to the location.

Fortunately for Maria Christopher and her entourage, somebody else (one of Father Bonelli's parishioners and a disgruntled ex-employee of the newspaper) called the police.

The two police officers set off in Retberg's car in the early hours that morning, having packed warm coats and extra changes of clothes in the boot, as they believed their stay in the bleak old village could stretch to several days.

Ian Green put all his things in first.

While Retberg wasn't looking, the wily sergeant placed another package in the boot of the car. It was a large case and looked almost like a set of golf clubs. It was quite heavy and wrapped up among large towels, fleeces and covered with bags containing clothes.

And Retberg just carelessly threw all of his things on top of Green's.

Having received this tip-off from Bonelli's parishioner, they arrived in Bathlum at about 10 am, then began to search for the exact address of the B&B that the proprietor had called from.

They eventually found it. They parked just outside and got out of the car.

And there they stood, shivering on a bitterly cold and windy winter's morning, tired and unshaved. Any passers-by would not have believed that those two dishevelled, scruffy gits could possibly be respectable officers of the law.

They went up the pathway towards the door of the place together and briefly glanced at each other as Ian Green knocked twice with a big, heavy, brass knocker.

Then, like in an eerie old horror movie, they heard an echoey *clip-clop, clip-clop*, the tread of heavy shoes, on a bare-tiled floor. And the door opened with a creak.

Two hardened police officers shuddered involuntarily.

And there standing in the open doorway was a tall, thin guy of about sixty, with thinning hair, a bony face, and a deep scar down his left cheek.

"Yes?" he said in a deep, husky voice.

Ian Green shuddered again. Somehow just then he expected a blinding flash of lightening and a deafening clap of thunder.

"Good morning, sir," said Retberg. "We're Retberg and Green from *The Daily Venus*. You called us yesterday."

"Oh, yes. My name's Victor Best," said the bony, old guy. "Where's my ten grand, then?"

"Uh-hum," Retberg coughed. "You will receive your reward when we find the girl we're looking for." He tried to look behind Victor into his hallway. "I think you said she was here."

"Not here, fool," Victor said. "There are two young girls, a woman and an old bloke."

"Where, exactly?" Retberg said sharply. He did not appreciate being called a fool by this old codger.

"Over there, prat." Victor pointed over their shoulders.

Retberg and Green looked round to see, across the road, a gap in the fence, and beyond that was a rough and rather muddy-looking field.

"Across the field, just over the hill," Mr Best explained. "There's the barn almost hidden behind a dense circle of trees. You'll see a car parked outside the barn, a large Mazda Estate car."

The two plain-clothed police officers looked at each other. That would be Bonelli's car, the one he once falsely reported as stolen.

"Right then," Retberg said to Ian Green. "Let's pop over there and take a look."

"So what about my money?" The twisted look of mistrust on Victor Best's face was quite evident and made the scar on his cheek stand out grotesquely.

"If we find the girl we're after," said Ian Green, "then we'll contact our chief editor at *The Daily Venus,* and he will send you a cheque."

"But..."

"Also," Green added, "there's a couple of con men who have been following us around. They will tell you that they are reporters from our paper, but if you tell them anything you won't get a brass farthing from us."

Retberg looked at Green and nodded approvingly.

"Okay, you tossers," said the bony proprietor, "but hear

this. If you welsh on me, then I'll call the cops." He laughed a horrible husky laugh. "That'll stuff you up."

Involuntarily, Ian Green laughed, but immediately stifled it, and changed it into a cough.

With an angry snort, Victor Best slammed the door shut.

"Nice bloke," said Ian Green.

"If he'd had called me a fool, or a prat, or a tosser again I would have decked him," Retberg said gruffly.

"What about a dopey nancy boy?"

"Oh, never mind that daft old sod," said Retberg. "Come on. Let's get going."

The two plain-clothed police officers began on their way, trudging across the muddy field.

*

Father Bonelli, Anna and the two girls were all sitting on their makeshift chair-beds. Anna was boiling some water on the camping gas unit, preparing cups of tea and some buttered buns, and the girls were just chatting quietly.

There came a knock on the rickety old barn door. Bonelli looked at Anna with a worried look on his face.

"You three lie low and stay quiet," he said as he went to the door.

He opened the door ajar. "Yes?" he said quietly, barely louder than a whisper.

Sitting there on a pushbike was a young boy of about twelve.

"Is this where the two girls are?" he asked. "The two pregnant girls?"

"No," Bonelli snapped at him. "Now clear off."

To Bonelli's annoyance the boy did not clear off. Instead, the cheeky youngster laughed.

"Firstly," he said, "it's my dad who owns this barn and the

field, so you can't tell me to clear off."

Giuseppe Bonelli gritted his teeth.

"Your father has let us this barn," he told the boy, "so I'm sure he wouldn't want you to give us any cheek."

The boy raised a hand. "Who's giving cheek?" he said. "Look, I know the two girls are here. "

"Right, I'm going to have a word with your father, you cheeky rascal."

"And the reason I'm calling is to warn you..."

"Warn me?" For a moment Bonelli forgot that he was a priest and started to feel a strong disliking for this boy, together with an inclination to lean forward and give him a slap. "What could you possibly warn me about?"

"Apparently," the boy began again slowly, "a reward has been offered by a daily newspaper for anyone who can give information leading to the discovery of one of the girls."

Father Bonelli sneered at the grinning lad.

"Oh, and you want the reward do you?" he said. "You little shit."

The boy looked genuinely hurt.

"No, man, honest," he said. "But there's a couple of reporters sniffing around. That's what I wanted to tell you."

"Oh, bloody hell," said Father Bonelli. "But how did they know?"

"Yeah, well," the boy continued. "One of the other guest house owners called them and said he's seen you."

"So they could come here soon?" Bonelli looked skyward and held his head in his hands.

"Two newspaper reporters are already here," the boy laughed. "They're on their way, on foot, over the field right now."

"Holy Moses."

The boy shrugged his shoulders.

"Being a good citizen," he said. "Just thought I'd let you

know." With that he swung his bike round.

"Listen, kid," Bonelli said, putting his hand in his pocket. "I'm sorry if I was a bit abrupt before." He pulled his hand out of his pocket to discover a ten-pound note.

He reached out with it to the boy.

"Here," he said. "Take this."

The boy looked at it and smiled.

"No, thanks," he said. "My old man would kill me if he found out I'd taken money off a priest. He's so strict."

Father Bonelli looked at the boy in surprise.

"How did you know I was a priest?" he said.

The boy touched the side of his nose.

"Ways and means," he said.

Then before riding off, the boy said, "Just answer me one thing. That girl, is she really going to give birth to the Son of God?"

Father Giuseppe Bonelli looked at the boy, realising there was no point in lying to him.

"Yes," he said. "She really is."

"Wow, and on the twenty-fifth of December too."

The priest watched the kid as he rode off. Then he slammed the barn door tightly shut and secured the bolts in it. He then turned to the girls.

"Well, you heard all of that," he said. "Boy, have we got problems?"

The two girls looked at each other in alarm.

"What are we going to do now?" Maria asked.

"The reporters will be here any second now," Bonelli told them. "They'll probably knock on the barn door, just like that kid did. I'll go to the door and make out I don't know what they're on about."

"No," Anna said suddenly. "They'll recognise you from photos in newspapers. And they've seen you on television. Remember?"

Bonelli brushed his chin with the back of his hand.

"I looked different then," he said. "I had a beard."

"Even so," said Anna. "I will go to the door when they knock. Don't worry. I'll get rid of them."

Father Bonelli thought about this for a moment, then realised that Anna was right.

He nodded. "Okay," he said. "Just open the door ajar like I did. The rest of us will lie low."

They didn't have to wait long. There came three heavy knocks on the door.

Anna glanced at the priest and the girls, then went to the door. She unfastened the bolts and opened the door ajar. She squinted out at the two men who looked like they'd been on a long hike.

She had never seen Retberg and Green before. When they visited the first time, she had remained in her own room while Bonelli and Maria spoke to them in the hall, and when they visited the second time, it was at Bonelli's house and she wasn't there at all.

"Yes," she snapped abruptly.

"Good morning, madam," began one of the men, holding out his warrant card. He was a broad and rather tough-looking individual. "I am Police Inspector Paul Retberg of the East Midlands Constabulary, and this is Police Sergeant Ian Green."

"Police officers?" said Anna.

"Yes, madam."

"Not news reporters?"

"Oh, no," said Ian Green. "They haven't been here, have they?"

"Who?" Anna stared at Ian Green who was also tough-looking, but not quite as tall or as broad as the other cop.

Ian Green gazed back at her blankly.

"Madam," said Retberg. "We have been sent here on a two-pronged mission. One, to protect you and the two girls, particularly Maria Christopher who seems to have disappeared off our radar since receiving death threats…"

Anna laughed. "My good man," she said. "This all sounds very dramatic."

"Actually, she has insisted that she is going to give birth to the Son of God."

Anna made a fairly convincing scoffing sound. "Sounds like some kind of fairy story."

"But also," said Retberg, "secondly, we will try to bring to justice the terrorists who have been attempting to kidnap her and kill her. So please can you confirm that Father Giuseppe Bonelli and the two girls are here?"

Anna looked at him squarely.

"I can honestly and categorically swear to you, inspector," she began, "that neither the priest you mention, or either of these mysterious girls are here. I've never heard of them and I'm here on my own, except for my sheep, so gentlemen I bid you farewell."

She was just about to close the door in their faces when Father Bonelli and the girls suddenly came up behind her and practically pushed her out of the way. They grabbed the barn door between them and threw it wide open, before bursting out to greet the two surprised police officers. The girls hugged them and the priest shook their hands.

Retberg looked at Anna. "Do these people jog your memory at all?" he said.

"Oh, you mean *this* priest," she said. "And *these* girls. Oh, I see."

"Thank God you're here," said Bonelli. "Have we got news for you? Are we in danger, or what?"

"And we've got news for you, too," said Retberg. "We've learned quite a bit."

They quickly exchanged all the latest news.

"My dear chaps," Bonelli said at last. "Do step into our

humble abode."

They stepped inside together.

"Yes, very humble," Ian Green commented as he looked around, hardly believing his eyes when he saw farmyard animals standing there looking at him. "But I don't understand. Why can't you just take the girls into hospital?"

Father Bonelli and Anna Gabriella then spent the next ten minutes explaining between them why it was not a viable option to take the girls, particularly Maria, into hospital.

When they finished, Retberg looked at Green and pulled a face as though struggling with what to do or say next. He looked round at the group of people in front of him, glancing from face to face, summing each of them up as he did so.

Personally, he thought that Bonelli was just eccentric. Anna was a charming lady but was gullible and clearly crackers, and Maria was having them all on, probably for a laugh. The only one who seemed to have any kind of sense was Debbie Shallis, and she was just going along for the ride, perhaps to see where it all ended up.

However, he and Sergeant Green had been given very clear instructions by their chief superintendent. Even the deputy chief constable had stuck his nose in. And those instructions, in short, were to protect Maria Christopher and, if at all possible, nick the terrorists.

"Well," Retberg said at last. "We had best go back to the car for now."

"Then what?" said Debbie.

"We'll have to find rooms," said Ian Green. "Then we'll be back tomorrow to decide on the best course of action."

"But there aren't any rooms," said Debbie. "We asked everywhere."

"There may have been rooms," said Maria, "but they just didn't want us in them."

"Even so," said Bonelli, "if you're well-equipped and well-prepared, you may stay with us."

After a moment's thought, to Ian Green's amazement, Inspector Retberg went up to the priest and clapped him on the back.

"I think that's an excellent idea," he said. "We have blankets and fleeces in the car, and tomorrow we can go into a nearby town, look for a general hardware shop and get some panelling for a partition to give the girls some privacy. "

After another quick look round he added, "And arrange for the delivery of an adequate portaloo."

Ian Green went up to Retberg and said in a hushed voice, "Are you crazy, man? My nuts are freezing off at the thought of it."

"Eh, we do have heating," Father Bonelli said encouragingly.

"I'm sure, but..."

"That settles it, then," said Retberg. Then more quietly to Green, "Look, we do need to keep a close eye, and what better way than to be right with them."

"Yes, but..."

"Oh, come on," said Retberg, growing tired of the debate. "We'll go get the car so we can leave it parked just outside here. Then we'll have everything we need right here."

After a few more irritable huffs and puffs from a disgruntled sergeant, Retberg and Green made their way back across the field and towards the guest house where they had met Victor Best, and to where they'd parked the car.

*

Victor Best had been looking out for them from the front of his house. Just moments before, two other men had turned up claiming to be reporters from *The Daily Venus*. The old guest house proprietor grinned savagely to himself having told them that if they didn't piss of then he'd call the police.

An angry hiss escaped from between his teeth, though, when he saw the two cops (who he thought were the genuine news reporters) return to their car.

And instead of calling on him and delivering his reward money they just drove off.

"Right," Victor said angrily. "We'll see about that."

He put on a pair of boots, thick gloves and a greatcoat, and was just about to leave the house when his wife, Helga, a fat chain-smoker, and usually with a glass of brandy in one hand and a cigarette in the other, called out...

"Where are you going, Vic?"

"Someone owes me some money," he said, and with that went out of the house and slammed the door behind him.

"You what?"

His drunk wife didn't hear because she was in the bathroom and had just flushed the toilet, so she was left in ignorance. She didn't know anything about Maria Christopher, or the future Saviour of the World, or of Father Bonelli.

And she didn't know, either, that she wouldn't be seeing her husband for the next three days and nights, and that when she did see him again she would learn more about the future of the world than most people learn in a lifetime.

CHAPTER FORTY-SIX

While Retberg and Green were collecting Retberg's car, Father Bonelli and Anna sat opposite the two girls and they enjoyed cups of tea and bread rolls. They were all talking about the options they had for the next stage of their journey.

Then while the girls continued to chat, Father Bonelli suddenly stood up and made the announcement that he had to collect something from the back of his car.

"Need any help?" asked Anna.

The priest looked at her. He had been hoping she'd say that.

"That'd be great," he said. "Thanks."

They went out to the car together. Once outside, Anna looked at Bonelli, puzzled.

"What is it?" she said.

"I need to tell you something," he said.

She looked at him with a worried face.

"While we are waiting with excitement for the birth of God's Second Son," he said, "we mustn't forget the danger that Maria is in. We can run, but we can't hide."

"From the Satanists?"

"Exactly."

"How could they find us here?" Anna asked.

"They'll find us," said Bonelli, "and we'll have to defend ourselves as best we can."

"We're lucky we've got Retberg and Green here," said Anna. "And they're armed."

"That might not be enough…" Father Bonelli abruptly

broke off, then he said, "Oh, talk of the devil."

Anna looked surprised, wondering what he meant at first, but when she looked round she saw the two police officers coming up the hill in their car.

Bonelli and Anna stood side-by-side and watched the car park next to the priest's Mazda. The policemen climbed out.

Retberg and Green saw them and walked towards them.

"We were just talking about you guys," Anna told them.

"Nothing defamatory I hope," said Retberg.

Bonelli decided not to waste time. He came right to the point.

"Anna was saying how assuring it was that you are armed, but I'm afraid I was pointing out that two police-issue pistols, plus my army-issue revolver, and even a few grenades, might not be enough."

Retberg opened his mouth to speak, but the enthusiasm of Ian Green beat him to it.

"As soon as we know when the terrorists propose to attack," he said, "we will have a fleet of helicopters at our disposal. They will base themselves somewhere within a mile of here and will be awaiting our command. They will be armed with machine guns, cannon and flamethrowers."

Anna's mouth hung open in astonishment, but still Father Bonelli was hesitant. "Even so…"

But his sentence was cut short with…

"You cheating bastards. Where's my ten-thousand pounds?"

They all looked round and there was Victor Best striding towards them.

Retberg and Green looked at each other and hung their heads.

"This is the prat who called the news reporters," Retberg told Bonelli and Anna. "And now he wants his reward."

Anna looked at him. She had just been thinking how well

things were turning out, but now...

It was Father Bonelli who found the solution.

"Of course, my good man," he said. "But you will get something of far greater value than a mere ten thousand pounds."

Victor looked quite taken aback.

"More than ten grand?" he asked, for confirmation that he had not misunderstood.

"Certainly of greater value," the priest confirmed.

"How do I know I can trust you?"

"Well, come here and I will be glad to explain it to you."

With a happy, but slightly glazed, expression, Victor approached the priest.

"Closer," Bonelli urged. "Still closer. This is extremely confidential."

Victor Best was ten years younger than Bonelli, but looked older, and his reactions were not quick enough to prevent what happened next.

Father Giuseppe Bonelli unleashed the most fearsome right hook that crashed against Victor's jaw with a sickening, resounding *crack*.

Retberg and Green stared in utter shock. Where the old priest packed the strength to deliver a blow like that, neither of them knew, but it would have floored a heavy-weight champion. Victor went crashing down like he'd been struck by a locomotive. The hotel proprietor was thrown backwards and would have careered straight into Retberg and Green if they hadn't dodged out of the way. He finished up landing flat on his back, completely unconscious.

"What the fuck?" Retberg said in bewilderment.

Father Bonelli shrugged his shoulders.

"Problem solved," he said.

"Hardly solved," said Ian Green. "What do we do with him now?"

"I suggest we keep him here, tied up, until after God's Child is born," Bonelli told them. "After that, he won't be able to do us any harm."

Retberg and Green, and Anna, all looked at each other, then they all nodded in agreement, albeit reluctantly. Between them they dragged the dead weight of Victor inside, much to the amazement of Maria and Debbie. Bonelli had already noticed some lengths of rope hanging up in the barn, so he used these to tie him up, and secured him to an iron gatepost in the corner of the barn.

Some moments later, Retberg and Green had a debate about the consequences of aiding and abetting a kidnapping, and of unlawful imprisonment. On reflection, however, they considered that this was all part of accomplishing the mission they had been given, and their actions would be considered a means to an end.

On the other hand, there was the possibility Victor's family and friends would begin to wonder where he was. If they had only known, though, the state of Victor's drunken wife, then they wouldn't have worried too much. Helga Best only had a vague awareness of her husband's absence and wasn't too concerned about it anyway.

The two police officers had an uncomfortable sleep that night with just blankets and pillows, so the next day they set off to a nearby town where they purchased two camp beds, sleeping bags, and some plastic panelling for makeshift partitions in the barn to give the girls some privacy.

They also paid two delivery men a generous amount to set up a temporary portaloo cabin which would be just adequate for their present requirements, all paid for, of course, by the East Midlands Constabulary.

At the same time, with no other means of communication at that time, Father Bonelli also set off. His mission was to send a telegram to his brother Lucciano. As soon as Lucci had positive news about the Satanists' plans, then he would send word.

Giuseppe Bonelli hoped he would deliver this in person.

*

By now the story of Maria Christopher and her Sacred Claim was a regular news item on television, radio and in all the newspapers. The story of the girl who was claiming that she had been chosen by God to give birth to His Second Son was now continuing to spread around the whole of the United Kingdom, and to other countries around the world.

And the reaction to this news, predictably, continued to be mixed.

The atheists did not worry Father Bonelli unduly. They always stated their opinions in a courteous manner, and even though they did not believe Maria's claims, they did not wish her any harm. Therefore, as far as the priest was concerned, they posed very little threat, if any.

What was deeply troubling him, though, were the nasty messages that had been sent by extreme religious fanatics. These people were so angered by the girl's claims that they sent her threats, with their intentions and methods described in graphic detail. Obscene torture, culminating in slow death, was among the milder ones. These were sent to her family home address and were reported to the police by her distraught parents.

There were other groups of Christians who did not threaten to take such drastic measures, but still sent messages condemning her for blasphemy and advising her that, for this, she would rot in Hell.

Strangely, this sparked an unexpected reaction from the neutrals, many of whom were teetering on coming over to her side. They defended Maria and challenged the religious lunatics by asking two questions.

Firstly, why have they always believed so adamantly that Mary from over two thousand years ago was telling the truth? It was quite possible (some would say probable) that this young girl who was about fourteen years of age, was made pregnant by being raped by a Roman soldier. Such attacks by Roman soldiers on young Jewish girls were commonplace, so quite a plausible explanation.

And secondly, why did they feel so strongly that Maria Christopher could *not* be telling the truth? To these newly found 'Defenders Of The Faith' it appeared strange that these Christians had dedicated their whole lives to this belief, waiting and praying patiently for the sign, then when it finally happened they didn't believe it.

Finally, there were the total believers. They were like children believing in nothing more tangible than the Tooth Fairy. But at the same time, these people were the most intriguing. Some folk actually envied them.

They demonstrated inexplicable, unshakeable belief, and loyalty to their religion. Practical and down-to-earth people would attempt reasoning with them. Dinosaur bones millions of years old and irrefutable evidence of evolution cut no ice with them. They would continue to believe that man just simply sprang into existence. Some still believed that the Earth was a mere five thousand years old, instead of five billion, and that God simply sprinkled the stars across the sky, a fete that took him just twenty-four hours.

Police Inspector Paul Retberg was an atheist who believed that if the peasants who wrote the Book of Genesis had any scientific knowledge, then they would never have dreamed of writing such nonsense.

But Maria Christopher loved these people, for they were among her best supporters. They indicated their sheer joy that this situation gave them. They didn't need proof. They just somehow knew what to believe. All they wanted now were daily news updates of the Holy Mother and her child with the hope that maybe one day they would actually see God's Second Son.

However, there was just one little problem for all these people.

Nobody actually knew where the teenage girl currently was.

*

Since the incident at the hospital, the young mother-to-be had disappeared, but for everyone's sake, Maria Christopher who was now heavily pregnant, needed to be found.

Retberg and Green were already aware that one tabloid newspaper, *The Daily Venus,* had decided to offer a reward of ten thousand pounds for information leading to her whereabouts, provided that the information came solely to themselves. They would then follow the girl's progress, interview her, film her, and eventually take photographs when she made her first public appearance with the Holy Child.

Since then, a journalist working for that newspaper had visited Maria's parents' house. Neither her mother or father knew where she was, so they were naturally very anxious about the threats made against their daughter. They told the reporter that they regretted their reaction to their daughter's claim and were actually starting to wonder if it was true after all, that she really had been visited by an Angel.

The headmistress of Our Lady's Senior Girls' School certainly seemed to believe it.

CHAPTER FORTY-SEVEN

It was in the early hours of the morning of the twenty-first of December that Debbie's baby was born, a healthy little boy weighing eight pounds and nine ounces. Immediately after the birth, Anna Gabriella remembered the very important part of her midwifery duties by recording the date and the exact time and weight of the child, although the official registering of the birth would have to be done at a later date of course.

It was Maria who was the first one to hold him. Debbie had suffered quite badly during a long, tough labour. Anna had had to probe around deeply, using quite a lot of the pain-killing Entonox gas, which was better than nothing, but nowhere near as effective had the young mother been in hospital, where the use of an epidural would have been an option.

And there was an added complication. The umbilical cord became wrapped around the baby's neck. Fortunately, Anna had dealt with several such cases of this previously, and was able to carry out the necessary procedure, but unpleasant nonetheless. There was a moment of panic that was enough to shake everyone up.

Debbie's screams of pain could easily have been heard across the field but nobody in any of the guest houses heard, or cared. Christmas party time was already well under way and that meant continual loud music until about 3 am.

Father Bonelli said a quick prayer, thanking God for giving Anna to him, but at the same time asking for forgiveness for having had sex with her.

But the birth was over at last and they were all very

much relieved. Inspector Paul Retberg passed around a bottle of wine for himself, Ian Green and Anna Gabriella to enjoy in celebration, while Father Bonelli found something a little stronger for himself in one of his bags. A bottle of Scotch.

They were all huddled together around the oil heater and the baby was wrapped in swaddling clothes. Then Anna went to her luggage in search of another item. She waded through her bags and through various supplies, which included a huge supply of tiny nappies.

She eventually found the item she sought, and unwrapped the little machine with its white, plastic casing and transparent pipes looping from it.

Maria had never seen one before. "What's that?" she asked.

The old priest smiled. He knew what it was. He'd seen ones just like it in use on many previous occasions.

"It's a breast pump," the midwife explained. "When a baby is just born, it helps the mother to generate her milk faster, until the baby can suck for himself. In the meantime, it will collect the early breast milk in tubes. We can give this to him with a syringe for the first day. Nothing much will come out at first, though."

"One problem." Father Bonelli gave a great sigh. "No power."

"This one runs on batteries," said Anna, "and don't worry, I've got an ample supply of batteries in my goody-bag."

Carrying the breast pump, she went over to Debbie who was still lying half conscious on a camp bed.

With the process that followed, Retberg and Green thought that it would be propitious to hide behind the partitions within their own 'room', finishing off the first bottle of wine between them.

Maria watched in fascination as the pump was connected and it began its rhythmic action. She was full of excitement and anticipation now, looking forward to doing this herself quite soon.

Just then, Debbie became fully awake and began to try to sit up, looking around her still confused with all the pain-killing gas, and wondering where she was. She looked down, then appeared even more confused to see a tube attached to one of her breasts by means of a suction pad.

Maria handed her the baby for her to cuddle for the first time.

"A beautiful little boy," she said, smiling with joy for her friend.

But Maria noticed, for the briefest of moments, Debbie's look of slight disappointment, having stated that she would prefer a little girl, but that expression changed immediately when she saw the infant's face.

"Oh, he is beautiful, thank you," Debbie said as she took him in her arms, cuddling him, kissing the baby boy on his forehead, and instantly loving him.

"What are you thanking me for?" Maria said. "You did all the work."

Anna adjusted the pump. "That's enough from one side," she said.

"Thank you, too, Anna," Debbie said. "It wasn't too bad, was it?"

"No, not too bad," Anna smiled, restarting the pump on the other side.

And at that precise moment, Maria felt her baby kick, like a little reminder that within the next three evenings it would be her turn. She was already certain of the date, and the actual time, of the forthcoming birth.

And the sex of the baby too. And she couldn't wait to be breastfeeding her own little baby boy. She was sure... no, she knew, that the baby was a boy.

"The birth of the Second Son of God," she whispered to

herself. It would be an event remembered forever. And then her smile broadened still further across her face when another thought occurred to her. *Somebody might even write a book about it.*

And then something just as exciting, perhaps more so. *The book might be adapted for a TV mini-series.*

*

Stargazers everywhere had been anticipating a rare and spectacular, event. Gazing up at the night's sky was like a thrilling journey back through time.

The event involved the three brightest planets merging. One of these was Jupiter. This was the first planet of our solar system to be formed nearly five billion years ago.

The giant, Jupiter, in his infancy was a destroyer, selfishly sucking up all the loose material for himself, snuffing out any chance that any other planet might have had to develop.

But then after many millions of years, he seemed to get bored with being the only planet orbiting our Sun. And so it was that he began to mellow like an angry, young man may do as he gets older. After many more millions of years another planet did materialise.

Jupiter found himself being encouraged by another gas giant who appeared on the other side of the asteroid belt, like a beautiful young woman who was falling in love with the angry young man, setting herself a mission to change, and tame him, and redirect his energy and strength.

She attracted him with her beauty and enchanted him with her glittering array of rings. He was confused, in two minds, but he was at last drawn to her by her incredible gravity. This new planet, Saturn, worked hard, and it took her a very long time, but at last she succeeded. Jupiter decided to give up his life of anger, aggression and destruction and join Saturn on her side of the asteroid belt.

His force of gravity, however, was even greater than hers, and from now on he would use this force for creative and protective purposes, rather than destruction. Sadly, though, he was unable to prevent the massive meteorite striking the Earth sixty-five million years ago, wiping out the dinosaurs.

Some would say, sadly, but others would say gladly, for if it was not for the winter that followed, and the New Dawn, then life, from which Man evolved, would never have begun.

And from then on, Jupiter, sometimes seen close to Saturn in the night's sky, would do all he could to protect the Earth, using his immensely strong gravitational pull to deflect objects approaching from outer space, objects that would have otherwise hit the Earth with more catastrophic results.

Now, Jupiter and Saturn had several little brothers and sisters, the brightest of these was Venus, a planet the same size as the Earth, but who lived close to the Sun.

They only saw her once in a Blue Moon, and occasionally, very occasionally, they all joined together, merging perfectly in the sky, creating a large, beautifully bright light.

Each occurrence similar to this one has become known as a Syzygy (Siz-a-je).

Astronomers everywhere, at that moment were watching the course of the planets, as this was about to happen very soon. The exact merger had been calculated to occur during the early hours of the morning on the twenty-fifth of December. There was excitement among them all, of course, but some people also felt great anticipation.

They thanked their lucky stars that they knew about it before the event, because these occasions were extremely rare, and during the last occurrence something wonderful and miraculous happened.

CHAPTER FORTY-EIGHT

It was three evenings later when everything seemed to happen at once. Late at night on Christmas Eve, Maria was getting anxious, uncomfortable and restless.

And as everybody's attention was focused onto her, the prisoner, Victor Best, began to renew his efforts, struggling against the ropes that tied his wrists and ankles. One of his ankles was also secured to an iron post.

He cursed loudly, realising that his efforts were futile. The ropes had been tied too well to be easily loosened. He continued to shout and swear, insulting his captors.

This continual uproar was starting to become intolerable for everyone, especially the two girls, one of them now just hours away from giving birth to a Heavenly Baby. The priest sat there praying. He believed that at the precise moment of birth, the Holy Infant would be instantly aware of his circumstances and surroundings so would not want to hear a torrent of obscenities.

Debbie's baby was progressing well and gurgled happily as he sucked the freely flowing breast milk, but Maria was getting more restless, and could not make herself comfortable.

And Victor's ranting did not help.

"How much longer do you think you can keep me here, you frigging bastards?" he shouted.

"Shut up, will you?" Ian Green shouted back at him.

But Victor had no intention of shutting up.

"You cocksucking bunch of piss-taking shit heads," he yelled. "You can't keep me here forever."

Maria could feel sharp pain starting up now. It seemed to keep building up, then ease off again, but each time it seemed to hurt a bit more than the previous time.

Anna held the young girl's hand, then looked at Father Bonelli.

"Contractions are more frequent," she said softly.

"Does that mean…?"

Anna nodded. "She's well into labour."

Father Bonelli looked at his watch. Nearly 1 am.

More shouting and vile language from Victor Best.

Maria shook her head irritably and fidgeted restlessly. She believed now, more than ever before, that she was a much privileged and holy young woman, one that people should respect and bow to. She shouldn't have to endure discomfort, inconvenience or any kind of irritation

At that moment she knew she was a superior and sophisticated being.

"Oh, can't we do anything about that arsehole?" she gasped, just as the pain eased off again.

Ian Green got up off his chair-bed and went over to Victor Best.

"Shut up, you," he said. "Or I'll gag you."

"You do that, you bastard," Victor said through gritted teeth, "and I'll go straight to the police."

This time Ian Green could not help laughing.

Inspector Paul Retberg came over and put his arm around his colleague, then they leaned their heads together and sang out in unison, in high-pitched voices, "We *are* the police."

Father Bonelli, Anna and Debbie all roared with laughter. Maria would have joined in if she had not been in increasing pain.

Victor stared at the two police officers for a moment, outraged, then continued to yell, "You absolute bent, corrupt, bastards. I'm going to the press, to the television, I'll tell them…"

As he continued in one, continuous spate of insults, abuse and threats, Retberg and Green became serious again.

"I suppose we could gag him," Ian Green said.

Retberg looked thoughtful.

"I don't know," he said. "Even so, I don't particularly want him here while Maria's giving birth."

Ian Green glanced round at Maria who was puffing and panting.

"And I don't think that'll be much longer," he commented. "By the looks of things."

Retberg nodded, then called over to Father Bonelli who was sitting on his chair-bed, taking a discreet sip of whiskey.

The priest looked up at him. "What's up, my son?" he smiled.

Retberg explained to him his concerns about Victor Best. They couldn't let him go yet, but they didn't want him to be there when Maria was giving birth.

Bonelli thought about this for a while as he listened to a further stream of obscenities from the foul mouth of Victor.

"No, I agree," he said. "It won't do. Let's put him tied up in the back of my Estate car."

"Good egg," said Retberg. "Ian and I will carry him. You open up the back of your car and we'll throw him in."

"I'll climb in with him," said Green, "and I'll check his wrists are still secure."

"Right," said Bonelli, "and I'll use the extra rope to secure his ankles to the boot lid catch."

Retberg made a decisive move toward Victor.

"Hopefully, by tomorrow, we can let him go, anyway," he said with a great sigh of relief.

But as soon as the three men laid their hands on Victor Best, the old proprietor kicked up a shindy. "You keep your dirty, corrupt paws off me, you bent bastards," he shouted.

Bonelli looked at Retberg. "Give him a few slaps if he doesn't come quietly," he said.

Victor immediately became quieter, then allowed himself to be carried, but he did not remain silent for long.

"I'm going to report this case of assault, unlawful imprisonment and corruption to your chief constable," he said.

"No witnesses, I'm afraid," Retberg said, shaking his head sadly as they carried the wriggling man out to the back of Bonelli's car.

"You bent pig."

But while they were outside, and in the process of this unceremonious transfer, there was one almighty scream from inside the barn.

"Quickly," said Father Bonelli. "Check all the ropes, then lock the car."

He threw his keys to Retberg, while Ian Green was hurriedly trying to make sure the prisoner was secure.

But in his haste he had left one of Victor's wrists with a little more freedom than before. As the boot of the car was slammed shut and locked, Victor gritted his teeth. He realised that his left hand had considerably more movement than before, and he grinned to himself. He was sure now that with a little bit of wriggling around he would be able to work his way free.

But as Retberg and Green chased after the priest into the barn, they put Victor Best right to the backs of their minds. And as they did so they heard Anna Gabriella shouting triumphantly...

"Praise to The Lord! The Son of God is about to be born!"

CHAPTER FORTY-NINE

For stargazers everywhere witnessing such a rare event would remain as a memory to treasure for a lifetime. People who were lucky enough to have sufficient equipment would photograph it, whereas others would be happy just to see it and keep it fondly in their memories forever.

The three brightest planets, Venus, Jupiter and Saturn, gradually merging perfectly together, and creating a brilliant light that lit up the early morning sky like one massive star.

*

It was a long, hard struggle for Victor Best, but he eventually made it. He got both his hands free, then it was relatively easy to reach down, and even in the darkness inside the back of Father Bonelli's car, untie his ankles.

The most difficult part of his escape was getting out of the car which Ian Green had locked from outside. He climbed from the large luggage space of the Estate car onto the back seat where he noticed that one of the rear windows had been left slightly open, only by about an inch, but leaving a gap just big enough for him to insert all his fingers. He then pulled down applying all his weight. As he did this, he could hear the mechanism inside the door creaking, then creaking a bit more.

Then the closing mechanism broke with a loud *Crack*, leaving the window to slide down freely.

Victor was a tall, but very thin, man, so he had no difficulty in climbing through, and simply allowing himself to drop to the ground.

Hurriedly he got to his feet. Apart from feeling stiff from three days of captivity, he felt okay and was sure he would soon loosen up. He set off at a moderate trot.

It was when he was running across the open field that he noticed something unusual.

Normally, in the very early hours of the morning, this whole area would be in pitch darkness, but now there seemed to be plenty of light. He looked up and could not believe what he saw. To his amazement there was the brightest star that he had ever seen, and he noticed how it cast a shimmering light over the barn, the one where the girl was giving birth to her baby.

And then, as if seeing the light in more ways than one, it occurred to him...

"My God," he whispered to himself. "It's true. Jesus Christ."

In his excitement, he shouted out loud, "It *is* true. It's *all* true."

And he was running again, as fast as he could now. He had to tell everyone, and as quickly as possible, *the New King was about to be born.*

*

When a baby is being born, it's literally all hands on deck, and privacy and modesty are forgotten about. From the start it looked like being a difficult labour for Maria. She was in a lot of pain. Father Bonelli frequently glanced at Anna and noticed the look of strain and worry on her face was gradually getting worse. And she repeatedly looked at him, too, as if she was about to say something, but then kept changing her mind, deciding to say nothing.

And she was gradually using up all the remaining pain-killing Entonox gas. She had painkillers in tablet form, too, which had also been purloined, but still Maria was screaming like a banshee. And with the mixture of tablets and gas, she was no longer in her right mind, using the most abusive and offensive language that the mother of God's Child should never use.

Debbie was close by, too, to offer moral support, but she also had her own little baby boy to look after.

Retberg and Green were remaining quiet in the background and out of the way, and they perceived that even the animals shuffling around in the barn were looking worried.

The midwife looked at Father Bonelli, then to Maria.

"Okay," she said. "Take a breather, then when I tell you to push…"

Maria screamed so loud and so long and so high-pitched, the old priest's ears clanged like a gong.

"Mind your own sodding business, you stupid, fat bitch," yelled the fifth-form schoolgirl. And then, using her powers of ventriloquism once again, in a man's voice, and sounding like it was coming from the other side of the barn, "Screw you, screw you."

Ian Green looked at Retberg. "Reminds me of that scene from *The Exorcist*," he said.

Once again Anna looked at the old priest, and he saw that the look on her face was now terribly concerned.

"We need to get her to a hospital," she said.

"No, you thick bint," Maria yelled. "I'm not moving. I'm having my baby here."

"But…"

"Are you deaf, you dopey old slapper?"

The middle-aged midwife took a deep breath, then looked up inside Maria's opening, gently inserting a finger as she did so.

"I can feel the top of the baby's head," she announced.

"Okay, let's try again. PUSH!"

The scream from Maria then was heard by three farmers who were just crossing the field at that moment, as they often did late at night, or during the early hours of the morning, just to check that all was well with the world.

*

The three farmers, Andrew, James and Thomas, did hear that long, loud scream and gazed at each other in wonder.

They had finished their evening chores and were about to say their goodbyes to one another for the night when they noticed what looked like an unusually large, bright star. They were just discussing this when a tall, thin man came running towards them, waving his arms, evidently excited about something.

He came along and practically crashed into the three farmers. He was out of breath as a sixty-year-old man would be, having run across the field. He was trying to tell them something and catch his breath at the same time.

"It's... it's... it's..." he spluttered and coughed.

"What's up, my man?" asked Farmer Andrew. "Who are you?"

"It's that girl," he managed at last through gulps of air.

"What girl?" inquired Farmer James.

"The one on TV."

All the farmers looked at each other.

"There's a girl on TV?" said Andrew, trying to make sense of it.

"In that barn."

Farmer Thomas looked at the man closely. "I doubt that very much," he said.

"I think he means there's a TV in the barn," suggested Andrew

"Oh, I understand now. And a girl has appeared on TV. Is that correct, olden?"

Victor was beginning to get his breath back now.

"She's having the baby," he said. "*Thee* Baby."

"That's nice," said James. "I get it now. She's going to have a baby and she's telling people about it on TV."

"I see," said Andrew. "That makes sense now."

"No, just listen," Victor said. "That girl who claimed that she was going to give birth to the Son of God."

The farmers looked at one another with puzzled frowns.

"Oh, right," said Thomas. "But I wouldn't believe that story. Not unless there was absolute, water-tight proof."

"And nobody knows where she is now, anyway," said Andrew.

"Well, you know now," shouted Victor. "I've just told you. She's in that barn, and she's having the baby right now. And it's true. She is having the Son of God."

All the farmers laughed.

"I think you've had a funny dream," said James.

"Or been hitting the bottle," Andrew suggested with a broad grin.

"I doubt all that's true anyway," said Thomas. "I need proof."

Suddenly, unexpectedly, Victor Best lunged forward towards Thomas, taking hold of him by the lapels of his jacket with one hand, and grabbing a handful of his hair with the other, forcing the startled farmer to look up at the sky – *and at the bright star.*

"What do you think that is, you stupid bastard?" Victor yelled. "A flying saucer?"

"Jesus," said Andrew. "We were just wondering about that."

"But that star," said James, "or whatever it is, that'll be seen for hundreds of miles around here. How do you know what it means? If it means anything at all."

Victor shook his head, blew out an exasperated breath, then broke into a run again, continuing on his way towards the guest houses where he hoped to meet some intelligent people who would listen.

The three farmers watched him go and, when he was at some distance, they turned to each other.

"Strange chap," Thomas said, irritably straightening his jacket.

"I wonder," Andrew said thoughtfully.

"Let's go take a look anyway," suggested James.

It was when they were within a hundred yards of the barn that they heard the longest, loudest scream. Thomas happened to glance up at the star and he had to admit it seemed to be glowing brighter now than ever. Again, the farmers looked at each other in amazement, then continued on their way towards the barn. As they got closer, from what they could hear going on – screams and other shouting voices – whether it was the girl as seen on TV or not, there was definitely a girl or young woman in the midst of giving birth. Why she hadn't been taken to hospital they could not imagine, and why she couldn't afford to be put up in a better place than a barn they didn't know that either.

However, after a brief discussion, they thought it would be an appropriate gesture and good manners to go back home then return with some gifts for the mother and her new baby.

CHAPTER FIFTY

When Victor Best returned to his guest house he was more breathless than ever. He could hear loud celebrations going on and so went straight through to the lounge bar.

On a Christmas Eve, and running into the early hours of Christmas Day morning, it was hardly surprising to see that many of the guests were on the way to getting blind drunk, some falling onto the floor laughing, shouting at the tops of their voices and swearing.

Victor's wife, Helga, with a large gin and tonic in her hand, looked up and registered a vaguely surprised look.

"I wondered where you'd gone," she said nonchalantly.

Considering that her husband had been gone for three days and nights, it didn't seem to Victor that she had wondered for very long.

"I bet you did, you bitch," he retorted.

"Where have you been, anyway?" She burped and hiccupped.

"If you must know, I was kidnapped."

"Oh, right." Another loud burp and a hiccup.

He was about to say something else to his wife, but then he decided on a better, more incisive, course of action. He pulled out the piano stool.

"Give us a tune, then, Vic," somebody yelled.

"Yeah," came from someone else. "How about a couple of verses of..."

What song he wanted a couple of verses of was never discovered as his sentence was cut short when a fat lad standing next to him turned round and vomited down his front.

The man with puke plastered down his front looked at the mess with disdain.

Victor climbed up onto the piano stool and stood on it looking down on his guests.

"Listen to me, everyone," he shouted. "Please listen."

"Go it, Vic," came a shout. "Give us a song!"

"Yeah!" from everyone in unison.

But somebody else shouted, "Come down off the stool and have a drink with us commoners."

"Yeah, why not? Mingle with the riff-raff."

More drunken laughter.

"It's a Holy Night," Victor shouted, having seen the light, so to speak.

"Get out of it!"

"No, really," Victor insisted. "It's true what that girl's been saying. Even at this very moment, God's Son is being born."

Helga tottered to her feet.

"Well, that's what Christmas is all about, I suppose," she said, not bothering to stifle another great belch. "Or so they say."

The drunken laughter got louder.

"Do none of you understand what I am saying?" Victor shouted. "On this very night, that girl we've seen on television, she is here. She's the one in the barn across the field. There's another girl with her, a midwife and a priest, and..."

"Go and lie down, Vic," somebody shouted, "before you hurt yourself."

But the laughter was beginning to die down now, perhaps because some of the guests could see that Victor was in earnest.

"And there's two police officers there," Victor continued. "I thought they were reporters, but they've been given orders to protect the girl against evil people who want to kill her."

The party atmosphere was now fizzling out as, gradually,

more people could see that Victor meant what he said, and he was stone cold sober, too.

"You're not having us on, are you, Vic?" someone said. "Just for a lark?"

Victor raised his arms and said in a slow, loud monotone, "The Son of God is being born this very night"

"How can we be sure?" someone ventured.

"There's the Great, Holy Star," Victor told them. "Come and have a look for yourselves."

And with that he jumped off the piano stool, then raced out of the room to the front door, and outside.

And all the people followed. There were about twenty of them, a mixture of men and women, most quite drunk, and some still laughing and swearing. One was vomiting onto the ground. Once outside some of the folk took this opportunity to light cigarettes.

"Behold," Victor shouted as he pointed up to the sky. "The Great Holy Star."

Then absolute stunned silence as they all looked up at the clear sky, and at the huge, bright object.

"Oh, my good Lord," somebody whispered. "It is true, then."

"There," Victor cried triumphantly. "What more evidence do you need?"

And as one body, the crowd of drunk people, suddenly rediscovered their voices, and staggered across the road together.

And with Victor Best in the lead, they began on their way across the illuminated field towards the barn.

*

"Push, push, push," shouted Anna Gabriella. "Don't give up now."

But Maria, for a moment, did give up, gasping for breath and crying. The mixture of painkillers was causing her severe confusion now, and she was beginning to hallucinate. The midwife's face was that of a goat. She had gnarled, twisted horns and her body was obese.

Anna momentarily held her hands to her face, unsure of what to do next. Maria's behaviour and language just then were giving the midwife more reason for concern.

Anna looked at the priest.

"We really need to get the baby out now," she said, "otherwise I am going to insist on taking her to hospital."

"No," Maria screamed in a hoarse voice. "You useless, fat goat."

"Whatever she says," Anna said, completing her sentence. "She will be rushed into theatre immediately where they will perform an emergency C-section."

"You absolute ugly fat biffer," Maria shouted in a man's voice that sounded like it was coming from the roof of the barn. "My God, I've seen a better-looking rhinoceros."

"Come on, Maria. One more time. This is it." This time it was Debbie who spoke.

She had placed her own sleeping baby down on the chair-bed. Rolled up blankets were added all around him for safety.

She held Maria's hand. "Squeeze my hand," she said, "and PUSH..."

Maria gritted her teeth and pushed, but again she stopped, screaming and crying.

Anna held the gas mask over Maria's face. Father Bonelli noticed that grave look of concern on the midwife's face again, but now more intense than ever.

"What's up?" he asked.

She held the mask over her own face and breathed in.

"We're nearly out of gas," she said.

"Oh, shit."

After a pause, during which Anna took a few deep breaths herself (as if it was her giving birth) she declared adamantly, "This is our last chance. Otherwise it's hospital."

"Come on, Maria. Please, one more time," said Debbie still holding Maria's hand. "Squeeze my hand and push one more time. Please give it everything you've got. PUSH."

Anna held the gas mask down, but there was then such a roar from Maria that neither Retberg or Green could believe it came from a teenage girl.

"Jesus, sweet Jesus," Bonelli shouted. "I can see his head."

"PUSH," yelled Debbie.

Another great roar, ear-splitting to those all around.

"PUSH."

"My God, the whole head's out, his eyes are open, he's looking around, he's just beautiful."

"PUSH, PUSH," screamed Debbie, her shouts now as loud as Maria's. "PUSH."

"Fuck me," gasped Father Bonelli, "He's out."

Maria was exhausted and in terrible pain. She fainted.

Anna Gabriella grasped the baby. She was relieved to hear the initial healthy cry, but left the umbilical cord for now, observing more urgent matters. Maria appeared to be torn quite badly down below and would require stitches. She quickly wrapped the baby up in a towel and passed the bundle to Debbie.

While the midwife was dealing with the afterbirth, Father Bonelli sat next to Debbie and just looked at the baby, hardly being able to believe that they had just witnessed the actual birth of God's Second Son.

Anna closely examined the bleeding, bathing the area with soft, warm cloths as she did so. She was relieved to see that the wound was not as bad as she feared. Just three stitches, she decided, would be enough. Quickly and expertly, she performed the necessary procedure.

She then put the unconscious girl in a comfortable position, covering her up carefully.

Then all her attention switched back to the baby.

Debbie passed the bundle back to her. Anna let the towel drop to the floor, then examined the umbilical cord. She snipped it, tied the knot, then attached a temporary clip.

And the midwife noticed something else, too. Something that she definitely had not expected.

By now Maria was regaining consciousness. Before wrapping the baby up snugly again, using a fresh blanket and clean swaddling clothes, the unexpected detail was covered up, but not before Bonelli had got the briefest of glimpses.

She smiled when she saw the surprise, and some confusion, register on the priest's face. Neither of them could have predicted this.

Maria sat up and reached out her arms to take the baby from Anna.

"Congratulations, my dear," said the midwife. "You have a lovely healthy child. A beautiful little baby *girl*."

CHAPTER FIFTY-ONE

Anna Gabriella made a note of the date and exact time of the baby's birth, along with the weight, just as she had done for Debbie's baby for registration purposes. Debbie's baby boy had already been recorded. Maria's little girl was smaller, but still a very healthy seven pounds exactly.

Maria was exhausted and even the breast pump would be a slow process. Debbie, though, was now producing enough milk for two babies, so the answer was simple.

Without being asked, Debbie picked up Maria's baby, holding her to her breast, even though the newly born tot wasn't able to suck right away. There was no protest from Maria. In fact, she actually seemed quite pleased with the arrangement.

While this was happening, though, Debbie's little boy woke up and started to cry. Anna went to pick him up, but then Maria sat up and called out.

"Oh, let me hold him."

"Yes, that's okay," Debbie said as she continued to hold Maria's baby to her breast. Likewise, there was no objection.

Anna smiled as she carefully handed Debbie's baby to Maria. The midwife looked from one to the other. The girls were quite happy holding each other's babies.

Maria looked at Debbie.

"He's such a sweet little boy," she said. "Have you named him yet?"

Still looking down at Maria's little girl snuggling up comfortably, Debbie said, "I've decided to call him Adam. It was my grandfather's name."

"I like it," said Maria.

"What about this little one?" asked Debbie.

Maria laughed. "All the names I thought of were boys' names," she said. "After all, I did expect the Son of God to be a boy. I'll have to give it a bit more thought."

Then unexpectedly, Anna who was still standing there, spoke as if to herself, and as though in a dream.

"The Daughter of God."

Those words just fell from her lips.

"Why not? This is truly amazing. You really have been blessed by Our Heavenly King."

Father Bonelli heard this and came over to them.

"It is true," he said. "We are now in the Blessed company of the Daughter of God."

"Come to think of it," Maria reflected, "The Angel did not actually say the Son of God. I'm sure now that He just said *Child* of God."

"Perhaps the Angel wasn't sure if it would be a boy or a girl," Debbie suggested.

Father Bonelli shook his head.

"No, he knew. But I believe now that if he told Maria that the child was a girl, then less people would believe her."

Debbie stared at the priest, annoyed for a moment, initially taking this as a sexist remark.

But then Father Bonelli explained. He held his hands tightly together as though in deep prayer.

"I would possibly have doubted it myself," he said, reverently bowing his head. "But now..."

Anna promptly went to his side, and they prayed together, both in gratitude and asking for forgiveness for their sins at the same time.

Then Anna said quietly, almost in a whisper so only the priest could hear, "Well done, Giuseppe. You were set a mission and I believe you have accomplished that mission admirably.

God will be well pleased."

Father Bonelli turned to her and also spoke quietly, "You're forgetting, we're not out of the woods yet. We still have the Satanists to deal with."

"Satanists?"

"Yes, and the most heinous demon ever to visit God's Earth. I have no doubt he will want to take the child, and then..." he broke off suddenly.

Police Inspector Paul Retberg looked at Sergeant Ian Green, shook his head slowly and drew a deep breath. While the priest and Anna Gabriella joined hands to recite the Act of Contrition, there came three sharp knocks on the old barn door.

"I'll get it," Retberg called out as he went to the door, wondering who it could be calling so early on Christmas morning.

It was the three farmers, Andrew, James and Thomas, and they came in bearing gifts for the new mother and Baby King, not realising of course that it had turned out to be a Baby Queen. They also seemed somewhat confused to see *two* young mothers and two babies.

James looked at Father Bonelli.

"I don't understand this," he said.

The old priest shrugged.

"Don't ask," he said. "It's a long story."

"Which one is the mother of the Son of God?" Andrew ventured.

Maria laughed. "I have just given birth to God's Child," she told them.

The three farmers looked at her as she sat there holding Debbie's baby, Adam. Then they all dropped to their knees, each doing a rapid sign of the cross.

Debbie, who was still holding God's Daughter, had to stifle her mirth. She pulled her blouse up to cover her breasts.

Anna moved forward and gestured towards the packages that each of the farmers were holding.

"What have you got there?" she asked with an uncanny feeling that she already knew what the parcels contained.

Andrew handed his parcel, the smallest of the three, to Anna. Maria's hands were full so the midwife unwrapped the package for her. There was a hard jewellery case inside. She opened this to reveal a pair of gold bracelets, each studded with diamonds. She showed them to Maria.

"My God," said Maria. "They must be worth a fortune. Thank you so much."

Then James handed his parcel, a much bigger one, to Anna who unwrapped it with a vague thought in her mind, wondering why frankincense should be in such a large packet. Usually the product came in little tubs, like yoghurt cartons.

The box inside, though, had a bright picture on the front. It contained the very latest PlayStation.

Debbie's efforts to hide her merriment was getting more difficult, so she decided to turn her entire attention to the little baby girl who was now fast asleep, but who continued to make contented sucking sounds.

Finally Anna reached forward to take the last parcel from Thomas. This was the largest of them all, although deceptively light, and turned out to be the most practical of all the gifts.

A jumbo, bumper packet of newborn babies' nappies.

So there they were, Debbie thought to herself. The three gifts that would go down in history, a story to be told and retold forever, indelibly etched on every person's memory.

Gold, PlayStation and nappies.

The list had a certain ring to it, she mused with a thoughtful smile.

Anna and Maria looked at each other and were just about to exchange suitable comments, when there came the most fearful commotion from outside the barn. People shouting, but worse than that...

People singing, but in shouting, drunken voices.

Both Retberg and Green rushed off together to investigate.

"Please, not carol singers," Retberg shouted as they dashed.

"Not at this time of night," said Ian Green.

And there, outside, was a rowdy bunch of about twenty people. At the front of them stood Victor Best. The police officers momentarily glanced over to Bonelli's Mazda Estate car, as if the answer to how he had escaped would be there.

And the whole scene appeared to be brightly illuminated. The crowd of people were all shouting together, but Victor stepped forward holding his hands up as if in surrender.

"I haven't returned to cause trouble," he told the officers, "because I know now that the Son of God has been born, and these friends of mine just want to see Him."

Retberg and Green exchanged amused glances, and Ian Green tried to disguise his grin, wondering whether it was necessary to tell Victor that the Son had turned out to be the Daughter.

"And how do you know that, all of a sudden?" asked Retberg.

Victor Best pointed towards the sky. "Because of *that*," he said.

Retberg and Green looked upwards to see what appeared to be the largest, brightest star they had ever seen.

Inspector Paul Retberg was just about to say something when, at that moment, Maria appeared at the doorway of the barn, still holding Debbie's baby boy, Adam.

It was not advisable for a young teenage girl to start walking around so soon after going through such a traumatic birth, but curiosity had got the better of her. She wanted to find out what the din was all about. She was wearing a shimmering pink nightdress that Anna had given her, and it reflected the light from the bright star, making it appear that she was shrouded in a Holy light.

Seeing her just appearing there, bathed in a soft, pink glow, even while staggering quite severely and bent almost double, Victor Best and all the drunken men and women dropped to their knees, worshipping her. Debbie's baby boy who, oblivious to the attention he was receiving just then, gurgled happily, burped and farted.

The three farmers appeared outside at that moment, too. They weren't quite sure what to do now. Nevertheless, they thought it would be wise to leave the scene quietly. They had done what they came to do, so completely unnoticed side-by-side, silently and discreetly, they just slipped away and were never seen, or heard of, ever again.

Meanwhile, the noise among Victor Best's crowd was just dying down to a murmur as they each prayed, earnestly but solemnly, for forgiveness for all their sins – sloth, greed, adultery and general debauchery – when there was another loud noise, the roar of a trials motorcycle, its engine revving as the bike skidded sideways up the frozen, muddy hill before coming to a sliding halt.

Father Bonelli then appeared through the barn door and went running over to where the rider was removing his helmet.

Neither Retberg or Green had ever seen the motorcyclist before, but they still knew instantly who he was. Giuseppe threw his arms around Lucciano and hugged him.

But Lucci's news, delivered in a rush, was not good.

"The Satanists, they're coming," he said loudly. "They already know of the Birth and, if they can help it, they will not allow the mother or her child to live. They plan to summon the most hideous demon, who will snatch up the New King in its claws, and then…"

"We won't let it happen," yelled a man from the crowd.

Lucci Bonelli paused for a moment, then concluded with,

"There will be a great, uncontrollable fire. The Satanists plan to snatch the mother and her child and throw them both into the blaze."

*

Both Giuseppe and Lucci, and Anna, and the two girls and their babies, were back inside the barn while Retberg and Green remained outside, making plans for their defence. They decided that they would need to go into town, acquaint themselves at the police station there, then get their helicopter squad assembled as near to their location as possible, and as soon as they were able.

As they mulled over details of their plans, they had forgotten about Victor Best and all the other people who were still hanging around. To the police officers' surprise, Victor approached them.

"So, there are evil people who want to kill the Son of God?" he said.

"You got that right," Retberg told him. "You and your friends had better get out of it. Just go home."

"We've all got guns," Victor told him.

Paul Retberg looked at him.

"Fully licenced, of course. Shotguns and rifles, mainly."

At that moment, Inspector Paul Retberg couldn't care less whether Victor had licences for his guns or not.

"No," he said. "Thanks, but I cannot let you get involved in this."

"Why not?" Victor demanded, standing there with a look of defiance.

Retberg turned to him, but spoke quietly, and patiently.

"Because," he began, "you and your friends will get yourselves killed."

Victor breathed hard.

"Okay," he said, "but at least let the girls and their babies come back to the house. I'm sure we will be able to make room for them."

The policemen looked at each other. Retberg did consider this suggestion for a moment, but then at length he shook his head.

"No, thanks," he said. "Now listen to me. You and your friends and guests, would be in very serious danger..."

At that point, all twenty-or-so people began to gather round. They seemed to be sobering up quickly and were listening to this conversation. They wanted to know what was happening.

Victor Best looked around at them, then back at the police officers.

"Do you know something?" he said. "I haven't done one decent thing in my whole useless life..."

"Oh, thanks a bunch," said his wife, Helga, who was sobering up more quickly now than most of the others.

Victor ignored her.

"... but now I'm going to put that right," he continued. "I want to help protect the Son of God against this demon, or Devil, or whatever it is."

Retberg shook his head.

"Just listen to me you utter idiot."

Victor turned round to his comrades.

"Who's with me?" he shouted,

There was a loud chorus of support from all around.

"Right," he shouted. "Go and get every gun you can lay your hands on, and as much ammunition as you can carry."

"*Yeah!*" came the loud reply from everyone.

"Then get back here as quickly as possible with all your camping equipment."

Finally he looked back at the police officers.

"We're with you to the end," he told them.

And despite everything that happened so far, and the terrible danger they were about to face, Inspector Paul Retberg's features broke into a humorous grin.

"You nutter," he said.

Sergeant Ian Green laughed but wondered what the next twenty-four hours would bring. He stopped laughing abruptly, and suddenly became serious, as though he had experienced a nightmarish premonition.

It was almost certain that not everyone would come through the next day in one piece.

*

Victor Best and his friends parked their jeeps and vans around the opposite side of the barn, together with two huge tents that they were setting up, so that their presence could not be detected from the hill which led from the main road.

Retberg and Green went to help them with their tents, and for a while even the Bonelli brothers lent a hand.

During that time, Father Bonelli approached Victor and apologised for hitting him.

"I probably deserved it," Victor said, as he took a mallet from his toolbox and began to hammer some rods into the ground for securing one corner of one of the tents.

"I was telling you the truth, though," the priest told him. "Your eventual reward will be of far greater value than ten thousand pounds."

Victor gave him a rueful grin.

"You'd better be right," he said.

Retberg got out his police radio and, once again, tested the signal. He had been able to charge the unit up from an attachment in his car.

The inspector and sergeant had been in touch with their own HQ via the local police station, and a fleet of eight helicopters had been deployed, prepared and stationed at an airfield less than one mile away. The cops explained to the Bonelli brothers how formidable the choppers' fire power was, but the two Italian men looked dubiously at each other. They did not appear confident that machine guns, and even cannon and flamethrowers, would be sufficient.

Father Bonelli looked around him. Come to think of it, he thought, neither would a crowd of local peasants carrying rifles and shotguns be much of a threat to the most evil demon.

And the priest had still not explained the full enormity of their situation to the policemen, that these were not just ordinary terrorists that they were dealing with.

These were Satanists. They made your average terrorists look like a bunch of choirboys.

*

They were well into Christmas Day and the hours were dragging by. The babies kept the girls busy with their ongoing needs, and Anna hung around to offer assistance whenever needed. She passed food and drink around that Father Bonelli had managed to obtain during the previous day, and Maria found an opportunity to apologise to her for all the things she had said during the difficult birth.

Anna simply laughed it off.

"I've been called worse things," she said.

And at this time, the Bonelli brothers and the two police officers were taking turns in keeping watch over the field from the barn door, open just wide enough to see through. At the same time, Victor Best and his crowd remained in their tents, also taking it in turns among themselves to keep a lookout.

It was late in the afternoon, and just starting to get dark again, when activity on the hill leading down to the main road, was detected.

Father Bonelli was the one on lookout duty at the time. "We've got company," he said quietly.

CHAPTER FIFTY-TWO

Father Giuseppe Bonelli was standing inside the barn door that was slightly ajar, but then he opened it a little more to gain a wider view.

It was now late in the afternoon, but despite the gradually failing light, because they were high up on a hill he could see over a good distance.

He had known that, at some point, the Satanists would arrive, and that their preliminary rituals would begin. Up until then, though, they did not know precisely when.

But now they did know.

The Holy Star was not shining brightly anymore. In fact, it appeared to have separated into three smaller stars, still quite bright individually, but nowhere near as bright as before. The priest, though, could still make out figures running around the field, many of them carrying burning torches.

Inspector Paul Retberg appeared and stood right behind the priest, squinting through the gap in the door so that he could also see out. Both he and Ian Green had their police-issue pistols now concealed in holsters under their jackets. He felt his weapon through his jacket, as though for reassurance, and nodded to Ian Green. The sergeant did the same and nodded back.

Retberg then got out his police radio and clicked the transmit button.

"Activity on the hill," he said. "We will observe for now. Stand by for instructions. Over."

"We hear you, sir," came a garbled reply. "Over and out."

Retberg looked at the Father Bonelli and gave a faint smile when he saw the old priest checking his firearm. He got a glimpse of the army-issue revolver. The last time that the police inspector had seen that it was on a TV screen, displaying a recording of the incident at St Mark's Hospital five months earlier.

And the priest's brother, Lucci, had a firearm, too, no doubt also 'borrowed' from the army. A machine pistol, almost as formidable as a regular machine gun, but for closer range targets. Lucci also had a belt of ammunition around his shoulder.

Then Retberg looked round at Ian Green.

"It was a shame you handed in those sawn-offs," he said.

"I have a confession to make about that," Green replied. "It is possible I may have forgotten to actually hand them in."

"What?"

"You know, what with one thing and another going on."

Retberg looked at him impatiently.

"Well, where are they, then?" he said.

"Up until yesterday they were living in the bottom of a wardrobe at home," Ian Green said with a look of innocence. "But now..."

"That's right, now..." Retberg's impatience grew worse. "Now. Where are they right now?"

"Only in the boot of your car," said the sergeant, grinning. "Together with a box of cartridges."

The Bonelli brothers looked from one to the other, while the police officers were clearly considering the possibility that they would be facing a bunch of armed terrorists. But the priest and his brother knew something that the police officers did not know.

Even though references to Satanists and demons had been made, the Bonellis could tell that Retberg had not taken this seriously. The situation was, though, that if the demon, Bael, did show up, they would need all the fire power they could get, and then some, and even that might not be enough. Even with Victor Best and his little army with rifles and shotguns.

Neither Retberg or Green noticed, at that point, Lucciano casting a quick glance over to Debbie, nor her nodding gesture in return. Even if they had noticed they would not have understood the meaning of it.

On reflection, Father Bonelli decided that they needed to make the best possible effort. Drawing in a deep breath he looked at the police officers.

"Get them," he said. "Get the shotguns, and all the cartridges."

The inspector got out his car keys and handed them to Ian Green.

The sergeant quickly nipped out through the barn door, and to the car which was parked just a few yards away. While he was out there, Victor Best appeared.

"We're ready to move," called out the guest house proprietor.

"Okay, get your people assembled," Green called back in a hushed voice, "but wait for our signal."

The police sergeant gathered up the leather bag containing the shotguns and ammunition then returned quickly to the barn.

"Good." Retberg took one of the shotguns, opened it and put in two cartridges, one in each barrel. He snapped it shut and handed it back to Green, then took the other shotgun and did the same.

The Bonelli brothers were watching, nodding with approval. The police inspector was clearly a man who knew how to handle a weapon.

Then Retberg and Green shared the remaining cartridges between them, putting them into their jacket pockets.

Paul Retberg then drew out his police radio again and

clicked the transmit button.

"We're moving in now," he said. "Stand by, Units One and Two."

"We copy. Standing by," came the crackly reply.

Hearing that brief exchange, Father Bonelli pondered, yet again, over whether this was the right time to advise the police officers of the full scale of the danger they were in.

He heaved a big sigh. On reflection, still not yet. He remembered his primary objective, and that was to protect Maria and her baby. He was to achieve that objective no matter what, and at all costs. The inspector, he considered, was a good copper who had, in turn, been given his instructions, and at this point, to attempt to explain about demons and Satanists would be of no benefit to anyone. Retberg had seen for himself what Bael had done to the man known as Tuan, but the policeman seemed to think it was just the work of some maniac.

Meanwhile, Anna and the two girls were sitting well inside the barn. Both Maria and Debbie were nursing their babies. Debbie was breastfeeding her little boy, and at the same time giving plenty of vocal encouragement to Maria whose baby girl was beginning to suckle well with the breast milk starting to come through.

Anna was watching them, marvelling at them both, but also wondering what the future held in store for them.

When Giuseppe and Lucciano, and the two police officers, called out announcing their departure, Anna called back to them.

"Please be careful," she shouted. "May God be with you."

The barn door slammed shut.

And then, for a short while, there was complete silence.

Anna and the girls were all quite scared about the threat of attack. They prayed together, which made them feel a little better because, after all, this was for the protection of God's Daughter, so they could hardly imagine that God would let any evil thing happen to them.

They sat there quietly and listened out for anything that could suggest danger.

After a while, a terrible commotion could be heard building up in the distance.

Then an awful *Boom* of an explosion, which made the ground inside the barn shake.

After another moment, to Anna's surprise, Debbie abruptly got up from her seat, and handed her baby to the midwife.

"Please look after him," she said. "There is something I must do."

"But what?" Anna and Maria said together.

"Father Bonelli and Lucci have given me precise instructions which I must follow exactly," Debbie told them. "Both of you must stay here."

"I strongly advise you to stay here, too," Anna advised.

"No," Debbie said adamantly. "I've got to do this. Our whole future depends on it."

Before leaving through the barn door, Debbie seemed to be searching through her belongings.

Anna and Maria watched her in astonishment as she found the object that she sought, and carefully drew it out of her case.

CHAPTER FIFTY-THREE

Victor Best and his band of friends followed the Bonelli brothers and the police officers, and it was when they were halfway across the field that the fire started. The whole field in the failing light of that late afternoon in the middle of winter seemed to be illuminated by the sudden brightness of the fire. The blaze created shimmering shadows against a crowd of at least a hundred men and women gyrating together in a wild circle. There didn't seem to be anything to burn, like dry wood or rotting rubbish, but the fire quickly began to spread.

Father Bonelli remembered what his brother had told him about a fierce fire when he arrived on a motorcycle the previous night.

"There will be a great, uncontrollable fire. The Satanists plan to snatch the mother and her child and throw them both into the blaze."

As the priest and the others drew nearer, they could see that some of the men were armed, while others who danced around the fire, along with the women, had now all removed their clothes. There was another, smaller group of people standing nearby, and these were wearing hideous masks that were like ugly reptilian faces. These people danced too, but not around the fire. They had something that they were wheeling out of a container on the back of a truck. It was some contraption on wheels, like a trolley, but whatever was on the trolley for the time being remained covered up with a large, grey blanket. Bizarrely, about six hooded figures knelt before it, seemingly worshipping it, while other trucks and vans parked there were being unloaded of various kinds of packages.

Father Bonelli drew out his gun and held it out in front of him. He began to walk down the hill towards the Satanists, and Lucci went with him, gesturing to the policeman to follow as he went. Victor and his people didn't need to be beckoned. They just went too, aiming their guns already, as though anticipating the need for immediate action.

Retberg and Green glanced at each other. The sawn-offs were formidable weapons at close range, but not accurate at this distance. Retberg held his shotgun under his arm, then drew out his pistol with the other hand, while following closely behind the Bonelli brothers. Ian Green did the same.

As the police inspector followed the priest and his brother, he was gradually becoming quite puzzled. If these terrorists were targeting Maria and her baby, why didn't they just get on with it? That way he and his sergeant, and the Bonellis, together with Victor Best's men, could handle them with their combined firepower, and that would be the end of it.

For Retberg that would mean loads of arrests and his next promotion he had been working so hard for would almost certainly be his.

Alternating thoughts raced through the police inspector's mind.

Maybe the Satanists realised now that they were so unexpectedly outnumbered (thanks, he had to admit, to Victor Best and his people) that they were cooking up some alternative sort of plan.

There was a lot of them, but only a relatively small group were armed.

Then he started to wonder what dancing naked around the fire was all about.

Weighing it all up he considered that maybe it was time to give the order for the helicopters to move in, all armed with machine guns.

He stopped and drew out his police radio again, but Father Bonelli stopped too, and looked round at the same moment. He took a rapid stride toward the police inspector and put a restraining hand on his arm.

"Not yet," he said. "We're not sure yet of..."

"What do you mean, we're not sure?" Retberg snapped. "These are terrorists, and..."

"NO!" the priest snapped back. "They are worse than terrorists."

Retberg tried to pull his arm free, but Father Bonelli's grasp was surprisingly strong.

The priest decided it was time at last to tell the truth.

"These are Satanists," he said. "They are planning on invoking a demon, the most vicious and destructive of all demons."

"But," Retberg managed to wrench his arm free, "our C.I. called them Satanists, even the deputy chief constable referred to them, but really, it's all complete bollocks."

"Guvnor doesn't believe in Satanists," Ian Green said. "He doesn't believe in God, or The Devil, Heaven or Hell."

"I'm a practical police officer, is all I'm saying," said Retberg. "I've no time for demons, or goblins, or..."

The priest cut him short, waving an impatient arm at him.

"If we just go ploughing in with helicopters and machine guns without knowing for sure what's going on," he said, "we will all be committing suicide."

Retberg stared at him, for a moment breathless with exasperation.

Victor Best's men had gathered round in a circle, not understanding what the argument between the priest and the police inspector was all about.

Father Bonelli looked around at them all.

"We mustn't lose this battle," he said. "If we do, Maria and God's Child will be slaughtered, and that will be The

End... for us all."

Victor Best stepped forward. "The End?" he said. "The End of..."

"The End of the World." Father Bonelli nodded slowly. "That's right, we are on the brink of the End of the World."

Retberg continued to stare at him, then angrily turned away, now out of Bonelli's reach.

"That's crap," he said, and before the priest could stop him, he spoke rapidly into his radio.

"To Units One and Two," he shouted. "Move in now. Beware, though, they are armed and they are cooking something up. Over."

"On our way. Over," came the prompt response.

"NO!" Father Bonelli shouted. "You fool, you've just signed their death warrants."

While Giuseppe Bonelli and Paul Retberg continued to argue, Ian Green suddenly yelped.

"Oh, my God. Look!" he shouted, pointing.

They all looked in that direction and saw that the masked men had moved towards the group dancing around the fire. They had brought with them the thing on wheels which had a cover over the top of it, the thing that they thought was some kind of trolley.

When it was uncovered Ian Green could see clearly what it was.

The Bonelli brothers both recognised it, having been trained to use them in the army.

"Oh, shit," Father Bonelli said, forgetting his holy status.

It was an anti-aircraft cannon.

Sergeant Ian Green suddenly stood rigid. He was peering intently through the smoke, concentrating on a man by the side of the cannon.

"And that's not the worst of it," he said, turning to Retberg. "See that man loading the cannon?"

Retberg also concentrated for a moment, then nearly choked on his next words.

"Bastard," he said. "Police Constable Gifford."

"They must have a radio for picking up your signal," the priest shouted. "Withdraw the helicopters immediately."

Retberg spun round in panic and confusion.

"Withdraw!" he yelled into his radio. "Stand down. Units One and Two, withdraw immediately."

But even as he shouted they could hear the sound of the choppers' rotor blades.

"Withdraw!" Retberg repeated, yelling wildly. "I tell you, get out of it!"

And now they could see the two helicopters coming towards them, over the hill until they were almost directly over the Satanists.

"Don't worry, sir," came a nonchalant drawl over the radio. "We'll deal with it. You just watch us kick their arse if they try anything funny."

"You don't understand," Retberg shouted.

"Don't worry, sir. We've had lots of experience dealing with dangerous lunatics."

"NO!" Retberg was screaming in desperation now. "They've got a cannon, some kind of rocket launcher."

But it was too late.

The helicopters were directly above the Satanists.

But then…

One moment they were there, the next moment gone, just two brilliant flashes of light, accompanied by two deafening *bangs*, and burning pieces from the explosions descending.

Paul Retberg's brain was buzzing loudly in shock and confusion, and then he lost control of everything completely.

He burst into a run, rushing down the hill towards the Satanists.

"You fucking bastards!" he screamed, and as he ran he fired

his pistol, but from that distance, and being in rapid motion, his shooting was wildly inaccurate, each bullet sailing harmlessly off into space. As he got closer to his intended target, the heat from the fire became more intense, but in his utter fury he kept going, wanting to avenge the murdered helicopter crews.

Ian Green, the Bonellis and Victor's people looked at each other for a brief moment with utterly hopeless expressions, but they had no choice now. They had to follow. They all ran down the hill together, chasing after the crazed police inspector.

As Ian Green ran, he felt like Rambo with a handgun in one hand, and a sawn-off shotgun in the other, but unlike Retberg he didn't shoot while running.

"Come on!" Victor Best shouted to his people. The whole crowd continued to run together, firing their rifles and shotguns as they went. Many of their shots found the intended targets accompanied by screams from the gyrating Satanists.

Lucci ran in front of Sergeant Green with his machine pistol and fired it into the crowd of the naked and masked people, many of them falling, several more yelling, some being injured, others just scared.

Giuseppe, not quite as fit as Lucci, momentarily fell behind, while Victor Best and his men continued with an all-out attack with their rifles and shotguns.

Meanwhile, Retberg continued to pull the trigger of his handgun until it clicked on empty chambers, then he just threw the gun to the ground, and took aim with the shotgun in both hands.

Then he saw PC Gifford still standing by the cannon.

"You lousy traitor," The words hissed from Retberg's lips as his finger tightened on the trigger, but then a shout of panic from the priest distracted him.

Standing still and taking aim, he didn't notice that the surviving naked and masked Satanists who were dancing around the fire were now working themselves up into a real frenzy.

Father Bonelli knew, with sheer terror in his heart, what that meant. He met up with Ian Green and Lucci who had, at that moment, arrived behind Retberg.

Victor and the others were not far behind. They huddled together as the fire suddenly spread and surrounded them. They were trapped.

Then a fierce wind began to blow like they were near the centre of a hurricane. Dust and dirt flew up into their faces, momentarily blinding them.

"What the fuck's happening?" shouted Victor Best.

"Just keep together," the old priest shouted back.

There was not much choice about that. There was nowhere else to go.

Then the wind began to die down, but the fire was still intense. The blaze was all around them, and gradually spreading. Unless there was some kind of miracle, they were all going to be engulfed in flames.

The ground beneath them begin to shake and vibrate as though there was to be an almighty earthquake. They could feel the ground tremble as if the sea was trying to come up through the hill. Retberg thought they must have been standing on a volcano that was about to erupt. The centre of the circle that the Satanists had formed in their dance rumbled. Then it exploded.

Then Father Giuseppe's darkest fears were realised.

From the ground before them a hideous creature emerged. It was like a giant toad, except its head was more cat-like, with a snarling mouth, drool dripping from its sabre teeth.

And the creature roared, coupled with the deafening noise of a storm brewing. Retberg and Green were having to shout to make themselves heard.

"What the fuck?" Retberg shouted, repeating Victor Best's unanswerable question.

Sergeant Ian Green stood close to him and yelled back, "Why don't you just tell him you don't believe in demons?"

But Retberg didn't hear him amidst the combined thunderous sounds.

The creature's body continued to grow until it was over eight feet high.

And as it changed from one creature into the next, it spoke in a loud, booming voice.

"The Daughter of God is now amongst us," it roared angrily, "and she will die, just as her subjects will, in agony, no more or less than they deserve."

Father Bonelli stepped forward, and as he did so Ian Green saw him take two objects from his jacket pockets. One was a golden crucifix which he held up in front of him.

The other object was a grenade.

"Bael," he shouted. "Heathen and spineless wretch of the deepest sewers and gutters of Hell!"

The creature roared angrily.

The priest waved the shape of the sign of the cross with the crucifix in his hand.

"In the name of God the Father," he continued, "and the Son, and the Holy Ghost, I command you to be gone."

He then pulled the pin from the grenade and threw it at the creature.

But the demon, Bael, appeared to deliberately catch it in his mouth.

The priest and the whole group of them threw themselves onto the ground, covering their faces with their hands.

Bang! Whoooosh!

They looked up, and there was the mocking grin of the ugliest cat-like face ever seen.

And laughing.

Bonelli struggled to his feet and continued to hold the crucifix up in front of him.

"It is God himself who commands you," he shouted. "Return to the gutter that you slithered from."

The crucifix suddenly became red-hot, then flew from the priest's hand.

Bael roared back a torrent of obscene, blasphemous abuse, at the end of which he added, "Now, let me help you die."

Retberg and Green, and Lucci and Victor and the others, watched in terror.

Father Giuseppe Bonelli rose up into the air as though being picked up by the scruff of the neck with invisible hands. Then he was forced closer to the fire, gradually closer and closer and closer, until Retberg and the others could see the flesh on his face burning, bubbling like a frying egg.

Lucci rushed forward brandishing his machine pistol, firing continuously at the demon's ugly head.

Then Retberg moved forward. He got as close as he could to the demonic monster and levelled the sawn-off shotgun into the hideous face.

Father Bonelli screamed in agony. He could feel his flesh burning off. He was now almost in the fire. He prayed for some miracle to save him from being burned to death.

Retberg fired both barrels of his shotgun at point-blank range into Bael's bulbous eyes. Victor Best and some of his group moved forward and in the next moment they were firing their guns too.

The invisible grip on Bonelli's neck was momentarily relaxed. The priest struggled desperately to free himself, feeling like his face and chest were on fire.

While still holding Bonelli with some evil, invisible power, he suddenly lunged forward with his giant, cat jaws and gripped Retberg's right arm at the elbow.

Then he crunched on it.

Retberg screamed as his arm was severed, pumping a shower of blood out as he was tossed to one side like a rag doll.

With a war-like yell, Ian Green also rushed forward, discharging both barrels of his shotgun at Bael as he did so. Most of Victor's men were retreating now, needing to re-load their weapons.

Bael then turned viciously on the police sergeant, but the priest, almost blinded, took out his army revolver, and rapidly fired all nine shots into the demon's head, and this created just enough distraction that Green needed to rush to Retberg's side.

Then Bonelli fell to one side, fainting with intolerable pain. Lucci rushed to his side. Thinking his brother must be dead, he just collapsed on top of him, sobbing.

Ian Green grabbed Retberg by the legs and pulled with all his strength to get him as far away from Bael, and from the fire, as possible.

CHAPTER FIFTY-FOUR

Back in the barn, a young girl and her middle-aged midwife trembled with fear. Maria Christopher and Anna Gabriella sat on their chair-beds, looking around the barn with nervous faces, being able to hear clearly the fearful battle that was raging across the field.

Maria looked at Anna, and when she spoke, it was in a quiet monotone.

"It might have just been a dream," she mumbled.

Anna looked at her without replying.

"The Angel visiting me."

There was another massive explosion that shook the ground.

"Oh, my good Lord," said Anna.

Maria was not sure if Anna had heard her. She sat there on her chair-bed for a moment longer, wondering whether to repeat her statement.

There was the sound of more gunfire – shotguns, rifles and pistols – followed by rapid machine gun fire. Then the earth seemed to shake with two more almighty explosions.

There was then a short spell of eerie silence before the sound of more gunfire.

Maria was now holding her little girl, and despite the noise in the distance the baby had miraculously gone to sleep.

Anna had just finished changing baby Adam's nappy, and he too had fallen into a comfortable and contented slumber.

The gas heater was being kept at a safe distance but was still blowing out adequate warmth.

They settled the babies down together on a chair-bed, placing plenty of rolled up blankets around them for security. As they did this, the battle raging on outside was still audible.

Both Maria and Anna looked thoughtfully at each other.

Then they both spoke at once.

Maria laughed nervously. "You first," she said.

Anna smiled. "I was just going to say, I wonder what Debbie's doing," she said. "It sounds like World War Three out there. I hope she's okay and knows what she's doing."

Maria just nodded, and a moment more went past as she finished arranging the babies' blankets.

Then she looked at the midwife.

"Listen, Anna," she said. "I've got to tell you something. It's about the Angel that visited me."

Another loud explosion from outside made them both jump.

"Oh, I do hope Debbie's all right," Anna went on, as though Maria had not spoken.

"The thing is," Maria said, "I've been thinking, it might have been a dream."

To Maria's surprise, Anna just looked at her, smiled and bowed her head. Then she leaned over and, in turn, gently stroked the babies' heads, first Adam, then Maria's little girl who was, so far, still nameless.

As she did this she said, "I know in my heart that this is the Daughter of God"

"But..."

"It was not a dream, Maria," she said. "It really did happen, so please do not ever tell anybody that again."

As the commotion from outside continued, Maria and Anna fell into a thoughtful silence. Anna kept looking at the barn door as though expecting to see somebody bursting through it at any moment, praying that it would be a friend, but fearing the most deadly foe at the same time.

"Have you thought of a name yet?" she asked, looking at Maria as if predicting the name she would choose. "A name that will suit your beautiful little girl?"

"A name I have always liked," Maria said. "Evelyn."

Anna smiled and nodded knowingly, and as she began to recite a prayer quietly to herself, she looked down at the two infants, a little boy and a dear little girl. Adam and Evelyn.

Outside a war was being waged. Good versus Evil, with The Devil's most dangerous demon violently demonstrating his intention to kill Maria and her baby, a heinous act that would have the most catastrophic consequences to the entire world.

If there had been any doubt about Maria's baby, in Anna's opinion, that settled it. How could it not be true?

The midwife looked down at the two babies, bowed her head, and finished her prayer with the sign of the cross.

Maria's little infant really was the Daughter of God.

*

Police Sergeant Ian Green pulled off his own jacket, then his ammunition belt, then his shirt, revealing just his vest. He tore the shirt into strips to make a tourniquet that he tied as tightly as he could around Retberg's severed right elbow, then he held the remaining stump up.

Victor Best and his army were engulfed in smoke that blinded and choked them.

Lucciano Bonelli crouched over his brother and, believing him to be dead, joined his hands and bowed his head. He was deep in prayer, praying for him to be brought back to life.

Ian Green desperately looked around him for any means at all that could help. He saw Retberg's police radio sticking out of the inspector's jacket pocket.

He grabbed at it, his hands shaking and sticky with Retberg's blood. He pressed the transmit button, but his voice was so tight with fear and dry with smoke that he couldn't speak.

He took a moment, taking deep breaths, fighting to get himself under control. He was almost crying when he spoke into the radio, and he was hardly able to hear his own voice with the demon's angry roar, and the insane chanting of the surviving Satanists.

Some of the demon's followers were dead. Others lay there injured, screaming in pain from gunshot wounds. The surviving ones just ignored their comrades' pleas for help.

Then he was aware that Retberg was trying to move and he too was crying out in pain.

Green looked at the radio in his hand and realised he still had his thumb pressed on the transmit button which would not allow any reply to be received.

He released it, then pressed it again, feeling ready now to speak, but even as he did this he was scared of what might happen, with the fate of the previous two helicopters still vivid in his mind.

"Sergeant Ian Green here," he was shrieking, while choking on another cloud of acrid, black smoke. "Please, urgent assistance required. Paul Retberg is seriously injured, and Father Bonelli. Over."

He then released the transmit button and pressed the radio tightly to his ear, the volume fully up, desperately trying to hear any response."

"We're on our way," came a garbled voice. "In the meantime, please advise extent of injuries."

The stunned sergeant was still struggling to speak. "The priest has third degree burns, and Retberg..." Green could hardly bear to say the words. "... Retberg's lost an arm."

"We can hardly hear you."

"For fuck's sake just get here."

"Armed Units, Three and Four, are on their way," came

the drawling response. "Don't you worry. We know how to deal with this kind of maniac."

Ian Green looked up at the hideous, eight-foot-high creature that looked like a cross between a giant toad and a hissing, spitting cat, but it's face was now changing into something far more grotesque.

Gradually its head and face changed into that of an ugly, snarling sabre-toothed tiger.

"No, keep away from it," screamed Ian Green. "Just get an air ambulance here urgently."

But even as he made this desperate request, looking round him he realised that this was impossible. The fire was completely surrounding them and was rapidly spreading towards them.

There was no escape now. They were all going to be burnt to death

"You hang on in there, sergeant," came the same drawling voice. "Rescue is less than a minute away. Whoever this feller thinks he is, we will kick his arse."

"It's not a feller," Green yelled. "It's a fucking demon."

"Take it easy, sarge. We're nearly there now."

"No, it's suicide."

"We have machine guns, cannon and flamethrowers. That'll teach the bastard."

Ian Green could already hear the helicopters' rotor blades, as Bael's grotesque roar gradually changed into hideous laughter.

When the two helicopters emerged through the smoke, the crews inside them expected to see some armed lunatic mowing people down while randomly swinging a machine gun around his head, but what they saw made them disbelieve the evidence of their own eyes.

One of the helicopters trained its water hose on the spreading blaze, while the other aimed directly at the monster. There was a deafening chatter of gunfire as its cannon and three machine guns commenced work, all firing together at the demon.

For a moment Bael stopped laughing, then he made a sweeping gesture with one arm as though slightly irritated.

And the two helicopters exploded simultaneously in a spectacular ball of flame, the burning debris floating to the ground as if in slow motion.

Ian Green sagged forward in dismay, their last ray of hope, he believed, gone.

He knew for certain now that they were all going to die.

And nothing short of a miracle could prevent it.

He felt something grip his hand. He looked down. It was Retberg's one good hand. With his last remaining strength Retberg yelled at him.

"Make a run for it! You can make it!"

"No, I'm not leaving you!" Ian Green yelled back.

"Oh, don't be such a hero," Retberg roared, but now on the verge of passing out again with the pain of his severed arm. "Just piss off, you irritating prat."

"You can't get rid of me that easily," Ian Green told him. "We're like brothers."

"Ha, ha," Retberg shouted. "That's a laugh. I've always thought how annoying you are."

"We'll get through this together." Ian Green was sobbing now, knowing that they were both going to die as the fire continued to spread rapidly towards them.

"Now just clear off," Retberg ranted on. "I don't need you, I don't even like you."

Not being able to tolerate the pain any longer, Paul Retberg passed out.

Sergeant Green was leaning forward over the stricken inspector. He looked round him, desperate for some kind of miracle. He went to tighten the tourniquet around Retberg's bloody stump, and as he did so he squeezed his eyes tightly shut in mental agony.

But when he opened them again, what he saw emerging through the blaze made him believe that he had already died.

He saw the form of a young girl walking through the flames.

The girl, a mere teenager, was dressed in a nightgown and as she walked she appeared to be pointing some kind of object at Bael, The Devil's most dangerous demon.

At first, through the smoke, Ian Green could not make out who the girl was, or what the object in her hand was, but as she came nearer, he realised.

The girl, without a doubt, was Debbie Shallis.

And in her hand, the object pointed at Bael?

It was a crossbow.

Bael saw her approaching and roared with laughter.

He'd already had more than twenty people firing rifles and shotguns at him from point-blank range, and a priest shouting words of exorcism and throwing grenades at him. Then helicopters had appeared unleashing machine guns and cannon shell, all with absolutely no effect, except possibly to annoy him slightly.

But, apparently, God's children were merciless and hadn't finished with him yet, for here was a mere slip of a girl pointing at him a crossbow, whose firepower was marginally more formidable than a bow and arrow.

"Shoot your bolt," he roared at the girl. "Then I will laugh as I tear you to pieces and leave you mutilated to crawl away. I shall watch as..."

Debbie Shallis ignored him. She knew what she had to do, and she had to concentrate fully to carry out her instructions exactly.

She raised the crossbow in both hands. Then, looking across the sights and closing one eye for accuracy, she aimed directly between Bael's bulbous eyes.

"Get the hell out of it," Ian Green shouted desperately. "Run for your life."

Lucci Bonelli was now kneeling next to his brother, hands joined, looking pleadingly up at the sky.

"Please God. Please God." he prayed.

Bael roared again, the most horrible roar of laughter that Ian Green would ever hear, but hardly noticed by Debbie who needed to make sure of her first shot, steadying herself as she aimed.

Then she fired.

The arrow, which had an unusually long, and wedge-shaped point, struck Bael cleanly between the eyes, going right through his skull.

The effect was devastating. He roared, a deafening sound, no longer laughing now, but like some mortally wounded prehistoric creature in agony.

He fell forward, then he tried to get up, while waving his limbs and turning clumsily. As he struggled to get up, the fire around them intensified.

In total shock and disbelief, Ian Green watched. He thought it seemed that the repulsive creature had been blinded.

Father Bonelli was regaining consciousness. Still in unimaginable pain he attempted to sit up. His brother Lucci tried to comfort him, to reassure him, but at the same time he needed to see the girl complete her task.

Debbie Shallis had fired her first arrow and was now reloading the crossbow with the second of three specially prepared missiles which she had secured around her waist by means of a belt.

"Shoot!" yelled Lucci.

But Debbie did not need telling. She had gone through this procedure a hundred times with the priest's brother.

She aimed carefully.

Then she fired the second arrow, its gnarled, twisted point

going straight through Bael's heart.

Bael collapsed in a heap, all of his evil humour knocked out of him now, but still, the next moment, he was trying to crawl towards the girl. If anyone had expected the most fierce demon to repent at the end they would have been disappointed.

He just continued to roar aggressively at her.

The next stream of obscenities and blasphemies were unprintable

Then he screamed, "I will tear off your little arms and legs, then I will twist your head round and round, slowly, ever-so slowly, until…"

With nothing left to fear, Debbie approached the fallen demon, and as she did so, she drew out the third and final arrow, and fitted it into the specially modified crossbow. The six-inch point that was welded onto the arrow was aimed at her third target, as instructed by Lucciano Bonelli.

Ian Green watched as if paralysed in a never-ending nightmare.

"DO IT!" Giuseppe and Lucci shouted together.

And for the first time there was terror in Bael's eyes. Lying there, unable to move, he saw the arrow and, at the very last moment, the thing that was attached to it. He reacted like he knew what it was.

"NO!" he roared.

Then Deborah Shallis, just turned sixteen and very recently having given birth to a beautiful little baby boy, stood there next to the demon, ready to carry out Lucci's final instruction.

She closed one eye, checking her aim one last time.

Then she fired.

She shot Bael right in the groin.

The next instant, the hideous form of the demon vanished in a bright flash of light and a shower of sparks, and lying there, dead, in front of the young girl, was a black cat.

Four more helicopters had been deployed and hovered over the fire, dousing the flames with their water cannon, while an extra helicopter – the air ambulance – landed. The pilot had seen Ian Green's frantic, wildly waving signal, and landed as close to the casualty as he could. Two paramedics with a stretcher came running over.

They quickly examined Retberg's injury, and Ian Green noticed the anxious looks they gave one another. Retberg had lost a lot of blood and required urgent surgery, but he would have died if his partner had not fitted the tourniquet so expertly. Ian Green's first aid training during Module Two at police college had been good. He remembered being told that day to pay attention, and he was glad now that he had done so.

At the same time, though, his stomach was churning with the shock of what had happened. Realisation began to sink in. What was going to happen now? What would life be like for a police inspector who'd lost an arm? A man who only ever wanted to be policeman, and an inspector who had been working hard for promotion?

But for now, Ian Green had to push those thoughts to one side. He needed to be as supportive as possible to his colleague… and his friend.

Retberg was placed on the stretcher and carried to the air ambulance. Injections were administered, and a mask feeding him pain-killing gas was placed firmly over his face.

As they slid the stretcher into place on board the helicopter, one of the paramedics turned round to Ian Green

"Okay," he shouted over the noise of the chopper's rotors. "We'll look after him, thank you."

"No, I'm going with him." Green shouted back.

The paramedic nodded. "Okay, you sit there."

Ian Green climbed aboard, sat in a seat just behind the

pilot, and strapped himself in.

Everything else was thrown into the cabin. The paramedics climbed into their seats. One of them slammed the sliding door shut as the air ambulance began to take off.

For a moment, Ian Green felt like his insides were coming up through his mouth. Once in the air, though, his stomach settled, and he swivelled in his seat to look at Retberg lying behind him on the stretcher that was fastened into a specially designed frame.

And the police inspector began to toss and turn and call out.

He was a bit delirious, the mixture of pain-killing drugs and local anaesthetic making him hallucinate.

"Ian," he called out. "Where the hell are you? Just like you to piss off and leave me to it, you cowardly bastard."

Ian Green unstrapped himself, climbed out of his seat, and knelt at Retberg's side.

"Here I am, buddy," he shouted over the chopper's noise.

"Where have you been?" Retbeg's voice sounded rough and dry. "I've been calling you for hours. We'll be late because of you, you useless, lazy bugger."

"Well, you see..."

Retberg's head snapped round suddenly. He opened his eyes and stared intently at the sergeant.

"Get out of here," he said. "Run for your life while you still can. Leave me to it."

"Not a chance," Ian Green told him. "You're stuck with me. If you don't like it, it's tough."

Retberg looked around him, then seemed to realise what the state of play was.

And he shouted, "I'm finished. My God, my career is over."

"Rubbish," Green shouted back. "You might have a scratch or two."

At that, Paul Retberg actually laughed.

"A scratch or two?" he shouted. "Take a look at me, you prat. How am I going to get my promotion now?"

Then Police Sergeant Ian Green leaned over the inspector, grabbed his lapels, and shouted back.

"Now you listen to me, you self-centred, self-righteous, self-pitying bastard. If Douglas Bader became a fighter pilot with no legs then you can continue to be a copper with one arm. We've got years of adventures ahead of us, and anyway, I wouldn't work with anyone else."

Paul Retberg reached out with his one hand and squeezed Ian Green by the arm.

"Well, if that's all you've got to say," he shouted, nearly choking now on his dry throat, "then there's no point in discussing it any further."

CHAPTER FIFTY-FIVE

Another team of paramedics were attending to Father Giuseppe Bonelli. He had got severe, third-degree burns, especially to his face, and these were so bad that he would be scarred and disfigured for the remainder of his life, but he still found the strength from somewhere to stand and walk.

When he was offered a free ride in a helicopter to the hospital, though, he thanked the guys but turned them down. He had seen Inspector Retberg being taken away in the air ambulance, and Sergeant Green go with him. He prayed that they would be all right, but his mission that he promised to complete, was not quite accomplished yet.

Maria and her new baby would still need him for protection for some time to come.

Her new baby, he thought. *The Daughter of God.*

On the arrival of more police officers, the surviving Satanists had suddenly dispersed, scattering in all directions. This was easy for the ones who managed to get their clothes on in time. Those disciples of The Devil mingled casually with crowds of people who, on hearing explosions, had turned up to investigate. The naked ones, however, were a little conspicuous, and were rounded up swiftly by some of the officers who had with them snarling dogs.

One police dog became over excited and lunged forward, grabbing the scrotum of a naked man, and continued to twist and gnaw until the dog handler came to the rescue with a tube of doggy-chocs. The hapless man, though, by that time had been virtually castrated and was in shock, squealing like a pig.

But all of Bael's remaining followers were now in shock, hardly able to apprehend what they had witnessed. Their Prince had been vanquished by a young girl. A child with a crossbow.

Father Bonelli and his brother looked anxiously around them, then relaxed when they saw Debbie Shallis walking towards them with a paramedic by her side. His arm was around her, holding a blanket around her shoulders. The young man had looked at her, puzzled as to why she was out on a winter's evening in nothing but a night gown and a pair of cheerfully designed slippers. She then gestured to him, thanking him, but assuring him that she did not require further assistance. He nodded to her, then began on his way back down the hill towards his comrades.

And she was still holding the crossbow. She waved it in the air when she saw the Bonelli brothers.

It was when she got closer that her expression changed.

"Oh, Jesus," she gasped. "Father, your face."

"Nothing that a smear of sun block won't put right," he said, wincing in pain as he opened his mouth. "But maybe a blister or two."

She shook her head solemnly. She wanted to hug him but realised that this would just hurt him more. She then looked down at the specially modified crossbow in her hand, then at Lucciano.

"It feels like part of me now," she said. "Here it is, Lucci. I'm going to miss it."

Lucci tried to laugh but it sounded more like a gasp of relief.

"It's yours," he said. "I always wanted you to have it."

"Okay, thanks. And…"

"Hey, excuse me!" came a sudden shout from down the hill.

Debbie and the Bonelli brothers looked round to see a fat, little man trotting up to them. He waved some sort of ID card at them.

"My name is Godfrey Turner," he said. "I'm from the *North East Gazette*."

They all looked at the fat, little guy, but he just turned his attention to Debbie.

"Are you the girl who walked through the fire?" he asked

Debbie laughed and shook her head.

"What are you on about?" she asked. "Walk through fire? Me? Are you drunk?"

"Those people over there," the man said, pointing. "They said they saw you walk through the fire."

Debbie looked round at each of the Bonellis, shrugged her shoulders, shook her head and pulled a face.

"Then you shot the monster," the reporter continued, not to be fobbed off, "with that crossbow there, then the creature disappeared in a shower of sparks."

"That is complete rubbish," Debbie said. "Now if you don't mind, I must be going."

Debbie began to walk away.

"But..." Godfrey Turner made a move to follow her.

Lucci stepped forward, blocking the man's path.

"The young lady says she doesn't know anything about it," he said.

The reporter looked at him, then at the priest, grimacing at his burnt and blistered face.

But then Lucci added quite courteously, "Now, we bid you farewell."

With that, the Bonelli brothers set off after Debbie who was now some distance ahead of them. They walked together, back towards the barn, leaving the reporter with nothing to report.

When the brothers caught up with Debbie, she looked round at them.

"I hope Maria's okay," she said. "And Anna, of course,

and the babies."

"Anna and Maria will be getting anxious," said Lucci. "They must have heard those explosions."

"And poor old Inspector Retberg," said Debbie. "I saw them putting him into the air ambulance."

As Father Giuseppe Bonelli continued to walk with his brother on one side, and the young girl on the other, despite the throbbing burning pain, he joined his hands together in prayer.

"We will pray for him," he told her. "Retberg is a tough bloke and I'm sure we will be seeing him again in the future."

*

The newspaper reporter, Godfrey Turner, who up until then had nothing to report, stood on the hill, angrily kicking his heels.

Looking round, he saw a group of dishevelled-looking men and women trudging up the hill towards him, all carrying shotguns and rifles.

"Oi, you lot!" he called out.

Victor Best looked round at his comrades, then momentarily held up his arms, electing himself as the spokesman.

"Well?" he said. "Who are you, and what do you want?"

The reporter from the *North East Gazette* introduced himself.

Victor Best looked at him. The guest house proprietor thought he resembled the Penguin from Batman, but he also considered that no publicity was bad publicity.

"Well?" he repeated sharply.

"Listen," said the reporter. "I was told by that other mob that the girl shot the monster with a crossbow. Did you people witness that?"

Victor Best and most of his crowd laughed.

"That is complete bollocks," Victor said. "It was us. *We*

shot the monster."

"You?" The tubby reporter looked flummoxed.

"Yes. First it was a boy, then a black cat."

"At first it just squatted like a giant frog," someone shouted out from the crowd.

"Then it turned into a large dog," shouted somebody else.

"Then a giant gorilla," added Helga, for once completely sober.

"Then an octopus."

Victor turned to the crowd.

"Shut up," he said loudly. Then he turned back to Godfrey Turner again.

"It turned into a giant sabre-toothed tiger," he said. "Then it attacked the policeman. We moved in with our rifles and shotguns, and kept firing at it until it dropped dead and turned back into a black cat..."

The reporter just looked at him.

"... and thereby saving the world. My name is Victor Best, by the way."

Godfrey Turner kept eyeing the tall, thin man who was holding his shotgun with its twin barrels resting on his shoulder. He then glanced round at the whole crowd of people who were also holding their weapons, looking like they were ready for more action at any moment if required.

The reporter didn't believe a word of it, of course, but that didn't matter.

It was still a bloody good story.

CHAPTER FIFTY-SIX

Two days after the heroic battle with the demon, Bael, quite a crowd of visitors arrived at St Joseph's Hospital on the north-east coast, and as the time gradually edged nearer to the afternoon's visiting hours, a queue formed in the corridor outside Ward 8B.

Ian Green was already in the ward itself, where he had been virtually continuously since the evening of Christmas Day. He had simply phoned his wife to briefly explain. He had no time for any argument on the subject. The loyalty and comradeship between police officers were top priority.

Police Inspector Paul Retberg sat up in bed to be examined. The surgeon who had performed the necessary emergency procedure that evening was, himself, doing the rounds, accompanied by a young nurse. They stopped at his bed to check on his progress.

Ian Green, who was sitting close by Retberg's bedside, moved his chair backwards to allow them better access around the bed.

The nurse walked around the bed, pulling the screen round with her as she went.

"So let's take a look," said the surgeon who then gestured to the nurse.

The nurse, barely nineteen years of age, and with her dark fringe just visible below her white cap, moved forward and began to undo the bandage from around the stump of Retberg's right arm.

As the bandage gradually came away with the nurse's

gentle round-and-round motion, the surgeon spoke quietly to the police inspector.

"I was able to save your elbow," he said.

Then the whole bandage was off to reveal the raw, stitched stump.

Ian Green had a glimpse of it. He grimaced and turned away.

Retberg, himself, could hardly bear to look, but he forced himself.

"Shit," he muttered under his breath. At that moment he could not accept that this was now part of him and would remain so for the rest of his life.

The surgeon peered closer, making satisfied, murmuring sounds.

"Yes, I'm quite pleased with that," he said. "It's looking good. That'll heal up neatly. You'll be back to work in no time."

"Back to work?" Retberg said. "Are you jesting? I'm a policeman."

"Yes, I saw it on your record," the surgeon said absentmindedly as he picked up the clipboard from the end of Retberg's bed. He looked at the notes for a moment, briskly added something to them, then placed the clipboard back into its position.

"Much pain?" he asked.

"A bit," Retberg said, "but you know, mustn't grumble."

"Well, that'll begin to ease off in a couple of days. In the meantime, the nurses will keep you topped up with painkillers. Okay?"

Paul Retberg nodded slowly. He felt that the mental pain he was going through was worse than any physical pain he could imagine.

"Right, then," the surgeon said to the nurse. "You may re-dress it now."

Then he nodded to Ian Green.

"And you," he said. "That was as good a tourniquet as I have ever seen. Basically you saved your buddy's life."

Then he turned back to Retberg.

"See you tomorrow, old scout," he said. "Then we'll decide when we can send you home. Okay?"

Retberg looked at the surgeon's cheery smile, just as the nurse started work on the fresh bandage.

"Oh, God," he said. "Home? What am I going to do?"

"Oh, don't be feeling so sorry for yourself," the surgeon said abruptly, his smile evaporating. "I've seen people far worse-off than you."

"Sorry for myself?" Retberg gasped. "I won't be able to cook, do the garden, service my car, tie my shoelaces, change a fuse..."

To Retberg's extreme irritation, the surgeon actually laughed.

"My friend," he said, "I assure you you'll be able to do all those things, and more, but just a bit differently."

"How?"

"You'll receive lots of help, advice and training," said the surgeon, "but in the meantime, I must warn you, by all accounts, there is one thing that cannot be done with one hand."

"Oh, no," said Retberg, fearing the worst. "What is it?"

"Well, it's the one thing that's impossible with one hand. Actually, come to think of it, it can be bloody tricky with two hands."

"But what?

"Change a baby's nappy."

Despite everything, Ian Green suddenly roared with laughter. It was very unlikely, he thought, that Paul Retberg would be called upon to change a baby's nappy in the foreseeable future.

Smiling broadly again now, the surgeon walked away.

"Thank you," Ian Green called after him.

Retberg looked at the nurse who had a look of deep concentration on her pretty, young face as she continued with replacing the bandage.

"I'll need help with everything," he told her. "Shopping, bathing, going for a pee."

"Don't be such a grumpy guts," she told him.

Ian Green laughed again. It wasn't what she said, but the purely honest way that she said it. The police sergeant occupied himself by opening the screen that had been closed for privacy.

"Grumpy guts?" Retberg said. "Will someone around here show a bit of sympathy, please? I've just had my arm bitten off by a demon appearing as a giant tiger, and all I'm getting is people calling me names and laughing at me."

"Oh, my poor love," came a sudden shriek from the opposite end of the ward. "What have you done to yourself?"

"Ah, now you see," Retberg said. "Here's someone with a spot of sense."

Retberg and Green, and the young nurse, watched as an elderly woman came running across the ward, but then sailed past Retberg's bed, and to the patient in the next bed, a frail-looking old man with a bandage on his head.

Paul Retberg shook his head and glared at Ian Green as a warning for him not to laugh. The nurse compressed her mouth into a tight line as she continued with the bandage.

Just then, another nurse came trotting along and called out, "Mr Retberg. You have another visitor."

Retberg and Green looked at each other, then glanced round to see who was coming.

It was Chief Superintendent Sutton.

Retberg looked up at the ceiling and closed his eyes.

"Shit," he whispered to himself. "I've had it now."

Sutton came in with huge strides and went straight to Paul

Retberg. He placed a bulky, white envelope on his bedside table and extended his hand to shake. Retberg looked at him for a brief moment before reaching out his left hand.

The chief super seemed embarrassed, but only briefly, then he coughed and pulled out a chair to sit on.

"Sorry, Paul," he said. "I heard you'd been slightly injured."

"Slightly," Retberg agreed. "Just a tinsy, winsy bit."

Sutton nodded to Sergeant Ian Green.

"And you," he said. "You're going up before the chief constable. You're in for a commendation, my lad. This could even go to Her Majesty the Queen for her honours list."

"Oh, well, that's just spiffing," Retberg said. "And what do I get? A top-of-the-range hook?"

The chief super then turned his attention back to Retberg.

"Ah, yes," he said. "We were going to have a meeting next week, weren't we? Your promotion board, but..."

"But now it's cancelled," said Retberg. "I guessed that one. Thanks."

Sutton coughed again, then took a deep breath before continuing.

"What I was going to say," he said quietly, "was that it's been postponed for two weeks. Can't let you have more sick leave than that, I'm afraid. I mean, you're not exactly ill, are you?"

"No, just minus a limb," Retberg said. "Nothing too serious."

"Exactly." The chief super waved a hand, clicking his fingers. "And that being the case, we will expect to see you when you return. Be bright and early that morning please. Monday, the 10th of January, 9 am sharp. The panel will include myself and the chief constable."

Retberg just stared at him. "So, I..."

Sutton leaned forward and spoke in a confidential tone.

"The word on the street," he said, "is that you are being promoted."

Retberg opened his mouth to speak, but all that came out was a tight croaking sound.

Sutton reached forward and shook the man lying there by his left hand again.

"Congratulations," he said. "*Chief* Inspector Retberg."

"Sir, I..." Retberg's voice was still dry.

At that moment, the nurse who was bandaging the stump of his right arm, leaned forward.

"All done," she said brightly, patting him on his other arm and, to his surprise she kissed him on the cheek. "And congrats on your promotion," she added.

She then stood up and walked away, giving Retberg a little wave as she went.

He raised his left hand and waved back.

After she'd gone he turned to the chief superintendent.

"I'm sorry, sir," he said. "I've been a rather grumpy old sod recently. It all began one winter's afternoon when a nasty demon from Hell appearing as a sabre-toothed monster jumped out in front of me and ripped my arm off."

Sutton laughed.

"Well, you've been through a lot," he said. "Not to worry. All the girls and boys from the nick send you their love and best wishes."

He then gestured to the large envelope he'd delivered.

"That's from everyone," he said.

Feeling somewhat sheepish now, Retberg reached for it, placed it in front of him, opened it and pulled out the get-well card that was crammed full of signatures and comments, but as he started to read them his vision began to go blurred. Most of the entries were simple *Come back soon* messages, and *Love and best wishes*, but other were cheeky or humorous. One read, *Get back to work on the double, you lazy bastard.*

Emotion got the better of him. He placed the card back on the table deciding to look at more of the messages later.

"Thanks, sir," he said. "Please convey my appreciation to everyone."

And then the nurse who earlier on had announced Sutton's arrival, came dashing in again.

"Mr Retberg," she called out. "You've now got *five* more visitors."

"Five?" Sutton said, looking at Retberg. "Popular fellow."

"That's nothing." Retberg found himself smiling for the first time in a long time. "You should have seen me when I had two arms."

"Seven, if you count the babies," the nurse continued. "I'll show them in."

Mindful of the hospital's 'two-visitors-per-bed' rule, Ian Green stood up.

"Shall I wait outside?" he asked the nurse.

"We'll make an exception on this occasion," she said with a wink. "Matron's not about."

Then all in a rush, in came Maria and Debbie, each holding their babies, followed closely by Anna Gabriella, Father Bonelli – who was hardly recognisable with cotton gauze plastered all over his face – and Lucciano.

Maria and Debbie sat on either side of Retberg's bed, leaned over and kissed him on either cheek, while the others were offered chairs by the nurse who then went out and left them to it.

To Retberg's further surprise, they passed to him their babies, Maria's little girl Evelyn on his left side, and Debbie's boy, Adam, on the right, where Debbie provided some assistance to support the child propped up on that side.

Then Maria did a polite little cough into her clenched hand to clear her throat in preparation for a short speech which she had rehearsed. Everybody, ten of them including Sutton, Ian

Green and Retberg himself, became still and quiet, as though anticipating the significant words that were about to be spoken.

Maria, who everyone now believed to be the mother of the Daughter of God, spoke.

"Thank you for your brave actions, Mr Retberg. You made a great sacrifice to protect God's Child from the most evil demon, and…"

"Oh, do call me Paul," said Retberg, smiling broadly now, looking down at each of the babies.

Evelyn looked asleep, but Adam's eyes were wide open and, the injured police officer was certain, studying him with a look of deep concentration.

"… and for that," Maria continued, "you will lead a healthy and active life, but when you eventually die you will go directly to Heaven."

"That's great," said Retberg. "Thanks."

"Also, Paul," It was Debbie who spoke this time, "we've got a favour to ask you."

"A favour?" Retberg looked from one girl to the other with a feeling of bewilderment, but also with an unexpected and inexplicable feeling of happiness.

"Yes," she said. "Will you be our babies' godfather?"

Time drifted past as everyone waited for Retberg's reply. The police inspector continued to lie there looking at the babies, and a strange drowsiness began to wash over him. Perhaps the warm atmosphere of the hospital ward had something to do with it, but he was warned this might happen at first while being under strong painkillers, and with his body gradually adjusting to the shock of losing a limb. He would sometimes feel sleepy.

The injured police officer began to lose consciousness.

*

The newly promoted Chief Inspector Paul Retberg sat alone in a room, empty except for a table in the middle of it, and the hard, upright, wooden chair that he sat on.

Each of the four walls had a window covered by a thick, net curtain, and this made the room seem quite gloomy.

There was only just enough light to see through the window directly opposite him. Beyond the dark net curtain was a mesh panel, like the semi-secret partition in a confessional.

And beyond that was the silhouette of a man who appeared stooped. The police officer could not see the features of his face, only a dark, moving shape, like a shadow, a broken-up image through the mesh, and even that was partly obliterated with a kind of swirling mist.

When at last a faint voice broke through the mist, this confirmed to Retberg that the man, probably a priest, or some other kind of holy man, was very old.

"You made a great sacrifice, Chief Inspector Retberg," said the old man through the mesh, his voice an almost inaudible croak.

Retberg squinted through the gloominess as he tried to get a better look at the shape behind the curtain. He leaned forward and momentarily looked down. He rested his left hand on the stump of his right arm. He had got used to having just one arm quicker than he imagined, and had adapted to various activities. His police career, rather than being over as he had originally feared, had taken off. He had been promoted to chief inspector, and there had already been speculation that he would soon be promoted again, to superintendent.

"Yes, Your Honour, Your Worship, Your..." He suddenly realised he did not know how to address this person.

"As a repayment for your extreme bravery and sacrifice," the man behind the mesh went on, "you will be rewarded."

"Oh, no, that's okay," Retberg said.

"YOU WILL be rewarded." The tone of the voice now

implied that there was no choice in the matter. Retberg would be rewarded whether he liked it or not.

"But..."

The next words stunned the chief inspector. They shook him rigid. He wondered if he was dreaming when he heard the words, yet at the same time he knew that this was real.

"You saved my son from The Devil."

Retberg went hot and cold. He began to sweat and couldn't speak.

"Son?" His head was spinning with confusion. "I thought, I mean everyone thought, that you had a daughter."

There was a soft, croaky laugh.

"As a reward, you will be given five very special powers."

"Special powers?" Retberg could only manage a whisper. "What, like a super hero?"

"Sort of," came a dry, rasping chuckle.

"And how will I know what these powers are, or how to use them?"

"When you most urgently need them," came the voice which suddenly adopted a clearer, commanding tone, "that is when you'll know what they are, and I tell you this, Paul... Paul Retberg... Paul..."

"Yes?

"Paul... Paul... Paul... Retberg."

"Yes, tell me, please tell me."

"Paul... Paul... Paul..."

Paul Retberg woke with a jump, and the first thing he did was to look down at the two babies, fearful that he may have dropped them."

"Paul," came Debbie's voice. "Mr Paul Retberg, sir. Wake up Paul."

"He's awake now, I think," said Maria. "You dozed off on us, Paul," she said.

Retberg quickly cast a searching glance around the whole

ward.

"The others have nipped off to the canteen," Debbie explained. "It's just us."

Maria and Debbie were still sitting on either side of him, just as he remembered before he had drifted away. And the babies were still in the same position, too.

Evelyn on his left side, was still asleep with her face relaxed and contented, but Adam on his right had the continued support of his young mum and carried on studying him with a look of firm concentration, not usually seen on the face of such a young infant.

Just at that moment, Ian Green walked in with a beaker of coffee in each hand, freshly bought from the hospital's canteen. He put one of them next to Retberg on his bedside cabinet.

"We go to all the trouble of visiting you," he said, feigning disgust, "and all you can do is go to sleep. Damned disrespectful I call it."

He expected a peel of laughter for his wit, but nobody seemed to have heard.

The girls were looking at Retberg, and he seemed mesmerised now by the two infants.

"Well?" said Debbie, with her head tilted to one side. "You haven't answered our question."

Retberg just looked at her, then at Maria. He seemed unable to speak for the moment.

"Will you be our babies' godfather?" This time it was Maria who asked the question.

"Sorry, girls," Ian Green said, shaking his head sadly, then taking a sip of coffee. "But godparents have to be people who do actually believe in God, and I'm afraid to say…"

The police sergeant broke off when he saw the strange, intense look that had suddenly appeared on Retberg's face.

"God…" Retberg gazed round at each of them. He knew he wasn't going crazy.

It was God who had spoken to him.

It really was... actually God.

"Well?" Maria persisted. "Will you?

The police inspector, shortly to become *chief* inspector, looked at Maria and Debbie in turn, then down at the two babies. Mistiness blurred his vision.

"It's my duty," he said quietly. "And it would be an honour."

*

TO BE CONTINUED...

ACKNOWLEDGEMENTS

Writing a story of this kind is rewarding, but it can be traumatic and stressful also, so firstly I would like to thank my young son Winston whose sense of humour and infectious laughter has helped me to remain sane;

To my brother, George. A 'born-again atheist." He gave me the inspiration for the basis of the beginning with one simple question: "What would happen if a young girl in present day times claimed she was visited by an Angel?"

Next, a big thank you to each of my two lovely daughters, Sabrina and Stephanie, for their input during the creation of this story. They made many suggestions and contributions, but I must mention a few of my favourites . . .

Steph's comments regarding the Angel's visit enabled me to create a far more effective sequence of events in the early chapters, and I loved her idea of 'spooky corridors' in the house where Tuan lived;

Huge gratitude also to Sabs for suggesting the undercover Satanist. This solved a problem - How would the Satanists know where and when the baby was being born . . ?

And more thanks to her for her contribution to the dramatic paragraph prior to Bael appearing;

Many thanks to Shipa Begum for the Religious Education, and for her Prayers;

And to another lovely friend, Alexandra Trocan. Her feedback meant so much to me. When she finished reading she told me she felt kind of sad she didn't have the next few chapters of The Sacred Claim to look forward to. Well, Alex,

I'm preparing Books Two and Three as quickly as I can;

Last but not least, to my beautiful wife, Maudlin, who supported me throughout. It was sometimes tough for both of us. Two or three hours of writing every single night for twelve months, and not once did she complain.

Lots and lots of love and thanks to you all. Joe.

*

Published previously by Joe Hartwell : Hunted Down